DECEIVE

DECLAN REEDE: THE UNTOLD STORY (BOOK 2)

MICHELLE IRWIN

COPYRIGHT

DEDICATION:

To Renee, who has probably been one of Declan's biggest fans before she'd even met him and has helped spread the word better than anyone.

To my family, who at different times have inspired different elements of this story.

To Angie and Cryssy, thank you for the help getting the word out there about Declan.

To those waiting with baited breath to find out what happened to Declan, I give you Deceive.

DECLAN REEDE: THE UNTOLD STORY

Decide (Book #0.5)

Decline (Book #1)

Deceive (Book #2)

CONTENTS:

GLOSSARY:

Note: This book is set in Australia, as such it uses Australian/UK spelling and some Australian slang. Although you should be able to understand the novel without a glossary, there is always fun to be had in learning new words. Temperatures are in Celsius, weight is in kilograms, and distance is (generally) in kilometres (although we still have some slang which uses miles).

Arse: Ass.

Bench: Counter.

Bitumen: Asphalt.

Bonnet: Hood.

Bottle-o: Bottle shop/liquor store.

Buggery: Multiple meanings. Technically bugger/buggery is sodomy/anal sex, but in Australia, the use is more varied. Bugger is a common expression of disbelief/disapproval.

Came down in the last shower (Do you think I): Born yesterday

Cherry (Drag racing) : Red light indicating that you "red-lighted"/jumped the start.

Cock-ups: Fuck-ups/mistakes.

Diamante: Rhinestone.

Dipper: See S Bends below.

Fairy-Floss: Cotton candy.

Footpath: Sidewalk.

Formal: Prom.

Fours: Cars with a four-cylinder engine.

Loo: Toilet.

Message bank: Voicemail.

Mirena: An IUD that contains and releases a small amount of a progesterone hormone directly into the uterus.

Necked: Drank from.

Newsagency: A shop which sells newspapers/magazines/lotto tickets. Similar to a convenience store, but without the food.

Off my face: Drunk/under the influence (including of drugs).

Pap: Paparazzi.

Paracetamol: Active ingredient in pain-relievers like Tylenol and Panadol.

Phone/Mobile Phone/Mobile Number: Cell/cell phone/cell number.

Real Estate: All-inclusive term meaning real estate agency/property management firm.

Ricer: Someone who drives a hotted up four-cylinder (usually imported) car, and makes modifications to make it (and make it look) faster.

Rugby League: One of the codes of football played in Australia.

S bends (and into the dipper): Part of the racetrack shaped into an S shape. On Bathurst track, the dipper is the biggest of the S bends, so called because there used to be a dip in the road there before track resurfacing made it safer.

Sandwich with the lot: Sandwich with the works.

Schoolies: Week-long (or more) celebration for year twelves graduating school. Similar to spring break. The Gold Coast is a popular destination for school leavers from all around the country, and they usually have a number of organised events, including alcohol-free events as a percentage of school leavers are usually under eighteen (the legal drinking age in Australia).

Scrag: Whore/slut.

Shout (referring to drinks or food): Buy for someone. "Get the tab."

Silly Season: Off season in sports. Primarily where most of the trades happen (e.g. driver's moving teams, sponsorship changes etc).

Slicks: A special type of racing tyre with no tread. They're designed to get the maximum amount of surface on the road at all times. Wet weather tyres have chunky tread to displace the water from the track.

Skulled: (can also be spelled sculled and skolled) Chugged/Drank everything in the bottle/glass.

Stiff Shit: Tough shit/too bad.
Sunnies: Sunglasses.
Taxi: Cab.
Thrummed: Hummed/vibrated.
Titbit: Tidbit.
Tossers: Pricks/assholes/jerks.
Tyres: Tires.
Year Twelve: Senior.
Wag: Ditch school.
Wank: Masturbate
Wankers: Tossers/Jerk-offs.
Whinge: Whine/complain.
Uni: University/college.

CHAPTER ONE

WAKING UP

A BANGING YANKED me from dreams of Alyssa. Of her panting beneath me as I kissed her. Of her body pressing against me.

The sound smashed through me, echoing the throbbing in my head. Or maybe it was the other way around; maybe my head beat a rhythm in response to the banging. I didn't fucking know. All I knew was that it was too fucking early to be awake and I didn't want to be bothered by anyone. Not when it felt like my whole body had been passed through a meat grinder.

Twice.

"Fuck off!" I called into my pillow, not giving a shit who it was. I wasn't interested in a conversation with anyone. Not until I'd had a handful of pain pills and at least another twelve hours of sleep. Maybe another bottle of whiskey.

When the door opened regardless of my wishes, I groaned in complaint. I lifted myself just far enough off my pillow to pull it out from under me and stuff it over my head, blocking out all light and sound. The movement stabbed at my ribs, which were sore along one side from multiple injuries. First a crash on the racetrack, and then a fall while I was in London trying to recover from the accident. A cry of agony slipped from me as my other side joined in the party, sending a cascade of pain rolling through my body before stealing my breath away entirely.

Unable to breathe through the torture, I stilled and did what I could to will the blinding ache away. One thing was certain, there was no way I was moving again — not even to get painkillers.

"Declan." My father's voice boomed through my skull, reminding me that I wasn't home in Sydney.

Instead, I was up in Queensland. Back in Browns Plains, the one place I'd sworn for so long to never return to. All in an attempt to woo back Alyssa, my one-time best friend turned ex-girlfriend. I'd spent so long pretending not to care about her that I'd almost convinced myself it was true. The wake-up call had come in the form of a battering on the racetrack by my subconscious mind. It was almost comical how pussy-whipped I'd become in the week I'd been home. I'd done almost everything she'd asked me to, and in response, she'd spurned me.

A groan rose in my throat as everything that had happened in the last few weeks came flooding back in. When it had, the aches in my body seemed meaningless compared to the ones in my heart. I'd been gone for so long, denying the parts of myself that wanted to think of Alyssa, that I'd missed so much in the lives of those I'd left behind. My thoughts turned to my son, who'd passed away days after his birth, and had been mourned by everyone but me because of the fucking secret-keepers, who included my own damn parents. It was a good thing my eyes were screwed shut under the pillow because otherwise they might have filled with tears.

My mind turned from death to life. To Phoebe, my daughter; already a little girl, even though I'd barely known about her for two weeks. I hadn't spent more than a few hours with her, and I didn't know whether I'd be able to after the way Alyssa had left the previous afternoon.

My throat grew clammy at the thought. The recollection of my attempt to make her see that I was here to stay and the subsequent anger that had burned through me in response to her walking away from me came crashing back. Fuck! I wanted to go back to sleep and forget about how I'd lost her yet again. I wanted to rush to her and beg her to take me back.

"Declan!" Dad repeated my name all too fucking loudly, his tone pissy and simmering with heat.

"I thought I said fuck off," I uttered in a breathless murmur before my voice was stolen by a fresh groan.

The pillow was ripped from my hands, causing a stabbing pain to radiate through my ribs again. I growled as it sailed across the room.

Fucking prick.

"I cannot believe the stunts you pulled last night. What were you thinking? Do you know what it could do to your career if you were caught? Not to mention what people might say about your mother and me with the way you arrived home. Do you have any sense at all?"

Taking my time in order to avoid more pain—not that it really helped—I rolled over onto my stomach to stop the influx of light burning my eyes even through my closed eyelids.

"What are you talking about?" Every syllable hurt. Every breath wheezed. My head still throbbed and I couldn't concentrate. *What the fuck happened last night?*

The absolute last thing I needed was a lecture. My father's tone made it clear one was coming regardless of whether I was willing to listen. Arguing with him would only delay the inevitable and quite possibly result in an explosion of anger from one of us. Probably me. It was better for me to lie there and at least pretend to pay attention. Even if I was really thinking about everything except what he had to say.

While he started to speak about some shit, I did my best to concentrate on his words but failed miserably. I opened one eye, wincing against the harsh light, and raised my head slightly off the bed. Ignoring the shooting pain in my sides as I turned, I looked over to where my father stood watching me with an expectant look on his face. With a groan, I closed my eyes and dropped my head again.

"Have you listened to a single word I've said?" he snapped.

I shook my head against the mattress. My dark auburn hair, overdue for a cut, fell into my eyes as I did.

A sigh escaped him seconds before he sat on the bed next to me. The jerk of the mattress as he sat down sent a fresh wave of pain rolling through my body.

"Son of a bitch," I muttered under my breath.

"Honestly, you're old enough to know better than this stuff."

I opened one eye again after something landed on the bed beside my arm. An empty scotch bottle met my eye and the throbbing in my head made a little more sense.

How much did I drink?

"Your mother explained how much you hurt her when we saw you in Sydney. I'd have thought you'd have learned your lesson about alcohol by now."

Even though I was barely awake, I was cognisant enough not to admit that it was a hell of a lot more than alcohol in my system when I'd apparently destroyed a cafe in Sydney rather than let Mum talk to me about Alyssa.

"And drunk-driving? What the heck were you thinking? And as if all that wasn't bad enough, coming home in the arms of that boy was the last straw. What will the neighbours think?"

Like I give a shit what your neighbours think. Instead of letting the words fly from me, I swallowed them down. My ribs protested the action. In fact, they protested every breath and tiny movement. I had no idea why they were so much worse than they had been any other day since I'd injured them—why the other side now ached just as badly. I only hoped the pain meant they were healing and not getting worse.

While I focused on the pain, more of Dad's words made it through my treacle-like mind and my confusion grew. *Drink-driving?*

As if a dimmer switch was being turned in my head, a little more of the picture grew clear. I'd gone to the Gold Coast after Alyssa had run from me when I'd made a reference to a future together. Then I'd . . .

Fuck, he's right.

I had driven drunk, hadn't I? The fact was I couldn't remember much of what'd happened after I'd stopped at the bottle-o for two bottles of whiskey. All I'd wanted to do was drown the bitterness that the sight of Alyssa walking away had burned into me.

Illuminated by the recollection, a memory niggled of kissing Alyssa. Even as it clarified, I knocked it down. There was no way Alyssa would have allowed me to kiss her that way under the rules she'd set when I'd asked whether we could try once more. She certainly wouldn't have kissed me back like my mind taunted. It had to be a dream, an extension of the dream I'd been having when Dad woke me maybe. Only, it didn't feel like a dream—my hands burned with the memory of tracing them along her body. My lips, though dry as fucking sand, felt heated and worked over.

While Dad droned on about responsibility and stupidity, I spent a minute going over Alyssa's rules again to be sure there wasn't something I'd missed that would explain the memory of the kiss.

First, one date for every psychiatrist session I had. Second, I had to wait for her to be ready to take things further, I couldn't fuck random chicks or I'd lose her forever.

And lastly, no using alcohol as a salve.

Oh shit!

I'd broken at least one of her rules—I'd drunk alcohol. To excess and in order to forget a problem. *Fuck!*

Worse, I'd had so much to drink that I didn't even know if I'd broken her second rule. The memory of Alyssa's warm body beneath me, of her honey-gold eyes meeting my turquoise ones in the instant before we kissed, of her breasts pillowing against my chest, made me think that *something* had happened while I was drunk. But what?

Maybe it was just a dream. I'd had enough of those about her lately. The theory made some sense. After all, the memory of my hands searching her familiar curves while she lay beneath me with her mahogany hair fanned behind her could only have happened in a dream. It just . . . felt too real in my mind for that to be the case. I wanted it to be real, but all I could do was hope to hell that I hadn't done something stupid with a stranger and had just imagined Alyssa in her place. If only I could remember a little more of the night.

As I nursed my aching head and sore body, I wondered whether Alyssa had a point about alcohol. Drinking so much only got me into trouble; it had certainly never done me any favours.

Something else Dad had said finally registered as I finished berating myself for being such a cock-up. "Wait! What fucking *boy*?"

"You'd have to ask your mother," he said with a dismissive wave of his hand. "All I know is that he all but carried you in from your car. Which is a mess, by the way."

At his words, I threw myself out of my bed. Even though my ribs and side stabbed me with even the smallest movement I made, and my head felt like I'd had cotton wool shoved into every spare inch, I had to see what he meant.

My baby? A mess?

I dragged my tired, sore arse through the house as fast as I could with the agony I was in and threw open the front door to get a look at the damage Dad was talking about.

At the sight, my stomach fell to my feet and I almost dropped to my knees. Along the driver's side of my once pristine black Monaro was a huge-arse scratch that went from fender to quarter panel. Around the main damage, the black paint was torn away to expose the bare metal underneath.

My lip quivered as I took in the image of the side mirror hanging on by little more than the electrics. My baby was thoroughly fucked.

"What the fuck happened?" I cried out as I headed back into the house, slamming the door shut on the sight behind me. If I looked at it for one more second, I'd lose it. I was used to seeing cars in various states of disrepair, but other people's cars. Not my fucking Monaro.

I met Dad halfway down the hallway.

"What happened?" I asked again.

"How am I supposed to know what you did to your car? It is a perfect example of what I've been saying though. If you hadn't been so irresponsible last night, it would still be undamaged, wouldn't it?"

I rolled my eyes as he used the opportunity to start his lecture again, only now I was too awake to ignore him and too sore and sorry for myself to put up with it.

"You need to think through your actions. How long do you think Sinclair will keep you on as a driver without a licence? If you lose that job, then what will you do? "

His words made me think of Phoebe. Of Alyssa. Of the life that I wanted to have; the one I wanted to deserve. The one I absolutely didn't deserve if I made stupid-arse choices like getting behind the wheel while I was drunk. It put the damage to my car into perspective a little, and my fingers unclenched from the fists they'd formed.

"I always told you not to settle down and ruin your life, didn't I? I said to make sure you practised safe sex. You obviously didn't listen to me."

Even though talking to him about whether or not I wrapped my cock was the last thing I wanted to do, the statement made me think of the fact that he hadn't told me about Phoebe and Emmanuel. He'd known about the pregnancy, about everything, and had kept it quiet. Mum had explained her reasons, but Dad . . . he wasn't bound by any such promise or desire to protect a relationship with Alyssa.

While he'd been something of a surrogate father to her while we were younger, just like her Dad had been to me, things had changed around the time she and I had shared our first kiss. From that moment on, Dad seemed to view her as a threat to my dreams and had not been overly welcoming toward her.

"Why didn't you tell me sooner?"

"Your mum promised Alyssa."

My gaze cut to his. There was no way that was the reason. "Don't pull that bullshit cop-out answer. Why didn't *you* tell me?"

The corners of his eyes pinched together and he frowned. It

seemed like he was issuing some silent challenge. I didn't back down though. After a moment, he raised one brow. "I didn't want you to be trapped."

My hung-over brain took a minute to process the intent behind his words. "You think Alyssa was trying to *trap* me?"

He lifted one shoulder in a half-shrug. "She wouldn't exactly be the first girl to use that trick to get what they wanted. There's plenty of girls out there willing to do anything to land men like us."

The ache in my ribs burned as my heart pounded against my chest without relief. My cotton-filled and swollen head throbbed in time with my rapid heartbeat. "Why would you even think that?"

"You made it clear that you had dreams elsewhere and then suddenly she came here and announced she was pregnant with your child. Come on, son, it doesn't take a genius to work it out."

I stood as tall as I could, until I towered over him. The movement sent stars bursting behind my eyes, but I didn't care. "You don't know shit about her."

"I know she's manipulative. Most of these girls are, son."

With great effort, I bit back on my rage and didn't just lash out at him with my fists like I had with others when they'd spoken about Alyssa.

"Watch what you're saying." My voice was a low hiss squeezed through my clenched teeth.

"You only have to look at the way she has all the boys running around after her. It's like she's the queen bee or something."

"Back off her," I seethed, as my fingers curled into my palms.

"You're making my point for me."

With my fists still clenched tightly at my sides, I closed the distance between us until my face was inches away from his. "Fuck off," I spat at him.

"You have her so high on a pedestal you can't even see how much she schemes to get her own way."

"She *schemes*?" The tight rein I'd had on my temper snapped. "You think it was a fucking scheme that *I* decided to stick my unprotected dick in her? You think it was a fucking manipulation that I was too much of a prick to take her calls when she needed me the most? You think it was a fucking ploy of hers that I haven't been able to have a single night's sleep without her living in my dreams? You think she somehow arranged for visions to show up in the middle of every fucking race to distract me? 'Cause you know what, Dad, I can't fucking see how she could have arranged any of that shit. I can't see how she had one ounce of control in any of those things. And I don't see how she's ever fucking tried to do anything other than try to make me a better person."

"So, Josh wasn't the one that beat you up that day?"

His question threw me and I took a backward step. "What?"

"After the formal, when I had to take you to the doctor. You were spouting some bullshit story about how you were mugged, but I'm not stupid. I know it was that boy Josh."

I blinked at him, trying to figure out what that had to do with anything. "Why does that even matter?"

"Well, you break up with Alyssa and then suddenly her big brother is beating you up. Tell me how that's not manipulating the situation."

"God, you're a fucking idiot. If that hadn't happened, I might have had to think long and hard about whether or not to go to Sydney. That made my decision easier. So if Alyssa was trying to *trap* me, why the fuck would she send Josh around here?"

Dad stared at me in stunned silence.

"You really wanna know why Josh came here? Because he fucking thought I raped her, that's why. Because all the shit you put in my head about not being trapped by our relationship bubbled to the surface on what should have been the best fucking night of my life and we argued about it. She took off in tears with a ripped dress in her hands and Josh filled in the blanks the way he wanted to."

"I didn't know." It didn't escape my attention that his voice didn't hold an ounce of apology.

"No, you fucking didn't. So shut the fuck up about shit you know nothing about."

He huffed but then collected himself and tried to appear in control of the situation again. "There is no point arguing about the past. However you will need to learn some respect if you expect to stay in our house. You will apologise to your mother and if I hear of you doing one more thing to upset her, I will kick you out on your arse."

"Yeah?" I raised my eyebrow. "Well, if I ever hear you disrespecting Alyssa again I will kick your arse."

He shook his head and curled up his nose. "You've still got it bad for that girl, don't you?"

"If you mean do I still love her? Then yeah, I do. And I'm going to go fucking tell her that right now."

CHAPTER TWO

PIECING IT TOGETHER

DESPITE MY WORDS, when I turned away from him I went in search of Mum first. As pissed as I was at Dad, some of his words had made sense. Not the shit about Alyssa of course — that was utter bull. But about the way I'd treated Mum. Ever since I'd left for Sydney, I'd been an absolute fucking jerk.

After a short search, I found her in the laundry. The way she was hiding behind the door made me think she might have been trying to avoid me. The thought made my heart ache almost as much as my ribs did.

"Want a hand, Mum?" I asked, trying to make my voice as apologetic and sincere as I could through the pounding in my head. I wasn't sure how to go about mending things with her. Truthfully, she probably didn't expect me to try, but I needed to grow a pair and grow the fuck up or I would never deserve Alyssa. I'd certainly never deserve Phoebe.

Mum turned to me. For a brief second, shock flittered across her features before being pushed down again. "No, thank you, love. I can manage."

There was no doubt in my mind that she wanted to chew me out over my stupid-arse actions the night before, but just like when I was a child she'd leave me be because Dad had already had his say. She offered me a smile, which I was certain was supposed to be a peace offering for both of them.

"Fine, don't say I didn't offer though." I smirked at her as I jumped up to sit on the laundry bench. It took me a moment to catch my breath after I had, and I wondered what the hell had happened. Before I could ask, Mum spoke again.

"You seem in a better mood than you were last night," she observed.

I shrugged. The truth was that I wasn't, but I was willing to try to be. If I didn't think of my car, or the shit Dad had said, I could stay in an almost decent mood. At least to the outside world. In my head, it was a different story. "Not really. But I gotta deal with this shit sometime, don't I?"

She shook her head as she folded a towel. "Declan, you really should watch your language."

And that's when I knew things were okay between us, because she was at ease enough to admonish me again. "I know, Mum. Look, about last night—"

She cut me off with a wave of her hand. "I don't expect you to be perfect, Declan. I know you've got a lot to deal with. Just try to remember that Alyssa does too and you're going off the rails will only add to her stress."

"I know. I think I might have really fucked things up last night. I . . . I can't remember what I did after I left the Gold Coast though. Between Dad and my car"—the thought of the damage entered my mind and I wanted to whimper—"I know something bad happened. Dad mentioned something about me being dropped off?" I let the statement hang in the air as a question and a request for more information.

"You really shouldn't drink so much," Mum lectured in response.

I frowned that she hadn't filled in the blanks. "I know."

"I thought we'd raised you better than to get behind the wheel like that?"

A knot of emotions rose in my throat, and I swallowed hard to shift them. The words were not that different from what Dad had said. Except where his comments were armed missiles of rage and bullshit, fired with a precision strike to rile me up, the soft disappointment that echoed through Mum's voice broke my heart and ramped up my guilt.

I hung my head. "I know. It was stupid."

"You're lucky you didn't kill yourself or someone else."

Without raising my gaze, I nodded. My lips turned down into a frown as I considered her words and the truth in them. Who knew what I could have done—*had* done, considering the damage to my car. I really was such a fucking idiot. "Never again, Mum. I promise." I drew a cross over my heart with my fingertips like a kid.

She grabbed my chin like she used to when I was younger, and forced me to meet her eyes. "That's all I need to know."

I offered her a half-hearted smile.

"Alyssa called for you earlier, but I didn't want to disturb you while you were sleeping."

There was an emotion in Mum's voice that made me wonder whether she thought I'd have a reaction similar to the one I'd had when she visited me in Sydney—when I'd been so off my face on drugs and booze and had been trying so hard not to think of Alyssa and home. When I'd threatened to kill my own flesh and blood just for mentioning Alyssa's name. God, I was such an arsehole.

All traces of my slightly decent mood were washed away. Although I wanted to apologise to Mum, I knew words wouldn't make a difference. The best way to do it was exactly the same way I would win Alyssa back—not fucking up again. Proving through action that I could be better. That I could do better.

One thing Mum's words gave me was hope. Alyssa had called

for me. Surely that meant she was still talking to me . . . for the moment at least.

If I'd fucked up too badly, and she didn't want to speak to me anymore, surely she'd just cut all contact like she did when we were in London. She wouldn't call just to tell me to fuck off out of her life, would she?

"And you should probably find a way to thank Flynn for bringing you home."

My attention shot back to Mum, all thoughts of London and the shit that went down there between Alyssa and me forgotten in an instant.

Flynn?

Flashes of the night before crossed my mind, but I couldn't remember Flynn. I ran the few things I could remember over in my mind again and again. A nosy neighbour in a pink velvet robe over a floral nightgown. Kissing Alyssa. Josh?

Kissing Alyssa.

Even though I couldn't recall it all—everything was a haze of fuzzy memories and drunken recollections—it was clear that whatever had happened, I hadn't shacked up with some random chick. The certainty that I hadn't broken that rule gave me another small glimmer of hope. Something told me that would be the most unforgivable of crimes, at least as far as Alyssa was concerned. If Danny Sinclair found out about the damage to the Monaro, or the fact that I'd been drinking before I'd crashed, I would probably be kissing my position at Sinclair Racing goodbye.

I would have to make sure the repairs were done to the car before I went back home to Sydney. Both Eden and Danny would be likely to stick their noses into my business to find out the dirty details otherwise.

As I wondered how the hell I'd find a good panel beater, and whether I might be able to get the car straight in, a thought struck me. I'd lost all track of time and had no clue how much time had actually passed since getting on the plane in London.

"Fuck, what day is it today?" I asked.

"Language, Declan. Honestly."

A smart-arsed grin twisted my lips. "In that case, what day shall I call this beautiful sunshine morning my dearest mother?"

"Smart-arse," she muttered under her breath.

"Language, Mother. Honestly." I chuckled.

She stopped midfold and took a playful swipe at me.

I jumped down from the bench to avoid her. When I landed, a fresh stabbing pierced both my sides, causing a vice-like grip around my chest, and I couldn't breathe.

"Fuck!" I wheezed as I doubled over, clutching my chest.

"Declan! Are you okay?" Mum's voice cut through the fog of pain that had surrounded me.

I tried again to draw in a breath, but it felt impossible. My heart rate soared, each thump increasing the agony in my ribs. When I struggled to get enough oxygen into my system, panic clawed at my throat and made it even harder to squeeze any air into my lungs. Turning around, I grabbed hold of the side of the laundry bench and tried to focus through the pain and creeping dread. Tears pricked my eyes as I fought against the ache radiating from my ribs to encompass my whole body.

"Declan?" Mum's hand came to rest on my side, ramping up the pain until it was almost unbearable, making it difficult to not cry out in response.

With a tender touch, she lifted my shirt. A horrified gasp crossed her lips. "Is this from last night?"

Distracted from my panic by her words, I followed her gaze to my left side. Fresh purplish-black bruises blossomed opposite to where the yellow-brown ones were just starting to fade. *Fuck.* No wonder I was so goddamned sore. Sucking down a breath, I shifted to get a better view of the bruises and winced when the lightest touch of my fingers sent a fresh wave of agony around my body. The pain swelled through me, twisting my stomach and making me want to hurl. Just the thought of the pain that would accompany the action was enough to make me swallow it down.

"I think you should see a doctor," Mum said. The concern on her face was clear. Her eyes flicked to the dressings on my arm which covered a cut I'd earned in London after another night drinking and I could see the worry running through her mind. She thought I was going to end up killing myself.

If I kept on my current trajectory, she wasn't far off.

Dropping my shirt to cover the bruises, I tried to ignore the pain. "It's okay."

"Decl—"

"Really, Mum, I've had worse."

Although she frowned, she didn't argue further. "Did you want me to get you something to eat?"

It took me a second to connect her response to my earlier question. She was changing the subject, and I was grateful. "Honestly, Mum, I'm fucking twenty-two . . . I can handle getting myself some breakfast." I looked back at her. "Thanks for offering though." It was the closest thing to "I love you" I could say to my mum without handing my balls back in and requesting a pussy.

Leaving Mum to her chores, I headed to the kitchen but decided I really couldn't face having anything to eat. Instead, I thought I'd investigate getting quotes on my car. Mum was probably right, I should go to the doctor about my new injuries, but if I didn't book the car in before too long, I risked it not being done if I needed to head home to Sydney. Plus, the longer I left it, the greater the potential for the elements to increase the damage.

Knowing I needed to clean myself up and wake up properly before I could go anywhere, I headed for the shower. I was halfway back to my room with just a towel around my waist when I heard my phone ringing in my bedroom. My thoughts immediately went to Alyssa. Hoping against all odds that it was her, I raced down to grab it before whoever it was gave up. I didn't even look at the display before pushing Answer and putting the phone to my ear.

"Hello?"

"Declan, it's Danny."

"Oh. Hi."

I heard him chuckle. "There is no need to sound so disappointed."

"I was hoping it might be someone else, that's all," I said, trying to push the fact that I was talking to my boss wearing

28

nothing but a towel out of my mind.

He hummed in response before moving on. "Now Declan, I was hoping you might be able to enlighten me on something?"

Taking not too deep a breath, I answered with care. I couldn't help the feeling that I was walking into a trap. "Yeah?"

"You flew back in from London over the weekend, correct?"

The certainty it was a trap grew stronger. Considering I'd had to organise the travel arrangements through Sinclair Racing, there was no way he didn't know I'd come home. After a moment of silence passed, I realised he was waiting for an answer.

"Yes." My voice squeaked as I said the word. *God, I sound like a pussy!*

"And we agreed that you would stay in London as long as necessary to sort yourself out?"

"Yes."

"Can you see where I might be a little confused?"

"Confused?" I parroted the word, feeling the epitome of it myself.

"Yes, confused. If you were supposed to stay in London until you got yourself sorted, and you are now back home, it would be logical to assume that you have sorted yourself out, would it not?"

"Umm—" I didn't get anything more out before he cut me off.

"But if you had sorted yourself out, I would have expected you to come back into the office to talk to me about returning."

"Well. See. The thing is . . ." I swallowed down the nerves, wincing as it sent a fresh shooting agony through my ribs. "Something came up."

"Like?"

"I bumped into an old girlfriend on the plane. She wasn't able to stay for an extended visit in London and I wanted to spend some more time with her." Why did I feel like a schoolboy explaining something to his father?

"And this girl. Is she helping or hurting your goal this silly season?"

"Helping." I couldn't tell him it was a bit of both. Frankly, I was a little terrified of climbing into the new car next year because I didn't know whether my visions of Alyssa would be gone, or if they would be replaced by visions of Phoebe instead. Maybe both turquoise and brown eyes would haunt me in unison. "At least I think so."

"And you're not thinking about jumping ship on me are you, Declan?"

"What? No fucking way. Sinclair is my home."

He hummed again before issuing a half-hearted, "Okay."

I felt like that was the crux of his call and the rest was preamble. My heart was in my throat as I asked a question that burned through me in response to his interrogation. "Why would you ask that?"

"I keep my ear to the ground. Sometimes I hear interesting things."

"Like?" My heart raced as I remembered Danny's wife, Hazel, watching my conversation with Paige Wood—the owner of Wood Racing, Sinclair's closest rival. I hoped like hell she hadn't told Danny, but I knew the chances of that were slim. She had no reason to hide it, even if it wasn't something I wanted discussed.

"Like the rumours that Paige Wood has been courting one of my drivers."

"Well, it ain't fucking me. And if she did, I'd tell her where to stick it." It may not have been the full truth, but I didn't need to stir things up more than they already were. The fact was that even though Paige had made it clear she had her eyes on me, I hadn't considered her offer seriously. The only reason I'd even stopped to talk to her was because I'd wanted some positive attention after the crash, and for an older woman she wasn't too hard on the eyes. Considering driving with Wood meant driving with the psycho motherfucker Hunter Blake, nothing she could have offered would have been worth the hassle. It would have also meant moving back to Brisbane, and at the time that hadn't been appealing.

Danny was quiet for a second. "That's reassuring to hear. Remember you still have a year left on your contract."

Wondering why he'd bring that up, why then, I swallowed down the lump in my throat and asked, "And then?"

"Well, that's up to you. Isn't it?"

"Meaning?"

"Meaning if you stop costing me so damn much money on the track, I'll consider renewing your contract."

"Thanks, that's very gracious of you." The sarcasm dripped off every word.

He chuckled, no doubt more satisfied by my returned snark than he ever would have been by words of reassurance. "Actually, I think that it is. You do know how much you cost me last year, don't you?"

"Not *exactly*," I said, "but I have a rough idea."

"Bear that in mind when you hit the tracks next year then, and we'll be fine. I do still believe in you, Declan."

His words were yet another reason why the offer from Wood Racing would never have been interesting to me. As much of a monster as Danny could be when it was needed, he also made his team a family. He made you feel like he cared and did whatever he had to do to keep everything working. "Thanks, Danny. And . . . thank you, for giving me some time to sort this stuff out."

"Where would I be if I strung out my best drivers every time they hit a rough patch?"

"Between Morgan and me? Without any drivers." I was being a smart-arse but Danny knew that side of me. It was who I'd been before Queensland Raceway. Before I thought Alyssa had moved on with someone else and the memory of her haunted me around the track. Before I knew that it was actually me, and a genuine growing love for the sport that held my passion, that had led her trackside.

He laughed heartily. "Exactly. Well, if there's nothing else?"

"Actually, there is *one* thing." An idea for a date with Alyssa had struck me and I knew Danny would be well placed to pull some favours and arrange it for me. I explained what I wanted to do, and he actually sounded excited as he agreed to help me with my request. All I had to do was organise my part and wait until Saturday.

And get my car fixed.

After I'd hung up, I dressed and then went looking for Mum

again. I needed her help to pull off my plan. When I found her, she was in the kitchen rearranging the cupboards.

I frowned as I watched her work. *Does she ever just stop and have a break?*

And I was going to add to her load.

"Hey, Mum?" I gave her my best puppy-dog look.

She didn't stop her incessant cleaning, but took a moment to glance up at me. "What is it?"

"What are you doing on Saturday?"

"Nothing I can think of. Why?" Her voice held just a hint of concern.

"I was wondering if you were available to watch Phoebe if Alyssa can't get anyone else."

She stopped and stood up properly, leaving her rag on the bench. "What are you planning?"

I winked at her. "Nothing . . . much. At least, nothing until I know for certain that Alyssa is willing to go out with me on Saturday." *Or at all.* "I'm just trying to make sure she doesn't have an easy reason for saying no."

"I take it you haven't rung her yet then?"

"No, I was going to call her after my shower but Danny rang instead."

"I hope it was nothing serious?"

I shrugged. "I'll tell you all my secrets when you tell me yours." I paused. "Actually scratch that, I don't want to know your secrets and you sure as shit don't want to know all of mine."

"Declan—"

I cut her off with a laugh. "Yeah, yeah, I know. Watch the language."

"Exactly. And ring Alyssa."

"Have you got her mobile number? I don't want to call Josh's house."

She sighed. "Will I regret giving it to you?"

"I'm not going to stalk her, if that's what you mean."

"And if she tells you that she's had enough and wants you to go?"

Fuck. I wondered whether Alyssa had said something along those lines to Mum during the phone call that morning. The question was on my lips, but I couldn't ask it in case the answer was yes.

Fuck me. I'd called in a favour from Danny that I hadn't really earned or deserved—one that would no doubt cost me in the long run—to organise my planned date with Alyssa. The entire fucking experience I was trying to put together for Saturday would be for nothing if she didn't want to see me again. My hand gripped at my hair, tugging the auburn locks with concern.

Mum shook her head lightly and chuckled. "Don't stress so easily. She didn't say anything in particular." There were times I thought Mum could fucking read minds or something—it was scary how intuitive she could be. "Between your behaviour last night, Flynn bringing you home, and Alyssa's phone call this morning, I guessed something must have happened between you two. I just want to know that if she honestly wants you to leave her alone, you will."

I nodded. "If she said that, and really meant it, I guess I'd have no choice, would I?"

She mulled it over for almost a minute before scribbling a number down on a piece of paper. Grabbing it off her with a grin, I headed to my bedroom, programming the number into my phone as I went to make sure I didn't lose it.

Just as I was about to dial Alyssa's number, my phone rang again.

Fucking popular today, aren't I? I sighed but then looked at the name displayed and was smiling by the time I pressed Answer. "Hello, Doc."

"Good morning, Declan. Are you ready for your first session?"

"Sure thing, Doc. Shall I call you back, 'cause I know you'll add a surcharge to my arse if you pay for an interstate mobile call."

He chuckled. "Are you implying I'm opportunistic?"

"I ain't implying anything, Doc," I said with a laugh. "I'm saying it straight out."

"Shooting straight from the hip, like always. Do you ever think that maybe that's what gets you into trouble?"

"Always." Despite the pain I was in, talking to Dr Henrikson made me almost buoyant. So long as I could convince Alyssa that my fuck-up with the alcohol was a one-off that would never happen again, I might be able to look forward to a date with her. After all, she'd agreed to a date for every session, and I was ready to have my first.

With those thoughts bouncing around within me, it was easy to ignore everything else. Okay, there was still a lot I had to arrange with Alyssa, but overall I was feeling pretty fucking elated. "I thought you were going to have Lucy call and schedule though?"

"I had a cancellation," the doc said. "I figured you were desperate to talk to me and wouldn't complain if I was the one to call in this instance."

"'Course not."

"So, tell me: where would you like to start?"

Fuck. I hadn't thought that far ahead. Alyssa had specified I try to sort myself out, but there was so much to sort. I didn't know where to start or how much to tell him. Especially not after what had happened in our last meeting—where I'd threatened him for trying to force me to talk about Alyssa. The truth was I hadn't really thought the whole therapy thing through. Sucking down a painful breath, I just let the first thing I could think of free. "I think I know why I was crashing?"

"Is that a question or a statement?"

"Um, I'm not really sure, I guess."

"Well, why don't you tell me what you think is causing it?"

"Alyssa."

I don't know what the sound that I heard down the phone line was. It might have been the sound of him choking on a drink, a cough, or possibly even him stifling a laugh. "I thought Alyssa was off limits?"

I *really* hadn't thought the whole therapy shit through. "She's, uh, she's not anymore."

"And why is that?"

I took a deep breath. "Because almost everything I need to talk to you about from here on in centres around her in one way or another."

"And why is that?" His voice definitely had a hint of amusement to it. He was probably just itching to mutter those four fucking words.

"Because I fucking love her. I always have, and I—I was running scared of that." Once I'd opened my mouth to start, the words escaped me in a rush.

There was a beat of silence on the other end.

"Just say it already," I said, to break the silence. Even though phone sessions weren't ideal, I was actually a little relieved not to have to see his expression. Although if I closed my eyes, I could easily imagine the smug smile that had to be lifting the ends of his moustache.

"I don't know what you are talking about."

"Yeah, right. You know you're itching to say it."

"It would be highly unprofessional."

"Fuck professional. Say the words. I dare you."

A chuckle echoed down the line. "I told you so."

I laughed. "See, doesn't that make you feel better?"

His laughter grew in response. "You really are in a good mood today aren't you?"

"I guess." I started randomly cleaning shit up in my room, pinning the phone between my shoulder and my cheek. Each time I bent over, a new pain shot across my chest. It was starting to become clear that Mum was definitely right—I needed to see an actual doctor before long.

"Why do you think that is?" Dr. Henrikson pressed. "What's so special about today?"

"Today is the first day of the rest of my life?" I couldn't even say the words with a straight face. "Isn't that the sort of shit I'm supposed to spout in these sessions?"

"You know you can say anything you want with me, it's just between us."

"I just . . . I don't know. I feel like something's shifted in the universe, know what I mean?"

"Go on."

"I've had the week from hell and yet I've survived. More than that, I know what I want now, and I'm ready to claim it."

"Do you think you deserve it?"

"Fuck no. No one deserves Alyssa, especially not me, especially not after what I've put her through. She's too good for every fucking person on this planet. But I want to work toward the possibility of maybe deserving her one day."

"It's not good to hold people up on pedestals, Declan. The higher you hold them in your regard, the further they have to fall when something goes awry."

"Yeah, but you haven't met Alyssa."

"No. But I'd like to if this is the influence she has on you."

"What do you mean?"

"Well, first there is the mood. You sound happier than I've heard you. Ever. And second, you've said a total of six cuss words the entire conversation. I used to be able to count that many per sentence."

Well, fuck me. Am I that obvious? "I guess she's calming me a bit. Although I think I may have screwed up last night. I don't really remember."

He sighed. "Tell me all about it."

So I did.

CHAPTER THREE

WALK AWAY

I HUNG UP the phone and took a minute to recap in my mind the conversation I'd just had with Dr. Henrikson. I'd expected him to ask me probing questions about why I was in Brisbane, why I wanted to talk to him daily, and mostly why I was drinking to excess again.

Instead, he simply listened as I told him the little I could remember about the previous night, then he questioned me about random stuff. What the weather was like, how long I was planning on staying in Brisbane; he never asked a single question about Alyssa and me. I was actually glad for it. I knew I needed to talk to him about my drinking, about Emmanuel and Phoebe, and Alyssa and everything else that was happening in my life. I hadn't wanted to go into an in-depth analysis during our first phone call after the way my last session had ended.

I didn't relish the idea of going over the twelve months that had passed in the meantime either. He seemed to sense that, or perhaps he just knew better than I did that I needed time to broach those subjects. He was the fucking shrink after all, and a highly recommended one at that. That's why he got the big bucks.

After I hung up, I felt as though a small part of the stress I'd been feeling was lifted. Between my mood and the phone call, I was feeling pretty fucking fantastic when I picked up the phone again to call Alyssa. It was only as I listened to the dial tone that I realised Dr. Henrikson had kept me on the phone and therefore would charge me extra for the cost of the call.

Fucker, I thought to myself in amusement. He was a great therapist, but definitely opportunistic. He never missed a single chance to get in extra billings.

"Hello?" Alyssa answered, obviously wary and not recognising my phone number.

"Hey. It's me."

"Mmmm-hmmm, so you finally decided to pick up a phone and call me did you?" Her irritation was clear even down the phone line.

God, I hope she'll let me apologise. I couldn't explain—there was no explanation or excuse good enough—but I could apologise. Again and again if I had to.

"Yeah. Sorry. I'm only four years late." I tried for the lame joke to break the tension.

There was a strangled sound, but then more silence.

"You, uh, you wanted me to call," I said, trying desperately to draw her back into a conversation. If it was any other woman, I was certain I'd be able to charm them into whatever I wanted. With Alyssa though . . . She had my tongue tied up in knots so big I was lucky to be able to get any words out at all.

"Right. So do you care to explain what the hell that was about last night?"

Shit. I knew I'd done something to fuck it up with her. If only I could fucking remember the conversation we'd had or what I'd done. "I'm sorry, Lys. I just . . . fuck. I don't even have an excuse. There is no excuse. I fucked up. Plain and simple."

"I thought you'd agreed to try my rules."

"I did, Lys. I *am*. I just fucked up. Please, let me try to make it up to you. And to Phoebe."

"Did you mean what you said?"

"When? About trying? Didn't I just say I did?"

"No, last night at Josh's. Did you mean what you said?"

I tried in vain to remember what I said. "Fuck. Look, Lys, I promised I'll be honest with you, and the truth is I can't remember anything I said last night. The last thing I can clearly remember is . . ." I trailed off, because the last thing I could remember was buying the alcohol and climbing into the car down the Gold Coast.

"Getting drunk?" Alyssa finished for me.

"Yeah," I agreed. "I'm sorry about that. I . . ." I couldn't finish because there wasn't an excuse. I understood that on some level. Although, it was easier to see how stupid and selfish it was when I had Alyssa on the phone and knew she was still talking to me. When she'd run away the day before, it had just felt like it was all too much and I had no other option. "Look, can I take you out to dinner?"

"What about our agreement?"

A small smile reached my lips as I sighed in relief. Alyssa was still going to hold me to the agreement. Which meant she still wanted to see me. "Already had my first session."

"Really? When."

"We finished about five minutes ago."

"And?"

"And what? You expect him to fix all my fucking problems in one hour?"

A hard bark of laughter echoed down the line. "No, I guess not. When are you talking to him again?"

Fuck. I knew I'd have to tell her this part sooner rather than later, but I'd been hoping to discuss it when she was in a good mood, not when she was pissed over something I did while drunk and stupid. "Tomorrow."

"So soon?" Her confusion was evident.

"I meant what I said, Lys. I know I fucked up last night, but I want to make up for that. In fact, the doc and I agreed that it would be best for me to talk to him daily for the moment."

"Uh huh, and I suppose that decision was in no way influenced by *our* agreement?"

"Maybe just a little," I admitted. I wasn't going to lie to her about it, but I also wasn't going to tell her that she was the only reason for daily sessions. Although I was starting to see benefits for myself too. After all, I had a reason to be better. I remembered London, looking in the mirror and wondering whether Phoebe should be saddled with someone like me in her life. I realised now that I wanted to be in her life, but it was more than that—I wanted to *deserve* to be in her life.

There was silence echoing down the line from Alyssa's end. I could almost picture her face and the way she would be spinning her hair between her fingers as she tried to decide whether or not she was happy about that.

"Don't worry, Lys, I'm not going to hold you to the agreement of one date for each session." It killed me to say it, but if it made her happier, it was the truth. "Of course I'd like to see you as much as possible, but I'm not going to make you do anything you don't want to."

She sighed. "Okay."

"So, can I pick you up tonight? I mean, if that's okay with you?"

"What about Phoebe? I'm not going to palm her off on people every night. She's my daughter, I want to spend time with her."

I began to feel hopeful that maybe I would get to see Alyssa as much as I wanted to; well, maybe not quite as much, because if I had my way I might not let her out of my sight again. "Bring her too."

"Declan, have you ever gone out to dinner with a three-year-old?" Somehow I could hear the frown in her voice. "It's not much fun."

"An early dinner then? Don't worry so much, Lys, I'll sort it out." *Trust me.* The words were poised on the tip of my tongue but I couldn't say them because that was part of our problem. She didn't trust me—and might not for some time.

"If you say so." I could hear the amusement in her voice now.

She'd come full circle from when we started the call.

"What time?"

"Um, five?"

"Perfect. Looking forward to it, Lys."

"Okay, I guess I'll see you later, Dec."

I love you, Lys. It was too soon to say it, so I bit the words back down. For the moment.

I would tell her when the time was right though. Just like I would tell her about the visions I'd had of her while racing. That although it wasn't her fault, every crash I'd had was because of her. I sighed. Despite ending the call on a positive note, just talking to Alyssa reminded me we still had so much to work out, so much trust I had to regain. Between that, the reminder that my car was busted to shit, and my aching side, my optimistic mood was positively dead.

More than anything, I wanted to show Alyssa that she could trust me. I would make the date perfect and stress-free for her. I would show her that I could plan ahead and be a . . . father. No, that I could be a dad. The only problem was I had no fucking clue how. I didn't know what I needed to organise for a three-year-old. Like Alyssa had pointed out, I had absolutely no freaking clue about kids. Luckily I knew someone who did and who just happened to be sitting out in the living room right now watching some shit on TV.

"Mum?" I said as I walked up behind her.

"Did you ring Alyssa?" The words were out before she'd even spun around.

Of course that'd be the first thing she asked. "Yeah. I just got off the phone with her. I'm taking her out to dinner tonight."

"It's not fair to take her away from Phoebe all the time."

"Yeah, Alyssa said the same thing. That's why I'm taking them both out."

Mum laughed. "Somehow I don't think your idea of a romantic date is compatible with a three-year-old."

"So I'll change my idea of a romantic date." I shrugged, and regretted the movement almost instantly when the pain in my side spread through my body again.

"Wow, Declan, is that the sound of you growing up that I hear?"

"Fuck off." I laughed to let her know I wasn't serious.

She shook her head but didn't say anything.

"I've never spent much time around kids. At least other than signing autographs, but that hardly qualifies as 'quality time.'"

"No, not really." I could tell Mum was struggling to keep the amusement out of her voice.

"So what the fuck do I need?"

"Well, first you need to clean up your language."

After making sure I was out of arms' reach, I said, "So no saying fuck, shit, arse, dick, or pussy then."

She shook her head again. "Declan, whatever will we do with you?"

I smirked at her. "Love me. It's all you can do."

She chuckled, but didn't argue.

"Second," she said. "You'll need to arrange a car seat. I know Alyssa has a spare one that she lends us when I look after Phoebe."

"Okay, car seat. I'll get one. I'll need it again anyway."

"You seem confident."

"I know how Alyssa feels about me, or at least I think I do. I mean, she hasn't sent me packing yet even though I did some stupid shit. That's got to mean something, right?"

"Maybe."

"Thanks for the vote of confidence."

"Just trying to keep you grounded in reality."

"I know the reality. I'm also trying to fix it."

"Fair enough."

Talking about reality reminded me of my earlier conversation with my father. "What's Dad's problem anyway?"

"What?" Mum was caught off guard by the shift in the conversation.

"This morning he was going on about how he thought Alyssa was trying to trap me."

She closed her eyes. "It's nothing for you to worry about."

"I think it is something to worry about if he's going to go around bad-mouthing the woman that I love and the mother of my child."

"I don't know what to tell you, Declan. I'm sure he's made his thoughts clear to you in the past." Her voice sounded . . . resigned.

I knew he'd always regretted settling down young, having me early, but it felt like there was more to it than that. "Are you trying to tell me he feels he was trapped somehow?"

"I don't know. You'd have to talk to him about it."

"I'm trying to talk to you."

"It's not my place."

"Are you okay, Mum?"

"I'm always okay, sweetheart. I can't tell you how happy I am that you are making an effort with Alyssa. She's a good person."

"Fine, change the subject, but I will find out what's going on."

"You'll need something to keep her entertained too."

"What?"

"Phoebe. If you expect her to sit nicely while you two eat, you'll need crayons and a colouring book or something."

Even though I knew it was just a distraction, I let the conversation move on. "Okay, so car seat and something to keep Phoebe occupied. Anything else?"

"I don't think so, dear. So I assume that means you are going out now?"

"Yep."

"You've still got the key?"

"Yep."

"Are you going to try to see a doctor about your side while you're out?"

"I'll try."

"Well, I'll see you later then." It was a dismissal and I understood why when she turned on the TV. Some daytime soap was on. I chuckled. Some things never changed.

I hunted for my wallet, phone, and car keys. Then I grabbed my sunglasses and hat because I decided to brave the Grand Plaza but still wasn't sure that I wanted to be recognised.

CHAPTER FOUR

REPAIRS

THE REMNANTS OF my somewhat happy mood were wiped away when I got outside and saw my car again. The scratch along the side—the one I'd caused . . . somehow—looked even worse than it had the first time I'd seen it. My Monaro was my baby, and I'd done everything I could to keep it pristine. Even though it was a few years old, there wasn't a scratch on the paint or the rims. At least there hadn't been until I'd fucked it up good and proper. After popping the locks with the remote, I ran my fingers across the exposed metal surface.

Fucking hell. It was just lucky that I'd only damaged the car. It was a miracle I hadn't killed myself or someone else.

Taking care not to hurt my ribs any further, I ducked down to examine the damage closer. The scratch had torn off the paint, but as I ran my finger over the worst of it, I found that it hadn't bent the metal too badly along most of the car. The front fender was rooted and would probably need to be replaced. Still, from what I could tell, the chassis wasn't bent. The car wasn't a write-off. It was the sort of damage that would take the boys back at Sinclair just a couple of hours to fix with their ready spare parts, willing hands, and array of tools. Considering they could repair a car overnight, it would have been an easy task for them. The longest part would be the paint booth. I didn't expect that any local smash repairers could get it done that fast, but there wasn't much choice. I needed it repaired before I went home.

Adding find a repairer into my mental to-do list, I climbed behind the wheel. When I did, I stopped and stared at the card on the dash. Sitting in front of the gauges was a card for Eastern Smash Repairs. I figured it was Dad's way of trying to mend the bridge between us. He was a car guy at heart after all. If anyone understood how much the damage hurt to look at, it would be him.

Putting my child seat shopping on hold for a little while, I headed toward the address on the card. At least it was close, so it wouldn't be a huge detour to, at minimum, get a quote.

A little less than five minutes later, I pulled up into the car park at Eastern Smash Repairs. It was more sophisticated and bigger than I'd expected for a suburban smash repairer. The front of the building, no doubt housing the admin offices, was all tinted glass, shiny aluminium, and navy walls. Four large roller doors faced the road, each one painted a pristine white. It certainly looked like the sort of place I could trust to work on my baby.

After I'd parked in one of the covered parking bays, I headed into the reception area. Chimes sounded when I pushed the door open and a young man who couldn't have been more than seventeen glanced up at me with a polite, welcoming smile at the ready. A second later, recognition lit his eyes and his smile widened. Behind his desk was a large plastic sign bearing the business name.

"Declan Reede," the receptionist said in awe as his eyes grew as wide as his smile.

"Um, hi."

He stood and practically leaped around the desk to get to me. "I was told to expect you, but wow, I didn't think I'd actually get to meet you." He stuck out his hand. "It's a huge honour, sir."

I shook his offered hand. "Just call me Declan."

After everything that had happened in the last few days, I'd almost forgotten my celebrity status. It had been so easy to get sucked into a well of darkness, that it was almost refreshing to see the hero worship on his face.

Although he looked like he might choke on his own tongue in his happiness, he nodded and repeated my name.

"You said you were expecting me?"

He nodded. "Mr. Olson said you might come in for a quote."

"Olson?" The name rang a bell in my mind, but I couldn't immediately place it. I was so certain Dad had been the one who'd left the card. Who else would have had access to my car to put the card on the dash?

Motherfucker! The answer struck me in an instant and I couldn't believe the interfering arsehole. "Flynn Olson?"

The receptionist frowned, his confusion clear on his face. Then he nodded. "Yes, Mr. Olson said you had some damage on your—"

Without waiting for him to finish, I turned around and headed back out the door. The chimes that had greeted me sounded again and drowned out the last of the sentence.

"Bastard," I hissed under my breath. As if it wasn't bad enough that he'd taken over my place in Alyssa's life, now he wanted to call the shots when it came to repairing my fucking car.

When I hit the car park, I saw the fucker kneeling down in front of my car inspecting the damage. One hand lifted to rub over his short, jet-black hair.

"What the fuck are you doing?" I called out.

He stood and spun on the spot, but the face that greeted me wasn't the one I'd seen with Alyssa at Queensland Raceway or the one from Emmanuel's graveside. It was almost but not quite the same. His eyes were the same as Flynn's, especially the way they narrowed at the corners as the man glared at me.

"Well, I was inspecting the damage so that I could give you a quote, but I don't need the hassle of rude customers so I don't think I'll bother."

"Just ignore his grumpy arse, Cain. It's me he's upset with,"

Flynn's voice called from behind me.

Cain . . . the fucker Alyssa had been with. I clenched my jaw tightly as I considered it. Images of his hands trailing paths through Alyssa's hair assaulted my mind. His tongue exploring her mouth. His body pressed against hers. Her hands—

My teeth ground together as I tried to push the thoughts out of my mind. *Fuck this, I don't need this shit.*

I didn't need to be there. There had to be other smash repairers around. I unlocked the car with the remote and moved toward it.

"Wait," Flynn said. His voice was closer than it had been. "I need to talk to you."

I spun on him. "Yeah? Well I don't have anything to say."

"Tough shit, because I do. And I'm sure Alyssa will be interested to hear of your unwillingness to listen."

I curled my fingers into a fist around my keys. *Motherfucker.* I sighed, forced my hand to relax, and locked the car again.

"Leave the keys with Cain," Flynn directed, as if he actually had some authority over me.

"Why—"

"There's no one better, that's why. At least, not nearby and maybe not at all. I'm sure you'll want that damage fixed before you have to explain it to Alyssa." His smug look indicated that he knew exactly what had happened. Added to Dad's words and Mum's assertions that I needed to find some way to thank Flynn, it was clear that he'd been there. Somehow, he'd found me and taken me—and my car—home.

That was the only reason I muttered, "Fine," and threw the keys to Cain.

Without another word, Flynn spun on his heels and headed back into the building. After balling my hands into fists again, I huffed out a breath to calm myself and then followed him inside.

He led me past the receptionist and into a spacious office. With a wave of his hand, he motioned toward two tub chairs along one wall. I stood in the middle of the room until he turned around. My fists curled and uncurled at my sides. I wasn't going to make it easy for the fucker.

"Just sit will you?"

I crossed to the chair and sat, letting out a huff as I lowered myself down. *This better be fucking worth it.*

He leaned against the desk and looked at me.

"Want a drink?" he asked, but his tone indicated it was a smart-arsed remark not a polite offer. I knew his true colours would come out as soon as we were alone.

"Fuck off."

"Charming. I can really see why Alyssa likes you. You've got that whole warm and fuzzy thing—"

I'd stood and crossed the room halfway through his sentence. "Shut the fuck up."

"You've got this whole nice-guy thing going on when it comes to her, but you don't fool me. You're a self-entitled arsehole."

I got up in his face, a sneer curling my lips. "I'm only an arsehole when people make me one."

He clenched his fists at his sides. "The only reason you're still standing right now is because I know how to control myself. Now, sit."

"You know what, it's not even worth it." With the sneer still cemented on my face, I reached for my car keys before I remembered Cain had taken them for his fucking quote. *Fucking shit!*

I stopped and clenched my fists before turning back to Flynn. "You wanna get to whatever point you wanted to make? 'Cause I sure as hell don't have all day to sit around and shoot the shit."

He raised one eyebrow at me. "What the hell was that last night?"

"What fucking business is it of yours?"

"Your drunk arse almost ran me off the fucking road before you crashed into that guard rail, that's what."

"Oh."

"Yeah. 'Oh.' Seriously, what the fuck were you thinking?"

Unwilling to explain my life to him, I crossed my arms and raised one eyebrow.

"Not only that, I don't know why you'd do that to Alyssa. She's trying—so damn hard—to trust you again for Phoebe's sake, and how do you repay her? By breaking her rules at the first opportunity."

"How do you—" I was going to ask how he knew that but there was only one way. My jaw clenched tightly as I thought about the fact that Alyssa had spilled our secrets to him. "She told you."

"Everything. From the whiskey to the whispered declarations. I know it all."

My fists clenched and unclenched against my legs. I itched to wipe the smug expression from his face. The fact that his brother had the keys to my baby—to my escape route—was the only reason I didn't. "Well, that's just—" *fucked up* "—great."

"Even if you hadn't agreed to follow Alyssa's requests, what the hell were you thinking getting behind the wheel in that state?" Before I could say anything in my own defence—not that there was anything I could say to excuse my behaviour—he continued on. "Do you know how many cars we have come through the doors here because of drunk drivers? Do you know how many lives have been lost because wankers like you got behind the wheel?"

"I didn't come here for a lecture."

"Well, stiff shit. If you're going to make stupid decisions, you're going to have to listen to one. What if it hadn't been me? I can control my car well enough when arseholes try to run me off the road, but what if it'd been another car you swerved toward? One with a family? You could have killed someone. What if you'd had Alyssa in the car with you? Phoebe?"

His words twisted in my stomach, writhing like snakes and increasing the guilt. "You think I don't know that?"

"I don't know. You were the one who—"

Holding up my hand, I cut him off. "Yeah, yeah, I know. And I really don't need to fucking hear it again."

"You do realise that if I hadn't been there, if I hadn't driven your drunk arse home, you might have been caught DUI? Anyone else would have probably called the police."

"What do you want, a fucking medal?"

He moved over to me and sat in the other tub chair. "You

know, each time I see you I find myself thoroughly confused over what it is that Alyssa sees in you. I still wonder what she'd say if she knew you almost ran me off the road."

I narrowed my eyes at him. "You didn't tell her?"

He sighed and looked away. "I was going to. And I still think she needs to know."

"Then why didn't you? After all, it'd earn you some points against me."

"God, you are such an idiot. This isn't a fucking contest."

Despite his words, it felt like one.

"She cares about you. God only knows why, but she does. If it was up to me, I'd be kicking your arse to the kerb over what you did."

"Are we done here?"

"You don't get it do you? I'm trying to help you out. I know Alyssa better than you do."

"No. I really don't think you do." I couldn't help the smirk that crossed my lips. Sure he might have her confidence for the moment, but there were things about Alyssa I knew that Flynn never could. Things that fuelled my fantasies and filled my nights.

"Whatever, man, I just want to know you'll stop doing stupid shit that can kill other people."

"Not that it's any of your business but no, it won't happen again. And you can tell Alyssa that when you speak to her."

He seemed to consider my words for a few moments, then he nodded. "Just know that if you do, I won't hesitate to call the cops and get your arse arrested for DUI."

Before I had a chance to say anything in response, there was a knock on the wall beside the open door. Without waiting to be invited in, Cain walked through and offered me a sheet of paper.

"I've got your quote," he said. "If you're interested, I can probably fit you in today."

"Are you serious?" The rest of my question, *Why on God's green earth would I leave my car with you?* died on my tongue as I flicked open the quote. I'd been certain it was going to be jacked up to twice the normal price, but it wasn't. In fact, it was a good few hundred less than I would have expected for the damage. "How long will it take?"

Cain and Flynn shared a loaded glance before Flynn nodded.

"I could probably have it back to you by Friday," Cain said.

"Friday. Huh." It timed out perfectly, but could I actually trust him with my baby?

Except, if I did, and they fucked up the Monaro worse than it already was, I could probably use it to my advantage. Alyssa would be pissed at them if they knowingly screwed me over. Plus, a bad word about their business by Declan Reede could probably cause them some grief. It was worth the risk to have my car repaired before Saturday with as little effort as possible.

"I guess I can leave it here, but then I don't have another car." I didn't add that I needed one to take Alyssa on a date.

"We can probably help out with that," Flynn said. "We have a few loaner cars."

He walked over to his desk and grabbed a leaflet. When he handed it to me, I saw it was for Eastern Car Hire.

"We actually run a hire company," he explained. "It's a good secondary source of income."

"Flynn's a wicked businessman," Cain said. "He came up with the idea after he finished uni last year. We haven't looked back since."

"It was easy to build on the back of his skills with the wrench."

That's fucking nice. Resisting an eye-roll at the mutual wank-fest, I nodded. Even though it killed me to ask, I found the words. "Well, what do you have available?"

Cain and Flynn grinned at each other and somehow I knew I was fucked.

CHAPTER FIVE

WILD ROSES

AN HOUR LATER, I was standing in front of a dizzying array of baby shit. I didn't understand how the fuck there could be so many different types of car seats. How the fuck was one significantly different to the others? All they needed to do was keep Phoebe safe, what the fuck else mattered?

I was in a big, faceless chain department store so there weren't even any ready assistants around that I could ask.

Each of the seats seemed to have weight ratings on them but how the fuck was I supposed to know what Phoebe weighed? She was little, that was all I knew. I looked around to find assistance, but the best I could do was ask at the CD counter. Which was unattended. Hoping someone might be in the little back room there, I rang the bell for help.

Not long after, a ghost from my past walked out to meet me. His dark hair was cropped short, and his once rake-thin body had expanded, but he was easily recognisable.

"Declan Reede!" Ben called in surprise.

There had been a time he'd been my best male friend, but I

hadn't spoken to him since I moved to Sydney.

"What the hell are you doing here?"

"Ben! Fuck, man, it's been too long."

"Yeah? Well, you knew where I was." His words were clipped. After the initial surprise of seeing me had worn off, he'd obviously decided he was going to aim for pissed off.

"True, bud. Sorry. It's been brought to my attention recently that I was an arse for the way I left."

"Just a bit." He dropped his voice. "You know about Alyssa, right?"

I nodded. "Yeah. Do you speak to her much?"

"Jade tried for a while, but Alyssa sort of froze everyone out as much as you did. I think it was because of the gossip. Arses like Blake Cooper and that bitch, Darcy. They made sure Alyssa's life was a living hell as soon as they learned she was pregnant. Of course none of them knew who the father was. The truth is most of them are still too stupid to realise."

"Of course, that means you know then?" I asked, to confirm my suspicion. "Because you and Jade were never stupid."

He shrugged. "Wasn't hard to figure it out, I mean we knew your plans. Then you're gone and Alyssa's pregnant."

He started to look a bit annoyed, as if he might take a swing at me. Then I realised what he probably assumed. It would have looked like I was avoiding them all to ignore my responsibilities.

"I—I didn't know." My admission was barely a whisper. I was still ashamed that the reason I didn't know was my own damned refusal to pick up the fucking phone.

"Serious?"

"Serious, man. I, well, I was a bit of a dick to Alyssa when she tried to contact me after I moved to Sydney." My voice faltered as the thoughts flitted through my mind. I shook it off as I remembered my mission. "But that's in the past now. Do you know anything about fucking car seats? I need to get one."

He raised his eyebrow at me. "It's like that, is it?"

"Hopefully." A small grin crossed my lips as I allowed myself to admit to the growing excitement about the date with Alyssa and

Phoebe.

"Sure, I know a bit," he said. "Give me a sec to get someone to cover me here and I'll help you out."

"Thanks. Oh, and I really am sorry for the way I left. But I'm home now, and I'm trying to fix my fuck-ups. All of my fuck-ups."

"It just took hitting half a dozen walls to knock some sense into you, hey?" He laughed as he walked into the back room. He emerged a few minutes later wearing a normal t-shirt rather than the uniform he was just in.

"I'm going to have lunch while I've got cover," he said in response to my quizzical look.

"Oh shit, don't let me take up your lunch hour."

"You won't. It'll take five minutes to get this seat. I assume you want one designed for a toddler?"

"You fucking know me too well." I laughed.

"I used to," he said sadly. It was man code for, "I missed you."

"Yeah." Which was man code for, "me too." "Hey, why don't I shout you lunch for helping me out?"

He shrugged. "I won't say no."

It wasn't long before he'd selected the "perfect" seat and we were at the counter paying for it. I tried to quiz him on why it was the right one and he gave me a stack of shit about anti-submarining straps, adjustable height, head support, seat-belt slots. I understood most of it in theory, but in terms of a fucking baby seat I had no idea. About the only thing I understood was that it had cup holders. Cup holders were good. Not that anyone would be allowed to eat or drink in my Monaro when I got her back.

We took the seat back to the car because there was no way in hell I was carrying a box that size all the way around the Grand Plaza. When the indicators flashed on the red five-door Barina hatch, Ben turned to me with a questioning look.

"Just don't say shit about it, okay?" I said.

He raised his hands in surrender. "I won't say a word. It's just not what I pictured you in." He smirked.

"Fuck off, it's a hire car. Mine's getting repaired."

"Are you crashing off the track now too?"

"Fuck you," I said, but the grin on my face let him know I wasn't serious.

As it turned out, Ben was a fucking champion and even installed the seat into the car for me. I definitely owed him a fucking meal for his help.

We went back into the centre and grabbed our old favourite, roast beef rolls, from the food court. I was surprised by just how easily we fell back into conversation. For a little while, we reminisced about high school and then I filled him in a little on what I'd been up to. Before long, I was bored with me and was much more interested in what he'd been up to.

"Well, I married Jade. We've got two little ones."

"Really? How old?" Even as the words left me, I wondered at what point exactly I stamped the daddy card and started asking questions like that. Usually my response to, "I've got kids," was, "Do I look like I fucking care?" but just then, I did care. I was genuinely interested. Which even surprised me.

"Two and a half, and eleven months."

"So that's why you're a genius when it comes to car seats?" I laughed.

He grinned at me. "Yeah, well, I had to do a hell of a lot of research. Jade dragged me around to a stack of shops before we settled on the seat that you've got for our oldest."

For a moment, I stood back and assessed my old friend. It had been a few years, and despite the physical differences, in my mind he'd still remained unchanged. Standing in front of me though, was a young man miles away from the teenager I'd left behind. "Wow. Married with kids."

"Well, you've got one yourself."

I shrugged. I wasn't going to go into the full details about why I wasn't on the birth certificate. Why she wasn't legally seen as my daughter. Or why I didn't feel like I deserved to be her dad yet.

"So what brought you back up to Brissie anyway?"

"Actually, Alyssa did. I went to London to get away for a bit and kinda ended up on a plane beside her."

He laughed. "So you tried to run away but fate had other

plans?"

"Something like that."

"Wow. I still can't believe you're here in front of me, man. I guess I should get your autograph or something while I got this chance."

"How about my phone number instead?"

He laughed.

"I'm serious, man. I told you I'm trying to make up for my mistakes. Losing contact with my friends is one of them. Maybe I can even bring Lys around one day."

"I'm sure Jade would love that. I know she's missed Alyssa, and we heard that Alyssa was leaving soon so it'd be nice to patch things up before then."

"Oh, Lys isn't going to London anymore. She didn't want to be that far away from her family, so she's staying."

Ben shook his head. "No, she's not. She's definitely leaving. Jade works for the real estate that Alyssa rents from. The day before yesterday she was in to discuss finalising the lease and talked about how hard it would be to leave. Jade was real upset when she came home."

"The day before yesterday?" I whispered.

Alyssa was leaving? Had she lied to me when she said she wasn't going to London? My mouth was dry and my heart began to thud in my chest. I was going to have a panic attack, I just knew it. I needed to get away from prying eyes before it could hit. Rumours of panic attacks could kill my career just as completely as crashing into walls.

"Um, Ben, I'm sure you're probably due back at work and I've gotta go." I quickly rattled off my phone number and he programmed it into his phone.

I almost ran through the centre back toward the car. As soon as I arrived I climbed into the driver's seat and tried to breathe. I turned on some music and tried to concentrate on the rhythm. My eyes hit the car seat in the rear-view mirror and I felt my heart rip in two. Alyssa was leaving Brisbane and wasn't going to tell me. Worse, there was no legal way I could stop her from taking Phoebe out of my life.

Fuck that!

I picked up my phone and rang my lawyer. After a fifteen minute conversation, I discovered I could go to court and contest the paternity to prove Phoebe was mine. The only problem was it would mean a potentially public battle with Alyssa. My lawyer also advised me that I would be liable for child support going back to Phoebe's birth, but I didn't give a shit about that. If I'd known sooner, I was positive I would have helped Alyssa out more. Although it worried me to think what would have happened if I'd found out about Alyssa's pregnancy during my worst three months.

As I hung up the phone, I decided I would wait Alyssa out. I would see if she'd come clean to me and tell me what the fuck was happening. Why was she discussing getting out of her lease as recently as two days earlier if she wasn't leaving? And if she was, why would she have told me she wasn't taking the London position? Was it just to stave off my panic attack?

I took a deep breath and started the car before remembering another item on my to-do list: something to keep Phoebe entertained.

For a moment, I considered going back into the shops, but I still felt the signs of an impending attack and I couldn't risk one of those in public. Not with my reputation already hanging by a thread. I breathed out and put the car in reverse. I would just have to deal with it. Whatever happened, I would just have to cope.

The thought struck me that I should probably find a doctor or something, but the pain in my ribs wasn't getting worse and the new bruises were no worse than the old ones. Until something happened to change that, the injuries could wait and just heal on their own. Why get shit on permanent record if it might affect my chances of getting to drive again soon?

As I drove, I saw a sign for a shop I would never have considered entering before but once I'd seen it, an impulse built in me. The sign across the door of a small shop front read Wild Roses Tattoo.

It was all too easy to recall the small dark markings on Alyssa's skin that symbolised our children, and I wanted something too. I needed to commemorate my son. Wanted to celebrate my daughter. Especially if she was going to be torn from my life too.

The thought cemented my plan and I slammed on the brakes so hard that a white Nissan X-Trail almost went up my arse. Ignoring the almost carnage around me, I turned into the car park for the small set of shops. When the X-Trail followed, I thought I was going to have some issues.

Great. Just what I fucking need.

Parking the little red Barina, I climbed out and waited for a confrontation with the other driver, but the doors didn't open. The windows were too heavily tinted to see inside, but the fact that no one climbed out of the car made me think maybe it was a coincidence. Shrugging it off, I found my way back to the shop. When I was inside, I glanced around at the artwork-covered walls and nodded to the woman behind the counter. I was thankful not to recognise anyone. Of course, that didn't mean they didn't recognise me.

"How can we help you today?" the receptionist greeted me. She was tall and lean, with spiked black hair, a piercing in her nose, and a full sleeve of tattoos up one arm. I thought it was safe to assume she was more into bikes than V8s, but even if I was wrong, it didn't show in her eyes if she did recognise me.

"Um, I was thinking about getting a tattoo done."

"Okay, have you got a design in mind?"

"Not really." Fuck, I hadn't thought this through.

"Well, you can have a look through our books if you like." She pointed out a stack of ring binders. I flicked the first one open and saw that it was filled with print-outs of various tatts.

"Have you done any horses?" I remembered the engraving from Emmanuel's tombstone. I didn't know what the significance of the horses was, but I knew they were important.

"Any particular style?"

"Style?" Fuck, I was so far out of my depth it wasn't even funny.

"Well, you can go for realism or tribal." She showed me a

sample of each.

"Tribal, I think." There was something beautiful and strong in the twisted black patterns of one of the designs she showed me. "Do you have any that are rearing?"

She pulled out another folder and flipped it open. I had to give it to her, this girl knew her job and was fucking good at it.

"Something like this?" She showed me a picture of a tribal horse reared up on its hind legs. It reminded me of the design on the tombstone.

"Yes, that's perfect. How soon can you fit me in?"

She chuckled. "You're eager."

"I just have to do this before I can pussy out."

After tapping on her computer for a moment, she said, "The earliest I can fit you in is a month from Friday."

I shook my head. "That's not going to work. It has to be soon. Today."

"We're booked out this afternoon."

"I'll pay you double if you reschedule them." I gave her a winning smile.

"I'm sorry, I can't just—"

"Call them and tell them that I'll pay for their tattoo if they take the appointment in a month's time."

"I'm not—"

"Please?" I cut her off and turned on the charm. "I really need to do this today."

She nodded. "I'll call them, but I can't guarantee anything."

Grinning that I'd at least won her around, I stepped back from the desk to let her do her thing. "Just see what you can do."

She turned and headed into a small office to one side of the reception desk. A little less than ten minutes later, she came back with a smile on her lips. "Looks like you're getting inked today."

"Fuck yeah. How long will it take?"

"Where would you like it?"

"Between my shoulder blades." Even as I'd looked through the designs, I'd settled on the position. I wanted it to be close to my heart but also somewhere I could hide it easily.

"And do you want that exact design?"

I shook my head. After seeing the design, I could picture the exact tattoo I wanted. "I want that and then a mirror of it alongside. I want each of the horses to have an initial on them and a date between them."

"Facing inward or turned away from each other?"

"Inward."

"What initials and what date?"

"A C and a P and the date is the eleventh of June."

She took the design out of the folder and went to the photocopier. Within five minutes, she had a drawing of the two horses side by side, facing each other. Then she quickly stencilled in the initials and the date. "Like that?"

I smiled. She had somehow managed to capture exactly what I was looking for on her first attempt. "That's perfect."

"Okay. Give me a few minutes to set up my station." She smiled.

Holy shit. The fact that she was actually the tattoo artist was kind of hot. Something told me she'd be wild in the sack. Only a few weeks earlier, I would have definitely tried for a post-tatt happy ending.

Now, I was a one-woman man. Or at least, I was trying to be.

A little while later, the tattooist came back out and led me into the back. She showed me her equipment, running me through her safety and hygiene practices. As happy as I was that it was all above board, I just wanted her to get going already before I pussied out.

"C'mon then, get your shirt off." Her lips curled into a flirtatious smile.

Meeting her eye, I peeled off my top with a smirk on my lips. Maybe I was a one-woman man, but that didn't mean I didn't appreciate being admired.

"Holy shit, what did you do to yourself?" she asked, as her eyes raked over my ribs, taking in the dark blemishes that covered my left side and the yellowish ones on my right.

"Uh, well, it's a long story."

"Well, it's a good thing we've got a bit of time." She pointed in the direction of the chair. "Let's get you comfortable and then you can spill."

My heart started to race when she pulled her chair in close and turned on the machine.

IT WAS a little after four when I finally left the tattoo parlour with an aching back and a list of aftercare instructions. Although the tattooist had been a willing ear, I hadn't told her everything. I'd told her enough to satisfy her curiosity without leaving her with enough gossip to sell as a story to *Gossip Weekly* or some other similar magazine.

As I'd talked to her about Alyssa, by hinting at a girl I was interested in, I'd come to the decision that I wasn't going to show Alyssa the tatt until it had healed. At least that way, she'd see it in the proper glory rather than as the weeping mess it could be for the next few days, according to the tattoo artist.

It wouldn't be that hard to hide it from Alyssa anyway. After all, it wasn't like she had any reason to look at my naked back. She'd made it pretty clear nothing was going to happen in *that* department for a while yet.

When I arrived home, the house was empty. Although I wondered where Mum was, I figured Dad was probably at work, considering he'd left late that morning just so that he could have his little discussion with me before going.

I scribbled a quick note on the whiteboard in the kitchen to let Mum know that I'd been home and not to worry about me. She already knew I had a date with Alyssa, so I figured I didn't need to stress too much about letting her know why I wasn't there.

Changing into something a little more formal, I couldn't help but laugh when I thought about the date I'd organised during a small break from the tattoo chair. It would show her that I could do romantic and kid friendly.

At twenty to five, I left the house. My nerves sprang to the surface as I considered the fact that it was technically our first date.

By the time I pulled up to Alyssa's house, my palms were sweaty and my mouth was dry. I hadn't been on a proper date in forever. Not since the formal. My usual nights out were a lot less formal and with more guarantees to score by the end.

Standing on her doorstep, I took a few deep breaths to calm myself. When I knocked, the door opened almost immediately to reveal two lovely ladies both wearing fine attire and beautiful smiles. Alyssa was in a soft pink dress that crossed over in front of her bust, enhancing her cleavage. It fell to just above the knee, but the material was so flowy it looked significantly shorter.

"Hello, you two," I said.

Alyssa smiled.

"Declan!" called Phoebe, waving enthusiastically.

"Are you ready to go?" I asked Alyssa.

"Yeah. I'll just go get my car keys."

"Uh-uh, I'm driving you tonight."

"Declan, I'm not going to put a car seat in a coupe in this dress."

Even though I was in the tiny Barina, I mentally pictured Alyssa leaning over into the backseat of the Monaro. The image had me gulping for air. When I saw that Alyssa and Phoebe were both staring at me, I pushed the picture from out of my mind. "It's all sorted, Lys. I told you I'm all over it tonight."

She raised her eyebrow and smirked at me. "If you say so."

"Trust me, I say so." Then I remembered one small problem. "Although I don't know how to fasten the child seat I got."

Alyssa laughed. "Yep, sounds like everything is under control."

I almost felt like she was waiting for something to go wrong, but she locked up the house and followed me to the drive without any further questioning.

"Uh, Dec, what's with—"

"It's nothing. My car just needed a tune-up." The words fell from my lips before I'd had the chance to consider whether lying to her was really the best option.

"Okay." When she spotted the brand-new car seat in the back, she paused for a moment but recovered quickly and helped Phoebe into it.

As Alyssa leaned forward to fasten Phoebe in she gave me the exact view I'd just been picturing, even if it was in the wrong car. The long lengths of her thighs were creamy and white and I wanted to run my fingers along them. Instead, I took a deep breath and climbed behind the wheel.

After Alyssa was in the car, she turned to me. "So where are we going?"

"It's a surprise."

I started the car and reversed out of Alyssa's driveway. The drive to our date took about ten minutes. Alyssa burst out laughing as I pulled into the car park. "We're a bit overdressed, aren't we?"

I smiled and shook my head. "We're dressed just right in my opinion."

Alyssa helped Phoebe back out of the car and then the three of us headed toward our date with the future.

CHAPTER SIX

GOLDEN ARCHES

AS WE CROSSED the carpark, Alyssa held one of Phoebe's hands and, at Phoebe's demand, I held the other. I couldn't believe how small and warm Phoebe's hands were as her fingers curled around mine.

"So do you want to line up?" Alyssa asked. "Or shall I?"

I shook my head. "It's five-star all the way tonight."

She laughed. "Five-star? At McDonald's?"

"Well, as five-star as Macca's can be. Come on, this way."

I led her through to the kids' party room. This had all been arranged with the manager when I called from the tattoo parlour. I pushed open the door and smiled when I saw everything was done to perfection. The long table was covered with a crisp white tablecloth and was adorned by a vase containing a dozen red roses. We'd barely sat when the waiter brought out our meals. I wasn't sure what Alyssa ate now, but I knew McChickens had always been her favourite so I'd ordered one of those for her and a chicken nugget Happy Meal for Phoebe.

"Kid friendly and romantic," I said triumphantly, indicating the room with my hands.

"Very good," Alyssa said with a growing smile. "You seem to have considered everything." She chuckled as if thinking there was something blatant that I'd missed.

"I don't want chicken nuggets," Phoebe complained.

Alyssa giggled again.

"What would you like then?" I asked.

"Pizza."

"They don't have pizza here, sweetie," Alyssa explained. "Declan was kind enough to bring us to dinner. I'm sure you can have chicken nuggets just this once."

Phoebe shook her head and started to whine a little. I felt my *perfect* night slipping away faster than my V8 could get off the line.

"Is there anything else you want?" I asked. "A burger maybe?"

She nodded. "Yep. Burger."

I called our waiter back again and asked for a cheeseburger for Phoebe. After it was placed in front of her she pushed it away. "Don't want that."

With a sigh, I looked to Alyssa for help. I wasn't sure what to do and I wanted to defer to her.

I was relieved when Alyssa touched her hand and spoke softly. "Just eat what you like, sweetheart. You can have something else later if you want."

"I want a milkshake."

I smiled. "That I can do." I pushed the chocolate thickshake I'd ordered toward her.

She took a deep sip and then beamed at me. Our perfect night started to get back on track.

Eventually Phoebe ate what was in front of her without too much complaint. Alyssa and I didn't talk much while we ate. Instead, Alyssa sat back and watched as Phoebe regaled me with stories about her day and her week. For at least half the time, I had no idea what she was saying but after asking "what" fifteen times, I'd decided just to smile and nod as she spoke.

Every time I looked over at Alyssa she was staring at us with an unknown expression on her face. It was not quite a look of longing, not quite a look of love, but because of the pain buried in her eyes, it was almost heartbreaking to witness.

"Are you all right with her for one minute?" Alyssa asked.

I nodded. "We'll be fine, won't we, Pheebs?" I winked at her. She giggled and nodded in reply.

Alyssa walked off and pulled out her mobile phone.

"I want more." Phoebe held up her empty cup. I ordered another thickshake for Phoebe and cleared off the rest of the table. Alyssa came back a few minutes later.

"Sorry, Mum asked me to check in with her when we got to the restaurant. I didn't want her to worry."

"She doesn't trust me, does she?"

Alyssa smiled at me. "No, not really."

"I don't know what it will take to convince everyone that I am here for good, but I'll do it. Eventually, I'll prove to everyone that I'm not going anywhere. I promise."

The look from before, the almost painful look of longing and desire, crossed her features again.

"I know." Somehow she made the two words sound more like, "I wish I could believe that."

It left me certain that I had a lot to prove to her too.

"Is everyone finished?" I asked. I was unable to shake the sorrow from my voice. Even though a few weeks ago I would never have considered the possibility that a date at McDonalds with a three-year-old in tow would be a good time, I'd actually really enjoyed myself.

Both Alyssa and Phoebe nodded.

"Did you want to go onto the playground?" I asked Phoebe, to delay the inevitable moment when we'd have to go home.

She nodded enthusiastically. "Yes, please."

Alyssa took Phoebe out to the playground while I went inside and paid for the meal, for the staff member, and for the room. I'd never paid so much for McDonalds before; in fact I probably could have fed a family of four for a week for what it cost, but it was worth it. At least the night hadn't been a total disaster, so I was happy.

Before I joined Phoebe and Alyssa, I grabbed sundaes for all of us and another Coke for Alyssa and me to share. I smiled tentatively at her as I sat beside her on the parents' seat inside the playground. She grabbed her sundae from me and I watched appreciatively as her tongue curled around the spoon to clear it of ice cream and chocolate sauce.

Phoebe climbed through the holes and around the ladders all the way to the top of the playground. There was something almost joyous in her simple act of play. An emotion built within me that I couldn't explain, a warmth that spread through my chest and lifted the corners of my lips.

Alyssa's hand was extended out onto the seat between us and before I realised what I was doing, I'd wrapped mine around it. She glanced down at our entwined fingers briefly but didn't pull away.

"I saw Ben today," I said, mainly to fill the silence between us.

She nodded, a sad look crossing her face. "How is he?"

I heard the unspoken questions, the desperate urge she had to get acquainted with her old friend, Jade.

"He and Jade are still together." I wasn't sure how much Alyssa knew, only that—from what Ben had said—she'd pulled herself away from them. "They have a couple of kids now."

She nodded. "Yeah, I know." Her thumb began to brush a trail along the back of my hand. I closed my eyes briefly, relishing her touch and the simple pleasure she gave me.

"He really wants to catch up with us both."

She nodded vaguely and watched Phoebe intently. "I want to, too. I just don't know if I can."

"What do you mean?"

"Do you know why I stopped talking to them? Why I prefer to spend my time with Flynn?"

Horrified by the overwhelming sadness in her voice, I shook my head.

"When you left, well, everything reminded me of you. Like I said before, it wasn't just a break-up . . . I lost my best friend. For a while, I tried to see everyone and pretend everything was normal, but it was different. We were no longer the awesome foursome. There was Ben and Jade the couple, and Alyssa the rejected one. I couldn't face it. I felt like a third wheel all the time. And then I found out I was pregnant and I just . . ." She closed her eyes and blew out a breath.

When she reopened them, her eyes had a hardness to them — as if she'd closed off the part of herself that felt the pain. I wondered how I'd never noticed the difference before. "And then Flynn came along one day and he was new. There were no ties to you. I could finally just be Alyssa, and not the one you left behind. It was refreshing."

I let go of Alyssa's hand and put my arm around her shoulders. I wasn't sure how she would react but she nuzzled into me as I squeezed her gently. I was beginning to see how much of a struggle it had been for her.

When I left, I'd forged a new identity for myself. I was completely free of all memory of her, of us, and any time I found something that was a reminder, I ignored it or pushed it away. But Alyssa had been faced with our past every single day. Her entire support network was saturated with memories.

"Did you and Flynn ever . . ." I couldn't even finish the question.

She laughed. "No. I tried once or twice but he's firmly in the other camp."

"Was there ever anyone else?"

"Not really. Just Cain."

I nodded. "What happened?" I didn't really want to know, but I needed to know her and that included learning about her past after us.

"I don't know. I guess I sort of thought I could have something with Cain, so I chased him. I learned pretty quickly that I really only wanted him because of his resemblance to Flynn though. He was like Flynn-lite. Then not long after we broke up, I found out he was in love with his boss's daughter, Kirsty. The way they are now, it's like they were made for each other. There's no hard feelings there at all."

"Why did you chase him so much?" It didn't really sound like the Alyssa I'd known.

She stared straight ahead and I could almost see thoughts formulating, so when she spoke, I knew each word was chosen with care. "When you're at the track and something happens, and you *know* you can't get first place, no matter how hard you work, do you try hard for second?"

"Of course." I was confused by her change of tack and wasn't sure where she was going with the question, but allowed her to go with it.

She glanced at me, and the intensity in her gaze burned through me. "And if you can't get second? You fight for third?"

"Yeah."

"But then, at some point, you realise third place might be good. It might be the best you can ever get, but it's never going to be first, no matter how much you might want it to be. Third place is never really going to get you anywhere."

"I don't understand." Even as I said the words, it hit me. I couldn't help the grin that crossed my face even though my heart broke for her. "Are you saying I was your first place?"

She smacked my chest playfully at my smile. Then she grinned in return. "Yes, you *were*."

"I'm offended," I mock-protested. I wrapped my arms tightly around her and began to tickle her lightly. "Am I still first place?"

"More like a consolation prize, I think." She managed to squeeze the words out between squeals.

Phoebe ran back over to us with a smile on her face. She wrapped her arms around Alyssa's neck while I held Alyssa's waist. I couldn't even begin to explain how right it felt to be together like a family.

I was forced to relinquish my hold when Phoebe climbed onto Alyssa's lap and started to eat her sundae. I watched as the two of them giggled and played, Phoebe feeding Alyssa occasionally.

In that instant, I knew my world would shatter if I was unable to see them again. The doubt I felt over Alyssa's apparent departure began to niggle in the back of my mind. I wanted to talk to her about it, but I didn't want to ruin our date—which had gone surprisingly well given its start.

After Phoebe had finished her sundae, she ran back into the playground. I put my arm back around Alyssa's shoulders and we sat like that in silence, both watching Phoebe running around, playing on her own. I felt the missing part of our life so sharply. I wondered whether Alyssa did too. A quick look at her face told me she did. I squeezed a little to let her know silently that I was there for her. That I understood.

Phoebe darted off the playground. "I want to go home, Mummy."

"What's the matter, sweetheart?"

Phoebe just shook her head before resting it against Alyssa's chest.

"Is she all right?" I asked. "She looks a little green?"

"I think it's just time to call it a night," Alyssa said. Despite the situation, I was pleased to hear the tinge of regret in her voice.

I nodded then held out my hand to help Alyssa to her feet. She clutched Phoebe to her chest as she carried her back to the car and put her into the car seat. As she bent over the seat I was once again afforded a view of her creamy thighs. I clenched my fists to stop myself from touching her and walked around to the driver's side.

"Everyone okay?" I asked when they were both loaded up and had their seat belts on.

Phoebe nodded from the back, but I was starting to get concerned about her; she was a definite shade of green.

"What did she eat?" Alyssa asked as I drove. "I only saw her with one small thickshake, some chips and then half a sundae."

I stared at the road. "Actually, I got her another thickshake while you were on the phone."

"Declan!" Alyssa groaned. "Does she look like she's big enough to fit two thickshakes in?"

She turned to the backseat and stroked Phoebe's hair.

"I'm sorry. She said she wanted another one, and well, I couldn't say no to her."

Alyssa bit her lip and looked back at Phoebe. I got the feeling the topic wasn't closed but she didn't want to say anything in front of our daughter. She stroked Phoebe's hair again. "Do you have a sore tummy?"

Phoebe nodded and her bottom lip wobbled.

"Don't worry sweetie, we'll be home soon then you can lie down for a bit," Alyssa said. "Declan, pull over!" she cried out a second later.

She said it with such urgency there was no way I could refuse. As soon as the car was safely on the side of the road Alyssa ripped open her door and pulled open the back door to get to Phoebe but it was too late. A stream of milky vomit came pouring out of Phoebe's mouth and down her front. The smell was wretched and a small part of my brain immediately worried about the state of the seats. It was just lucky that it wasn't my car.

"Fuck!" I shouted as an instinctive reaction.

I climbed out of my seat too, pulling it forward to give more room in the back. Alyssa and I juggled our way through the vomit to pull Phoebe from the car seat.

"You help her, and I'll see what I can do about cleaning this up," I said. I pulled my shirt off and used it to soak up as much of the vomit as I could from the baby seat.

The floors could wait until we got back to Alyssa's house, but I didn't want Phoebe to have to ride the rest of the way home in a pool of sick.

As Alyssa loaded a still wet, and quite miserable-looking, Phoebe back into the car seat, I wound down all the windows so that we'd be getting fresh air into the car because quite frankly the smell was making me feel utterly nauseous.

I smiled apologetically at Alyssa and she just shook her head slightly. I could have sworn she uttered the word, "Honestly," under her breath.

A short, quiet, stinky ride later we were in front of Alyssa's house. She ran to the door and unlocked it returning with half a dozen old towels. "You better clean the car out before it gets too dry. I'll take care of Phoebe."

I felt a little insulted that she wanted me to worry more about the car than I did about Phoebe, but ignored it because I knew she was a bit pissed at me for giving Phoebe that extra thickshake.

I cleaned the interior of the car as best I could, pulling the once lovely new car seat out and hosing it off. Then I dampened one of the towels, spotting it on the cloth seats to soak up the rest of the vomit.

It took me close to half an hour to finish. When I was satisfied I'd cleaned up as much I could, I opened the car right up and left it to dry. I bundled the towels up, together with my vomit-soaked shirt, and took them back inside.

I stood waiting for Alyssa in the living room, feeling self-conscious because I didn't have a shirt on. I could hear her down the hall, singing softly to Phoebe. Then I heard the song finish and Alyssa whisper, "I'll be right outside if you need me."

"Okay. I love you very much, Mummy," Phoebe's small voice called.

"I love you too, sweetie."

Their simple, honest declarations of love warmed my heart but at the same time made me feel like an intruder in their home. I waited at the end of the hall as Alyssa walked out of Phoebe's room, a soft smile of contentment on her lips. She stopped in the hallway when she saw me. Her eyes swept over me in a quick appraisal. "Oh God, Declan. I'm sorry. I completely forgot you used your shirt in the car. I'll see if I can find you something to throw on while I wash yours."

I nodded. "Do you want me to put these somewhere?" I held up the bundle of clothes.

"Just throw them in the basket and put your shirt in the washing machine—" She pointed to a door which I presumed housed the laundry. "—I'll put a load on in a second. We'll get your shirt washed and back on before you go home." She laughed. "People might talk otherwise."

"They'll talk anyway, you realise."

"Yeah. I know," she said with a sad edge. No doubt she knew it better than I did.

I went into the room she pointed to and worked out which

machine was the washing machine and I threw everything in. I was walking back to the living room when I heard a door shut and a slight gasp from behind me.

"Declan? Did you hurt yourself again?"

At first I thought she meant the fresh bruises on my ribs, but then her fingers traced the outline of the bandage that still covered the tattoo. I blushed. I hadn't anticipated showing her quite yet. In fact, I had no idea how she'd take it.

"Um, no. I . . . ah . . . I . . ." My voice dropped to a whisper. "I got a tattoo."

"You what?" she asked. "When?"

"Today. Did you want to see?" Her hands were still on my back and her skin felt too good so close. I needed a distraction and showing her my tattoo was perfect.

"Should I be scared? You didn't do anything crazy did you?"

I laughed. "Besides get a tattoo in general? No."

I felt her gently lifting the bandage and she gasped. Her hand came to rest on my shoulder, just beside where the horses now took pride of place on my back. She remained quiet behind me and I was worried it was the calm before the storm. I was so stupid—I didn't even think about how Alyssa might feel about the work I'd had done. I was just so desperate to make something permanent in my life. A moment later, she pressed the edges of the bandage down once more, covering the tattoo.

When I turned slowly to see her face, to figure out what she was thinking, she had tears in her eyes and was chewing her lip. She looked seconds from losing it and I worried that maybe I'd overstepped some boundary I hadn't known existed.

"Lys, are you all right?" I asked.

"It's beautiful," she whispered. "Why did you do it?"

"I wanted a permanent reminder of my children."

Alyssa dropped the shirt she was holding and fell against my chest, sobbing. I moved her over to the couch and sat with her, just holding her until her tears began to subside.

"Do you mind?" I asked her.

She shook her head. "Do you know how long I've waited and

dreamed that one day you'd come back and say words like those?"

"You dreamed and waited for me to get a tattoo?" I knew it wasn't what she meant, but I also understood that the moment needed a little levity.

She gave a half-laugh, half-sob. "No, you jerk. I—"

"I know, Lys. I've proven myself to be an arsehole a hundred times over. Let me prove that I can be the man you need me to be, yeah?"

Fresh tears rolled down her cheeks. "Are you sure you're not going to regret it?"

I wasn't sure if she meant the tattoo or my promises, but either way the answer was the same. "Never. I only have one regret now."

She didn't ask what. I wondered whether it was because she knew it was leaving her, or because she was afraid it was something else.

"Was tonight okay?" I asked. I was afraid she would hate me for the disaster it had turned into.

"It was a start," Alyssa replied through her tears. Then she shook her head and barked out a hard laugh. "Although, why did you give her that second thickshake?"

"A start is good?" I wanted to clarify.

"Yeah, a start is good. But it doesn't make up for last night."

"I know. It was stupid . . . I was stupid. I just—" I cut myself off because I knew there were no excuses to warrant what I'd done, not in Alyssa's book. "I fucked up."

"You did. But you also said some things I think I needed to hear."

"Like?"

She shook her head. "I think that's better left alone for now."

More than anything, I wanted to know what she'd needed to hear, what it was that had put her in, not so much a good mood, but an accepting one. At least one which had given her a willingness to go along with my idea of a date.

"Lys." I said her name in a quiet whisper, certain my next words would be a mistake but unwilling to deceive her any longer. "The Monaro isn't in the shop for a tune-up."

She pulled away from me with a frown.

"I didn't mean to lie to you. I just didn't know how to tell you the truth."

"Which is?"

"There was an accident."

She practically leapt to her feet, her eyes tracing my body and settling on the fresh black blemishes on my side. "Fuck, Declan. Those bruises? What happened?"

After her reaction, I almost regretted telling her the truth because I still had to admit the worst part. "I don't remember."

"You don't remember?" She paced to the window before spinning back around to shout, "Jesus Christ, Declan, did you drive last night?"

Staring at my lap, mostly because I was unable to stand looking at the anger and disappointment in her eyes, I nodded.

Throwing her hands in the air, she covered the distance between us as her lecture started. "You could have killed someone, Dec. God, you could have killed yourself. How could you have been so stupid? I didn't see a car last night. I thought you must have walked. Jesus Christ, if I'd thought you were driving, I would have driven you home. What if you'd killed someone?"

If it had been anyone else, I would have told them where to shove it, but I understood her anger was at least partially linked to her worry. "I know. God, I know it was stupid. And I don't even know what happened. All I know is Flynn found me and—"

"Flynn? He knew about this?" She paced away from me again. "I spoke to him this morning and he didn't say a damn thing about it even though he knew?"

"I don't know what to tell you, Lys." It was the moment to throw him under the bus if I wanted to. It was so tempting, if only to score a few points considering how many I'd probably lost with my err in judgment. Only, I couldn't do that—to Alyssa. "I don't think he meant to hurt you. He probably just didn't want to make you unhappy."

"Yeah, well, he didn't do a very good job." She slumped onto the couch beside me.

"I didn't mean to hurt you either."

Her eyes fluttered closed and a small exasperated sigh left her.

"I know there's no excuse. I'm not going to try to make one. All I can do is promise it won't happen again. You mean too much to me to fuck it up over something so stupid."

We sat in silence. After a moment, another small sigh escaped her and she glanced up at me. "I just don't know how many chances I can give you, Dec. Not with Phoebe around. I—I can't let you hurt her."

Her words were agony to hear, but strangely, I understood. If it was someone else hurting Alyssa or Phoebe, even accidentally, I would kick their arse. "At least one more?" I said, offering a small smile—the sort that usually got me anything I wanted.

Alyssa gave me a begrudging smile in reply. "Maybe *one* more."

"I promise, no more fuck-ups."

Despite the fact that she nodded and curled into me, I didn't think I had her entirely convinced. The truth was I had no idea what Alyssa was thinking, but my mind raced with everything that had happened in the last few days. Ben's assertions regarding Alyssa's lease flooded into my mind and my heart raced at the thought that I could be losing my little family before I had a chance to win them back.

"Are you going to take Phoebe out of the country?" I asked. My voice came out in a choked whisper.

Alyssa pulled away and looked at me. "No. Why would you ask that?"

"You're breaking your lease." It came out in a more accusing tone than I'd anticipated.

Alyssa looked surprised. "Yeah. I told you I was offered a job."

"Yeah, but you also told me you weren't taking it."

"No."

My brow pulled together in a frown. It didn't make any sense. She had told me exactly that.

"I told you that I wasn't moving to London, not that I wasn't taking the job."

"What?"

She sighed. "You really don't listen do you?"

"What the fuck are you talking about?"

"Pembletons offered me a job in their Sydney or London office. London's just too far from my family. I'm moving to Sydney in February."

With three sentences, my world flipped upside down. A smile beamed across my face at the thought. Alyssa was moving to Sydney. She would be close to me when it came time to return home. There would be no need to decide between Sydney and Alyssa.

When she moved, everything would be fucking right with the world.

CHAPTER SEVEN

CLUELESS

I COULDN'T WIPE the fucking smile off my face and I couldn't believe my luck. Alyssa wasn't leaving the country. She wasn't taking Phoebe away. Better yet, Alyssa was wrapped in my arms. Even though it put excess pressure on my side, and hurt like a bitch, I couldn't ask her to move. While she remained still, the pain in my side abated until it was bearable. Especially with her in my arms. Neither was she trying to shift away from me. The scent of her coconut skin cream was right under my nose; it smelled fucking terrific as she leaned into me.

It was exactly what I'd been missing for four years.

I was home.

She tucked her legs up underneath her and nestled into my shoulder. Her hair brushed across my chest as she nuzzled close to me. I didn't know what Alyssa was thinking as her hand gently wrapped around my arm. Her touch felt so good. Peaceful.

I closed my eyes and blocked out the last four years, pretending none of it had happened. The formal was just yesterday and I never freaked out after it. We were just happy together and I'd never hurt her.

It was a nice fantasy.

We sat like that for a while. Half an hour or more passed before either of us dared to move. Silence emanated from Phoebe's room so I assumed she was asleep, but I really didn't fucking know.

Alyssa's hand came up to her face as she wiped away the last of her tears. As she swept her cheek, her hand brushed across my chest. My abs tightened, and a fresh pain stabbed my ribs, but if I said anything I risked breaking whatever spell was keeping her in my arms.

When her skin stroked mine, it was soft and warm. An involuntary moan rose in my throat. Her touch was so perfect, eliciting a fresh wave of tension through my stomach and a flutter of nerves across my skin. Nothing I'd experienced had ever compared. Nothing *could*.

I opened my eyes and looked down at her. When our gazes locked, I saw she'd been staring at me. She gave me a small smile and played with the ends of her hair when she discovered she'd been caught. I smiled in response and ducked my head a little without thinking through the move.

Alyssa echoed my movement, tilting her head back and parting her lips. I grazed my own lips against hers and rested them there for a fraction of a second. It wasn't quite a kiss, but our lips definitely met. I didn't dare push it any further. Pulling apart, I rested my forehead against hers. With my eyes closed, I breathed in her presence. It was calming and soothing, and just perfect.

While my eyes were still closed, Alyssa made her move. Her tongue pushed forward and traced along my bottom lip. I groaned again, wondering if she knew exactly what she did to me. Opening my eyes, I was greeted by the lust dancing behind her gaze.

Every muscle in my body was primed and ready for action.

Every muscle.

Taking my time, giving her the chance to stop me if she wanted, I slid my tongue forward to greet hers. Her eyes closed and it was her turn to moan. My arm moved from her waist to her hair and my fingers trailed it. I used the hold to guide her closer, drawing her to me until there was barely a breath between us. Her hands gripped my shoulders, the increased pressure sending a sharp ache down my side. A moan ripped from my lips, but the sound seemed to spur her on. I wondered whether she'd mistaken it for lust—I wasn't game to tell her otherwise. The pain was bearable—just—and worth every second to be able to kiss her again.

With her hold on my shoulders, she gripped tighter, as if she couldn't decide what she wanted. Like she was pushing me away even as she moved forward into the kiss.

I was seventeen again, with the images of the life Alyssa wanted in my head. University. Career. Marriage. Family. Only now, I wanted it too. I still wanted to race, but I'd proven that could be a career.

Maybe I didn't have to choose; I could have it all. The thought raced through my mind, and sent a course of fresh desire rushing through my body.

There was a long road to walk, but I wanted to prove to Alyssa that I could do it. Which meant knowing when to slow down. Like right then. I was sore, bruised, and freshly tattooed. Alyssa still didn't completely trust me. Nothing would be served by continuing down the path of seduction, even though I really wanted to. Sleeping with Alyssa so soon would only prove that I was an arse who couldn't keep it in his pants.

Even as I battled to maintain control, my body reacted instinctively and my hands traced down to her neck. She pulled away from me but only to tilt her head up and issue a breathy sigh.

My lips moved to her exposed throat, tasting and sucking her smooth skin. Another wanton groan slipped past her lips. Her hands clasped my neck, pulling me closer still. A garbled cry at the fresh wave of agony down my side made it as far as my lips before disappearing against her skin. It was torturous, but I didn't want it to stop.

My kisses reached her shoulder and I desperately wanted to keep going, to push the material out of the way and continue down to explore her breasts. With an effort worthy of a Bathurst win, I finally gathered up enough control to pull away from her. As I did, I sank back against the armrest, trying to put some distance between us.

Only, Alyssa followed my retreat.

Her torso twisted and stretched to lie on top of me. Her hands threaded into my hair and she pressed her lips to mine again. Before I could fight it, I was lying beneath her on the couch, her warm body resting between my legs and my hands positioned on the small of her back. It made my ribs ache, and my back burned where it was pressed into the couch, but I couldn't ask her to stop because she might.

She was on top of me, in front of me, all around me. Despite the pain rolling over my body in waves, I couldn't complain about a damned thing. Over the top of her thin dress, I drew small circles, tracing the tiny dimples near her tailbone. She pressed her hips forward, grinding lightly against mine.

"Oh, fuck," I whispered into her mouth.

I grabbed at her hips, pulling them over mine, relishing the feel of the pressure. It was almost enough to take away the pain of my ribs. I had never wanted anything, or anyone, more than I wanted her in that moment.

"Shit, sorry, that must be painful," she said as she pushed herself up so she was sitting on my lap. With a tender touch, she leaned over and, just like she had in London, kissed each of my ribs.

The part of me that was screaming resistance was getting smaller with every passing second, and with every swipe of Alyssa's tongue against my skin. My fingers played at the hem of her dress. It would be so easy to pull it off. Then I'd be able to feel her skin against me once more. I'd see her in whatever underwear she was currently wearing.

Just the thought of it made me groan in anticipation. It had only been a few weeks since we'd been together in London, but it felt like years. Placing a hand on either side of her hips, I played my fingers upwards, inching her dress higher and higher.

A loud beeping sound broke the silence in the house. The noise wasn't so unbearable that I couldn't ignore it, but it was enough to distract Alyssa.

"Oh, shit," she said, as she climbed off me.

Standing in front of me, she smoothed down her dress and ran her fingers through her hair. Her gaze shifted from my face to my crotch and back again. A moment later, blushing brightly, she walked off in the direction of the noise.

I stood quickly to follow her, adjusting myself to find some space in my pants as I went. As we passed the spot where she'd dropped the clean shirt earlier, she ducked down and picked it up before throwing it back to me, all without turning her head in my direction. I slid it on without a second thought. Obviously my bare chest was making her uncomfortable and that was the last thing I wanted.

It was only as I reached the laundry a split second behind her that the obvious question came to me.

"Why do you have a man's shirt?" I asked, as she opened the machine lid.

Alyssa turned to look at me. "It's Flynn's," she said, as if the question was absurd and the answer obvious.

"Why do you have Flynn's shirt then?" I wondered whether the fucker made a regular habit of coming to her house and getting shirtless.

She rolled her eyes. "You're kidding me aren't you?"

"What?"

She reached into the washing machine to pull out the clothes. "You aren't seriously still jealous of Flynn, are you?"

Am I? In a way, I was. At least a little. Not because I thought the fucker was into Alyssa or was a threat to me in *that* way. But he had almost four years of Alyssa's life that I'd never have.

He had three years with Phoebe that I'd never get back.

He was in their lives in ways I had never been—in all the ways I wanted to be now that I knew the truth. I wondered if he'd been there to experience all of Phoebe's firsts. Had he held her hand and helped her with her first steps? I felt physically ill at the thought.

It should have been me. It would have if I'd just picked up the damn phone.

Wouldn't it?

Before I got a chance to consider the answer to my own question, Alyssa huffed, bringing my attention back to her. "Seriously. You never listen properly do you?"

"What?" I expected to get a lecture about how Flynn was gay and there was nothing between them, so her next statement confused me.

"I said to put the towels in the basket and your shirt in the washing machine."

"So?"

"What did you do?"

I thought about that. I'd come inside and ... *fuck*. I'd just thrown everything in the washing machine. It was my turn to blush. "Sorry."

She pulled out my shirt. It was covered in multicoloured fluff.

"What happened to *that*?" I asked.

"*Someone* put towels in the washing machine with it."

"Oh."

Shaking her head, Alyssa examined it. "It might be salvageable," she said. Then she put my shirt into the dryer on its own. "Hopefully this will get rid of some of the pilling." She cleaned some dust out of a cover on the front of the dryer and pressed some buttons to start it.

I was lost and wasn't afraid to tell her so. "Thank you for this. I don't know what I would have done otherwise. Probably left it for Mum to do in the morning."

She laughed and shook her head. "You are pretty clueless about all things domestic, aren't you?"

I put my arms out to her in apology. "I'm pretty clueless in lots of things. But I'm trying."

She considered me for a minute, then nodded. "Yes, you are trying." She stepped into my outstretched arms and wrapped her arms around my waist. It didn't escape my attention that she was being careful not to put too much pressure on the bruises on my side.

I rested my cheek on the top of her head. My breath came in

long, shaky gasps. I wanted her so badly. Just being near her was driving me crazy. I felt myself losing the semblance of control I'd finally achieved, and knew it would be a mistake to stay any longer. There would be no way I'd be able to resist turning on the charm and trying to get her into bed with me. The way her heart pounded against my chest as I held her tightly, I didn't think it would be a massive challenge. I dropped my arms and stepped back.

"Alyssa, I'd better go."

"Why?" She seemed shocked.

I tucked a loose strand of hair back behind her ear; she closed her eyes and sighed as our skin made contact When she looked back at me, her breathing as unsteady as mine, I smiled.

"That's why. I don't think we should . . ." I trailed off, sure the look in my eyes and straining crotch were enough to communicate to her what I didn't think we should do. Even though I really, *really* wanted to.

She nodded. "No, we definitely shouldn't," —she bit her lip and her voice fell to a whisper—"at least not yet."

I ducked down and our lips met in a chaste kiss.

"Can I see you tomorrow?" I asked. Then I added, "Only if you want to though."

"Sure," she breathed. "You'll need to come back to get your shirt anyway."

"Oh, and while I remember, are you free on Saturday?"

"Why?"

"I want to take you somewhere, just the two of us. Then I'd like us to go out on Sunday, as a family."

She shook her head. "I'd like to, but I don't know if I'll be able to get a babysitter at such short notice."

"Mum's going to do it," I said. Only after the words were out did I understand that it might sound like I'd been working behind her back. "That is, I asked her if she wouldn't mind if no one else could."

Alyssa looked shocked but didn't say anything.

"What is it?"

"Your mum agreed to have Phoebe on a weekend?" she asked

with a frown.

"Yeah. I mean I thought you said Phoebe went around there a bit, so I . . ." I trailed off. The look on her face worried me. "I'm sorry. I didn't think you'd mind."

"I don't, as such. It's just . . . your mum doesn't usually watch Phoebe on weekends, that's all."

I felt my eyebrows pinch together. "Why not?"

"No reason, I guess." Her voice was full of stress and her eyes brimmed with concern.

I cupped her cheek. "There is a reason, what is it?"

She squeezed her eyes tightly shut. "Please don't"—she inhaled deeply—"don't make me explain. Not now."

I hated seeing her in this much pain—especially knowing it was my fault, even though I didn't know the reason. "Okay. No explanations necessary tonight. But when you are ready, I'll be here."

"I hope so," she whispered.

"No, not *hope so*," I replied. I lifted her chin so I was looking directly into her eyes. "Alyssa, when you're ready. I *will* be here."

She looked deep into my eyes as if trying to hunt out the lie.

I wanted her to believe, to understand. I kept eye contact. "I am not going anywhere." I emphasised each word, hoping she would believe me.

She nodded. "Okay."

I pressed my lips gently to hers again. "I'll see you tomorrow. Call me when you are ready for me to come over."

She smiled. "Okay, Declan, and . . . thanks."

She threw herself into my arms and kissed me goodbye properly.

I shot her a quick smile as we pulled apart. She stepped back and leaned against the washing machine for support. Her lips were twisted into a goofy smile and her eyes seemed to scream of the things she wanted to do.

I knew the feeling.

Breaking away from the spell of her gaze, I walked to the car on shaky legs. When I reached it, I checked that the seats and carpet were dry, and wound the windows up. There was a slight lingering smell, but if it moved Alyssa and me on to the next step, the cleaning bill would be a small sacrifice to make.

"MUM, I'M home," I called as I entered the house.

"How'd it go?" she replied from the kitchen.

"Good." I walked up behind her. "Actually, no, not just good. Great." I leaned against the kitchen bench, not willing to jump up and risk a repeat of the morning.

"That's good. Did you all have fun?"

I laughed. Vomit, attitude, and McDonald's weren't really my idea of *fun* but it was a good night regardless.

Mum turned slightly to look at me. "What happened to your shirt? That wasn't the one you wore was it? It's too big on you."

Nice, I thought. Of course she would notice that. "Phoebe got sick in the car."

"Oh no, is she all right?" The concern and love in her voice was evident.

"Apparently she'll be fine; she just had too much to drink."

Mum nodded.

We lapsed into silence for a few minutes, the only noise being the sloshing of the dishwater as she washed up.

"Are you still 'right to watch Phoebe on Saturday?" I asked, breaking the silence.

"Definitely."

"And you really don't mind?"

"No, I really don't mind. Why?"

"Alyssa just said something about you not usually watching Phoebe on weekends."

She shrugged and the dishes in front of her were suddenly very interesting. "I guess I haven't. I've never thought about it too much."

Her voice was a little too dismissive, her actions a little too blunt. She was lying.

"Bullshit," I said. "What the fuck is going on?"

"Declan, please! Watch your language," she snapped. She grabbed a tea towel and dried her hands. She threw it onto the bench. "And I said there wasn't a reason."

"Mum, cut the crap and tell me."

"Just leave it." She stalked out of the kitchen.

Half a minute later, I heard a door slam down the other end of the hall. I sat stunned for a few seconds. I tried to remember a time Mum had ever snapped like that before. There was more to this fucking situation than everyone was telling me. It made me more determined than ever to find out what it was but there was no fucking way I was going to walk into Mum and Dad's room just then to find out. I didn't know if Dad was home or not, and Mum was obviously in no mood to talk.

I looked at the half-washed dishes and decided to try my best to finish them. I hadn't been lying to Alyssa when I said I was clueless. Usually, I just ate with the team or grabbed something on the way home. I didn't cook and I certainly didn't clean. Like everything I didn't want to do, I just paid people to do it for me. Just then though, I wanted to help Mum in whatever way I could. At least it would be one less thing for her to stress over later. I left the pots because I had no fucking clue how to clean them, but did the glasses and plates and left it all to air dry in the drainer beside the sink.

After I'd finished, I locked up the front door and poured myself a glass of Dad's whiskey, on the rocks. I took it to the bedroom and locked the door behind me. Then I spent the next little while reliving the memory of the things I'd done with Alyssa in London.

CHAPTER EIGHT

JAMMED

HAVING SLEPT THROUGH yet another uninterrupted night, I woke late on Thursday morning. I didn't know what it was about being home, but I hadn't slept so restfully for nearly four years. I was so used to the insomnia, the constant waking, and the nightmares, that it felt almost hedonistic to get so much sleep.

In fact, it left me feeling fantastic and ready to face the world. I grabbed the empty glass that'd held the whiskey from my bedside table and headed toward the kitchen. I was halfway down the hall when I heard Mum's voice in a hushed whisper.

"No, don't worry. He won't be here over the weekend. He's got other plans."

I stopped dead in my tracks and listened to the one-sided conversation.

"I know. It'll be fine. In fact it'll be nice spending some time with her." Mum paused then said reassuringly, "Yeah, I'm sure." Her voice dropped even lower. "Listen, I know it's not my place but I'm glad you two are trying. You are good for him." She gasped. "He didn't."

I walked a little further so Mum could see me. Her eyes widened slightly with surprise and she abruptly said goodbye and hung up the phone.

"Who was that?" I asked, trying to sound politely disinterested. I had a very strong suspicion I knew *exactly* who it was, but I wanted to see if Mum would lie about it.

"It was just Alyssa," she replied.

"What, were you two getting your stories straight? Making sure you know exactly what to tell me?" All this secrets and lies bullshit was beginning to grate on my nerves.

"It's not like that," she objected. "She just wanted to make sure I was okay to watch Phoebe."

Narrowing my eyes, I assessed her carefully. She clearly wasn't going to give me any extra information even if I pushed hard on the issue. I shrugged. "Whatever."

I banged the glass on the bench, causing Mum to jump a little. She was definitely wound up. "A parcel arrived for you," she said, no doubt to distract me. She pointed to a huge-arse box near the front door.

Walking to the box she'd pointed out, I checked the sender's address and smiled. Danny had come through for me, like he always did, but I couldn't believe he'd paid for overnight freight on it. Then again, knowing Danny it would probably come off my next pay cheque.

The sight of the parcel made me think about the team. The time off, reconnecting with Alyssa—even if we were still a little up in the air—it all felt fantastic, but I was also ready to go home. I was ready to return. In fact, with the newfound knowledge of Alyssa's upcoming move, I was actually anxious to return to Sydney.

We could begin again there—together. I wanted to celebrate the progress we'd made. I wanted to shout from the rooftops that Alyssa and I were going to be together. The sentiment was fucking miles ahead of where we actually were, but I was certain we would get there. Our date had been proof of that. Despite the disasters, we'd managed. We would manage. We would face the world together.

The love that still existed between Alyssa and me despite the hurt was evident in everything we did. It would overcome our issues, I was sure it would.

Then there was the chemistry. *That* was going to kill me before long, but the exquisite torture was worth it. I wondered how much longer I could be in her presence without dragging her to the bedroom, caveman style.

In fact, just thinking about her filled my mind with visions of our time together—and what visions. It was hard to believe that we'd only been together twice. I'd slept with a couple of casual flings more than that. But Alyssa was no casual fling, and she was worth waiting for.

Every second of our time together was etched permanently into my memory, whereas all the other girls melded into a blur of remorse. If I could take back every one of them I would, but I couldn't. All I could do was prove to Alyssa she was all I ever wanted. All I would ever want. And I had a few ideas of how to do it.

Pulling open the box that Danny had sent, I grinned at the contents. A note rested on the top of the pile with Danny's handwriting.

All organised for Saturday as requested.

At the sight, I desperately wanted it to be Saturday already. The thought brought me back to the present, to the secrets Mum and Alyssa were hiding. I took the parcel down to my room and dropped it on the bed before heading back out to Mum. "I'm going for a shower. I need to go to Alyssa's later to get my shirt."

"Okay."

"And Saturday's definitely okay?"

"Definitely."

I walked straight into the bathroom and locked the door behind me. Something was happening and it was starting to get on my nerves. Why were they trying to hide whatever the fuck it was? I showered and dried off as fast as I could.

Wrapping the towel around my waist, I walked back into my room to find some clothes, formulating a plan as I went. Mum had said "he" wouldn't be here. I knew she wasn't referring to me because Alyssa knew my plans. There was only one other he I could think of, and I needed to know why it mattered whether Dad was here. I dressed in a pair of slacks and a short-sleeved shirt; I needed to be presentable for a visit to the city.

When I walked back into the kitchen, the glass was gone from the counter. It was an additional indicator that something was wrong—Mum always cleaned when she was nervous.

"I was thinking about talking to Dad about some possible investments. Is he free on the weekend?"

"No, he's going away for business tomorrow night. He won't be back until Tuesday," Mum said, with a degree of caution. I think she was waiting for the "inevitable" explosion and demands that she tell me what was going on.

I wasn't going to give her that though. It was clear I'd get more information through subterfuge than outright honesty. "Oh, that's too bad. I guess I'll have to go into his office to talk to him. I really wanted to get this sorted."

"Sure thing, dear," she said. "I'm sure he'll be able to fit you in. Just give the office a call first and make an appointment. He'll be glad to know you're willing to start doing something with your money."

I resisted the eye-roll. There was a fucking team of brokers that worked for Sinclair Racing and handled that shit for me. I was sure they were ten times better than any two-bit banker could be—even if that two-bit banker was my father.

"Yeah, I'll be sure to call first," I said, knowing full well I wouldn't.

"By the way, Alyssa said she's free whenever you are ready, if that means anything to you."

I nodded. Although I was glad she'd called early to ask me over—it meant she was as anxious to see me as I was to see her—I couldn't see her just yet. She'd asked me not to push her about the situation with Mum, and I wanted to respect that request, but I knew if I went over there right away, I *would* push her. Whatever was happening, I had a goddamned right to know. It was easier to wait for a few hours until I had it sorted before going to Alyssa's.

And I would fucking get it sorted.

"If she calls back, can you tell her I'll be over later? I just have some errands to run first."

Mum's gaze shot to me. "Errands?"

"Oh, you know, I still need a couple more outfits if I'm going to be here until I'm due back for testing."

"When's that?"

"January."

"You're staying until January?" Mum asked. Her shock was clear in her voice. It occurred to me that we'd never discussed exactly how long I'd be in town for, and I hadn't really asked for permission to stay.

I dropped my head, suddenly worried that maybe she wouldn't want me around for that long. "Yeah. Well . . . I mean . . . if it's all right with you, I'd like to."

She walked over to me, placing one hand on either cheek and pulling my face down to look at her. "You're welcome to stay as long as you want. I just didn't realise you'd be here through Christmas."

Christmas? Holy fuck. I hadn't thought about Christmas. I felt the colour drain from my face.

My first Christmas as a father.

My first Christmas with a family.

How the hell was I going to do that? Would Alyssa expect me to dress up as Santa and all that shit? Would we have to spend time at her family's house? The thought of it terrified me. Alone with Josh and "killer" Curtis. Worse—*Ruby*. I knew I would have to face them all sooner or later, but frankly later suited me just fine.

Before I could go into panic mode, I cut off the thoughts. Christmas was still a month and a half away, I could worry about it then. For the moment, I needed to focus on the here and now, otherwise I risked screwing things up with Alyssa again. In the here and now, I needed to find out what the fuck was going on between Alyssa, Mum, and Dad.

"Well, if that's settled," I said, stepping out of Mum's grasp,

"I'm just going to go . . . run those errands."

She furrowed her brow at my evasiveness, but just said, "Sure."

I climbed into the hire car to head into the city. The smell of the vomit was worse than it had been the night before. Winding down all the windows, I hoped to get some fresh air through the car.

As I turned onto the motorway, the wind swept through my hair. I drove for all of ten minutes before I came to a grinding halt in the last dredges of peak-hour traffic. The sun beat through my windscreen and I cursed myself for the clothing choices I had made. Not that I'd had much choice in the matter, with my limited supply.

I glanced over at the car next to me to see someone staring slack-jawed through their window. Once I'd glanced in their direction, they waved frantically and the passenger rolled down their window.

"You're Declan Reede, aren't you?" they shouted across the divide between our cars.

Fuck me. During my time in Sydney, I'd almost forgotten what it was like to be anonymous. My time in London and in Browns Plains had almost brought it back to me. Especially the last few days with Alyssa. I'd felt normal again—just a boy trying to woo his girl. It was nice. I hadn't realised how nice until that moment, sitting in a car that was the equivalent of a fishbowl. A small, Barina-shaped fishbowl at that. All around me, people's gazes seemed to light up with recognition. I sank deeper into my seat, trying to hide away from them.

The worst part was that I hadn't thought to remove the child seat, so it was sitting in the back of the car as evidence of my new life. I could almost hear the thoughts of everyone around me as they pondered the development. The gossip mill was already starting to grind around me. Maybe I was being paranoid, but I wanted to avoid that part of my life coming anywhere near Alyssa or Phoebe. I had two choices: I could either leave the windows down and endure the stares, or wind them up and allow the lingering smell of vomit to cycle through the air-conditioning. Either way, I was going to be stuck in traffic for a while yet and both choices had their drawbacks.

In the end, the sun made my decision for me. By the time the traffic had crawled halfway into the city, it was too fucking hot to have the windows down any longer. Sighing, I raised the windows up and set the climate control, adjusting it to as low a temp as I could. Ducking my head, I let the cool breeze from the vents run through my sweat drenched hair. When I caught sight of myself in the rear-view mirror, at the mess my hair had become, I tugged my hand through it a few times to try to tame the unruly strands, but nothing seemed to work.

After a while, I gave up and simply rested my head in my hand and leaned my elbow against the driver's window, contemplating just what the fuck I was doing. Yeah, I was heading into the city, but to do what exactly? Walk up to my father's work and ask him the questions I was dying for an answer to? Could I do that? Should I?

I flicked the radio on to distract me. If I allowed myself to overthink it, I might never find out what was going on. I'd never know why Mum didn't usually have Phoebe on the weekends. Why Alyssa had called to check that it was okay, and why Mum had needed to reassure her.

The car inched forward along the highway and I felt my courage dissipating a little more with every passing minute. The radio did nothing to quell the doubts creeping into my mind or the sick sensation in my stomach.

My phone rang loudly in my pocket and vibrated against my leg, causing me to startle a little. I gathered my bearings, pulled my mobile from my pocket, and pushed Answer before flicking it on to speaker.

"Hello?"

"Declan. It's Dr. Henrikson. I'm calling for our appointment."

"Oh fuck, Doc, I forgot."

He chuckled a little. "Is now a convenient time? Or would you like me to call back?"

"No, now's fine. Or at least, it's as good a time as any other."

"Perfect. So what would you like to talk about today?"

I rolled my eyes. *Where do I begin?* "You're the shrink. You tell me what we should talk about."

"Why don't you tell me a little bit about Alyssa?"

She was a topic he'd been itching to discuss in Sydney, and I'd always shut him down. His constant prompting to talk about her was the reason I'd stopped seeing him. No matter how many times I'd told him she was off limits, he wanted to know more. Now, he'd get his wish. "Like what?"

"How did you meet?"

"At school." Even though I'd decided to be an open book, it was hard to put into words everything that Alyssa and I had once shared.

"Just 'at school?' Won't you elaborate?"

There was no point in evasion. If I was serious about trying to get better for Alyssa—for Phoebe—I needed to talk as honestly as I could. With those thoughts burning though me, I told him about the first time I met Alyssa, when we were six—how she was a walking contradiction and I'd been immediately enamoured.

"And then what happened?"

"Then we became friends. For about eight years that's what we were. Friends. Best friends. We shared everything. Barely a day passed when I didn't see or speak to her." It was confronting, recalling exactly what Alyssa and I had once shared. I didn't think I could articulate exactly what we meant to each other—even back then, long before we discovered our mutual attraction, long before girls stopped having germs—Alyssa was always there for me. According to all the other boys back then, I'd been risking cooties every time I spoke to her, but I never cared.

Just thinking about it all made me want to smile, and made me want to cry.

The beep of a horn behind me reminded me that I was driving. Lost in the past, I'd tuned out and the traffic had moved on. In fact, it was gaining speed. I pressed down on the accelerator as I continued to talk to Dr. Henrikson.

"She was there for me through everything. No one else knows this, but there were quite a few nights when we would sneak out after everyone was asleep and meet at our park bench. It was never planned, but somehow we both seemed to arrive within minutes of each other. I don't know how to explain it, Doc, in fact it probably makes me sound like a fucking looney, but it was like we were linked. Like we could communicate without words."

"That doesn't sound unreasonable. Many people would say they have a similar connection with their partners."

"Maybe, fuck, I don't know. All I fucking know was that whenever I needed her she was there for me. Always. And I was always there for her . . ." I stopped. I couldn't continue on that train of thought, because it wasn't true. I hadn't *always* been there for her. The opposite was true—I'd deserted her during the one time she needed my support most.

"What are you not telling me, Declan?" I should've known better than to assume the doc wouldn't hear my pause.

"I abandoned her," I choked out. My eyes stung and I was finding it hard to concentrate on the road ahead of me. I watched the taillights of the car in front as carefully as I could and followed their line.

"When?" Dr. Henrikson asked in a strangely calm, almost hypnotising voice. "How?"

"When I moved to Sydney . . ." I couldn't say any more. There were no words to explain the shame I felt. A sob ripped from my chest instead.

"Declan?" Confusion laced his tone, and it was easy to understand why. He'd heard me rage, and scream, and swear, and argue. He'd never once heard me cry.

"I fucked up, Doc." Another sob ripped out of my chest but the tears were merely swelling. None had fallen yet. Thank fuck. "I fucked up real bad. So bad that I don't even know how to begin fixing things. It's all my fault. If I hadn't left her . . . God, things might be different now."

"What do you mean?"

"I'm sorry, Doc. I . . . I can't . . ."

"Would you like to stop for today?"

Did I? I felt like it was cheating Alyssa if I didn't complete the session, but I couldn't keep going either. At least, not while I was driving. I was already finding it difficult to even see the car in front through the tears that hazed my vision. Eventually I found my voice enough to manage a small, "Please."

"Declan, you know I would like nothing more than for you to clear the air on every issue. But you must do it at your own pace, or it could be counterproductive. If you feel something is too difficult to discuss, we can approach it another day."

"Thanks, Doc."

"Would you like to pick this up tomorrow, same time?"

I didn't think I really did, but I knew I would have to talk it over with him eventually or else I might as well kiss any hope of rekindling with Alyssa goodbye.

"Please."

"Okay, we'll pick this up at the same time."

I knew he would still charge me for the full hour—and for the cost of the phone call—but I didn't care. I needed to get off the phone.

Throwing my phone onto the passenger seat, I bit my lip to fight off the tears that were still threatening. Once again, I felt dangerously close to a panic attack. Doing everything I could to turn my mind off the ways I'd let Alyssa down and get back in control of myself, I weaved through the traffic as quickly as I could before taking the Elizabeth Street off-ramp. Parking in the city was always expensive, but at least I wouldn't have to worry about public transport when I was finished my meeting with Dad.

I glanced down at the clock on the dash, it was just before eleven. As I drove along Elizabeth Street, my heart thudded in my chest. I'd completely forgotten that the Suncrest Hotel was right above the car park I'd been aiming for.

The fucking Suncrest Hotel.

The last time I'd been there was when disaster struck.

When I left Alyssa.

The night of our school formal.

I hadn't stayed at any Suncrest hotels since then, but this one in particular I couldn't handle. Focusing on the car park entry, and *only* the car park entry, I was determined to get in before I broke down. It was all too fucking much.

I ripped the ticket from the machine, glad they had the

unmanned booths now. The boom gate opened and I drove underneath. Without even looking at what parks were available, I headed straight for the bottom level, twisting around the ramps and corridors without letting myself concentrate on details. I only stopped when I saw a group of unoccupied parks clumped together in one spot. After I'd pulled up, I slammed my fists against the steering wheel in frustration. Why the fuck had I come here? Ugly reminders of the formal were everywhere I looked. Every level of the fucking car park was the same—each one looking exactly like it had been when I'd had to drag my sorry arse from the hotel room after Alyssa had left.

Every agonising second of that dreadful walk rushed back into my mind. What should have been a short walk to the car with Alyssa at my side on the best morning of my life had instead felt like a funeral march after the death of our relationship. I couldn't even feel satisfied over the fact that we'd made love for the first time the night before. In fact, I felt sickened at the fact that it happened right before our break-up.

I recalled with perfect clarity how, somewhere between the lobby and level P3, I'd resolved that regardless of anything else that might happen, I would win Alyssa back. That I wouldn't run away and leave it as we'd left it. I'd hoped that with a little space, we'd come back together to discuss uni and my contract with Sinclair Racing again, and come to some sort of compromise. Of course, when I'd reached that resolution, I hadn't counted on Josh waiting by my door to beat the shit out of me.

My breathing came in ragged heaves as the panic attack that had been threatening for so long hit with full force. The reminders of the past were too much. It was all too much. Somehow the last two weeks had simultaneously been the best and worst of my life.

I couldn't do it though. I couldn't cope with everything I was facing. How could I win Alyssa back when all we did was hurt each other? Even if we got past that, how could we ever have a future with the obstacles in our way? Her family hated me, she'd admitted as much.

They would never forgive me.

I would never forgive me.

Twisting in the seat, I pulled my legs up to my chest, ignoring the biting pain as the steering wheel dug in to my shins, and the stabbing that shot through my side. Putting my head on my knees, I tried to breathe but it didn't help. Nothing helped. I couldn't stop the thoughts that were consuming me for long enough to draw oxygen down into my lungs. A vicious cycle of heartbreak and doubt.

Wrapped around myself, one thing was certain: I was going to die. And a fucking car park in the city was going to be the cause.

Fumbling with the door, I reached the handle and yanked it open. I half-climbed, half-fell from the car and landed on all fours on the concrete. Struggling for air, I pushed the door shut to remove it from my path and crawled to the front of the car. Squeezing myself between the front bumper and the concrete wall, I tried to hide from the prying eyes of passers-by. Once hidden, I sat staring at the blank concrete and leaned against the car, dropping my head back to rest against the bumper as I tried to get my breathing under control.

What the fuck am I doing?

Hours later, that may have only been minutes or even seconds, I felt my breath begin to return, bringing my sanity along with it. I was able to remind myself that despite the odds, Alyssa was willing to give it another go. *She* was willing to try to forgive me, even if her family couldn't accept that. That was what mattered.

Standing, I drew one more shaky breath, steeling my nerves and my resolve. I would find my father and talk with him, find out what the hell Alyssa and Mum were hiding. Then I would use that knowledge, and all of the information at my disposal, to work hard until I earned Alyssa's forgiveness. Until I deserved it.

Without glancing back or around me, I locked the car and headed toward the elevator. One more reminder of the night it had all fallen apart might have been enough to kill me. Not for the first time, I wished I could turn back time and make it all better. Do it the right way the first time.

Inside the elevator, my eyes scanned the levels and my finger hovered over the buttons. An idea formed. Maybe I *could* make it better. I couldn't actually turn back time, but maybe I could do the next best thing.

Making up my mind, I pushed the button for the hotel lobby rather than the shopping centre entrance below. I gulped nervously and said a silent prayer that my plan would work.

As the elevator doors opened, I planted a smile on my face and walked up to the concierge. I saw recognition light up his features immediately. The look was enough to leave me hoping it would be like shooting fish.

An hour later, my plan was set into motion and I didn't even have to organise a fucking thing. It was likely the hotel manager would have eaten his own shit if I'd asked him to. Sometimes the whole celebrity thing wasn't so bad, especially when you could call on favours from fans by greasing the right wheels with a few autographs and a couple of happy-snaps.

After heading back down to the food court in the shopping centre beneath the Suncrest Hotel, I had a quick bite to eat. While I ate, I thought of the week I had planned out for Alyssa. If it wasn't the best fucking week of her life, something was wrong. I grinned stupidly as I imagined the look on her face. I very nearly turned straight around and headed back to her house to see her. But then I remembered I'd actually come to the city with a purpose.

I cleared my table and walked out into the Queen Street Mall. I knew the route to Dad's work by heart and my feet trailed along the familiar path while my mind wandered elsewhere.

As I passed Post Office Square and approached the building that housed his bank, my eyes scanned the small cafe across the road. I couldn't say what had initially drawn my attention, but once I looked there, I couldn't turn away. My hands clenched into tight fists at my side.

I couldn't believe what I was seeing, but it was there plain as day.

In that moment, I saw everything.

I saw him. Then I saw her.

And then I saw red.

CHAPTER NINE

COLLAPSE

"WHAT THE *FUCK* do you think you're doing?" The words left my lips as soon as my brain had taken in the details of the scene.

Even as I spoke, I tried to work out which part of the scene I found most disturbing. The fact that my father had his hand in another woman's lap, the fact that she was feeding him and he was pulling all sorts of ridiculous faces as he licked the fork clean, or the fact they were doing it out in public, without any shame. As if it was just a normal relationship, and not a filthy fucking affair.

Despite all of that horrid detail, there was one thing more disturbing.

Much, much more disturbing.

And that was the fact that the girl was Hayley Bliss. One of the members of the blonde brigade who'd been in my year at school.

As if signalled in on cue, a tonne of questions and doubt smashed into my brain. Was Hayley the first and only, or just the latest in a string of lies? Had there been others like her over the years? Countless others? Had all of the late nights and the weekends away when I was in school been because of affairs? My stomach turned at the thought, and I felt sorry for Mum, stuck at home doing all the housework while Dad was off shoving his dick into a scrag.

At the sound of my shouting, Dad looked up. I wasn't sure whether it was because he recognised my voice though, because almost everyone in the cafe raised their head at the noise.

I tuned out everything around me except for him and her. My sole focus was on my father and his floozy. I didn't even watch for cars as I stormed across the busy intersection.

Dad leapt to his feet, knocking over his chair in the process. It clattered loudly behind him. "Declan? What . . . what are you doing here?" He looked around between me and that tramp, as if willing himself to understand. Or maybe he was just trying to come up with some bullshit excuse.

I didn't stop my charge until I was in his face. In the same motion, I raised my hand and fisted his shirt collar. Using it as leverage, I lifted him to my level. It hurt like a sonofabitch but I didn't give a shit. He needed to pay. The look of terror on his face was evident. For years, he'd always managed to maintain a certain level of authority, even as my height towered over his. It was only during the last week that his power had waned. I couldn't say at exactly what point I'd lost my respect for him, but it was definitely sometime between his words about Alyssa and the sight of him with *her*.

I'd been raised believing that marriage was for life, and that vows were sacred—special. That you made promises and kept them for life. That was part of the reason I'd been so fucking terrified of my feelings for Alyssa. To discover that the very person who taught me that—the same man who'd claimed he had to give up his dreams to get married—was off on dates with a whore half his age . . .

"What. The. *Fuck*. Is. Going. On?" My face was right in his as I spat the words at him.

When I finally tore my eyes away from him, I turned to look at Hayley. She was still sitting at the table with a look that rested halfway between fear and amusement.

Before I could do any serious damage to him or myself, I pushed Dad out of my way in disgust.

When I turned on her, Hayley gave a nervous giggle and said, "Um, hi, Declan. I, ah, didn't expect to see you here. Although Robbie had told me you were back in town."

Robbie? What the fuck. I took a step toward the table and she shrank back in shock. Her eyes widened as she speedily moved her chair backward, as if getting ready to run at any second.

My head swung back and forth between her and my dad, not trusting myself to talk. I knew that in my current mood a stream of invective would be the most conversation I was capable of. Not that they didn't deserve it. Both Dad and Hayley kept their eyes on me. Both wary as if I were a hungry predator preparing to strike.

I took a deep breath, trying to calm myself, but the red haze still filled my vision.

"Will someone tell me what the fuck is going on here?" I shouted, kicking out and knocking over the table in front of Hayley. She screamed and leapt out of the way as the contents went flying, spraying coffee or chocolate or something all over the ground and on some of the surrounding patrons, who all fled as quickly as they were able.

"Calm down, son," my father said, placing his hand on my shoulder. Knocking his arm off roughly with my elbow, I twisted out of his grip.

"Don't touch me!" I spat at him.

His eyes darted from side to side, making me partly aware of the gathering crowd. It wasn't enough to stop me though. I couldn't give a fuck about anyone watching, I just wanted answers.

At the same time, I really didn't want to know.

"Does Mum know?" I asked through gritted teeth. My heart pounded against my ribcage so hard I was surprised that it wasn't audible to everyone nearby.

"Can't we go somewhere a bit more discreet to discuss this?" Dad asked, glancing around once again.

"Does Mum know?" The words burst from me as I picked up

the nearest chair and hurled it at the wall. Screams from the bystanders filled the air, but I couldn't care less. Anger burned through me and I needed to release it. At least it was only a chair and not Dad's face. For now.

Dad hung his head. "She knows."

"Does she fucking know it's with a slut who's three months younger than me?" I growled. "I mean, what the *fuck?*" I picked up another chair and threw it to punctuate my sentence. Someone behind me put their hand on my shoulder.

"Sir," a calm but authoritative female voice said from behind me. I shook my shoulder free of the loose hold.

Dad squared up in front of me. "Hayley and I are in love, Declan. In a way I've never truly felt about your mother."

A different hand rested on my shoulder, once again trying to turn my attention away from my father. A male spoke this time, "Sir, we're going to have to ask you to—"

Ignoring whatever it was he wanted to say to me, I shook free of the hold. Despite voices murmuring around me, words like damage, police, and leave, my focus remained pinned to Dad. "Are you fucking kidding me? You are screwing *Hayley*, and you have the gall to call it love? She's the town fucking bicycle for fuck's sake. Worse, she's younger than *me*—your fucking son! All of that and you have the nerve to tell me you're in love?"

I was dangerously close to losing control, but was surprised when Dad did first. I saw his fist the second before it connected with my jaw. The impact hurt, but I'd had worse. Morgan and I had swung at each other often enough over the years to leave me more than ready for a fight with my middle-aged father.

I retaliated—hard.

Grabbing at the side of his head, I caught a fistful of his hair and yanked his head backward. My other fist flew at his face with all the power I could muster. At the last second, he yanked himself away from my hold, but my fist still connected in a glancing blow.

Without waiting to recover, I threw myself at him in a tangle of limbs. My chest protested the movement, but I couldn't stop myself. He landed a blow along my left side, and the breath rushed out of me as I gave a strangled cry. It didn't stop me though. It only gave me motivation to hit harder, faster.

Fuck him!

My fists smashed into his body again and again until I felt myself being pulled off him. I struggled against the arms that had me, kicking out and knocking over more tables. Everything was tinged in red and I was beyond all reasoning.

All I saw was the object of my fury in sharp relief. Everything else was a blur. I heard murmurs of conversations, and screaming, and the sun reflected off the metal tables over and over, flashing in my eyes each time.

Before I could process what was happening, I was being dragged back across the road. My father stepped forward and embraced Hayley fucking Bliss. As if he was fucking *comforting* her. At the sight, I went to launch myself across the road at him again. How *dare* he do that to Mum? How could he be so brazen and uncaring as to flaunt his fucked-up relationship in public?

Before I could make my point again, two meathead security guards from the building that housed the investment offices of the bank, including Dad's office, stepped in front of me. They were obviously the ones who'd dragged me away. Without me realising it, I'd been backed into a corner by them. I could have tried to fight my way out, but I didn't really like my chances. Instead, I turned toward the wall and butted my head against it, focusing on the pain of the brick biting into my forehead to take the mind off my burning rage, aching side, and twisting stomach.

I kicked off from the wall to face the security guards again. They stared impassively at me, as if daring me to try to run. I knew they had no legal power to hold me against my will, but they were also big enough to beat the shit out of me if I tried to make a break for it. While I was cornered, a police car turned up and two officers climbed out. Dad stepped straight up to them and shook their hand. Ever in control.

Ever the slimy bastard, more like.

I turned back toward the wall and let loose a roar of primal anger before pounding my fist against the brick, just imagining it as my father's face. I pulled my fist back and shook my hand—the action had fucking hurt and only made me madder.

I spun around again when I heard *his* voice barking out instructions to the guards. They turned and left, and suddenly I was face-to-face with the man who had been my hero while I was growing up.

The man I now despised.

Without even thinking about it, my fingers curled into fists at my sides. My knuckles protested. They were swollen and sore and wouldn't form a fist properly, but it would be enough to do some damage.

"I've smoothed things over with the cafe owner," he said. "He's agreed not to press charges if the damage is paid for."

"Like I give a shit," I spat at him. "How could you do it?"

"I've told you, son—"

I cut him off. "Don't you fucking *dare* call me that! You need to be a fucking father before you get to call me son."

He sighed and pinched the bridge of his nose—a gesture I'd actually learned from him. "Declan, go home and calm down. I'll talk to you about this later."

"Like fuck you will." I wanted to smack his smarmy face again, but instead I thought of Phoebe. What sort of father would *I* be if I kept it going? If I wasn't the bigger man by walking away?

I took a deep breath and stared him down. Shifting my gaze behind him, I saw Hayley cowering near the building entrance. When I looked between them it occurred to me that I had never hated two people more in all my life.

"You are fucking dead to me," I spat as I shoved him away. "Stay away from me. Stay away from Alyssa. And stay the *fuck* away from Mum. You don't deserve her. You don't deserve any of us."

Before he had a chance to respond—and before I had a chance to lose the sliver of control I had on my temper—I turned and stalked away. Even then, it was only thoughts of Alyssa and Phoebe that stopped me from turning around and kicking his arse. Well, thoughts of them and the fact that I knew the two boofhead security guards would be there waiting if I did.

I may have been angry but I wasn't fucking suicidal.

I made it back to Post Office Square before my lungs threatened to collapse on me. Anger still coursed through me and I had no way of releasing it. My fingers began to shake as I felt my breath leave me entirely. While my legs felt weak beneath me, my brain began to muddle. Needing to get out, get *away*, I picked up my pace and headed back in the general direction of the Barina.

By the time I hit the end of the Queen Street Mall, I was practically running. While I raced toward freedom, I drew quick laboured pants through my teeth.

I needed . . .

I fucking didn't know what I needed.

I just needed to get away. I needed to forget. I needed to wipe the image of my father's intimate interactions with Hayley fucking Bliss out of my mind. Questions I really didn't want the answers to raced through my mind on an endless track. Why was she in the city? Did she work with him? How long had he been fucking her? Did it go back to high school?

A shudder ran down the length of my spine.

I took the stairs into the Suncrest Shopping Centre two at a time before screeching to a halt at the bottom when I saw a sign.

A way to cope.

The only way I knew how.

The temptation of the pub—the sweet siren's call—was too great and I couldn't resist. Hiding my bloodied hand behind my back, I nodded briefly to the bouncer. I didn't want him to stop me, or ask me questions, because questions led to thoughts and I didn't want to think about Dad, or Hayley, or anything really.

I wanted to bring on oblivion.

Oblivion and ignorance.

When I reached the bar, I didn't hesitate. The order for a triple shot of Jim Beam was on my lips the instant I had the bartender's attention. Past experience had told me that a couple of those would get me sufficiently blotto as fast as possible.

The bartender slapped the drink down in front of me and I

tossed him a twenty. Closing my eyes, I took a deep breath, trying to clear the images of *him* and *her* from my head.

I reached for the glass and raised it to my lips, ready to wipe it all away.

As I did, a new picture entered my mind.

Phoebe.

Phoebe and Alyssa, smiling and waving.

The look of disappointment in Alyssa's eyes as I'd told her about driving while I was under the influence.

I can't do this!

The glass slipped from between my fingers before I could comprehend what was happening. I opened my eyes just in time to see it hit the ground—crashing against the metal footrest that ran the length of the bar and spilling amber liquid everywhere.

"Fuck!" I jumped backwards, but it was too late. The splashing liquid went as high as my knees and soaked into my pants.

"You all right, mate?" the bartender asked.

"Um, yeah . . . um . . . no . . . I—I'm sorry. I've . . ." I turned and fled without a second glance.

I COULDN'T say exactly how I'd ended up at Alyssa's. I had no recollection of reaching the car or climbing in. Neither was there a memory of driving out of the car park and onto the freeway.

I didn't even know how I managed to get out of the car and into the house. All I knew was that when I'd left the city, I'd had a burning need to be in Alyssa's embrace. It was a new, healthier way to find the oblivion I sought.

Sometime after I'd stumbled through the door, my anger long burned away and tears flooding my eyes instead, I found myself coming back to reality. My chest still heaved from the weight of the sobs that had started while I was driving back from the city. I had no recollection of how long we'd been in our position, with me lying on the couch with my head in her lap, before I finally rolled onto my back and stared up at my personal angel.

She brushed the hair from my eyes, and ran her fingers along my cheeks to brush away the remnants of my tears.

"Hey, you," I said.

"Hey, yourself." She smiled softly at me and brushed her fingers through my hair again. "What's wrong?"

I shook my head. I'd finally composed myself enough to talk—I couldn't tell her that my entire world had crumbled. Again.

Everything that I'd known to be true, no longer was.

Everything kept piling up on top of me, forcing me to shoulder one burden after another. Dad's affair was one burden too many.

"You scared me before," she said matter-of-factly, "barging in here like that."

"I'm sorry," I whispered. "I just didn't know where else to go."

It was true; I had no idea how I was going to go home or face Mum. She'd known about Dad's affair. She'd known about all the disgusting things my father did while at work—probably more than I ever would.

My heart plummeted as my memory started to work and reminded me of the phone calls between Mum and Alyssa. The whispers and secrets. Had Alyssa known too?

She must have, it was the only thing that made sense.

"You . . ." I rolled off her lap and was across the room an instant later, staring at her accusingly. "How could you, Alyssa? How the fuck could you keep that from me?" Without thinking about why I was doing it, I shouted at her. My voice was wild and hysterical.

Standing to follow me, she looked back at the hallway, as if seeking an escape path, before turning back to me. She held her arms in front of her, palms upturned. I took it as a silent plea for understanding.

"How could you!" I screamed again.

"Declan," her voice was low and calm, "I don't know what you are talking about."

"About him. About fucking Dad and his little whore! You knew, didn't you? You knew and you never fucking told me."

She looked down the hall again. When she turned back, her

face was full of anger.

"Watch your language!" she hissed.

"Fuck that! Why didn't you tell me my own fucking father was sleeping with Hayley fucking Bliss!"

Alyssa's jaw fell open and she gasped loudly. "What?"

I froze. Her expression of surprise looked genuine, but could I trust it?

"You didn't know?" My voice was full of the disbelief I felt.

She shook her head. "I really didn't," she whispered. "How long?"

I took a step away from her, until my back pressed against the wall. As soon as I felt the support behind me, my legs gave beneath me and I slid down to the floor. I wrapped my arms around my legs and laid my head on my knees.

"How could he do that to Mum?" I sobbed. "How could he say he loves that little slut?"

Kneeling in front of me, Alyssa's hand enclosed my own, and she enticed me to raise my head just a little. She put her hand on my cheek. "Why don't you have a lie down? It sounds like you've had a bad day."

I wanted to laugh at the understatement, but I just didn't have it in me. There wasn't a single thing about my life that was the same as it had been a few weeks ago.

Just a few short weeks and everything was different.

I was hit with a paralysing fear of how short life really was. How quickly things could change. I climbed forward onto my knees and clutched at Alyssa. I placed one hand on either side of her face, and pushed my fingers into her hair. I caught her eyes with mine. A last sob escaped my throat before I managed to stifle them.

One of her hands shifted to the back of my neck and the other held my waist. She pulled me against her, and cradled me to her body and moved to help me stand. I resisted the pull though, instead taking a moment to relish her embrace. Taking a few deep breaths to calm my breathing, and never breaking eye contact, I pressed my lips to hers in a gentle, chaste kiss.

"I love you, Lys," I whispered as I pulled away. My gaze was still locked with hers, and I knew she'd heard every word. "You were right when I said I loved who you used to be. But you were wrong about one thing; I do love who you are now too."

"Come on," she said, apparently ignoring my statement. "Let's get you into bed. Things will look better in the morning."

I shook my head and nuzzled into her neck. "This won't. I don't know if this will ever be better. How am I supposed to deal with this shit?"

"We deal with things because we have to," she said, the pain in her voice evident.

I felt like an arse because as bad as the revelation over Dad's affairs was, it wasn't half as bad as the things she'd had to face.

"It's called life, Declan." A sad sigh left her as we stood and she led me to the hallway. "At some point you just have to learn how to deal with it," she added quietly, her voice almost sarcastic.

There was no way for me to answer her that wouldn't make everything worse. So I didn't. Instead, I let her guide me to wherever she wanted me to go. I was a little surprised when she walked past the spare room door. Sounds that seemed far too bright and cheery for the day issued from behind that door. I knew it was still only early—far too early to be going to bed—but I couldn't care less. I wanted to cocoon myself in there, preferably with Alyssa, and block out the rest of the world. The rest of the world hurt like fucking hell and it was easier to block out that pain with Alyssa beside me.

After I'd climbed out of my still bourbon-soaked pants, I slid between Alyssa's sheets and curled in on myself. She helped and supported me as best as she was able, muttering something incoherent as she worked. When I was in bed, she grabbed my pants and headed out the door.

Once again, I found it hard to breathe. By the time she returned, I was seconds away from another panic attack. As if she sensed my rising angst, she ruffled her fingers though my hair and curled around me. I grabbed her hand and held it around my body. Right then, I needed her to survive. It felt like she was the only thing tethering me to reality. Sooner than I would have expected, I felt myself drifting toward unconsciousness.

The last thing I heard was Alyssa's soft voice whispering in my ear, no doubt assuming I was already asleep. Her voice was filled with sorrow as she said, "Why is it you can only tell me how you feel when you're drunk?"

I wanted to argue, but I was too far gone. My protest came out as a garbled murmur.

CHAPTER TEN

INTERRUPTIONS

I FELT THE bed shift and opened my eyes to try work out where exactly I was. The night was too thick to allow my tired and sore eyes to see anything. Pulling myself up onto my elbows to try to get a better view, I heard a small voice call through the dark.

"Sorry. I didn't mean to wake you." It was Alyssa.

"Hi," I said, feeling that it was a completely inadequate statement considering what had happened earlier. "What time is it?"

"It's just after eleven."

"And you're just getting to bed now?" I asked, my fuzzy brain trying to work out the events that led me to being in Alyssa's bed. Slowly things started to come back. "Weren't you with me before?"

She laughed a little as she climbed underneath the blankets. "Yeah. But it was too early for me to go to bed."

A beat of silence fell between us.

"I didn't have the same benefits as you when it came to falling asleep," she added in a voice as bitter as it was muted.

"What benefits?" I asked, confused. By now Alyssa was lying in bed beside me and it was seriously clouding my ability to concentrate on anything but her, and how I really wanted to reach out and hold her. And how I really shouldn't reach out and touch her.

"Like being drunk," she whispered into her pillow, as if confessing her sins. I could hear the tears in her voice.

"I—I wasn't drunk, Alyssa."

She sighed, her exasperation clear. "I've heard that before. You 'weren't drunk' but you've been drinking. Just like when you came to visit me at Josh's."

"No—"

"Dec, please," she begged, cutting off my protest. "Don't lie to me. What did I tell you when we had our talk? I want to trust you, but how can I if you're just going to lie to me?"

I turned completely onto my side, ignoring the crushing ache it caused in my ribcage. The position allowed me to meet her eye, because I wanted her to know the truth. "Alyssa, listen to me. I wasn't drunk. I didn't drink today. At all. I wanted to. God knows how much I fucking wanted to, but I didn't. I stopped."

"And let me guess, you just happened to smell of alcohol because you spilled it on yourself. Do you think I came down in the last shower?"

With a sigh, I turned away. It would be harder to get her to accept the truth than it would be to apologise for the lie. Regardless, I wanted her to know the truth.

"Didn't you just say you were going to try to trust me? Think about it, Lys, what reason do I have for lying now? You're here in bed with me even though you think I was drunk. Why would I try to convince you that I wasn't, if it's not true? What more would I get from it?"

"I'm hardly in bed with you, Dec." She sighed. "I mean, sure, I'm in bed with you, but I'm not *in* bed with you."

"I'm glad you cleared that up." I chuckled.

"I had nowhere else to sleep."

"Not that I'm complaining, or want to leave, but I could always take your spare bed if you'd prefer."

"No!" she said, a little too quickly. I smiled. She didn't want me to get out of her bed. In fact, she sounded almost desperate for me to stay.

I moved a little closer to her, and her breath hitched. It was hard to tell in the darkness but I could have sworn her eyes closed for half a second before they fluttered open again.

"Just stay over on your side," she said. I couldn't tell what the emotion I heard in her voice was—it almost sounded like desire, or maybe need, but that didn't marry up to her words.

"Really," I said. "I don't mind going to your spare room if you think it would be easier. I mean . . . I saw that the bed was made and everything when I was here yesterday."

"It's not really a spare room."

"What do you mean?"

"It's . . . it's Flynn's room. For when he stays over to help me out and stuff. I guess it doubles as a spare room when he's not here but no one's ever really stayed in—" She'd started to babble and I held up a hand to cut her off.

"Flynn's room?"

She nodded and cowered against the pillow.

"Flynn's *room?* He's got a whole fucking room at your house?"

"Declan, you need to understand the relationship I have with Flynn. He helps me out. Sometimes he's the only thing that keeps me sane. And he's always there for Phoebe. That's just easier when he can stay over whenever he likes, especially if he's looking after her late or in the morning."

Then the other part of what she'd said hit home. It doubled as a spare room, *"when he's not here."* I lost it. "Fucking hell, Lys. You mean that fucker was here the whole time? I was fucking pouring out my heart and fucking soul to you and that fucker heard everything? I bet he was having a merry old fucking laugh."

"No, Declan, it's not like that at all. He was here anyway and then you came in and he took Phoebe into his room. I didn't want you to scare her, not if we are going to tell her the truth soon."

Alyssa's words stilled me. "Tell her? You mean, who I am?"

"Yeah. I mean, if you're serious about staying, I'll have to. She's so clever, she's going to realise something soon and I don't want her to find out from someone else. I just don't know how to do it."

"Do you think it'd be okay if we told her together?" I asked. She was trying to redirect me, I could tell. I wasn't sure I wanted to drop the Flynn subject, but I was also reluctant to climb out of the bed if our argument spiralled any further.

"Maybe."

It wasn't quite the answer I'd hoped for but in the end, I allowed the subject to be dropped. I could always bring it up again in the morning. She turned away from me and settled into a comfortable position.

I waited a few minutes, trying to fall back to sleep, but it felt so wrong to be so close and yet so far away from her. When I moved a little closer to her, she settled back into me. Taking it as an invitation, I snuggled against her and pulled her close. Wrapping my arm around her waist, I guided her back so that I was spooning her properly without putting too much pressure on my ribs. It reminded me of times when we'd slept over at each other's houses when we were teenagers. We'd always start in separate rooms, but sometime around midnight we would sneak across the hall for a few hours to spoon with each other before crossing back to our own separate rooms before our parents woke.

"This is just like when we were young," she said, echoing my thoughts.

I chuckled against her, tickling the spot at the base of her neck and sending a small shiver rippling down her spine. I laughed at her reaction to my breath; it hadn't changed over the years.

"Let's play pretend then," I whispered into her hair. "Just for tonight let's pretend that we're back there again, that none of the shit that's gone down in the years since has happened. It's just you and me against the world like it always was."

"Instead of you and me against each other like it has been lately," she said sadly.

"No, Alyssa, it's not like that. I don't ever want to fight you. You protect me. You and Phoebe are the reason I didn't drink today. The only reason I stopped before I did."

"You really didn't drink this afternoon?" Her voice was still sceptical.

"I really didn't."

She rolled over in my arms and I was aware of just how close she was to me. Her breasts ended up pressed against my chest. Her thighs, which were uncovered, lay against the length of mine. I groaned as my body became hyperaware of her nearness. I tried to pull away from her a little to allow room for growth, but without making it seem like I was distancing myself from her.

In the darkness I saw her eyes searching my face, presumably trying to find evidence of the lie.

"What can I do to prove it to you?" I asked. "Try me. I guarantee I don't smell or taste of alcohol," I joked, puckering my lips.

"Well, if you are willing to subject yourself to that sort of test, you must be telling the truth," she teased back.

"Oh yeah," I said sarcastically. "Kissing you would be real torturous."

"Really?" she asked. I could hear the smile in her voice. "Well, it's a good thing you won't be doing it for a long time."

I picked up on the opening she had left. "But I will be doing it eventually?"

She mock-punched me.

"It's funny," I continued, "it didn't feel that torturous yesterday."

"Declan Reede, you're an arse." She laughed.

"Isn't that why you love me?"

She froze, her entire demeanour shifting in an instant. I wondered what had caused the shift.

"You really weren't drunk earlier?" she asked.

"No. I honestly didn't drink anything today. I dropped the glass I was going to drink and ran from the pub. In fact, I can probably make some calls and get the footage if you want."

"So everything you said earlier . . ."

"Was true. Induced by stress, maybe, but true. I meant every word."

She chewed on her lip and her eyes found mine. I could see into the depths of the honey-gold irises, even through the gloom that shrouded the room. Raising my hand, I coaxed her lip from between her teeth with my thumb.

Understanding dawned on me, and I saw what it was she was asking. Her words earlier came back to haunt me. *"Why is it you can only tell me how you feel when you're drunk?"* I wanted to prove her wrong and knew only one way.

"I, Declan Reede, world-class arse, love you, Alyssa Dawson, exquisite goddess, with all of my heart. I love who you were. I love who you are. And I have no doubt I will love whoever you grow to become."

She watched me balefully for a few minutes and then spoke so quietly I almost didn't hear. "Thank you."

Leaning forward, she kissed my cheek gently and then pressed her head against my chest. She breathed deeply and I closed my arms more tightly around her. It hadn't gone unnoticed that she hadn't told me she loved me back. I was torn apart by that fact; part of me recognised it was still too early for her and understood, but part of me—mostly my ego—was bruised and damaged. After the day I'd had, I really needed something solid in my life to cling to. I wanted that something to be Alyssa and me.

"When will we tell Phoebe?" I asked.

Alyssa was quiet for a while and I wondered if she hadn't heard or maybe she was ignoring me. I was just about to ask again when she answered with a sigh.

"Sunday?" she answered, but it almost sounded like a question.

"Sunday's good." I answered. I could see Sunday working. I wanted a family day on Sunday anyway—I would give Phoebe the best day of her life and then Alyssa and I would tell her that I was her father.

My breath caught in my throat just thinking about it. Terror gripped me—what if she rejected me? Or didn't like me? Or hated me for leaving Alyssa? Logically I knew she was too young to feel those things now, but what about in years to come? Could I ever make it up to her? I wanted to try, but I wasn't sure if I would be able to succeed.

I was lost in my own thoughts and fears for so long that Alyssa had fallen asleep and was snoring softly against me. I gently shifted her so she was facing away from me again and wrapped my arms around her, pressing my face into her hair and drawing comfort from our proximity. I stayed in that position, awake and planning out the various ways we could tell Phoebe for at least an hour before I finally succumbed to sleep myself.

MY FINGERTIPS brushed against something soft and delicate. I stroked back and forth a few times, trying to work out exactly what they were rubbing against. A soft moan sounded out nearby. Opening my eyes, I found that my hands were currently residing inside Alyssa's pyjamas and my fingers were playing along the underside of her breasts. For a second, I worried what she must think. The moan had sounded like it was issued in pleasure, but I couldn't be certain. I raised my head to look at Alyssa's face but realised quickly she was fast asleep still, her lips parted but drawn into a small smile. Slowly, reluctantly, I drew my hand back from her skin and pushed myself up to a sitting position.

Swinging my legs out, I sat on the edge of the bed and rested my elbows on my knees. I cradled my head in my hands, and tried to process all the events of the last twenty-four hours. I knew I needed to go home eventually, but I had no idea what I would say to Mum. What could I say? I was disappointed in her, in Dad, in everyone who had known and not done a damn thing about it. But wasn't that a bit fucking hypocritical, considering my own actions? Then again, nothing I had done with intent while sober was as bad as what he'd knowingly chosen to do.

I wanted to wake Alyssa up and quiz her on why Mum didn't have Phoebe on weekends if it wasn't because she knew about Dad and Hayley. I believed her when she told me she didn't know; the look on her face and her reactions were enough to convince me. But that still meant there were too many secrets and too much lying bullshit going on.

I wanted to get all our cards out in the open. To know about everything I'd done to hurt Alyssa during my darkest times, but I also wanted to know about the other secrets people were still hiding from me. Dragging my hand through my hair, I stood. I had nothing to get changed into but decided my shirt/boxer combo was modest enough not to scare Phoebe if she surprised me when I left the room.

At the door, I turned back to take in the sight of Alyssa before leaving her. She was curled up in a ball and the smile from earlier was gone. A frown had replaced it. I wanted to rush back over to her and smooth the worry off her brow, but I wasn't sure how Alyssa would feel about me doing something so intimate if she woke up and caught me. I opened the door as quietly as I could manage and went in search of the toilet.

After I'd drained the main vein, I walked out to the kitchen. I saw something move in the living room out of the corner of my eyes but chose to ignore it as I opened the fridge, taking in the contents. I grabbed out the juice and turned around to hunt for the glasses, pushing the door shut behind me.

I started and then groaned when I ran into the hulking form of Flynn. He crossed his arms and glared at me, like I was supposed to be scared of his pansy arse or some shit. Okay, so maybe I was a little—I knew he could probably beat me down if he wanted to—but I wasn't going to let the fucker know it.

Trying my best to ignore him, I set about hunting through the cupboards for a fucking glass. I probably could have just asked him, he had his own fucking room there after all, but I didn't want to give him the satisfaction.

"What are you doing here?" he asked, his tone rough, rude, and unapologetic.

Ignoring him, I poured myself a glass of juice. As I drank it down I could feel his eyes boring into my back. After I'd finished drinking, I put the glass down on the bench and turned around. He was staring at me, clearly waiting for a response.

"That's Alyssa's business," I said with a shrug.

"Alyssa's business is my business," he said in a voice of ice. "So what are you doing here?"

"Things are gonna start to change around here, *Flynn*." I said his name like a curse. "You're not going to be number one in Lys's life anymore."

He scoffed.

"What the fuck do you find so funny?" I asked, stupidly getting in his face.

"I was never number one. I don't *want* to be number one."

"Whatever. Just know that things are going to change."

To my surprise he laughed. "You just don't get it do you? After our last conversation, I thought maybe you might, but you don't. I hoped maybe you'd learn, but you're just a fucking idiot with his head up his own arse."

I wanted to ask him what the fuck he meant but I couldn't bring myself to do it.

"You know the way Alyssa used to talk about you, I honestly thought you were a decent guy who deserved to be in their lives. That was the reason I left you the birth certificate. That was the reason I convinced Cain to fix your car."

"You know nothing about me," I hissed icily.

"Clearly," he said. "The media certainly got a few things right though."

"Fuck the media."

"You should leave Alyssa alone."

"Why? Give me one good fucking reason."

"Goddammit, what do you think she's going to go through when you fucking kill yourself with your stupidity?"

"Fuck off."

"You're inflicting all your issues on Alyssa. Hurting her."

"That's what you do when you are a couple, you share your issues."

"Maybe, but you're not a couple."

"We're fucking trying to be. If only every other fucker wouldn't stick their noses in and keep fucking trying to ruin things for us." I made my point by poking his chest with each word. If I wasn't in Alyssa's house, I probably would have smashed his face against the cupboards by now.

He laughed. "The funny thing is you do a good enough job fucking things up yourself."

"What the fuck is that supposed to mean?"

"Turning up here drunk like that. Honestly, man." He shook his head at me.

"Just keep your fucking nose out of my business. She knows the fucking truth about yesterday and really that's all that fucking matters. I'm not going to justify myself to you. I really don't fucking need to."

"Will you two please just stop already!" Alyssa called from the hallway. Her voice was quiet, but deathly and filled with tears.

I shot Flynn a look intended to kill. He fucking couldn't leave well enough a-fucking-lone, could he? Now Alyssa was pissed at me again. After we'd found our way to an amicable place before falling asleep the night before. It was like we were back to square fucking one again, and it was his fault.

I turned to comfort Alyssa but somehow that fucker got there first and walked her back down the hallway away from me. As he wrapped his arms around her, he whispered an apology and asked, "We didn't wake the princess did we?"

Alyssa shook her head. "No, thank goodness—"

They disappeared into Alyssa's room and the closing of the door cut off the rest of her sentence.

"Fuck!" I cried, kicking at the kitchen cupboards.

Leaning my weight against the counter, I tried to steady my breathing. Flynn was going to be a fucking problem. Alyssa's family was going to be a fucking problem. No one seemed willing to give me a fucking second chance.

Except for her.

The thing was, I understood their anger. I'd fucked up big time where Alyssa was concerned. I knew it. It didn't seem to matter to any of them how hard I was trying to fix it though. It meant nothing to them. In their eyes, I was still just the big fucking arsehole trying to hurt her.

My anger made me twitchy. I needed to lash out. To do . . . *something*. I couldn't stay still any longer. Couldn't stand in her kitchen looking at the closed fucking doors without wanting to tear something apart—preferably the arsehole who'd taken her away from me.

I had to go. There was no fucking point staying when Alyssa was already upset with me—all I would do was fuck things up more. I hunted quickly for the essentials—wallet, car keys, phone, and pants. I found a scrap of paper and wrote Alyssa a note.

I meant what I said last night.

Call me.

— D

I pinned it underneath a magnet shaped like the letter P in a prominent position on the fridge. Then I rinsed the glass I'd used and left it to dry beside the sink.

After unlocking the front screen door using the key that was already in the lock, I crept out of the house as quietly as I could. I climbed into the Barina and felt a surge of regret. Why did that fucker have to rile me up so fucking much? That morning could have been a fucking magnificent morning, based on how Alyssa and I had been the previous night. I slammed the car door shut in frustration. The anger was direct at myself, at the world, at Flynn, at everyone and everything.

Releasing a frustrated growl, I turned the key in the ignition and slammed the car into reverse. By the time I reached the end of the road, it was clear I had nowhere to go. I had no one I could go to.

I could go home, but I still didn't want to face Mum. There was nowhere else I needed to be. Without thought, I drove through the streets until I ended up outside our old school. I parked the car and climbed out. There was only one place I could go to get any peace of mind: our park.

I walked the short distance as quickly as I could. My phone started to ring just as I sat down in at the table. I pulled it out anxiously, hoping it would be Alyssa because it'd been almost an hour since I'd left her house. I hoped she had kicked that fucker out and we could talk properly. My face fell as I read the number on the screen. It was only Dr. Henrikson. It was earlier than he'd called before, but I wasn't going to argue with his schedule.

"Good morning, Declan," he said after I answered the phone. "Are you feeling better than yesterday?"

The events of the previous twenty-four hours crashed down on top of me and my voice croaked as I responded, "No, not really."

"Are you ready to continue our discussion?" he asked.

Part of me wanted to say no, to hang up and pitch the phone across the park, but instead I swallowed down a painful breath and said, "Yeah. I think I'm ready now."

CHAPTER ELEVEN

IT'S SEMANTICS

"WHY DON'T YOU tell me what happened?" Dr. Henrikson asked in his smooth tones.

With the story on my lips, I found myself recalling sessions in his office; his voice hypnotic, soothing. In that moment, it occurred to me that we never actually talked about anything real. We'd talked about bullshit like what happened during races, about clubs, about life in Sydney, about the things I'd done while high—at least the things I could remember. It was clear now though that I'd had no life in Sydney. I wasn't *living* there, and I'd never hurt this much there either.

"Doc," I said. "This story, it's real fucked-up. I . . . I don't know where to begin."

"The beginning is usually the best place. You were telling me about how you met Alyssa yesterday. Why don't you tell me about how you fell in love?"

He was trying to ease me into the harder stuff, that much was clear. I decided to try and let him. He was the shrink after all. Plus, I didn't know if I'd ever be able to get the rest out otherwise. How could I just come out and tell him the things I needed to say when the lump in my throat was so large I could barely swallow?

"I guess a part of me always knew I loved her," I said. "Even if I couldn't admit it to myself. When I was fifteen . . . Well, it just kind of happened one day. The school year was coming to a close and we'd finished a big test, so we wagged our last class and went to our park."

The air felt heavy as I spoke, as if the world around me held its breath while I whispered my secrets.

"That first kiss," I said, closing my eyes as the memory washed over me. When I opened them again, I paused and glanced around me. It had happened no more than a few metres from where I sat. My lips burned at the memory, scorched forever by Alyssa.

"Even now, I don't know who actually started it. I think it may have been me, but I'll never know for sure. We had one of those movie moments, you know? Where you pause and stare at each other's lips for a second that feels like forever, then slowly, one of you starts to move forward, before pausing once more to assess the situation, then . . ."

I stopped as the memory overtook me again. Her lips had been so warm against mine. She'd thought I had lots of experience, but she was the first girl I'd ever kissed like that. Despite the lack of knowledge on both our parts, we just fit. It was perfect.

"What happened then?" Dr. Henrikson asked, pulling me from my thoughts.

"Well, that was it. From then until I left Brisbane, Alyssa was the only one for me." It wasn't entirely true. There had been the extremely brief, terribly regrettable week with Darcy, but I preferred not to linger on memories of that. Even if both Alyssa and I had been with someone else at the time, our hearts had belonged to one another.

"So would you say you had the perfect relationship?" he asked, his voice reserved.

"Hell no." I laughed a little as memories played through my head. "We fought like wild cats. We probably broke up at least once every few weeks, but we always found our way back to each other, at least eventually. There was never anyone else. Not really."

"So why did it end?"

"A lot of reasons, I guess. I had the contract for Sinclair Racing. She wanted me to go to uni. Neither of us was willing to compromise."

"So that was what ended your whole relationship? Just a disagreement over where life was headed?"

"Well, that and her brother beat the shit out of me."

"Why?"

I sighed. "Because he thought I raped her."

"Why did he think that? Is that what Alyssa told him?"

"Fuck no. Josh is" — I tried to think of the right word to describe him — "a little overzealous sometimes. He jumps to conclusions way too easily. Alyssa and I fought after our first night together and she stormed out in her nightclothes with a ripped dress. She spent the whole trip home crying too."

"And so he confronted you about it?"

"No, he beat the shit out of me. He didn't even let me say anything. It was what ended up making my mind up about moving to Sydney. I only saw Alyssa once more after that, at least until recently."

"You believe Josh is the reason you moved to Sydney?"

"Well, he was a big part of the reason."

"And if he wasn't there, waiting on your doorstep, what would you and Alyssa have done about your departure?"

I couldn't answer. I knew the answer, but I couldn't say it out loud.

"Do you think you might have left anyway?" he prompted.

"Yes." My voice was small and weak in my own ears and yet I knew it was the absolute truth. "But I would have tried harder to make things work with Alyssa."

"Would you? You always seemed quite certain that you liked the life you had here, the . . . freedoms it afforded you."

"I don't know, Doc. I mean I was young and fucking stupid, and terrified of the power she had over me. Whenever I was in her

129

presence, I just wanted to lock us both away in our own secret bubble and never have to face the world again. That frightened the hell out of me."

"It sounds like you two were pretty intense."

I chuckled. "That's one word for it."

"So what happened next? Did Alyssa just let you go?"

All traces of the good mood that was building inside me at memories of Alyssa and me fell away as I remembered what happened next. "No, she, ah, well . . . I ignored her phone calls for almost a year before she finally stopped calling."

"Is that what you meant yesterday? When you said you abandoned her."

I closed my eyes to hold back the tears and nodded, stupidly forgetting I was on the phone and that he couldn't see me.

"Abandoned is a very strong word, Declan. Why do you think you chose that word specifically?"

"Doc, the . . ." A sob ripped through my chest. Taking a deep breath to get myself back under control, I continued. "The things she went through."

"Like what?"

"She lost a child . . ." *My son*, I finished in my head.

"That's a terrible thing for anyone to have to go through, especially if you had been there for her in the past. But it doesn't explain the use of the word abandoned, or is there something more?"

I sobbed again. My chest burned with a lack of oxygen. My eyes stung with tears that refused to fall.

"She lost *our* child." I launched straight into the story Alyssa had told me, not trusting myself to pause for breath or I risked stopping entirely and collapsing in a heap. When I finished there was silence on the other end of the line.

"Declan, I would like for you to come in and see me as soon as you are able. In person."

"Sure, Doc." I was certain Alyssa would make me stick to the sessions for a while anyway and to be honest, I felt just a tiny bit lighter after telling him the story. It would never be forgotten, and I didn't know if the pain would ever go away, but it had helped in some miniscule way to talk about it.

"Where are things at between you and Alyssa at the moment?"

"Fuck, Doc, I don't know. Things were fucking great last night but then this morning . . . that fucker got in the way."

"Who?"

"*Flynn*," I said his name like a curse. "He can't fucking keep his opinions to himself. Not even when he knows nothing about what's going on!" I ranted. I stood and paced a tight circle around the table. Just thinking about that morning, about Flynn in general, was making my blood boil. Especially when he and his brother still had my Monaro in their care. My free hand clenched and released in time with my steps in a useless attempt to alleviate some of the tension.

"And who is Flynn?"

"He pretends to be Alyssa's friend. I don't fucking know what his deal is. Apparently he was there for her when . . ." I growled loudly before walking over and punching a tree just for being in my line of sight.

"When you couldn't be?"

"Yeah." I choked on my frustration as I shook out the pain in my fist.

"I take it he means a lot to Alyssa?"

"I guess so."

"Why do you feel so antagonistic toward him?"

"Because he's a wanker," I snapped.

"You don't think part of the problem is jealousy?"

"Fuck, Doc, he's living my fucking life. He's living in her goddamn house for Christ's sake! According to the world at large he's Phoebe's father. She's *my* fucking daughter, and yet he gets the benefits. I don't want him in her life."

"I think we need to discuss this at a later stage," the doc said, trying to calm me. "Why don't you tell me what happened this morning?"

"I was there, at Alyssa's," I seethed. I wasn't able to remove an ounce of venom from my voice, just thinking about the way things had turned that morning made my body shake with anger. "And that fucker started having a go at me over shit that he knew nothing about. Then when Alyssa came out and was upset at both of us, he fucking comforted her. He fucking wrapped his arms around her and led her away. And she let him."

"Did you talk to Alyssa about it afterwards? Explain why it made you upset?"

I paused. "No. I haven't spoken to her since."

"Why not?" he asked, sounding genuinely surprised. "Surely, you talked to her before you left her house?"

I closed my eyes and shook my head, trying to clear the doubts and fear that were creeping up. "No, I . . . couldn't."

"Why not?"

"Because he was with her."

"You didn't stay to talk to her?"

"No. How could I? How the fuck could I wait there knowing that his arms were fucking wrapped around her and she was taking comfort from him."

"Declan, that would have been the sensible thing to do."

"What the fuck, Doc? I thought you were supposed to be on my side? I thought you were supposed to be helping me and not fucking telling me how to live my fucking life."

"All I am saying, Declan, is to try to put yourself in Alyssa's shoes. Do you think she would have wanted you to stay to talk about things?"

I thought about what he was saying, and what Alyssa herself had said about not trusting me. "Fuck, probably. Sorry."

"It's not me you need to apologise to. As you pointed out, I'm just here to help you. Unfortunately though, I do have to get to my next appointment."

"Will we talk again on Monday?"

"Would you like to talk to me again on Monday?"

I barely gave it a thought before I answered. "Yes."

"Then I'll call you on Monday. But I would really like to schedule an in-person meeting as soon as you get back to Sydney."

"I'll let you know my plans as soon as I know them."

"No problems, Declan. We'll speak on Monday then."

I'd barely hung up the phone when it rang again in my hand. I answered it without looking at the screen.

"What are you doing tonight?" An overly excited voice exclaimed in my ear before I even had a chance to say hello.

"Hello to you too, Eden." I chuckled. It was hard not to be swept up by the infectious joy in her voice.

"Oh, fine then. Hello. What are you doing tonight?"

"I don't know, Edie, I don't really have any plans." Other than grovelling at Alyssa's feet until she'd forgiven me for being a fuckwit.

"Ha! Wrong. You're picking me up from the airport, that's what you are doing."

"What are you talking about?" I pinched the bridge of my nose. Fucking great. As if things weren't fucking hard enough at the moment. The last thing I needed was Eden's particular brand of friendship.

"I'm getting on a flight to Brisbane at around five, and I need you to pick me up just after five thirty."

"Why are you flying to Brisbane?" I tried not to sound too blunt. It didn't really work. A suspicion over the reason was growing within me, but I didn't want it to be true.

"Duh, to see you, silly. It's been too long."

I sighed. "It's been three weeks. I saw you at Bathurst, remember?" Even though I'd said the words, I didn't want to remember. Thinking of Bathurst and the shithole my career had fallen into made me more depressed than ever.

"Yeah, but I don't just mean physically *see* you. I mean go out like we used to. Have a good time. I kind of think you need it."

There was no point arguing with her, as much as I wanted to. Knowing Eden, she'd already booked and paid for every event and drink she had on her agenda. With a sigh, I gave in. "What time?"

"Just be at the airport at five thirty. I'll be through security and out as quickly as possible. I'll be flying in on Virgin."

"Sure thing, Edie," I said, resigned. "Have you got accommodation?" I knew she would, but it was the question she'd be dying for me to ask.

"Of course! I'm staying at the Suncrest."

Of course, she's staying at the fucking Suncrest Hotel. Why wouldn't she be? "How long?"

"Just the night. I've got to get back ASAP for the preparations for the Bahrain race."

Fuck, I'd forgotten about the Bahrain race. I'd travelled with Danny and Morgan a little more than a month earlier to scope out the track and the conditions. I'd been fucking looking forward to that race so badly. Now, I would miss out.

My entire body longed to be back behind the wheel of my V8. It was what I knew. It was what I wanted. When I closed my eyes, I could almost see the track stretching out in front of me. I could almost hear the rumble of the motor. I couldn't wait until I was back in the saddle. Maybe when Alyssa moved to Sydney, I'd actually be able to have it all.

"Okay. I'll be there," I said, as if I had a fucking choice in the matter. I had to admit though that the idea of a tiny link to my former life was a little exciting. It was like the two parts of me were slowly drawing closer together.

Eden's plans had pretty much made up my mind that I needed to go back to Mum's. I had to, mostly because Eden would have a pink fit if she saw the clothes I was in. Between the sleep-crushed shirt and unironed pants, I was a fucking mess. With a sigh, I picked myself off the ground.

I glanced around the park once more, taking comfort in its familiarity, and readied myself to confront the mother who'd been lying to me since I arrived back in Brisbane—and who the hell knew how long before then.

FOR A long time, I stood staring at the front door. Minutes passed while I let my indecision still my feet. Should I use my key and just go inside, or knock and wait to be invited in? How could I confront her? Just shout and scream until she told me everything, or try to pretend I knew nothing, just like she did?

I had no idea what to do, so I just fucking did what I always did. The way I always did it—with no thoughts, no consideration, just balls to the wall and a bravado I didn't really feel. With a breath as deep as my protesting ribs could take, I reached for the door handle.

I found Mum sitting at the dining table looking frazzled.

As soon as she saw me she threw herself across the room at me and wrapped me in her arms. "Oh, thank heavens! We've been so worried about you. Your father told me about yesterday, and then Alyssa said you were there last night. But then you just disappeared. Everyone's been frantic with worry over you."

"I just needed time to think."

She let me go and walked back to her seat at the table. She looked at me expectantly, like she was waiting for . . . something, but I had no idea what.

"Declan," she began.

I held up my hand to stop her and asked her the only question I wanted the answer to. "Why are you still here, Mum?"

She looked at me blankly. I wasn't sure whether it was because of the bluntness of my question or because she genuinely didn't understand what I was asking.

"I'm assuming that little whore isn't that bastard's first," I said.

Mum gave a small headshake, confirming my suspicions.

"Then why are you still with him? I don't get it, Mum. Don't you have more respect for yourself? I mean, fuck!" I slammed my fist on the table to drive home my statement.

"It's not that easy," she murmured.

"Fucking hell! It's exactly that easy. He's a fucking prick and you shouldn't have to put up with it."

"Declan, he's still your father. Please, just calm down."

"Not until you tell me why you're still here. Fucking supporting him at that. Even now you can't find one bad word to say about him, can you?"

"Of course I can, Declan," she snapped at me. "There probably isn't a bad word in the entire world that I haven't thought about him at one point or another. But you idolised him. You followed his every footstep from the moment you could walk. How could I ever shatter your world like that?" The sadness in her eyes echoed the truth in her words.

All the breath in my body left me in a rush. "You stayed because of me?"

"Of course, Declan. You're my son. You're the most important thing in the world to me. Even now, with you all grown and living your own life, you're still my little boy. There was no way I could be selfish and break up our family."

"But after I went to Sydney, why didn't you leave then? Why stay?"

She stared at her hands, which were knotted together on the table. "Where else could I go?"

I moved closer to her and knelt at her side. "You could have lived with me for a while. I would have helped get you back on your feet."

She shook her head sadly. "I don't think you would have. I think that's how you feel now, but that's Alyssa's influence." A small smile lifted the corner of her mouth. "She's good for you."

I smiled a little too, but it fell almost immediately. Alyssa was good for me, and I just kept fucking it up. I decided that it was time to get everything on the table, while Mum was talking anyway, and find out what the deal was with Alyssa and Phoebe and the weekends. No more bullshit and half-truths. Those had fucked everything up enough as it was. "Why don't you look after Phoebe on the weekends?"

Mum either understood I wasn't backing down, or she just didn't have the energy left to fight. "Just lots of little reasons."

"Like?" I shifted to sit in the seat beside her as my side began to ache.

Mum sighed. "Do you know you were born six months after your father and I were married?" she asked. At first I thought she was trying to change the subject.

"So?"

It was her turn to raise her eyebrow at me.

Slowly realisation dawned on me. "Are you saying that you and Dad got married . . . *because* of me."

She nodded.

"I was an accident?"

"No." Her voice was emphatic, but then her brows knitted. "Well, technically. I mean, you weren't expected or planned, but I would *never* call you an accident."

"Semantics." I wasn't planned. When I stopped to consider it, everything was obvious in hindsight. Like working out why a crash had happened in the moments after the car had hit the wall. It was the reason Dad and Mum had married early. *I* was the reason. All of Dad's whispered warnings made more sense. They weren't cautionary tales of what *might* happen, they were regrets over what had happened.

Mum moved her hand over mine. "No, it's not semantics. You may not have been planned, but you were loved from the minute I found out I was pregnant. I was overjoyed."

I didn't miss what she'd said, and also what she'd left unsaid. "*You* were overjoyed and Dad . . . felt trapped?" I guessed.

"Not at first." Her response was a whispered admission.

"But eventually he did?"

Mum's eyes turned glassy, picturing what exactly I didn't know, but her voice was emotionless when she spoke. "We were married at eighteen. It didn't take long for him to feel like he was stuck at home while his friends were able to go out and live it up. I think that made him a little resentful."

"Toward me?" I felt like I had been punched in the stomach. As much as I hated him at the moment, he was still my father. Hearing that he resented my existence stung and made me hate him even more. *Will Phoebe feel that way about me one day?*

She shook her head and reached out to stroke my cheek gently. "No, it was never toward you. He loved you with every fibre of his being. He still does. It was everything he had to give up to provide a stable household for you."

"Like racing?"

She nodded.

"That's why he said all that crap the other morning." I had meant it as a question, but knew it so absolutely that it came out as a statement. "And why he warned me to be careful so often?"

Mum looked away.

My blood turned to ice. Had he said similar things to Alyssa? Was that why she was uncomfortable around him and didn't bring Phoebe around on the weekends when he might be home?

"What else?" I asked. My voice was small and weak, lacking all the anger that burned just below the surface.

Mum's eyes fell back on me for a second before dropping to the floor.

"What else happened?" I asked, more loudly. "Did he fucking say something to Alyssa? After everything she went through, did he accuse her of trying to trap me?"

"No, he's never said anything like that to Alyssa. At least, not that I'm aware of."

"Then what did he do?"

"Nothing," Mum whispered, before picking up a rag that was sitting nearby and cleaning the table, wiping it in small, tight, anxious circles.

"What did he do?" I asked, kicking away from the table. My entire body was on alert. I was ready to turn around and hunt the fucker down. I had no idea where he was going for his "business trip" but I had a sudden desire to know and to go there. To introduce him to both my fists again and again.

Mum pressed harder as she cleaned the table.

"Tell me," I commanded, thumping my fist against the table. The noise resonated throughout the house and a small exclamation of shock left Mum's lips.

After her initial squeak of surprise, Mum fell silent. I wasn't sure if she was trying to protect Dad or not betray Alyssa. I'd scared her often enough with my lack of control, she'd likely only give up the secrets if she thought I wouldn't fly off the handle in response to them. The calmer I was, the more likely it was that she would tell me the details. I swallowed down the emotions clawing at my throat and tried to release the tension in my body.

"Please." I forced the word past clenched teeth.

"It was just little things—lots of little things—that made Alyssa feel uncomfortable."

"Like?"

"You have to understand the full situation. I already felt like I'd lost you. I couldn't stand to lose Alyssa and the twins as well."

"What did he do?"

"I didn't want to drive her away. So after it all happened, it was just easier for her not to be here when he was. To come during the day while your dad was at work. Alyssa seemed okay with that solution too. We've stuck with it ever since."

"What. Did. He. Do?" Each word hissed through my teeth as I tried everything I could to keep my anger in check.

"I told you, just little things. There wasn't anything specific."

I pulled at my hair and decided to pull out the big guns. With a sigh, I leaned against the table. "Mum, please, I need to know. I'm trying to gain Alyssa's trust and I think if I know everything she's been through, it'll be easier."

She eyed me sceptically. "You'll overreact."

My heart struggled to pump the ice-cold slush that filled my veins. I tried to keep that chill out of my voice. "No. I won't. I promise."

"It's really nothing."

"Fucking hell, Mum!" I snapped, slamming my fist onto the table again. "Just fucking tell me."

"He used to compliment her," Mum whispered, almost silently. I had to strain to hear the second part. "Especially once the pregnancy hormones kicked in."

That didn't sound too bad, and I wondered why it would be something to keep Alyssa away. I struggled to think of what pregnancy hormones did but I knew so fucking little about that shit that nothing came to me.

"And he accidentally walked in on her in the shower one day."

"What?" Mum's words cut through all of my thoughts, and I needed to know more because it didn't make sense. "Why would she shower here?"

139

"It was when she was about six months pregnant. She'd had really bad morning sickness through the early months. She was finally getting past it, or so she thought. But then she had a bad bout when she was here one day."

Her words layered a fresh serving of guilt over the ones that already surrounded my heart. I hadn't been there for Alyssa during those hard months. Whatever had happened to her because she was trying to keep a relationship with my mother was my fault.

"I loaned her some of your old clothes and offered her the shower."

I clenched my fists at my side. "Then what happened?"

"Are you sure you really want to know? I don't think the specifics are important."

"Like fuck they aren't." I needed to know whether I just needed to hurt Dad, or whether I needed to murder the fucker.

"All I know is that he was in the bathroom when she got out of the shower," she said. Then added in a guilty rush, "I'm sure it was just a misunderstanding though. He said he'd only just walked in."

"Misunderstanding, my arse," I whispered with barely contained rage.

Mum rested her hand over mine, no doubt trying to show me some support. "After that, Alyssa never felt comfortable here with him around. I never questioned her, not if it meant I still got to see her and Phoebe."

The only sound I could hear was the grinding of my teeth. Mum's words were a reminder that I hadn't only left Alyssa behind. The more I learned about the way things had been at home, the more I regretted my actions. It was no wonder Mum hadn't gone out of her way tell me the truth about it all. It wasn't the sort of thing she could just say over the phone.

Dad, the dirty prick, was getting around with a scrag younger than I was. Who knew what other fuckery he'd gotten up to over the years. My fingers curled into fists at the thought. My hold on my temper was tenuous at best. It took everything I had to keep my heart rate under control. Any additional revelations would push me over the edge. Without another word, I turned and walked away from Mum to my room.

Halfway down the hallway, I stopped. I didn't turn around to look at Mum when I spoke. "You *will* leave him. I'll make sure of it."

Mum didn't say anything.

Closing my eyes and releasing a frustrated breath, I spun back toward her. "You deserve better than the way he's treated you."

Without waiting for an answer, I turned around again and headed for my room. As I walked down the hallway, I passed a framed photo of us as a family. It was taken in my senior year, about three months before I left for Sydney. The three of us were all fucking smiles and happy family.

It was a fucking lie.

I yanked it off the wall and hurled it at the other side of the hallway. The glass sliced into the photo, scraping a line down my fuckwad father's face and halfway through my own.

Burning from within, I moved to my room and slammed the door closed. Leaning against the wooden surface, I took a few breaths in a useless attempt to calm myself. The fact was my words to Mum were as fit for me as they were for Dad. Alyssa deserved better than the way I'd treated her in the last four years. Better than I'd treated her just that morning. Growling as my frustration bubbled over, I punched the wall. The crunch of plasterboard beneath my fist didn't satisfy my need to break something.

Kicking away from the door, a primal cry flew from my lips. Without a thought, I grabbed the box on my bed and dropped it against the closed door. I ripped the doona off my bed and threw it to one side before twisting to yank the drawers out of the bureau, hurling them across the room one by one. Clothes went flying in all directions.

Still burning with the need to punish myself, my dad, everyone, I pushed the bureau over and kicked the side. It was the punishment my father deserved. The punishment I deserved. I took every ounce of it out on my room.

By the time I was finished, my clothes were strewn across the room, splinters of wood from the bureau covered the floor and bed, and the wall bore three new fist-shaped holes.

Panting with the effort of tearing my room apart, a need built in me to get out. I needed to see Alyssa. I needed to apologise to her for my father, for me, for everything.

Grabbing any clothes I could get my hands on, I threw them into an old bag I found at the back of my closet. Then I found an outfit to change into and headed for the traitorous bathroom.

Even as I entered the room, I felt sick as I wondered what the hell Alyssa had been through in there. Had Dad been spying on her? My stomach roiled at the thought.

After I'd showered and dressed as quickly as I could, I grabbed the bag I'd packed and headed for the door. Mum wasn't anywhere to be seen, but I figured she was probably hiding from the sounds of my rage. Regardless, I wouldn't come back again until it was absolutely necessary.

CHAPTER TWELVE

A CHANGE

WHEN I REACHED the Barina, I jumped inside and just drove, not thinking about where I was going. Instead, my mind was stuck in the past. Stuck on Dad and his whores. Stuck on the countless women I'd been with, and how I was no better than him. Stuck on the future, and Eden's visit. She'd been my unexpected ally and saviour when it came to my job. She'd always hated what I did. It wasn't just the drugs she protested against either. She'd been vocal about the girls, about the alcohol, and about my lack of respect for myself.

I had no doubt Mum had filled her in on everything that had happened since I'd arrived back in Brisbane and about Alyssa. I had no fucking clue why Eden was flying up, but I was certain I would get the third degree about everything live and in person as soon as she arrived.

Which left one question: should I subject Alyssa to that? Eden could be very full on, and I could only imagine she was already picturing herself as Alyssa's best friend just because of what Alyssa meant to me. It would be easier to introduce Alyssa and Eden on

Alyssa's terms, and not on the Friday afternoon before our big fucking date. If our big fucking date was even still on.

The more I thought of it, the more annoyed I grew that Eden had picked that night of all nights to come to Brisbane for a flash visit. She had to have known what was happening for my date. There wasn't much that happened at Sinclair Racing at all without her knowledge. If I hadn't known better, I would have thought she was Danny's fucking daughter or something. But it was common knowledge that Danny and his wife, Hazel, had been unable to have children.

In the end, it was the thought that Eden was almost certainly hoping to get the inside scoop on Alyssa that made my mind up. It was too much to ask of Alyssa to put up with that after everything else. I decided I'd go meet Eden, but I wouldn't introduce her to Alyssa. At least, not yet. Maybe I could convince Eden to come back again before Christmas, after Phoebe knew the truth and things were a little more . . . settled.

If they get settled.

Pulling the car over on the side of whatever the fuck street I was on, I glanced at the clock on the dashboard. A little less than an hour had passed since I'd left Mum's house, almost three since I'd left Alyssa's. Yet, Alyssa hadn't called despite my note. I wondered what it meant. The thought caused a flurry of questions to race each other in my mind.

Should I call her? Or did she not want me to? Was that why she hadn't called yet? Or was that fucker Flynn still there? Had he convinced her not to call me? Had he convinced her not to see me anymore? My heart thumped painfully at the thought. Before I had a chance to think it over or panic, I pulled out my phone and called the mobile number Mum had given me.

"Hello?" Alyssa said, her voice high-pitched and her breathing ragged.

"Hi," I replied timidly. I didn't know what reaction to expect.

"Dec," she breathed. "God, are you all right?"

"I am now." It was amazing how much calmer I felt just listening to her voice.

"What the hell was that this morning?"

"I'm sorry, Lys. I just . . . I saw you in his arms and I just . . . I—I just couldn't cope." I hung my head as I acknowledged that fact.

"Gah, you have to stop this being jealous of Flynn bullshit. Don't you see I have no interest in him outside of friendship? And I've already explained that he has *zero* interest in me in that way."

"It's not a matter of me being worried that he's trying to fuck you."

"Nice." Her voice was full of venom and raised in anger.

"Sorry. I didn't mean it to come out like that. It's just . . . well, he's living the life I should be fucking living. It should be me there to comfort you when you are upset. It should be my name on the fucking birth certificates."

She was silent. I knew why. There was only one thing she could say and it was sure to inflame the conversation even more. It was my fault I wasn't living that life.

"Look, can we just fucking start over? Hey, Lys. How are you, I'm okay for now, but I really want to see you."

She giggled a little. "I can't today, Dec. I have to work."

"Work?"

"Yeah, it's what those of us who don't have million-dollar contracts do to afford mortgages, food, and clothing."

"Smart-arse," I said. "I just meant you haven't mentioned it before."

"It's a part-time job in the local shop, hardly worth discussing."

I got a picture of Alyssa in a cute little outfit behind the check-out of the corner store we used to go to. I smiled at the image. "So check-out chick to world-class lawyer."

"Actually, we prefer the term product-currency transfer supervisors," she joked.

"That's a mouthful." I laughed.

"Better to be a mouthful than a handful."

I almost choked on the laughter as I processed what she'd said. I heard her laughter on the other end of the line.

"I really am sorry I left like I did this morning," I said, knowing it would drag the mood down, but feeling that it absolutely had to be said.

"Why don't you come around tonight?" she asked. "I finish work at seven thirty."

"I can't, I have a teammate flying in from Sydney to meet up with me before they start preparations for Bahrain."

"Oh," she said, and I could hear the disappointment in her voice. The sound was like music to my ears.

"But I'll be there first thing in the morning to pick you up."

"Is your Mum still 'right to look after Phoebe?"

"Umm, I'll have to check . . ." I trailed off.

"What did you do?"

In response to her question, I squeezed my eyes shut. I was so fucking sick of everyone always assuming the worst of me. Maybe in this instance it was warranted, but the assumption still pissed me off. "I'll check with her, but I'll be there tomorrow morning to pick you up regardless."

"Okay, Dec, I'll trust you to arrange it." It sounded like that trust was resting on thin ice.

"I'll be there early. Get a good night's sleep 'cause it's going to be a long day."

"And you won't tell me where we are going?"

I smiled. "Of course not."

"Fine. Be like that." I could hear the pout in her voice.

"I'll see you tomorrow, Lys."

"Okay, Dec."

"And Lys?"

"What?"

"I love you."

"I'll see you tomorrow." She hung up the phone.

It was the second time I'd confessed my feelings with her knowing I wasn't drunk, and it was the second time she hadn't said anything back. I dwelled on the implications for a few minutes before deciding I would simply have to show her a fucking fantastic time tomorrow so she wouldn't be able to resist telling me. I didn't care if it was too soon after we'd decided to try again, because it was the truth. Why hide behind bullshit and lie about how I feel just because someone else dictated that the timing was wrong? More than that, I was sure she did love me, at least on some level, even if she couldn't admit it. I'd fucked up and been forgiven once too often for her not to feel something. Not that it gave me free rein to fuck up anymore.

Before I did anything else though, I needed to go and do some more apologising.

I pulled up in front of Mum's house—I refused to think of the idiot who was my father at all anymore—and took a deep breath. It was time to pull on my big boy pants and get my fucking arse in the house and apologise to Mum.

I knocked softly. When there was no answer, I used the key to unlock the door. Walking into the house, I looked around for Mum but I couldn't see her anywhere. I passed the portrait in the hall; it was still exactly as I'd left it. Taking care not to cut myself, I picked up the fragments of glass and carried them to the bin. Then I moved the picture so that it was leaning up against the hallway, turning it so that our faces, frozen in perfect smiles, were staring at the wall. I listened out for any noise to indicate that Mum was home. I heard nothing at first but slowly I noticed a soft, rhythmic sobbing sound echoing down the hall from under Mum's bedroom door.

I knocked softly on the door. "Mum?"

I heard a clatter and a few bangs before Mum opened the door. Her turquoise eyes conveyed a deep sorrow I'd never seen before. She blinked a few times at me before her face fell into a smile. It was almost believable, but the sorrow in her gaze gave her away.

"I'm sorry, Mum," I said, hanging my head. I was ready for her to yell and scream at me for destroying her house.

She sighed and ruffled her hand through my hair before using it to lift my chin so that I'd meet her eyes. "You have nothing to apologise for. You have been under so much stress lately. I'm surprised it took you this long to snap."

"I'm not just apologising for that"—I lifted my hand and pointed to my room's closed door—"I'm saying I'm fucking sorry for everything that I did before I left, for everything that happened when I was in Sydney. I abandoned you, and I abandoned Lys, and

I'm fucking sorry for it all."

"I think we all made mistakes in the last few years. Let's just move past it, shall we?" Her smile widened a little but it still wasn't believable. I could sense that she wanted to drop the conversation though.

"Fine, if that's what you want."

She nodded.

"I have to go out tonight. Eden is flying to Brisbane and wants me to show her around."

"Eden is coming?"

"Yeah. She's not staying though, she's just here for the night. But you already knew this didn't you?" I still figured Mum and Eden were orchestrating something.

Mum shook her head. "No. I really didn't. I mean, I rang her this morning when no one knew where you were and your phone was engaged. But I just wanted to know if she'd heard from you."

"Well, obviously she's decided I need to talk, or some shit. I'm not sure. She's only getting in sometime between five thirty and six so I don't know how late I'll be. To be honest, I'll probably just crash with Eden at the hotel if the night goes the way they usually do."

"Okay."

I nodded. "Are you still all right to look after Phoebe tomorrow though?"

She smiled widely, and for the first time I believed it. The difference between the genuine smile and the one she'd worn earlier was remarkable. "Definitely. In fact, I'm looking forward to it. I might have to clean up a little first."

"Let me do it," I offered.

She laughed. "You? Clean?"

I grinned in response. "Well, let me pay for someone to clean it."

She waved her hand to dismiss me. "Don't worry about it. It'll give me something to do while I rattle about the house on my own."

I kissed her forehead. "You're too good to me."

She shooed me out of her room.

"Oh, and that package from Danny? I'll need that in the

morning." I chuckled to myself. I knew Mum would have seen the contents by now.

"Declan, you're not taking Alyssa—"

I cut her off. "Yep, I sure am."

"Well, that should be interesting."

"I know." I grinned as I said goodbye and headed back out the door.

I'd barely made it to the Barina before my phone rang. When I checked the screen I didn't recognise the number. For a moment, I was going to ignore it, but decided I needed to find out who it was while I still had a few hours up my sleeve.

"Mr. Reede? It's Brenton from Eastern Smash Repairs. I'm calling to let you know that your vehicle is ready to be collected."

My mouth split into a grin. It could have been a trap by Flynn to draw me into an argument, but I really doubted he'd let his company's name be dragged in the mud just to have a go at me. "When can I come in?"

"Whenever you are free, sir."

"I told you, just call me Declan. I'll be there in fifteen."

FLYNN WASN'T at the repair shop when I arrived. Brenton, the receptionist I'd met the day I'd dropped the car off, completed all the paperwork, took the payment, and handed over the keys. I was actually a little relieved that I didn't have to deal with either of the Olson brothers.

After I had the keys in my hand, I inspected the repairs and had to admit, albeit begrudgingly, that they'd actually done a good job. It was impossible to tell where the scratch had been and the mirror was firmly in place. Then I moved the car seat from the hired Barina back into the Monaro—with a little help from Brenton.

Sliding back in behind the wheel of my baby felt like coming home. For a moment, I just sat and absorbed it all. The smell of the leather seats filling the cabin, the feel of the wheel beneath my hands. I traced my fingertips along the dashboard and issued a contented sigh.

It put me in such a positive frame of mind that I got a new urge to see Alyssa, even if she couldn't spend any time with me.

I'D BEEN to three local shops and still hadn't found Alyssa. I glanced at the clock and figured I had time to check one more before I really needed to get a move on to go pick Eden up at the airport.

At the fourth, I had some success. When I walked through the door, I spotted her behind the counter, smiling and chatting animatedly with the customers she was serving. I stood back, where she couldn't see me, and watched her for a while. It was nice to see her that way—happy and seemingly carefree. Every now and then though, between customers, she would glance at her hands with a look of concern on her face. I wondered if it was me causing the worry that marred her features or something else.

When I'd made my decision to find Alyssa, I didn't have a plan for a particular conversation in mind. I just knew I needed to see her again before I went into the city for a night out. I needed to capture and carry with me a fresh memory of her perfect honey-gold eyes, of the curl of her lips, and of the way she lit me up from the inside.

I grabbed a can of Coke from the fridge—not that I particularly wanted anything, but a purchase gave me a reason to speak to Alyssa for a few minutes. Unfortunately, Alyssa seemed to be serving a little old lady who did her entire week's shopping at the shithole little store and it was taking forever. Instead of going to the other cashier, I let a handful of people cut in front of me. Finally, the old biddy finished and I practically ran to place my item in front of Alyssa.

"What're you doing here?" she asked.

I shrugged. "I had to see you."

"But you're seeing me tomorrow."

"I couldn't imagine waiting until then to see you."

She smiled. The sight of it made my mouth dry and my

stomach clench with anticipation. "I'm at work. I can't exactly stop and talk to you."

"I know." I brushed a loose strand of hair off her face, tucking it back up into her ponytail. "But I had to see you anyway."

She blushed bright red as she slipped back into professional clerk mode and gave me the total.

I handed her some coins, ensuring that my hand brushed along hers as I let go of them.

"I'll be there early tomorrow. I checked with Mum and she's still good to look after Phoebe."

"Sounds good, Dec. I'll see you then."

"Bye, Lys."

After I'd left the shop, I held on to the picture of her smile and drove toward the airport.

FORTY MINUTES later, I was standing in the airport, cap and sunglasses on, trying to avoid the glares and glances of the passers-by as they realised who I was. I wished I could just meld into the wall and be ignored like the rest of the faceless masses. Instead, I was reminded once more that I couldn't just be anonymous.

A squealing from the baggage carousels pulled me from my thoughts. "Declan!"

I looked up and smiled when I saw Eden bouncing toward me. She dragged her bag as she ran toward me. At the last second, she dropped it and launched herself into my arms. Her legs came around my waist as she gave me her patented full-body hug. When you were around her as much as I was you got used to them quickly. I gritted my teeth as her legs brushed against the bruises on my ribs.

I dropped her as quickly as I could before pressing my hand against my ribs.

"Oh shit, Dec, I'm sorry." She sounded genuinely contrite, but then a second later her enthusiasm had returned in force. "You ready to go?"

She bounded off in the direction of the car park. With a sigh, I moved to collect her abandoned baggage. I shook my head as I picked it up. Morgan had spoiled her. She expected all men to bend over backwards for her like he did. I didn't even think she fucking realised what she was doing.

I caught up with her quickly. "Did you have a good flight?" I asked.

She stepped into the sun and cast her face up to the sky. "Yes, but I'm so glad to be off. I hate planes."

"You never seem to complain when we fly around for racing."

"That's different."

"Why? 'Cause Morgie-worgie's there to protect you?" I teased.

"Protect . . . have hot sex in the airplane toilet—whichever one you want to go with." She said it so casually and without an ounce of embarrassment. That was the thing about Eden, hanging around so many men meant she could talk trash like the best of us. Very little embarrassed her anymore.

I curled up my nose. "Edie, that is way too much information. You know you're like a sister to me, and I do not want to think of my sister having sex."

She laughed and then shrugged. "As if you don't know what we do anyway. I know Morgan pretty much shares everything with you. You tell him your conquests, he tells you his."

She turned on me and walked backward. "Speaking of which . . ." She raised her eyebrow in an expectant way.

I knew it. She'd flown to Brisbane just to get the goss on Alyssa. "There's nothing to tell, Edie. Really."

"If you say so," she said. I wasn't stupid enough to think the topic was going to be dropped.

"So where to then?" I asked.

"The Suncrest Hotel first. Then I've got plans for us."

I laughed. "Why doesn't that surprise me?"

"Because we're friends, and you know me too well. Just like I know you." She cast me a meaningful look as I put her suitcase in the boot. She opened the passenger door and climbed in.

When I climbed in the driver's seat, I saw her casting a long glance back at the child seat in the back.

"Well, that's a change," she said, turning back to the front again as I started the car.

I remained silent. What could I say?

We drove for about five minutes before she spoke again. It was the longest Eden had ever been silent in my company.

"Is it a change for the better?" she almost whispered.

I didn't look at her as I nodded. "Yeah, I think it is."

CHAPTER THIRTEEN

A NIGHT OUT

AFTER TWENTY MINUTES, I pulled into the car park that had been the scene of my panic attack just the day before. Although my heart started to race a little, I managed to contain myself by putting on my poker face and taking a few calming breaths. I might have been friends with Eden, but we weren't close enough that I'd allow her to see me *that* fragile. After all, I still had an image to protect around Sinclair Racing. As it was, my reputation was going to take a hit with the daddy card, but I didn't really give a shit about that. That didn't mean I wanted to be seen as a complete fucking pussy though. Father and pussy-whipped partner, fine. Freaking out in a random car park, not so much.

It was too much to hope that Eden wouldn't notice the slight pause I'd taken before driving into the car park, though.

"What's wrong?" she asked as soon as the car was stopped.

I feigned innocence "What do you mean?"

"I know you well enough to know when something is wrong. It's just you and me here now. No Morgan, no team, no family. Just two friends. What's wrong?" She placed her hand on my knee in a calming gesture.

I closed my eyes and leaned my head back against the headrest. "I'm fine."

"No really, Dec. Tell me."

"No really, Edie. I'm fine."

Not wanting to let her push the issue, I shoved open the car door and climbed out. Without stopping, I headed straight to the back of the car to get her suitcase and my bag out of the boot.

Eden was just a few steps behind me when I reached the call buttons for the elevators. She didn't ask whether I was okay again, so I hoped she was willing to drop it.

The silence was stifling as we rode up to the hotel. When the elevator doors opened, I stood back and waited with the bags while Eden went to the counter and checked in to her room. Swallowing down, I looked around. The familiarity of the hotel put me on edge. All of the memories of my night with Alyssa, and the consequences that followed, flooded into me. I paced in front of the bags as emotions coursed through my body unchecked.

The concierge from the previous day was on again and he gave me a small, polite wave as I continued to pace. I nodded and gave him a small smile in reply. It was a much-needed reminder of the plans I'd set into action and my smile naturally curled my lips at the thought. It didn't completely dispel the discomfort of being in the one place that held so many memories, but it did give me something else to focus on.

"So, tell me all about Alyssa," Eden demanded as she led me to the elevators up to the guest rooms.

My smile grew more natural. My cheeks ached from the shit-eating grin as I thought about Alyssa. "She's fucking great, Eden. I mean, she's smart, and beautiful, and just fucking . . ." I couldn't find adequate words. "She's perfect."

Eden looked at me with unconcealed shock as she reached for the elevator call button. "Wow."

I furrowed my brow at her. "What?"

"Well, I just . . . I never realised just how much you actually cared for this girl."

"What do you mean?"

"It's written over every part of your face, and in every movement you make. You've got it so bad for her."

I rubbed my hand along the back of my neck. "Yeah, I think I do. I, uh, I think I always have."

The elevator arrived and the doors opened. We stepped in and Eden leaned against the silver bar that circled the mirrored walls.

Looking at my reflection brought back memories of the ride I'd had to leave the hotel room after Alyssa had stormed out the morning after our night together. My smile fell into a frown as the recollections haunted me. So many mistakes. So much heartache. My fists clenched at my sides as Eden's mouth began to run.

"Good. I'm glad it's working out. It's funny, 'cause I always knew someone out there was the right girl for you. The way Kelly spoke about your relationship with Alyssa, well, it all sounded so out of character for the Declan Reede I knew. Part of me always wondered if maybe she was telling stories, or was mistaken in just how much you cared about each other. But I don't know, I guess I couldn't help but wonder whether maybe you were still pining for Alyssa."

The walls of the elevator felt like they were closing in on me, forcing all the guilt I felt over everything that had happened since I'd left for Sydney came rushing in on me.

Eden continued to babble and I tuned her out as best as I could. She could talk under wet cement when she went on one of her tangents. Obviously my love life was one of those tangents. "I can't tell you how happy I am that you two are making a go of it. And God, your daughter! You'll have to tell me all about her too. I was so worried when you were sent to London. Honestly, I wondered if you would actually come back. I thought Danny's plan—"

She stopped talking, which drew my attention to her last words. Her face drained of all colour as I tilted my head trying to process the last words she had said. *I thought Danny's plan . . .*

"Danny's plan?" I asked as my heart sank to my toes. "About putting you in the new car. It's great, isn't it?" Eden said quickly— too eagerly for it to be the truth. Not to mention it didn't make sense in the context she'd used the words.

"Don't even try that, Edie!"

She gave me a sideways glance. "Are you okay?"

"That depends," I said, trying to remain as calm as I could despite the bile rising in my throat and the painful thudding of my heart against my ribcage. "What the fuck was Danny's plan?"

"I really shouldn't be telling you this."

"Eden," my voice held a warning, "I thought we were friends?"

"Of course we are." She rolled her eyes.

"Then why not tell me all about this lovely plan of Danny's." I tried, and failed, to keep the sarcasm out of my voice.

She sighed. "Don't you think it was a huge coincidence that you ended up next to Alyssa on that flight? For the second leg too? Like a mega, huge fucking coincidence? The sort that doesn't ever really happen in real life?"

Feeling like the wind had been forcibly knocked out of me, I stepped back until I fell against the back wall of the elevator.

"Are you . . ." I couldn't find enough breath to talk.

Eden's next words confirmed the horror that was running through my head. "Danny arranged it, Dec. He found out about Alyssa's job offer with Pembletons and her trial in the London office. He just tweaked a few of the arrangements so that you ended up next to her on the way."

"Why?"

"Are you kidding me? There isn't a single person on the team who couldn't pinpoint the fact that your career was fucking flying high until one race meet, near your home town. Then all of a sudden, you couldn't even finish a race. It wasn't hard to connect the dots. Especially not with what your mother had told me."

I turned and grabbed the railing for support, dropping my head between my arms. Eden's hand rubbed my lower back in comfort. The walls were definitely getting closer, and the ceiling too. I was boxed in with nowhere to go and nowhere to hide from the truth. "I'm sorry, Dec. If I'd known about your daughter, if Danny had, we probably would have tried something different."

"Why?" I repeated. My brain was having trouble processing

exactly what she was saying.

"Danny thought that maybe if you could see Alyssa again, it might help. That if you could be forced by proximity to speak to her, it would help you get past whatever was causing the crashes. With the amount of money you cost him in repairs last year, can you really blame him for trying anything? A few plane tickets were a drop in the ocean compared with a complete rebuild every race."

I shook my head in disbelief. "How did he know about Alyssa's offer though?"

She smiled sadly at me. "You haven't looked at your employment contract lately, have you?"

I didn't understand what she was asking.

"Pembletons is the firm that represents Sinclair Racing. Danny was in the offices when Alyssa was in for her week trial in Sydney. Apparently, Alyssa's mood fell after she saw him. When Andrew Kent spoke to Alyssa about it, she admitted to knowing you and told him a very condensed version of your history. When Andrew raised it with Danny, telling him how small a world it was, Danny put two and two together."

"Why?" I asked. My voice was without volume and I wasn't even sure I expected an answer.

Everything that had happened over the last two weeks, meeting Alyssa again, London, Phoebe, *everything*. It was all because Danny couldn't keep his fucking nose out of my fucking business. Because he had to play puppet master to everyone. He'd done it so often in the past, with so many little things. It was a big part of the driving force behind the team's success on the track. But what right did he have to interfere with my personal life? What right did he have to play with Alyssa and me like we were pawns in some sick game of chess?

My blood boiled, and my breath grew short. Images of everything that happened played over and over in my head. It burst from me in a rush and I slammed my fist into my reflection in the mirror. The glass cracked under my fingers with a dull thud. I leapt away, my heart racing and my hand sore.

"Why?" I screamed, turning to face Eden. My face was

contorted into a mask of hatred, displaying the anger that burned inside me to the rest of the world. "What gave him that right?"

Eden cowered away from me. I'd never once seen her scared of me. Even when I was at my lowest and she'd confronted me about it, she hadn't been scared. The terror in her eyes reflected the betrayal I felt in my heart. The last two weeks, the fucking hurt, the pain, the secrets and fucking lies. All of it was because fucking Danny thought he knew better than everyone else.

Arsehole!

The elevator dinged, signalling we were at our floor and Eden composed herself.

"Come on, Dec," she whispered as she guided me away from the wall. "Let's get you cleaned up. Then we can go out and talk." She picked up her suitcase and grabbed my hand as I followed her out of the elevator.

She swiped the card to unlock the hotel room. I hadn't stayed in one of these rooms—especially not in *this* hotel—since my night with Alyssa, and I was shocked to find they hadn't changed much at all. Practically everything was exactly the same as it had been four years ago. Even the shitty lamps on the bedside tables were the fucking same. It was all too much.

Pulling free of Eden's grip, I headed straight for the bathroom. The instant I was through the door, I slammed it shut behind me and twisted the lock. Then I raced to the toilet and lost the contents of my stomach. Over and over, I threw up until I was dry retching. When my stomach finally gave up trying to purge the anger from my body, I retreated to the door and pressed my back against it.

As I sat, staring at nothing and seeing only Alyssa, one question ran in a loop around my head.

Why?

A few minutes later I felt the door vibrate behind me rather than hearing the knock.

"Declan?" Eden's soft voice floated in through the door. I expected to hear revulsion or disgust in her voice, but instead there was just sadness and worry. "Can I come in? Or will you please come out?"

After another couple of breaths, I stood to gather my thoughts. I splashed my face with some cold water, rinsed out my mouth, and rubbed my hand along the back of my neck. Then I adjusted my shirt, as being pressed against the door had irritated the fresh tattoo on my back. The permanent reminder of my children. Children I may never have known about if it weren't for Danny's misguided plan.

If I really thought about it, I knew he was just trying to help me in his own way—albeit as a puppeteer with a fucking shitload of tangled strings. Strings he hadn't known existed. Without his interference, I'd still be in the dark and still wouldn't know about Phoebe. It was that thought that made me see I should probably find a way to thank him.

I flicked the lock on the door and looked Eden up and down. Her whole body was frozen with anticipation. She didn't know what to expect. Neither did I.

Trying to show that I'd be calm, I moved closer to her. "I think we should sit," I said.

She nodded, clearly not daring to speak.

"Want some fresh air?" I asked, pointing to the small balcony that came off the room and overlooked the city.

Eden nodded again and I indicated for her to go first. As soon as she hit the balcony she sat and perched on one of the chairs.

"Declan . . ."

I held up my hand to cut her off. "Edie, I want to tell you something. I just don't know how to start."

I was going to be as honest as I could with her. At some point between unlocking the door and arriving on the balcony, I'd decided I would take her on as a true confidante for perhaps the first time ever. We both seemed to recognise that a major shift in our relationship had just started. Eden had gone from a teammate with whom I hung out regularly, to a true friend with whom I was willing to share my darkest secrets. One of very few.

"Dec, no matter what you tell me. I'll be there for you." She wrung her hands together as she spoke. "That's the real reason I'm in Brisbane. I guess I figured you weren't at your best right now. I mean, between your mother's phone call this morning and you asking for Dr. Henrikson's number the other day, I just figured . . ." She trailed off.

I couldn't tell her how close to the truth she was. She shifted her chair a little closer to mine and grabbed my hands in hers.

"I think of you as my baby brother. You know that, right? I'm here for you. Always."

Her statement shocked me, but the depth of emotion in her eyes made me see it for the absolute truth that it was. I didn't know what words I could respond with—didn't even know how to start. I settled for something simple. "Thanks, Edie."

She ruffled my hair to lighten the mood. I growled playfully at her and then she clasped my hands again.

"So . . ." She raised her eyebrow at me and held up my cut knuckles.

I sighed and pulled one hand from her loose grasp and began to scratch my back without thinking. "I don't even know where to fucking begin."

I pulled myself away from her completely and stood against the railing, looking down over the busy mall below. Bending forward, I let loose a grunt of frustration. I spun around to look at Eden again. She was sitting patiently, waiting for me to be ready to continue talking.

"I told you a little bit of the story already. About Phoebe."

Eden nodded and beamed. Obviously she was anxious to get on to that topic. I thought of Emmanuel and Alyssa, and decided to dwell on Phoebe for a little while longer. I grabbed my wallet out of my pants and pulled Phoebe's photo from it. I handed it to Eden, who took it eagerly.

"Oh, Dec. She's beautiful. She has—"

"My eyes." I cut her off. "Yeah, I know."

I shuddered when I thought about my initial reaction to seeing the photo. To knowing instantly that she was my daughter because of those eyes.

"She's so beautiful, Edie. And smart as a fucking whip too."

Eden looked over the photo for another moment before

handing it back. I stared at it as I continued, drawing comfort from those soft, gentle eyes staring out at me. Even in this photo it felt like she could see into my soul, but it didn't feel like I was being judged.

"What I haven't told you though is that when I left Brisbane, Alyssa was pregnant with twins."

"Twins?" Eden's face lit up, but then fell on seeing my expression. I didn't know what I looked like, but I knew what I felt. I put the photo of Phoebe back in my wallet because I could swear her eyes had turned accusatory. Eden walked over to me and wrapped her hands around my waist. I dropped my forehead to her shoulder and took comfort in her presence. In her friendship.

"What happened?" she asked in a quiet voice.

I told her what Alyssa had told me. When I finished the story I was surprised to see the tears on her face, matching my own.

"I had no idea," she whispered. "I'm so sorry. How is Alyssa now? I can't even imagine . . ."

"Alyssa's . . ." I tried to think of the best word to use. "Strong." I hoped to God Eden knew what I meant. I didn't know how to articulate it better than that. There were parts of Alyssa that were broken beyond repair, but she had the inner strength to pull together the damaged parts and continue to live. To love.

I pulled at the collar of my shirt again. It was really starting to irritate the fuck out of me.

"What is it?" Eden asked. "You've been playing with your shirt on and off since you picked me up. Did you use the wrong washing powder or something?"

I shook my head and turned around. I pulled the collar of my shirt down a little to show her the now uncovered, but quickly scabbing, artwork on my back.

"Wow," she said. "Can I get a better look at that?"

A week ago, a month, I might have told her to fuck off, and that I wasn't getting half-naked in front of her. But I was proud of my children and wanted to show her that. With my back still turned to her, I undid the buttons on my shirt and pulled it off. A second later, I felt her fingers tracing along the outside of the design.

"It's just beautiful." She wrapped her arms around me and rested her head against my shoulder. "Thank you for sharing this with me."

I nodded. Like I'd noticed with Dr. Henrikson, sharing with Eden had taken another tiny weight away. So small it was barely noticeable, but enough to help my frame of mind.

After we stood like that for a few more minutes, I decided the mood had been too heavy and serious for too long. I owed it to Alyssa to let go of my stress for a while so that I could show her a good time tomorrow. With Alyssa in mind, I twisted my body, grabbing Eden into a headlock and mussing up her hair.

"Declan, you jackass!" she squealed, trying to yank herself from my arms. "We almost had a grown-up moment then."

"I know, Edie," I said. I let her go and ran back inside the room. I glanced around it—I still had find a way to get rid of the images of Alyssa the morning after the school formal, but Eden was doing a good job of keeping me sane at the moment. "So, what have you got planned for tonight?"

"Dinner at the Sunshine Room, and then daiquiris at the casino." She grinned widely.

"Eden, you know I'm a dude right? This—" I grabbed my crotch. "—qualifies me as such. Dudes don't do daiquiris. Those are girly drinks."

"Oh, but look at those pretty locks of yours, Dec." She jumped up and grabbed a handful of my hair, which was rapidly getting out of control without my regular trips to get it cut. "I'm sure I could put a nice barrette in there, maybe slip you into a turquoise dress to match your eyes. With your inch-long lashes and pretty pout, I think you'd make a hot chick."

I scowled at her. "You know you are just about the right weight for me to pick up and toss over that balcony."

She smirked at me. "I'd like to see you try."

I feigned a shrug and walked away, before quickly running back at the last minute and throwing her over my shoulder. I carried her back outside and sat her on the railing, with my arms wrapped around her to ensure she didn't accidentally slip.

"Declan Reede, you fucking arse, let me down," she screamed as she clung tightly to my shoulders, squeezing her eyes shut. "You know I hate heights."

"What were you saying about me?"

"That you are a manly man who has no feminine aspects at all."

"Exactly," I said, before pulling her back off the balcony rail. I flipped her around me and put her back on her feet. She smacked my chest before running into the room. Before I could follow her inside, she slid the door shut and locked it. She stood on the other side of the glass and poked her tongue out at me.

"Oh, you are going to get it, Edie!" I shouted.

She pretended she couldn't hear me, making ridiculously overemphasised gestures of cupping her ears.

"All right, you've had your laugh," I said. "Now, let me in."

She shook her head and laughed.

I clasped my hands together and held them in from of me. "Please?" I begged, pushing my bottom lip out.

"Uh-uh."

"What do I have to do to get back inside?"

She tapped her chin. "You have to say Morgan is the best driver at Sinclair Racing."

"Oh, I see," I said, laughing. "So for me to come in, I've got to lie. Yeah, that's not gonna happen."

She shrugged and started to walk off toward the bathroom. I'd been on the road with Eden enough to know that her in the shower "getting ready" usually meant a good hour or two. I debated whether I wanted to remain on the balcony with no entertainment for that long.

"Fine," I said with a sigh. "Morgan McGuire is the best driver at Sinclair Racing."

She unlocked the door and slid it open a little. I pushed my way past her and heard the door slide shut again after I'd passed.

"Apart from me," I added, before ducking for cover.

"You're lucky we've got reservations. Otherwise . . ."

"I'd like to see you try something." I winked.

She poked out her tongue at me one last time before

165

disappearing into the bedroom to get ready for our dinner. A second later she came back out, carrying a suit bag.

"I brought a suit from home for you. I figured you wouldn't have packed one for London."

Giving her a half-smile, I thanked her for thinking of it. At least I wouldn't look a complete shambles beside her no-doubt perfect appearance.

I pulled my shirt back on before I sat on the couch and flicked on the TV. For a moment, I debated ringing Alyssa while I waited for Eden. I really wanted to hear her voice again. It wasn't hard to see that I was already completely and utterly pussy-whipped but couldn't find it in myself to care. I pulled out my phone to ring her but when I saw the time, I stopped myself. She wouldn't finish work for another hour.

Not really focused on anything, I flicked through the channels for a while. I knew Eden would be a little while yet. Half an hour later, I grew bored of the TV. I walked over and knocked on the bedroom door.

"What time were the reservations for?" I asked through the closed door.

"Seven thirty," Eden called back.

Because it was a little after seven, I figured it was time for me to get ready. Within ten minutes, I was ready to go, just as Eden pulled open the bedroom door to reveal a red dress, coiffed hair, and face full of make-up. She could have been heading out for a red carpet event rather than a casual night on the town.

We walked the short distance to the Sunshine Room, with Eden talking non-stop about Morgan the whole way. I just smiled and nodded in the appropriate places—at least, I think they were the appropriate places. I really didn't know for sure.

Eden gave her name at the door and we were ushered through to a table. She watched me meaningfully as I sat across from her.

"So," she said after a moment. "Tell me everything about Alyssa."

One meal, four hours, and eight daiquiris later, we finally stumbled back to the hotel room, giggling. I don't know what was funny—I wasn't sure if it was the palm trees in front of the casino, the dumpsters we passed in Elizabeth Street, or the hushed whispers of the hotel clerks as we passed them. Whatever it was, it had Eden and me in hysterics until we finally collapsed side by side onto the couch, unable to breathe.

"Thanks, Eden," I said when I was finally able to draw some breath. "I had fun tonight."

It was the truth. It was nice to have a night without the stress of a potential relationship and without worrying about upsetting anyone with what I said. For the first time in weeks, I could just be me. Eden could like it or lump it—stay or fuck off—and it wouldn't really matter. The drunker we got, the more we insulted and teased each other. The barbed words didn't affect either of us, because it didn't matter. Neither of us gave a shit. We would still be teammates and friends at the end. There was no bullshit between us.

With Alyssa, I felt like I was walking on fucking eggshells all the fucking time. I hoped the date I had planned might fix that. Eden knew all about my plans from Danny and had offered me a few suggestions to tweak them. Suggestions I was more than happy to implement.

"I'm going to bed, shithead," Eden said with a giggle as she stumbled to the bedroom. We'd never agreed that I was staying the night, but we didn't need to—it had been an unspoken agreement between us.

"Whatever, bitch." I laughed.

"I gotta be at the airport early in the morning," she slurred. "I got an early flight."

"You gotta be at the airport early 'cause I got a fuck-hot date to get to and I am not missing that for shit. If you're not ready, I'm leaving you here."

"Touché." She pointed at the ceiling and did a funny little pirouette, twisting her legs around each other until she was tangled and fell unceremoniously on her arse.

I didn't stand or offer to help; I couldn't, because I was laughing far too hard. I'd end up on my arse if I tried. My laughter continued until one of her shoes sailed over my head. Then I stared blankly at the wall where it hit for a few seconds before I couldn't control the laughter anymore and it burst out again. I heard Eden giggling once more as she shut the bedroom door.

With a goofy smile on my face, I laid myself out along the length of the couch and thought about the night. It was almost fucking perfect; the best escape I could have asked for to help cope with all the shit that I'd had to deal with lately. I was actually happy Eden had taken time out of her schedule to come to see me. I'd gathered fairly quickly that this trip was actually impacting her preparations a little, but she'd been worried about me. There was only one thing missing from the evening that would have made it absolutely perfect—Alyssa.

I pulled out my phone, stifling another giggle that rose to my throat—Eden had forced the fucking girlie drinks on me, and now I was fucking giggling like one. I wrote Alyssa a text to let her know I was thinking about her even though I couldn't be with her.

After putting my phone on the coffee table in front of the couch, I let my thoughts of Alyssa take over my mind. I fucking wanted her—so badly. The forced celibacy hurt more than I'd expected it to. I was happy to respect her wishes, but goddamn did I want to re-enact our London night as soon as I could.

The alcohol coursing its way pleasantly through my system was making me so fucking horny it wasn't funny. I rubbed my hand up and down the length of my thigh, desperately aching for Alyssa's touch to soothe the fires that erupted there. I pictured her as she had been that afternoon when I'd seen her at the shop. Professional, smiling, blushing, and fucking gorgeous. My hand had just made its way up the length of my thigh and grabbed my shaft when my phone rang. I grabbed it quickly, thinking it might have been Alyssa.

"We need to meet." I didn't recognise the voice. It was female, but it definitely wasn't Alyssa.

"What? Who is this?"

"It's Ruby."

Fuck. I sat bolt upright. "Why?"

"I need to talk to you, now."

"Well, you've got me on the phone now."

"No. In person. Can you meet me down at the Grand Plaza?"

"Ruby, no offense, but why the fuck would I meet up with you when it could be a fucking set-up for an ambush by that boofhead husband of yours."

To my surprise she laughed. "No Josh, I promise."

"I can't anyway," I said, bristling. I still didn't know what she was ringing for and I wasn't sure if I could trust her. "I'm in the city with a teammate. I can't just leave. Edie needs a lift to the airport in the morning."

"Too bad, I need to talk to you before this big date you have planned."

"Well, unless you're willing to drive your arse into the city, I'm afraid you're shit out of luck."

"Fine," she said. I thought she was ready to hang up. "I'll be there in half an hour. I'll meet you at the McDonald's at the end of the Myer Centre."

"Fuck, really?"

"Yes, really. I told you, Declan. I need to speak to you."

Why did I get the feeling this wasn't going to be any good?

CHAPTER FOURTEEN

PRELUDE TO A DATE

MY KNEE BOUNCED uncontrollably as I sat on the marble stool at the end of the Myer Centre. The cashiers at the twenty-four hour McDonald's kept giving me awkward glances. I wasn't sure whether it was because they recognised me but were too afraid to approach, or if they thought I was a crazy person getting around in a crumpled suit, mumbling to myself, and doing a one-legged jig.

The agitation working its way through my body grew stronger with every passing second because Ruby was apparently due at any time. At least, she was due if she hadn't decided to stand me up and make me wait unnecessarily at the end of the Queen Street Mall until I'd had enough.

Glancing around again, I tried to see if any of the vehicles around could be hers. Not that I knew what she drove, or what to look out for. There was so much I didn't know. I had no clue what she wanted. No idea when she would arrive. The simple fact that she wanted to meet scared the crap out of me. Especially considering Alyssa had already confirmed her family hated me. That meant whatever Ruby's intentions were, they couldn't be good.

I tried to focus on anything but the worry running through my head. It was impossible though. I thought about Eden, back in the hotel room, oblivious to my night-time rendezvous with Alyssa's sister-in-law. I hadn't wanted to wake Eden to tell her where I'd gone, but I hadn't wanted to steal out unannounced either. In the end, I'd left a note just in case the meeting was an ambush and I ended up buried in the middle of a state forest somewhere. At least Eden would be able to tell the police who I'd met with. Despite that precaution, I expected her to sleep through to morning without any knowledge that I'd gone out.

Forcing myself not to worry, I focused on the people rushing around me. It was a bit of a surprise that the streets were still so busy at a little after midnight. I expected it in Sydney, but Brisbane had always been more of a large country town, where everything closed by ten. It had obviously grown up in my absence. It boded well for me that there were so many people around. At least if it was an ambush, Josh would have a harder time trying to stuff me in a boot if there were witnesses handy.

Just as I was about to give up waiting, a cherry-red '69 Mustang pulled up in front of me. It was a nice car, and I couldn't help admiring its sleek lines. It was no Monaro, but it was still a fine piece of iron. The blonde in the driver's seat leaned across the car and the passenger door flew open.

"There's nowhere to park around here. Hop in," Ruby's voice called. It looked like she was alone. If she was, at least I'd be able to handle her if it turned nasty. I ducked down and double-checked the backseat just to be safe. Josh was too big to hide easily.

"Just get in the fucking car!" Ruby snapped.

This is for Alyssa, I thought as I climbed into the passenger seat. I hadn't even reached for my seat belt when Ruby accelerated hard down the road.

"What do you—" I started to ask, but Ruby cut me off with a glare and a raised palm.

I sat in the passenger seat and stewed. The way Ruby had treated me was ridiculous. The fucking bitch hadn't even spoken since telling me to get in the car. Ten minutes later, we were pulling up to a park overlooking the usually muddy-brown Brisbane River.

The water shimmered black in the night. Once the engine was off, Ruby climbed out of the car and walked to the railing without another word or backwards glance.

I lost my patience as I followed her. "Ruby, what the fuck do you want?"

"I was about to ask you the same thing," she seethed as she spun on me.

I pinched the bridge of my nose. "What are you fucking talking about?"

"What do you want from Alyssa?"

"How is it your business?"

"Alyssa is my sister. That makes it my business."

"Fuck! Alyssa must be everyone's fucking business. Seriously. Why can't she be her own business?"

"We care about her and want to make sure she's getting what she needs."

"Well, I'm so fucking happy that everyone else has figured out what the fuck they think she needs. But what about what *she* thinks she needs? What about what *she* wants? What about what *I* want? Where is her fucking privacy in all of this? Or mine for that matter?"

Ruby's blonde hair fanned out behind her in the wind as she closed the distance between us. "You don't deserve shit"—she emphasised her point by poking my chest—"not after everything Alyssa's been through in the past four years."

"You're right, I *don't* deserve shit!" I shouted back. "I definitely don't deserve someone as pure and fucking fantastic as Alyssa. But she wants to give me one more chance, and you know what? I'm selfish enough to let that happen."

"Of course she wants to fucking give you another chance. She's never been able to let you go. But fuck, Declan, what do you think it's going to do to her when you leave again? You take her out, sweep her up in the romance of it all, and promise her all these things. It's going to crush her when you go again and we'll be the ones who have to pick up the fucking pieces."

I crossed my arms. "The answer to that is simple. I'm not

leaving. I'll never be able to leave her again. I love her."

She scoffed. "If that's how you really felt, well, you wouldn't have left in the first place, would you?"

"I left *because* I felt like that, because I felt . . . fuck it! I don't need to explain myself to you."

She shrugged. "Maybe you think you feel that way, but I don't think you know what love is."

I was going to interrupt her and tell her to fuck off, that she didn't know how I felt, but she held up her palm again and raised her voice as she continued.

"Regardless, I just want to give you a piece of friendly advice. Me to you, so to speak. If you hurt Alyssa in any way, then you'll have to answer to me." She raised her eyebrow before grabbing my shirt and pulling me in close, her lips practically brushing the side of my ear as she continued. "If you take Alyssa out on whatever date you have planned for tomorrow and build her hopes up, just to crush them, then I will personally ensure that you feel every ounce of pain you cause her."

Holding my hands up in surrender, I backed away. I'd been worried about an ambush by Josh, but I'd clearly been worried about the wrong person. Ruby was one fucking scary bitch. When she released me, she started to head back to the car. Did she really think she could say that shit and then just walk away? There was no way I would let her have the final word. Not like that. I grabbed her shoulder and spun her around.

"You've had your say, now I'm having mine."

The soft light coming from the CBD across the river lit her features so I could see every minor detail. She raised her eyebrow at me, as if shocked that I would dare speak back to her.

I didn't allow her to interrupt. "I fucked up. I know it—you know it—the entire fucking world knows it. But I'm here to right my wrongs. I'm here because I fucking love Alyssa. I love her. I fucking adore every inch of her with every fibre of my being. I refuse to let anything stand between the two of us anymore. It's bad enough that I have to prove to her that I love her and that I'm not going to hurt her again. I refuse to be forced to explain it constantly to the rest of the world as well. That's between her and me."

Ruby's face was a mask of incredulity, her lips twisted into a snarl as if more poisonous words were poised right behind her red lipstick.

Before she had a chance to speak, I continued. "Respectfully, you and the rest of her family, the rest of the fucking world in fact, can kindly fuck off and leave us be until we've sorted ourselves out."

For a few long seconds, she looked at me without saying anything. Then she laughed.

"Well, fuck!" she said. "You've certainly grown some balls. Do you mean it though? That you love her? That's the part I am finding hard to believe. You walked away from her so easily."

I laughed without mirth, the sound harsh and out of place in my throat. "You have no idea what I went through to walk away from her."

"So enlighten me." She walked back over toward me, but gracefully slid past me and stood near the railing.

"Why?"

"'Cause I can be your ally or your enemy. The choice is yours." She climbed up onto the railing, perching herself on top, and looked at me expectantly.

"What's the difference?"

"The difference is whether I tell the rest of the family to back off or close ranks."

"Like I give a shit. I told you, the only one who can get rid of me now is Alyssa. I'm here until she orders me away."

"Like that will ever happen," she mumbled under her breath. "Still, you have to admit the path will be smoother if Josh isn't blocking you. Or Dad."

I thought about it for a second. Killer Curtis on my side. Josh staying the fuck away and not threatening me with violence. I had to admit it sounded easier. Climbing onto the railing next to Ruby, I sighed. I turned my body to face the river so that I didn't have to look at her while I spoke.

"I don't owe you explanations," I whispered. "But it would be nice if you leave us alone for a little while. For Alyssa's sake."

"Bullshit you don't need to explain." Ruby turned around to face the river as well.

"I didn't say I don't need to explain. I said that I didn't owe *you* explanations. I owe them to Alyssa."

She turned to me. Her expression was softer than I'd ever seen it before. She seemed to consider me for a minute before turning away again. I didn't know what she was seeing, but her eyes were focused on a spot in the distance. All I could see were a few small boats with flashing lights to indicate their location. "I never thought I'd see you so . . . grown up. You were always so fucking cocky. Nothing and no one could touch you. And then everything I saw on TV and in the magazines only convinced me that you were a bigger arse than ever."

I stayed silent. My eyes trailed to the spot she found so interesting, but I still saw nothing.

"I know a thing or two about people making mistakes when they're young." I got the feeling she wasn't talking about me anymore—not really. "Mum was young when she had me, and I've never even met my father. Fucking bastard ran out the minute she found out she was pregnant. I guess if someone were man enough to try to correct a mistake . . ." her voice trailed off.

I looked closely at her face, seeing the tears that were moistening her eyes, but I knew would never fall. She probably wouldn't even acknowledge they were there. I was at a complete fucking loss about what to do. We were having a heart to heart that I hadn't expected to have. Watching her eyes glisten in the soft glow, I debated my action for a second but then put my arm around her shoulder to offer her some comfort.

My touch seemed to rouse her from her thoughts. She pulled away from me, quickly climbing back over the railing and backing away. "What the hell do you think you are doing?"

I followed her over the guardrail and stared blankly at her. "I fucking thought we were having a moment."

She sighed. "I came to deliver a message." She seemed to consider what happened for a second then turned on her heel and headed back to her car. "Message delivered."

She climbed into the driver's seat and started the car. When the car started to edge forward, I was sure she was going to just drive off and leave me there in the middle of fucking nowhere.

An exasperated sigh issued from her open window. "You coming or not?"

I ran to the car, confused and trying to process what happened. Something fundamental had shifted in the world. Then one key thing Ruby had said hit me. I couldn't believe I hadn't noticed it earlier.

She's never been able to let you go.

The statement lit my face up with a smile even as it broke my fucking heart. After I'd walked back to the hotel, and settled back onto the couch, I didn't sleep much. My mind was too busy ticking over with everything Ruby had said. Even when I was finally able to shove that out of my mind, I was too excited and nervous about my date with Alyssa. I was so wound up thinking about it—about her—that I couldn't find comfort.

In the end, the only way I could get some relief was to stop trying not to think about Alyssa. Instead, I let her invade every part of my conscious mind. Without much thought, my hand worked its way down my body, and I was soon stroking my length as visions of Alyssa danced in my head. Her face, her smile, even the scent of her coconut skin cream—every part of her drew me in and held me captive. Better yet, there were only a few short hours before I would see her again.

That was the thought that sent me tumbling over the edge. With a barely stifled moan, I came across my hand and stomach. After relaxing back, and allowing the peace that invaded my mind to take over for a few moments, I cleaned up quickly before falling into a few short hours of peaceful sleep where Alyssa was wrapped in my arms.

I woke to a high-pitched voice "singing" in the shower. After taking in my surroundings and seeing I was still in the hotel, it struck me what the noise was. It was a good thing I'd never had any interest in Eden; her voice alone would send me packing. I was still laughing about it when she emerged from the bedroom, dressed and towel-drying her hair.

"What?" she asked with a smirk.

I shook my head. "Nothing."

"Tell me." She pouted.

"No way, I value my manhood and everything that goes along with it too much."

She narrowed her eyes at me, then quirked her eyebrow. "Speaking of your manhood and everything that goes with it . . . you might wanna put the car back in the garage." She nodded her chin in my direction and then started laughing as she began to throw her belongings back into her suitcase.

Glancing down, I saw what she meant. My prominent morning wood was hidden only by my boxers—and barely hidden at that. My pants hung low on my hips with my zipper wide open.

Tucking myself back into my pants, I did up my zipper before dragging myself off the couch. It was only when I stood that I felt the effects of my night of drinking. A headache pounded just behind my eyes and my mouth tasted like arse.

The last thing I needed before my big date was a hangover. Worse, butterflies were doing loop-the-loops in my stomach making me feel nauseous. I put it down to an empty stomach after a long night of drinking. Coffee, food, and a few painkillers would hopefully make it a little better. If not, being with Alyssa again would definitely help.

At the thought of Alyssa, the butterflies turned into dive-bombers, smashing against the walls of my stomach. It was as if I was nervous about seeing her again, but that couldn't be the case. What I had planned for the day was perfect, wasn't it? I was going to be back in my element, albeit with Alyssa by my side, but that only made it better. If nothing else, I was going to show her my world—my life. That thought had me floating into the bathroom with a change of clothes. I needed to shower and shave before our date.

An hour later, I pulled in to the airport to drop Eden off. I offered to escort her all the way through to check-in but she argued with me, telling me in no uncertain terms that she was a big girl and there was no point in keeping Alyssa waiting. She pecked my cheek and wished me luck as she climbed out of the car.

Before I drove off, I glanced at Eden waving at me in my rear-view mirror with a knowing smile on her face.

When I stopped for a quick bite to eat on the way back to Browns Plains, I popped a couple of paracetamol to shake the remnants of the pounding headache from a night on the daiquiris.

As I closed the distance to Alyssa's house, my hands started to shake and I had to grip the steering wheel tighter to stop the quivers. It was ridiculous how nervous I was. It was only Alyssa after all, but then again . . . it was Alyssa. With everything else that had happened, it felt like the date was a last chance attempt to be together. If I fucked up, she would be lost.

When I pulled up in front of her house, I saw the curtain ruffle. By the time I turned off the car, she was already locking the door, with Phoebe standing beside her. Both of them were smiling broadly. Clearly they'd been waiting for me. I checked the clock to confirm I wasn't running late.

I wasn't.

Without even stopping to think about my actions, or whether it was a good idea, I ran from the car and pulled Alyssa tightly into my arms. It felt like I hadn't seen her in a week, even though it had only been a day. I placed one hand behind her head and buried my face in her neck, breathing deeply, before turning my face and kissing her softly on the cheek.

"I missed you," I whispered against her skin. Her eyes closed and she took a deep breath. I could see her mouth turning up into a smile. After I knew she was happy, I knelt down beside her, and turned my attention to Phoebe.

"Hey, Pheebs," I said quietly. Her eyes met and held mine as she gave a small grin.

"Declan!" she squealed, throwing her arms around my neck and surprising me. "I'm going to see Aunty Kelly today."

I gave Alyssa a quizzical look. "Aunty?" I mouthed.

Alyssa shrugged and glanced at Phoebe. I guessed it meant she wasn't willing to say more while Phoebe was around.

"Do you like Aunty Kelly?" I asked.

Phoebe nodded and her ponytails bounced in time with her enthusiasm.

"That's good, 'cause I have it on good authority that she's very excited about spending time with you." I stood back up. "You both ready to go?"

Alyssa seemed anxious, but they both nodded. I indicated my car and Phoebe ran over to it and smiled at me.

"Do you like my car?" I asked her, because she'd only been in the tiny Barina the last time I was with her.

"Yes!" Her eyes lit up.

"Well, hop in. We'll go for a quick spin before we go to Aunty Kelly."

I helped her into the backseat and then stepped back so Alyssa could do up the child seat, granting me exactly the view I'd fantasised about before I'd taken them on the date to Maccas. It was everything I'd imagined it would be, but with my sweaty palms and dry mouth, I couldn't really enjoy it as much as I'd thought I might.

Alyssa climbed into the passenger side and gave me a small, nervous smile as she put her seat belt on. I leaned over and tucked a strand of hair behind her ear, giving her what I hoped was a calming look. The flutters in my stomach had gone from loop-the-loops to full aerial acrobatics, including death-dives and barrel-rolls.

For a few minutes, I drove around the local streets. Each time we reached a set of lights, I took off hard, mostly because it elicited a round of giggles from Phoebe. After a ten minute joyride, I pulled up at Mum's and waited beside the car while Alyssa helped Phoebe out.

With a wide smile firmly in place, Mum opened the door almost the same second I finished knocking. Phoebe dashed into her arms, and they gave each other a hug. I was amazed to see the relationship they had despite the struggle of having to dance around my mistakes and my fuckwit father. Mum whispered to me that the box I needed was in my room.

I left the three of them to say their hellos as I walked down the hall to grab the box Danny had sent. Other than the few dents, holes and scratches in the walls, the room was completely straightened and it was impossible to tell the extent of damage I'd caused in my rage. Making a mental note to thank Mum later, I took the box out to the car, ignoring the strange glances from Alyssa as I passed.

"You ready to get going?" I asked her when I returned to the house.

She took a deep breath before swallowing audibly. After a moment, she nodded. She seemed to recognise, like I did, that today was pivotal for our relationship. I hoped after today we could stop the pussyfooting bullshit and just be together. We needed to decide whether we were going to have a relationship or not, and move on either way. My heart ached at the thought that it might go wrong. There was a chance Alyssa might run after today. But I could only hope for the best and do what I could to sway her in my direction.

"What was in the box, Declan?" she asked when we were pulling out of Mum's driveway.

I smiled at her. "You'll see. I promise."

"When?"

"Soon. Real soon."

After all, it was only a little under an hour's drive to Willowbank.

To Queensland Raceway.

CHAPTER FIFTEEN

QUEENSLAND RACEWAY

"SO, *AUNTY KELLY*?" I asked Alyssa, to break the silence in the car.

She shrugged. "It was just something we agreed on after the twins were born. We could hardly call her Nana. Not without telling the whole town that I was your loser ex-girlfriend who—"

"Don't," I said, cutting her off.

"Don't what?"

"Don't ever call yourself that."

She shrugged.

I grabbed hold of her hand and brought it to my lips. "No. I won't let you refer to yourself that way. You are the woman who's held my heart captive for years, even if I was a fuckwit and didn't see it."

Out of the corner of my eye, I saw her shake her head as her tears fell. "I haven't though. I wasn't enough for you."

I checked my blind spot, ensuring no one was in the lane next to me, then swerved into the emergency stopping lane and pulled the car to a hard stop. Before she could resist, I turned her and gently cupped my hands around her face. "You can't think that. This—all of this shit—it's about me. It's my fault and has nothing to do with you. You were always too good for me. Too pure and wonderful. You held my heart in your hands from the first moment I saw you, and that scared the fuck out of me."

She closed her eyes, and the tears fell in earnest. "You left. So easily. And you never once called me or asked anyone about me. I didn't hear from you for four years . . . except the email."

Her pain was etched onto every line of her face and clear in the timbre of her voice. I needed to explain the one thing that I had only just recently understood myself. "I left . . . and I *couldn't* ask about you. Don't you see? If I'd asked about you, if I'd allowed myself to believe for even one second that I still cared about you, I would have been back in Brisbane in a heartbeat."

I gently brushed the tears off her cheeks before leaning forward to kiss the salt trails left on her face. My eyes closed as I tasted her sorrow on my lips. It was a palpable presence around her, and I knew the path to *us* would only be accessed by confronting it.

Her fear and mistrust were born of that sorrow. They were the walls and gatekeeper, protecting the entrance to her heart and soul. I saw it clearly in that moment. I couldn't say exactly when I had grown the fuck up and understood that fact, but I knew that it could only be a good thing. A positive thing for myself, for Alyssa, and, most importantly, for Phoebe.

I gave Alyssa one final chaste kiss on the mouth before pulling back and taking in her beauty. My thumb grazed along her right cheek and she leaned in to the touch. "You may not believe in me, but believe in that. Believe in my touch and our love. I know you feel it too . . . that *thing* that happens when we come together. I've never found that with anyone else."

She opened her mouth to talk, her eyes filled with self-doubt, but I pressed my finger lightly to her lips to silence her.

"And I don't want to try. Not ever again. I'm not my father, Alyssa. I am committed to you . . . to us. Until the day you send me away."

"Declan, I . . ." She trailed off with a sigh and put on a smile, which was obviously forced. "I'm sorry I brought it up. Let's just go to Willowbank."

"Okay, that's—" I stopped when I realised what she said. "Wait, why do you think that's where we're going?"

She laughed, and it almost rang true. "You think I don't know the way to Willowbank? I mean, honestly, what else is out here? Not to mention you look like a schoolboy who's just been told his school is closed for the day."

I held up my hands in protest. "Fine. You caught me," I said jokingly. "Do you still want to go?"

"I'm still willing to see what you're going to subject me to," she said with a smirk. Her smile turned more genuine, and I made a silent oath to keep it there all day. Grinning, I winked at her, put the car in gear, and then pulled back out onto the highway.

Once the car was back up to speed, I reached across and grabbed Alyssa's hand. With a smile on my face, I rested our joined hands on my lap. She didn't attempt to pull away or shake off my grasp, which made my smile wider. After a few minutes she did break away, but only for long enough to turn on the radio before placing her palm back where it had rested on my thigh.

The radio proved to be the perfect distraction, and soon we were both singing along at the top of our lungs. The radio station was doing an "All Naughties" music special, playing all the songs we'd fallen in love to. I took it as an omen that it was going to be a fuck-awesome day.

I pulled into the car park and stopped in front of the sign that read, *V8 Experience*. Alyssa turned to me with a dazed look on her face.

"Is this . . . is that what we're doing? Are you driving us around the track? In one of those?"

"No," I said, with an innocent smile on my lips.

She breathed out in relief.

"You are."

Her jaw dropped, and her eyes widened. "Really?"

I jumped out of the car and ran around to her door before she had a chance to open it. "Really."

"So then . . . what's in the box?" she asked, with a little bit of fear—or possibly anticipation—in her voice.

"Your suit and helmet. And mine."

When she looked at me she had a wide grin on her face.

"*Really?*" her voice was high-pitched, almost a squeal. The doubt I'd felt over my choice in date evaporated.

"You want to check it out?" I asked, and offered her my hand.

As she nodded, her excitement was evident and rippled through her. Her fingers clutched tightly around mine. I led her to the back of the car and pulled open the boot. Resting just inside was the box that Danny had sent up—complete with two Sinclair Racing race suits and two matching helmets.

"Can I?" Alyssa asked, her hands already extended halfway to the box.

I shrugged. "The small one is yours to do with what you will. Although, I do hope you'll put it on and go for a spin." I ran my eyes over her body, just imagining her curves squeezed into the suit. My dick sprang to immediate attention. I turned toward the bumper so that my *situation* wouldn't be obvious to Alyssa. Then I reached for the box and positioned it to provide coverage.

"C'mon," I said, nodding toward the office.

"I'm not going to have to drive with someone else am I?" she asked, glancing around anxiously.

"Alyssa, look who you're with!" I said, pretending to be offended. "Danny's organised the lot. I'm going to take you round and show you how to do it. Then it'll be your turn. You'll just have to trust that I'll keep you safe and listen to my instructions carefully."

"So are we really going on the track?"

I put the box down on a bench. "This track and the car are ours exclusively for the next four hours. Obviously the safety people have to be around, but other than that, we'll be left completely alone."

"Wow."

I smiled. I knew this date would either bring us closer or drive a bigger wedge between us. Judging by the wide-eyed expression on her face, the day was going exactly as I'd dared to hope.

"Through there to get changed," I said as I threw her suit at her. "Just make sure you leave your t-shirt on underneath, otherwise it'll chafe like a bitch."

She giggled a little as she caught the suit and disappeared into the ladies' room less than a second later.

Yep, she was fucking excited. My heart skipped a beat or two at the thought.

After she'd disappeared, I grabbed my own suit and headed to the men's room. I dressed as quickly as I could because I didn't want to leave Alyssa alone for long with the number of wolves that were no doubt hanging around the track. I'd seen the draw of female drivers often enough. There was something about a sexy girl in a tight-arse driving suit in control of a fuck-hot V8 that just did things to men.

When I left the men's room, I stopped short. Alyssa was waiting for me and walking was no longer an option. She was red-hot; so hot she was on fucking fire. I'd seen plenty of women wearing a race suit, and none of them even came close to looking as sexy as she did.

She'd taken her hair out and was shaking it loose, sending the curls flowing down over her shoulders. The black of the suit contrasted deliciously with her milky skin. I swallowed as hard as I could to remove the lump in my throat, but nothing was going to shift the one in my pants.

She must have heard my steps, because she started talking to me.

"What's the matter?" she asked as she turned toward me. "Cat got your—"

She stopped short as her eyes raked over my body. For the first time ever, I felt self-conscious in my race suit. I'd done promotional shoots with at least a dozen grid girls, but no one had ever made me feel so attractive, and at the same time attracted me so much, as she did in that instant. I felt the need to run over to her and mark her as mine in any way possible. Particularly in any way that including rubbing up and down against her lemur style. Instead, I gave her an unsteady smile and released the breath that was stuck in my throat. "You ready?"

She nodded, but her lip quivered and her hands shook.

God, she's going to be the death of me. Reaching for her helmet, I slid it under my arm and closed the distance between us. When I was close enough, I kissed her forehead then whispered, "Trust me."

I didn't know if she understood that I meant in general, and not just on the track, but either way, she nodded as I slipped her helmet on.

Reaching for the box again, I grabbed my own helmet before linking arms with Alyssa and leading her out to the V8 we'd be driving. It wasn't quite as powerful as my own ProV8, but it was a Tickford XR8 that had been modified with high-performance ECU and was race prepared with roll cages, safety harnesses, race seats, and slick tyres. It was going to be a decent enough ride and would definitely give Alyssa the closest possible experience she could have to my life. At least until I could convince Danny to let me take her out in one of our cars.

"Just remember, I'll run through everything first, take you on a couple of laps, and then I'll hand it over to you," I said to her as I opened the passenger door. The most important thing for me was to keep her relaxed and excited. If the experience wasn't a good one for her, I might never be able to truly make her understand why I loved racing so much,

With wide eyes and a nervous smile, she looked around the relatively bare interior. Once she'd settled into the race seat, I leaned into the car to strap her into the racing harness. As I did, I took extra care to ensure all the straps were tight enough to be protective, but loose enough that they wouldn't cut off her circulation. To check, I ran my finger down the lines of each strap, first following the length from shoulder to waist across the front of Alyssa's chest. Both of our breaths grew shakier with each extra inch of her body my finger travelled along.

When I moved to check each of the straps that rested across her hips and the ones along her inner thighs, my gaze met hers and I lost my mind. Her eyes stared at me, practically unblinking but filled with lust that scorched straight through any sense of self-control I had. All I wanted to do was kiss her and then maybe use the restraints for something a little more fun . . .

My mouth went dry at the thought, but before I made a suggestion which might get me into trouble considering Alyssa's whole wait-until-I'm-ready rule, I reined in my desire and continued with my safety checks.

I gave the buckle one final pull to ensure it was secure before reluctantly withdrawing and moving to the driver's side.

For the next half hour, I ran through some of the key aspects of driving a race car. I showed her how to keep to the racing line, how to approach the corners, and where to hit the apex for maximum exit speed. I ran through braking techniques and general car control.

During the first two laps, she clung tightly to her harness. Because of her nerves, I didn't push the car as hard as I knew it could go. Instead, I concentrated on training her and trying to show my natural passion for the sport. Watching her carefully, I saw the moment when her nerves broke and she allowed the excitement to creep back in.

That was the moment I knew she was ready to take control. I pulled the car up and helped release her harness. When I guided her out of the car, she clutched at my arm. It was as if her nerves were back in force now that she knew she was going to be in control.

"Are you sure I can do this?" she asked with a shaky voice.

"Lys, baby, you can do any fucking thing you want." I didn't even think about the endearment until it had slipped past my lips. Her eyes widened slightly, but she said nothing about it as she slid into the driver's seat.

Once again, I helped her do up her harness, taking extra care while checking the straps this time. Not because she hadn't been safe the first time, but because it gave me a chance to touch her without complaint. As I slid my hand between the strap and her breast, I watched her face. When I ran my fingers beneath the straps on her hips, I bit my lip and held my breath. The breath released in a slow, steady exhale as I checked the strap between her legs. I might, or might not, have imagined the small, low moan that she issued in response to the caress of my fingers.

Fuck, I wanted her.

I had never wanted anyone more in my entire life.

Before I could completely lose control and do something she would make me regret—like kiss her—I pulled myself out of the car.

On the way back to the passenger side, I adjusted the hard-on growing in my pants. Once I slid into the seat, I did up my own harness. "You ready?" I asked.

She nodded, but I could see how tightly she was gripping the steering wheel. I placed my hand over hers and gave it a gentle, reassuring squeeze until I felt her relax under my hold. Then I drew my fingers down her arm and placed my hand on her shoulder.

"You'll do great," I assured her. "Just remember what I told you."

"What? All of it? What if I forget something?" she asked, concerned and perhaps a little frightened. "What if I crash?"

I laughed. "I'm here, Lys, I'll help you through it."

During the first lap, she almost killed the car by going too slow. I tried my hardest to bite my tongue so that I didn't snap at her to just put her fucking foot down already.

The second lap was a little better.

By the fifth lap she was starting to relax into it and was averaging 120 down the straight. I wanted her to push it even harder. With encouraging words, I coaxed her faster each time until finally, on her tenth lap, she hit 200 klicks an hour down the straight.

She pulled over shortly after, her whole body shaking with adrenaline. I unbuckled myself and practically fucking ran to her door. The combination of her speed and killer looks was enough to do me in, but I had to let her know how fucking proud of her I was.

Before I had a chance to help her out she'd already undone her straps and virtually leapt out of the car into my arms. Our helmets met with a clash, so I quickly pulled mine off and placed it on the bonnet. Alyssa followed suit before throwing her arms around my neck again, squealing like a little girl. Even though my ribs weren't healed, and still ached like fuck, the pain was totally worth it.

She was so close to me and smelled so fucking good. Her body rubbed against me as she did her celebratory dance, and I couldn't resist her anymore. I wrapped her body tightly in my arms, pulling her against me with all my strength.

Without hesitation, I claimed her lips, walking her backwards until I'd pinned her between my body and the car. The instant I made the move, I expected her to slap me or to pull away, so I was fucking shocked when the tip of her tongue traced my lips. With a groan, I ground my hips against her.

If she'd had any doubts about exactly what she did to me that action alone had to have erased them. I was so fucking hard it was painful. I needed her. My fingers traced gently through her hair as she tilted her head upward to allow for better access.

My other hand ran along her back and cupped her arse. I hitched her leg onto my hip and she moaned against my mouth. It was like my own private cheer squad, spurring me on to greater heights—or in this case toward greater depths. I pulled away from Alyssa for half a second, to ensure she was willing to partake. Her eyes were dark with lust and her lips plump and red from our hard kisses.

The sight called me to her, and I was so ready to take her then and there over the bonnet of the car. Clenching my fists, I resisted with every part of me but the one that stretched forward as if to reach for her.

"Oh, fucking hell," I whispered, as I took another step back. "This wasn't what I planned. I just wanted to show you my life—my passion. I don't want you to think . . ."

She cut me off by throwing herself into my arms and kissing me with a passion so fierce it was impossible to resist.

Before I even understood what she was doing, she slid down the zipper on my race suit, and pushed it open and off my shoulders. She planted small kisses across my chin and down my neck. Her fingers played along the bottom edge of my t-shirt, teasing my stomach maddeningly with her warm skin.

"Do you know what these suits do to me?" she asked, her voice husky and seductive.

"Oh, fuck, Alyssa," I moaned. "Tell me."

She pushed me away, and not wanting her to be uncomfortable, I took a few steps back. With a sexy smirk, she peeled the zipper open on her own suit. It was evident pretty fast that she wasn't wearing anything beneath it except a bra. The suit formed a V of nearly bare skin from her shoulders to her waist. I wanted to run my tongue along that patch of skin.

Or fall down on my knees and worship at the temple that was Alyssa.

Instead, I stood, wide-mouthed and powerless as she stalked toward me like a predator.

Her body called out to me, and I finally gathered my senses enough to run my hands into her suit, trailing my fingers along her bare skin. Kissing her again, I ran my fingertips along the patch of skin at the base of her spine. I pressed my t-shirt-covered torso against her bare chest.

The warmth of her body radiated though the thin material, and I knew without a doubt I had to have her—often and repeatedly. It was the only thing that could help save my sanity. I wondered if I could get a script from the good doctor for that: Alyssa Dawson, sunny-side up, repeated at least three times a day until cured.

And if that was my medicine, I didn't ever want to be cured.

With a regretful sigh, I pulled back from the kiss. Even though I was unwilling to back away completely, I knew all too well how many people were around. With any other girl, I wouldn't have given a shit. But this was Alyssa. And she was too fucking pure to be screwed in the middle of an open racetrack in full view of the safety staff.

I zipped her suit back up, but not before running my finger from her belly button to her chin, and then from her chin to her ear.

"Do you want me to show you how it's *really* done now?" I whispered in her ear.

A shiver raced through her. I wasn't sure which emotion dominated her features the most—fear or excitement. But she nodded once and so for the third time in as many hours, I strapped her into the car. This time took the longest as I checked, double-checked, and triple-checked her straps, taking all the time I could to enjoy the sensation of my hands on her body.

After I was in the driver's seat, I took her for a genuine lap, at proper race speed. Trying to impress her, I hit the track like someone was on my tail. I fought hard for the line against imaginary competitors. Through the straights, I drove hard and fast, braking deep into the corners, and cutting across the racing line.

Alyssa alternated between fits of screams and giggles as she was thrown around the passenger seat. I couldn't deny I had enjoyed every fucking second. It'd been far too long since I'd been able to properly stretch my racing legs. The fact that she was beside me, enjoying every second, just made it sweeter than ever.

After a few more laps, I pulled to a hard stop in front of the office. Then I turned and grinned at Alyssa. I couldn't believe that we'd been at the track for almost four hours—it felt like five minutes.

I was euphoric and she was grinning.

And the day had only just begun.

CHAPTER SIXTEEN

LIFE'S A DRAG

LIKE A CAT rising from sleep, Alyssa stretched her hands out above her head languidly. After dropping the car back with the track officials, we headed down to a secluded spot for an intimate picnic. We'd eaten, and then taken a moment to just enjoy one another.

With her warm body tucked between my thighs, I couldn't have been happier. Her shoulders rested across my hips, and her fingers raked my sides. I chuckled as she tickled my ribs. She dropped her head back, resting her chestnut locks against my stomach. She smiled a little and tilted her head so that she looked up at me. When she noticed I was watching her she flipped herself over and her smile widened.

"Thank you," she said. "For this morning and for today. It's been . . ." She trailed off with a sigh.

"Perfect?" I asked, hopeful.

She offered a small smile and nodded. Then she crossed her arms across my stomach and rested her head back down on them. I ran my fingers through her hair, brushing it all to the side so I had an uninterrupted view of her face.

"You're so beautiful," I said to her.

She swatted my stomach lightly, but I wouldn't be deterred. We'd had a perfect morning at the track, followed by a picnic in a quiet, and most importantly, secluded little corner of the Ipswich race precinct. I'd left explicit instructions that we were not to be disturbed by anyone, for any reason.

Which was a good thing, because almost as soon as I had unfolded the blanket, Alyssa had pulled off the top half of her racing suit and tied the sleeves off around her waist. She pulled a t-shirt on almost immediately, but not before I had a good look at the ivory planes of her back.

As if driven by the memory, my hand dropped from her hair to the collar of her shirt. My fingers dipped in and out as I rubbed a small circle there, relishing in the feel of her silken skin.

In response to my touch, Alyssa gave a small moan of approval, which spurred me on further. I rubbed my hand along her back over the top of her shirt. She groaned again. Each time she did, her chest vibrated against my groin, sending shivers of desire through my entire body.

She had to know how she was affecting me because my erection was pressing hard against her breasts. My hand went to her chin, lifting it up so that she was looking at me.

"I love you," I told her.

She looked me in the eye and smiled. Then she dropped her head back onto her folded hands. She closed her eyes and seemed lost in thought. I dropped my head back to the ground and closed my eyes. Even if she still couldn't say it, I was sure she felt the same way about me. After all, she'd put her trust in me around the track. She'd allowed me to push her boundaries and get her driving up over the 200-kilometre mark.

Lost in my own thoughts, my hand ran absentminded trails from her hair to her shirt and back again. I thought nothing of it when she shifted her weight—she'd been wiggling and moving most of the time she'd been lying between my legs anyway.

It wasn't until soft lips touched mine that I realised she'd shifted her entire body on top of mine. I opened my eyes to see her grinning at me from above. Once she knew she had my attention, she dropped her lips to my ear.

"I love you, Declan Reede." She whispered it so quietly I was almost sure I was hearing things.

Then her lips crashed onto mine, and her tongue pressed forward. I opened my lips and allowed her tongue into my mouth. Her hair fell in curtains around our faces as we became consumed by each other. I reached down between us to untie the knot in her race-suit—it was pressing hard against my stomach and was uncomfortable. Alyssa gasped as my hand slipped inside the suit to grab hold of the knot. Her mouth pressed harder against mine, and she moaned into me.

That small moan was it for me. I reached around her, pulling her closer. Then I flipped us over so she was pinned beneath me. I pushed her t-shirt up and tasted the skin of her stomach. I groaned in ecstasy. She tasted so fucking good. My hands explored north of where my head rested, pushing the cups of her bra up and releasing her breasts to my waiting fingers. I rolled her nipple gently between my thumb and forefinger. My mouth longed to join my hands, but was too busy exploring other parts of her stomach. Finally, with a trail of kisses, I climbed up her body. My head scooped low and tasted her breasts.

"Perfect," I breathed against her skin as my fingers traced the constellation tattooed near her heart.

She pushed her head back, bucking her hips and exposing her neck in the process. My mouth found her throat, my lips grazing and gently nipping at her skin. My hands parted ways; one ran to the back of her neck, supporting her head by resting against the base of her skull. The other traced a straight line between her breasts, over her stomach, and down into her racing suit without hesitation.

My fingers trailed across her panties. The heat radiating from her was exquisite. I claimed her mouth with mine again as my hand pushed down under the material covering her pussy. With a soft touch, I brushed my fingertips across her wet and ready flesh. A groan escaped me in unison with hers as I dipped my fingers inside her, first one, then two.

Alyssa's breaths became heavy pants against my mouth. I pressed my body against my hand, grinding my crotch against hers, sandwiching my fingers deeper inside her and rubbing my palm over her clit. Sucking her bottom lip into my mouth, I grazed my teeth along it.

With desperate thrusts, she pushed closer to me, sending my fingers deeper still.

Shifting my body away enough to move my hand, I grazed my thumb against her clit as I thrust against her again and again. She tipped her head back as a sigh of ecstasy escaped her lips.

Dragging her closer to the edge with every movement of my hand, I watched her face as she tensed in my arms. With a desperate moan, she came around my fingers. The sight and sound of it left me desperate for more. I pulled my hand out and rested it on her hip as I kissed her throat again.

"I want you so badly, Alyssa," I whispered, unthinkingly, against her hair.

"I'm yours . . .," Alyssa breathed back. Then, almost silently, she added, "Please . . . be careful with me."

A small tear in her eyes told me how honest her request was.

I kissed the corner of her eye. "Always," I told her, reverently. "I'll never hurt you again."

I wrapped her tightly in my arms, and twisted so I was lying on my back before pulling her in to my side. Her hand moved up to my face and her fingers grazed along my chin. She dropped her head against my shoulder.

"Just see that you don't," she murmured into my chest.

In response, I pulled her closer to me. The more time I spent with her, the more it became clear that I could never intentionally hurt her again. I could never leave her side again, because I needed her like air.

We lay there alongside each other for a few minutes more. We were both sleepy from the sun and food, and were soon completely relaxed into each other. I didn't want to move from the perfect slice of heaven we'd created in our private little corner, but I also knew we needed to get a wriggle on if we were going to make the second part of my date.

With a sigh, I pulled myself away from Alyssa and moved to my feet. Once I was standing, I turned and offered Alyssa my hand. "Coming?"

"Where?" She narrowed her eyes at me as she accepted my offer and rose to her feet.

"To our date: part two." I tied the arms of her racing suit back around her waist again as I spoke.

She laughed. "There's a part two?"

I raised my eyebrow at her. "Damn right there's a part two, and it's going to be a drag."

I laughed at my own pun, but Alyssa just stared blankly at me for a few minutes before recognition of what was right next door lit her features.

"Of course. It had to be that," she said.

"Of course. I mean, why pass up the opportunity while we're here."

"You know it won't be my first time?"

I cocked my head to the side. "Really?"

She blushed. "Yeah, Flynn brings me down a bit. He's quite into it."

"That's right, he drives a fucking ricer Silvia or some shit, wasn't it?"

She patted my chest. "Be nice."

I clasped to her hand and pulled her into my arms, leaving her fingers resting against my heart.

"I can be nice," I said. "But only because I get to do this—" I pressed my lips to hers, pushing my tongue forward and running it along her upper lip.

Her lips parted, and I brushed her tongue with mine. I deepened the kiss, bringing my hand to her hair. When I drew away from Alyssa again she was breathless, her eyes hooded with lust. I just smiled and winked at her, before pulling the picnic blanket up off the ground and shoving it into the basket. I'd have to thank

Eden later for arranging this part of the day; it had been one of her last-minute suggestions.

Linking my hand with Alyssa's, we walked back to my car in silence. I began to wonder whether I was being selfish by dragging her to do the things I wanted without checking that she was happy to do it. Once we reached my car, I opened the boot and put the picnic basket inside. Alyssa slid into the passenger's seat without another word.

"If you'd rather go home, we can," I said as I climbed into the car.

She smiled at me, and shook her head. "No, I've enjoyed myself today. It really has been," she gave a small sigh, "perfect."

"And you want to go to the drags? I mean, I just thought that we're kitted out in the suits anyway and we even have the helmets."

"It's fine, Dec. I told you, I've been with Flynn before."

"Yeah, but have you driven?" I asked excitedly, almost guaranteeing I knew the answer.

She bit her lip and nodded.

Fucking son of a bitch! My brows knitted together in a frown.

"So when Flynnie-poo brings you down here, which one of you races powder-puff?"

She closed her eyes and took a deep breath. I could see the pain that I'd finally shifted begin to form on her features again.

"Fuck!" I exclaimed, drawing her eyes back to me. "Just forget I said that, okay? Please? I'm sorry . . . I just . . ." *Can't fucking stand the fact that Flynn has stolen everything in my life.*

I couldn't tell her how that sentence was going to finish.

I turned to her. "Please?" I repeated, more softly. "I'm sorry."

"It's fine, Dec. Let's just go to the drags." Her voice held a certain resignation that I knew, and hated.

I shook my head. "I'm not moving this car until you forgive me. I was an arse and I'm asking you to accept my apology."

Her lip twitched just a little, and then she smirked. "You were an arse."

"And?" I prompted.

She sighed. "And . . . I forgive you. At least, so long as you promise to try to get along with Flynn," she added quickly.

"I promise to *try*." I said.

"Fine then, let's go."

I grabbed her hand and kissed her knuckles lightly. "Thank you."

After driving the short distance to the Willowbank Raceway drag strip, I joined the queue of cars that were there for the Street Meet. The tension in the car was still palpable, but Alyssa seemed as content to ignore it as I was. I couldn't believe that I'd fucked things up so soon after our fuck-awesome date, part one.

I paid our entry and drove into the pits. Alyssa sat quietly, playing with the stereo, while I began to unpack all the unnecessary shit from the car, putting it all to one side so that I could lighten the car and get a better time. I'd just finished unpacking the baby seat when I looked up and saw a familiar shape climbing out of a gunmetal-grey Silvia S14 which, judging by the number stuck in the window, was a regular here.

It took me all of two seconds to work out who it was. Fucking Flynn.

"Fucking perfect," I muttered to myself. I wasn't looking forward to facing him so soon after I'd had to endure watching him take *my* role to comfort Alyssa.

"What's the matter?" she asked, turning her head. If I'd hoped she wouldn't notice the fucker, I was disappointed almost immediately. She sighed audibly.

"It's fine, Lys," I said, through gritted teeth. "Do you want to go see him?"

I decided I would try to be the bigger man, the better man. The fucking best man. I knew I was, I just had to get Alyssa to see it.

She bit her lip, and I could see her desire to say yes warring with her anxiety about my possible reaction.

"Really, Lys, if you want to see him, it's fine. Go. I'll finish unpacking the car, and then run it to scrutineering."

"Are you sure?"

Breathing heavily through my nose so that I wouldn't swear, I nodded. I could do this—I could be the supportive person Alyssa needed me to be. With my arms crossed, I watched as she waved at him before walking over to his car. The fucker picked her up and gave her a giant bear hug.

I turned away and let loose a stream of invective when she smiled widely and laughed at something he said. It just seemed so effortless between the two of them. It was the way we used to be. The way I wanted us to be again. The way we almost were when no one else was involved.

After yanking out the spare tyre and my toolbox, swearing and cursing the whole time, I shoved them onto the ground in our pit area. When I'd finished, I risked a quick glance back at Alyssa and Flynn. He was pulling on the sleeves of her racing suit, and they were both laughing. Fucking arsehole. I'd hoped that this would be a good date for Alyssa. To show her part of my world and why I found racing so addictive. But she just found it all so fucking hilarious instead.

I'd opened myself up to her, and she was fucking laughing with that fucker about it.

Kicking the tyre, I let loose a low growl. Then I climbed into the car, started the engine, and headed off to the scrutineering shed, kicking up dirt as I went. In my rear-view mirror, I watched Alyssa. Her body was leaning against Flynn's car, and she was talking to him still, but her eyes followed my car the whole way. I raked my hand through my hair as I thought about the disaster the date had become. The thing was, I wanted to fix it, but I had no fucking clue how.

Climbing out of the car, I passed my helmet and paperwork across for the officials to check. I popped the hood so they could check the engine mods and exhaust system. They wrote the class and temporary number in white shoe polish on the rear passenger-side window and told me I was good to go. I double-checked that I'd signed Alyssa up for the powder-puff event. The thought of her taking control of my car scared the shit out of me. No one else ever drove my car. Usually I didn't even allow valets to touch the steering wheel. Especially considering it'd only just come back from being repaired—the last thing I wanted was new scratches.

In the small gesture of handing over control, I was trying to show my trust in her—my love for her. I'd told her as much so many times in the last few days that saying it again would mean little, so I had to show her with my actions instead.

I drove back to the pit area and saw that Flynn had shifted his car to be in the space next to me. Fucking great. As if it wasn't bad enough knowing he was there, I'd have to deal with him all fucking night. Alyssa jogged over to me when I was parked and pulled my door open. She knelt in front of me, placing one hand on my thigh.

"Try," she whispered to me, before pressing her lips to mine. "For me."

Closing my eyes, I allowed my body to take control for a few minutes. I needed to stop overthinking it. I needed to focus and think of it like a race. In my professional life, I was used to being on an opponent's arse on the track, trying to get by. If I rode hard enough, and was patient enough, they would usually make a mistake eventually and allow me to pass.

It was the same thing here. Before long, Flynn would make a mistake, and Alyssa would stop wasting her time with him.

"Anything for you, Lys," I whispered against her lips, before opening my eyes again.

She smiled at my compliance. Her hand came into my hair. "Thank you, for trying."

"It's not too late to go home if you want?" I offered, even though I was anxious to get out on the strip and kick the fucker's arse, but if Alyssa wanted to go I would.

"Are you kidding?" she said. "I wanna see what ET this thing gets."

Despite my shock that she even knew what an elapsed time was, I couldn't help the smirk that crossed my face. "Shall I go lay a time now then?"

She nodded and smiled. "I'll be watching from the stands."

"No," I said, grabbing her hand. "Come with me. At least until you have to get out. I don't want to wait in the lanes alone."

"Okay."

ONCE WE were in the lanes waiting for our turn on the strip, I turned to Alyssa. "You know what? Why don't you take first go?"

She shook her head lightly. "No way."

"But you said you'd driven here before?"

"Yeah, but only in my old Cortina. Flynn convinced me to bring it the first time we ever came down."

"So Flynn's never let you drive his car?"

She laughed. "Are you kidding me? As Flynn always tells me, there are two things of his I'll never touch, and one of those is his car."

"What's the other?" I asked, my curiosity getting the better of me.

I glanced over toward Alyssa; she was bright red and stifling a giggle. I thought about it for a second. My nose crinkled as understanding dawned on me. I didn't want to think about her hands and that fucker's cock.

She laughed heartily at something she saw on my face. Then she shrugged. "I told you before, there's no competition." She placed her hand on my thigh, running it up to my crotch and pulling it away at the last second.

"Well, that decides it. You're taking the first run," I told her.

"I'd rather not. I mean, what if I break something?"

I shrugged. "If you break something then I'll kill you," I deadpanned before laughing to show I wasn't being serious. At least, not completely. "Relax, you'll be fine. You just drove at over two hundred ks around a racetrack. This is a simple straight line. It's easy. There are really only three things to remember. Accelerate, change gears, and brake."

"You're sure? Most guys are like uber-protective of their cars."

"I'm sure," I said, but it sounded like a lie even to me. "I mean, yeah, I'm one of those guys. But I trust you, Lys. I know you can do this."

On hearing my affirmation, she squared her shoulders and nodded. "I'll do it."

I spent the next five minutes running through the finer details; when to take off, halfway between the second and third amber light usually worked for me; when to change gears, I told her speeds to change at rather than having her worry about listening to the engine, and how to change gears quickly. When we got to staging, I climbed out of the car, and she jumped in the driver's seat. She nervously clutched the steering wheel, like she had in the race car. And like then, I reached in through the window, placing my hand over hers, and held her until she relaxed a little.

"Good luck," I said as I gave her a peck on the cheek. "When you get to the end, just drive around and I'll meet you by the tower. I'll get your ET slip."

She nodded, and the look of fierce determination on her face was just so goddamned sexy. I tore myself away as she wound up the window. Then I ran off the track to stand in front of the tower and watch her pass. It may have only been practice, but I had a fucking hard-on watching her control my car. She launched it hard and drove it smoothly down the track for a 14.6 second pass. I smirked as I saw the time. Fuck Flynn and his 14.8.

Pussy.

I walked over to the tower to wait for the slip to give to Alyssa. Once I had it, I turned to go meet her.

"Reede!"

I scowled when I heard my name called from behind me, but only because I knew the voice. I turned, forcing my face to form a smile, and walked back to Flynn.

"I see you picked your car up and have managed not to trash it in another DUI yet."

I snarled at him, and bit back the "fuck you" that I wanted to say. Instead, I released my breath and said, "It was a good repair job."

It almost killed me to be complimenting him or his brother, but at least I could say that I'd tried.

"Nice pass," he said with an air of forced civility.

"Yeah, that wasn't me," I said innocently, as I waved the elapsed-time slip.

He scrunched his forehead briefly, then he raised his eyebrow and smirked. "Oh, you think you're so clever, don't you?"

I shrugged. "I don't know what you are talking about. I'm just here to show *my* girl a good time."

Before he could react, Alyssa pulled up in front of us. She practically bounced out of the car to meet me.

"What did I do?" she asked, breathless. "It felt so fast."

"You did a 14.6, baby." I made a show of wrapping my arms around her and pulling her lips against mine. I was sure not to overdo it—it wouldn't do to have Alyssa thinking it was just a show for the fucker's benefit. The fact was, I would have done it regardless, but it felt good to fucking show him what I could offer her that he never could. "Do you want to go back 'round so I can have a run?"

She nodded and I wrapped my arm around her shoulder to lead her back to the car without a backwards glance toward Flynn.

Score one, Declan Reede.

CHAPTER SEVENTEEN

IT'S ALL ABOUT THE STRATEGY

I COULDN'T BELIEVE how fucking awesome the date had gone. The morning and afternoon were just . . . well, I didn't think Alyssa's choice of the word *perfect* was too strong. Then, just when I'd been worried about the whole thing being derailed by the appearance of Flynn, it had actually turned out to be a blessing in disguise.

Every step of the way, I'd done exactly what Alyssa asked me to do—I'd *tried*. I *tried* not to be insulted at the barbs Flynn sent my way. I *tried* not to punch his face when he made a comment about my racing suit. And I *tried* not to be upset when he pulled a 14.5 out of his arse, beating Alyssa's time.

Mostly, I was successful.

Of course, it helped that for each insult Flynn issued Alyssa seemed to grow more affectionate.

When he said my arse looked good in a racing suit, she ran her hand over it and pressed her mouth to mine. When he made a supposedly off-the-cuff comment about deadbeat dads, Alyssa wrapped her arms around my waist and quizzed me on what I had planned for our family day the next day.

In retaliation to Flynn's childish crap, I decided to show him again what I could offer Alyssa that he never could . . .

And again . . .

And again.

Alyssa didn't issue a single complaint when I wrapped my arms around her or kissed her.

Even when we were wrapped so tightly around each other we were practically fucking each other against the side of his car, she never whispered a word to stop me. Sure, I was marking my territory and letting the arsehole know she was mine, but at the same time it felt so fucking unbelievable to touch and kiss her that it was hardly torturous.

Making the date even better was the fact that Alyssa's on-track ability in the powder-puff division was nothing short of amazing. Especially considering she hadn't raced in a long time and never in a performance vehicle like my Monaro. The truth was the most important aspect of dial-in drag racing was a good reaction time and consistent runs. She had both of those in spades.

Each run, she came within a fraction of a second of her dialled-in time. She only bowed out in the third round, technically coming in fourth place. I almost fucking died when I saw the cherry in her lane that indicated she had taken off a fraction too early. But she was happy with what she'd achieved, and that was enough for me.

Personally, I was pleased with the times I'd achieved during my own practise runs. I found a consistency which had seen me through four rounds and led me to be head-to-head with Flynn in the fifth.

Driving my car onto my side of the track, I let it rip and then dropped my clutch. The tyres lost traction in the water on the track and my tyres smoked up. I risked a glance at Flynn's car as the thick plumes of smoke rose from my rear tyres

My helmet restricted me a little, but I could see well enough to notice the smart-arse look on his face. I snarled at him as my car shot forward from the burnout and sailed past the Christmas tree.

Putting the car in reverse, I rolled backwards to prepare for staging. Flynn pushed his car forward into pre-stage. With practised care, I inched my car forward into pre-stage, ensuring I didn't slip it straight into stage. After all, I didn't want to go in first. That needed to be his honour, but only because it was a way to increase my own chances at scoring a win.

Because he was in a turbo, he needed to spool it up as much as possible before leaving the line to get maximum power, but if he revved his engine too much he would risk overheating it. It was a timing game, but by forcing him to stage first, I could ensure he had to wait the maximum time in stage. Plus there was the psych-out factor of being the first one in. He revved his engine hard but didn't move any further forward. With just the top pre-stage light on in both our lanes, I waited patiently.

Finally he jumped forward and the stage lights were lit on his side. I had thirty seconds before I needed to be there, or I would lose the race before we even started.

Let the mindfuck begin, I thought.

Breathing through my nerves, I waited. Ten seconds. Twenty. Flynn revved his engine hard again, trying to spool the turbo enough to give him a good time down the track.

Idiot.

I let twenty-five seconds pass, and waited for a dip in the revving of Flynn's engine, before I finally pushed my car into full stage. Almost as soon as I did, the Christmas tree lit up. Because I'd dialled in a time of 14.2 against his 14.5, I had a 0.3 second delay before I had to leave the line, meaning I had to chase Flynn down.

Amber-amber-amber fell on his side, and then, so quickly the difference was almost imperceptible, the lights fell on mine.

He launched his car hard.

I hit my accelerator between the second and third ambers on my side of the tree.

Once I left the line, I risked a quick glance in my rear-view mirror. The green lights were on for both sides of the track. I blew a quick sigh of relief.

Part one, get away clean, was a success.

Part two, chase him down and get ahead of him, was just beginning.

As the seconds passed and my car sped, I edged closer and closer to him. At around the hundred-foot mark, I was level with his rear quarter-panel. Then his passenger door. Finally, I closed in on the nose of his car. I snapped through the gears as quickly as I could, using my left foot to hit the clutch. My right foot barely lifted off the accelerator before slamming straight back down.

Despite the speed of the run, it felt like time had stopped. It was midtrack, just over eight seconds into the run, when I saw him dropping away behind me, agonisingly slowly, but he was going.

I was ahead.

I was winning.

Fuck yes!

By the end of the quarter-mile, I was half a car ahead of him. As I slowed down, I gave myself a mental fist-pump. I'd shown that arsehole what it takes to be a real fucking race-car driver. With a smile on my face, I checked my rear-vision mirror to see the light on the time boards that would confirm my win.

As I did, my jaw dropped and I slammed the brakes on hard, pulling the car to an almost complete stop. What I saw was impossible.

The win light was on, but in *his* lane.

Flynn's car continued to roll smoothly off into the distance in front of me, turning the corner at the end of the braking area and disappearing out of sight. I stared blankly at the board behind me. My head was reeling. Two questions, "What the fuck?" and "How?" played on an endless, alternating loop through my mind.

Eventually, I put my car back into gear and edged it around the end of the braking area. I watched from the end of the road as Alyssa ran to Flynn's car, elapsed-time slip in hand. He jumped from the driver's seat and pulled her into a bear hug. I ground my teeth as he kissed her cheek. I wanted to ram my car into the back of his. The fucker! How dare he kiss *my* woman like that, especially after what had just happened.

I still couldn't understand how I'd lost. To him.

Everything in my fucking life went to him. No matter what I did, I came in second place to him. I just couldn't win. I could never win. Not with Alyssa, or Phoebe, or anything else in my life. I may as well cut off my balls and hand them to him, considering he seemed to own everything else I cared about.

I revved my engine loudly and rolled the car forward a little further. I watched as Alyssa disentangled herself from Flynn and glanced back at my car. I stared impassively as a wide grin came across her face and she waved the slip in front of her. Flynn walked off toward the tower. It became clear then that even though she'd gone to his car, she'd actually grabbed my slip. Maybe she didn't care that I was the loser. I frowned in confusion. She ran toward my car, not even pausing for a second before pulling open the door and jumping into the passenger seat. Instead of sitting, she leaned across the car and claimed my lips.

"Congrats, Dec." She grinned at me.

I grew even more confused. Why the hell was she congratulating me? "I fucking lost, didn't I?"

"Only because you *smashed* your dial-in time." Her enthusiasm was a little contagious, and I felt my lips curling up . . .slightly.

"What'd I get?" I asked. I reached out to grab the elapsed time from her, but she pulled it away at the last second and giggled.

I narrowed my eyes at her. "Tell me," I commanded.

"Or?" She raised her eyebrow and giggled again, hiding the slip of paper behind her back.

"Or . . ." I pulled the car out of gear and reefed on the handbrake. I twisted in my seat to get leverage and leaned across the car, pressing my lips to hers. I kissed her deeply, pushing her into the passenger door. I snuck my arms around her waist as she moaned into my mouth. When she was sufficiently distracted, I snatched the piece of paper off her and sank back into my own seat, trying to calm my raging hard-on. The slip announced my elapsed time was 13.9. My smile grew at the sight.

Fuck yes!

It was the first time I'd had a sub-14 run. Not that dragging was a common pastime for me, but I'd gone often enough to be fucking elated with the time.

Between my time and Alyssa staring at me with come-fuck-me

eyes, the fact that I'd lost began to mean little. I felt like throwing the ET slip out the window and fucking Alyssa right there and then, but I couldn't. Instead, I put the car in gear, released the handbrake and drove back to the pit area.

"Did you want to watch his last race?" I asked her. "I'll pack up while you do."

She shook her head and smiled at me. "I'd rather help you. It's been a long day and I think I'm ready to go home."

I nodded. As much as I hated the date to be over, I was ready to head home too. I packed as quickly as I could. I'd just finished securing the spare wheel back into the boot when a thought occurred to me. Sitting against the edge of the boot, I turned to Alyssa.

"It was a good day though, yeah?" I asked, feeling uncertain about my choices again. "You enjoyed it, didn't you?"

She walked over to me and pushed her body between my legs. Then she ran a finger from my forehead, down my nose and rested it on my lips. "You are so cute when you're insecure."

I laughed. "Declan Reede is *never* insecure."

She quirked her eyebrow at me.

I shrugged. "What? I got a rep to protect."

She giggled and dropped her hand before kissing me softly on the lips. "It was a good day."

I wrapped my arms around her and rested my forehead against her chest. "I'm glad."

I lifted my head and captured her lips. My eyes closed of their own accord as I pushed my tongue forward. My entire body was aware of her proximity.

I wanted her so badly.

A small groan and parted lips told me she was just as anxious for me as I was for her. Regardless, her rules ran through my mind. It was all up to her, but if she wanted to take it further I would be there in a heartbeat.

If not, well, I'd have to work something out or have an ice-cold shower.

Cupping my hands along her chin, I pulled her mouth harder

against mine. I wrapped my legs around her hips, pinning her to me. I relished the sensation of her taste and smell.

It was only when I heard an engine revving beside us that I became aware of my surroundings again. I ran my fingers into her hair and exhaled heavily.

"Let's go home," I whispered, releasing the physical hold I had on her.

She nodded.

"Go say goodbye," I said, nodding in Flynn's direction. "I'll finish here."

It took less than fifteen minutes to get everything else back in the car. I didn't worry about changing back into normal clothes because we'd be driving straight home to Mum's to pick Phoebe up anyway, so I figured I could shower there.

Once I was finished, I waited for Alyssa. I watched as she and Flynn laughed about something and wished again that it could be that easy between her and me. I decided to be the bigger man—again—and walked over to them.

"Congratulations, Flynn," I said stiffly.

I may have been trying, but that didn't mean I could find it in myself to be overly friendly. Especially not after the way things had gone down the previous morning.

"Umm . . . yeah, thanks, uh, Declan," he said in response, clearly shocked at my words. "Are you leaving now?"

He looked briefly to Alyssa and mouthed something. She nodded slightly, as if in response. It was almost like there was some secret between the two of them.

"Yeah, Alyssa and I were just about to go," I replied, wrapping my arms tightly around Alyssa from behind.

I didn't even realise that I was rubbing my hard-on against her arse at first. But then she pushed back against my cock.

I imagined pushing my cock into her from that angle, with my hands cupping her breasts, and groaned in response to the mental image. Alyssa stifled a giggle as I pressed my hips forward against her once more.

"Are you ready?" I asked, with my lips against her neck.

"You don't know how ready I am," she replied in a breathy whisper that sent aches running through my body.

Damn the hour-long drive home.

ONCE THE car was enveloped in the darkness of the night, it was even harder to take my mind off Alyssa. In my peripheral vision, I saw flashes of her face lit by the headlights of oncoming cars. My car was filled with the heady scent of desire, with an undercurrent of sweet sweat from the race suits. Every breath I drew filled my mind with thoughts of Alyssa. She was making me mad with desire.

Even though the plan was to just drop her off at home after collecting Phoebe, I didn't know how I would be able to do that without some way of relieving my tension. It would have been so easy to pull the car over to the side of the road and beg for something—anything—to help my situation, but I didn't. Instead, I reminded myself that technically it was our first real date. At least, the first outside the vomiting disaster at McDonald's or the friend-only shopping trip.

Surely it wasn't right to fuck her mindlessly on the first date, no matter how desperately I wanted to.

We were halfway home when my phone rang. I answered it on the hands-free, relieved to be back in my car and where things were set up my way. It was Mum letting me know Phoebe had fallen fast asleep and that it might not be a good idea to wake her. After a quick discussion, the three of us agreed we'd leave Phoebe undisturbed at Mum's because the next day was going to be a big one with the things I had planned. It was going to be big for all of us.

For the rest of the drive, Alyssa sat playing with her hair. Even though it was the last thing I wanted to do, I planned to drop her off at home before going back to Mum's house to shower and sleep. I figured I could bring Phoebe around in the morning and collect Alyssa on our way out. It would mean being alone with Phoebe, but I was sure I'd be able to cope with that for the length of the drive from Mum's to Alyssa's.

When I'd pulled into Alyssa's driveway, I climbed out of the car and grabbed her clothes out of the boot. Like me, she was still in her race suit.

I followed close behind her as she walked to her front door. Not knowing we'd be out as long as we were, she hadn't left her porch light on, so the black beneath the eaves was almost absolute. I could only see a vague outline of her body. Yet, I could tell the she was regarding her feet with great interest.

"Well—" I started.

"Would you like—" Alyssa said at the same time, slowing raising her head to look at me.

"You go," I told her.

"Would you like to come in for a drink?" I could see her eyes clearly despite the intervening night. They stared at me, pleading silently for something as she continued to play with the ends of her hair.

I nodded before raising my hand to still her motion. The movement drew me closer to her and I couldn't resist the call of her lips. I dipped my head and drew her lower lip between mine, sucking on it for a second before rolling my tongue across the plump surface. In response to my touch, her eyes closed, and her breath hitched. My own breaths were unsteady, but it wasn't like the gasping lack of oxygen of my panic attacks. This was a type of breathlessness I enjoyed. The type I only ever experienced around her. I stepped back away from her, ready to follow her inside. In the darkness, the memory of her taste lingered on my mouth.

With shaking hands, Alyssa pulled her keys from her bag and raised them to the door. The tremors grew more pronounced as she struggled to find the right key. Just like I'd done earlier in the day, I put my hand over hers to steady it. The thrill that passed between us was almost too much to handle. I stepped closer to her, pressing my front against her back. She leaned into me, and all thoughts of keys, doors, and drinks were forgotten.

The black of night surrounded us like a blanket, cocooning us in our own private world. With my free hand, I brushed her hair over one shoulder before I pressed my lips to her neck. She murmured my name as she moved her head to grant me better access.

Reaching around to the front of her, I slowly drew down the zip on her suit until I'd undone it completely. My hand crawled from the zipper to her stomach, working its way beneath her shirt. I moaned and increased the intensity of my kisses on the curve of her neck as my fingers found their way to her nipples.

The keys left her hand, but the jingle when they hit the ground was easy to ignore when her fingers reached backward to caress my hair. She guided me closer to her, twisting my face against her neck. Possessed with need, I licked, sucked, and nipped at the skin of her throat.

Pulling her closer to me, my hands worked with only one intention—nudity. I yanked at the arms of her suit, pulling them away from her delicate skin. I worked the back of her bra, releasing the clasp. My mouth only left her throat for the briefest of moments as I swept her t-shirt off over her head.

I gathered both of her hands in mine and pinned them against the door in front of us. With my lips exploring her shoulders, I dragged one of my hands down over her body. Inch by inch, I trailed my fingers over her arm, down her back and then around to caress her warm breasts. My fingers played with her nipples, and I watched every movement over her shoulder.

"Dec." My name flew from Alyssa on end of a breathy moan.

I couldn't wait any longer. I needed to possess her, to take her the way I'd longed to since London. It was an almost unstoppable primal urge that built from deep within. Only she could stop me now; there was no way I could stop myself.

My free hand pushed down on her suit until it fell to puddle around her ankles. The almost non-existent moonlight seemed to search out Alyssa's skin as desperately as I did and shimmered off her. The radiant beauty of it spurred me on. One word from her and I would have stopped, but all she offered were soft mews and moans as my fingertips and tongue explored her body.

My mouth moved from her neck to her shoulder and across her

back as my free hand began to work on freeing me from my own confines. As I stripped off my suit, I released Alyssa's hands, but she compliantly left them where I'd placed them. She didn't turn or move except to push her body back against me. I wondered whether perhaps she was as concerned about breaking the spell as I was.

The moment I'd removed all barriers between us, I used my knee to spread her legs a little, grazing across her arousal in the process. She was warm and wet and ready for me.

Nothing could stop me. I needed her—I needed *us*.

I grabbed hold of my shaft and ran the tip down toward her heat. Her head fell forward until her forehead rested against the door. I could tell she had her lip between her teeth again by the way her moan was stifled. With an indrawn breath to stop my own desperate moan, I pushed forward into her, filling her completely.

It wasn't the way I'd planned our first encounter of our new relationship, but I was powerless to resist her even one second longer. Bracing my hands on the door, each placed slightly above her head, I surrounded her. She moved her hands to intertwine her fingers with mine before pushing her body back to meet me as I thrust forward into her again.

"Fuck, Lys," I murmured as I kissed her jaw, her cheek, everything I could lay my lips on.

I'd been waiting for the moment for so fucking long and there was no way I'd be able to make it last, especially not with the way she was pushing her arse back against my cock. I couldn't care though. In that moment, I was selfish, taking her and possessing her with little regard for anything else besides my own desperate need as I took pleasure from her body in hard, fast thrusts.

I shook loose of one of her hands, and she laid her palm back on the door as she pushed into me again. My hand grazed along her body, desperately needing to touch every inch of her skin, to commit it all to memory as if this were a one-time thing.

She whispered my name reverently over and over and I couldn't restrain myself. My hands wrapped around her body, and I lifted her against me. As she braced herself against the door, one of my hands came to rest against her throat; the other brushed her clit. Her head fell back onto my shoulder as I nibbled on her earlobe. My desire for her rose to heights I'd never imagined seconds before I came hard into her.

As I came, my breaths were nothing more than rough pants against her neck. I was hyperaware that she'd not been granted the same release, but I was spent. Releasing her from the hold I'd had her in, I braced my hands against the door again, and whispered her name repeatedly into her neck like a prayer to heaven.

My breathing began to steady, and the strength returned to my body. "Fuck, Lys, I'm sorry," I whispered.

"I'm not," she murmured, as she twisted to kiss my cheek.

When I'd collected myself, I pushed off the door and slid my hands down her back, running my fingers across her hips and down the backs of her legs. Then I dropped to the ground to collect the keys, fumbling in the darkness to find them on the doorstep.

Finally, I heard the rewarding jingle as my hand brushed past them. I clutched them, desperate to get inside and show Alyssa that I wasn't just a selfish arse by loving her properly all night long.

As I worked my way back up to a standing position, I ran my tongue across the back of her thighs and kissed the base of her spine. Then I placed the keys in her hands because I had no idea which key fit in which hole. She fingered through them quickly in search of the right one.

Her hand was steadier than it had been when she pushed the key into the lock. She stepped out of her suit and through the now open door. She turned back to me, her naked skin still reflecting softly in moonlight, and I knew I was done for.

I'd told her once that her body was her temple, and I was determined to worship there repeatedly and exclusively. Starting straight away.

Stepping forward, I swept her into my arms and kissed her with all the passion that burned through my body.

Lifting her over the threshold, I kicked the door shut behind us, leaving our discarded clothes where they lay on the porch, casualties of our lust.

CHAPTER EIGHTEEN

BREAKTHROUGH

I PUSHED ALYSSA further into the house, tasting her mouth and pulling her body against me as we went. We collided with the wall, and I ground against her. My fingers found their way into her, gliding in and out to a rhythm I'd long ago perfected. Her mouth opened wide as her eyes shut, and her head tipped back against the wall. My palm grazed against her clit as I pushed into her over and over. When I felt her tightening around my fingers, I withdrew them.

She whimpered softly. "Please," she begged, pushing her hips forward.

"Soon," I whispered against her hair as I kissed her temple. "But first . . ." I bent down, grabbed her around the waist and threw her over my shoulder. The movement sent a shockwave of pain down both sides my ribs, but I didn't care. Nothing was going to stop me taking her and claiming her every way I could.

Laughing and squealing, she mock-protested in my arms as I carried her down the hallway. I pushed open the door to the bathroom and placed her on the floor in front of the shower. It was one of the old shower/bathtub combos, and ever since the first time I'd seen it the first night I'd stayed at her house, I'd dreamed of doing exactly what I was about to.

I turned on the water, checking it to ensure the temperature was just right. Once it was, I turned to look at Alyssa. She stood waiting patiently, playing with her hair. Confusion was printed on her features. With a reassuring smile, I offered her my hand and helped her under the water. After a day of sweating in the suits, being under the water felt like fucking heaven.

Without releasing the hold I had on her, I reached for the soap and washed her perfect body. I paid particular attention to her breasts, using my soft palms instead of the rough loofah on her delicate skin.

As the water washed away the soap, I pressed my mouth to her wet nipples, tasting her as I sucked the water into my mouth. I reached for her shampoo to wash her hair, but she swatted my hand away. Grabbing hold of her hand, I brought it to my lips.

"Please, let me make up for the front door," I whispered against her skin. "I want to worship every inch of you."

Panting with need, and with a quiver racing through her, she gulped and gave a tiny nod in response to my words.

I lathered up the shampoo in my hands before running my fingers through the length of her hair. Being so close to her; touching her so intimately, but yet so innocently, was driving me crazy again. I grew hard again, but I worked to contain myself. Pushing thoughts of claiming her again out of my head, I rinsed the shampoo from her hair and repeated the process with the conditioner. Alyssa moaned as my fingers raked against her scalp and again as they ran down her neck.

After I finished with her hair, I curled my finger under her chin and used it to guide her lips to mine. I kissed her lazily, taking my time to experience the sensation of the moisture on her lips and the difference in her taste under the warm water. My hands explored her body as I kissed my way down her chest once more. I spent some time circling there, nipping and licking the water from her skin.

With her eyes closed and her fingertips tracing through my wet hair, she murmured and muttered desperate pleas for me to take her.

I couldn't . . . not yet. There was something I wanted to do first.

Wrapping my hands around the tops of her thighs, I pushed my face against her stomach, kissing an agonisingly slow trail down to her pussy. I licked my lips in anticipation as I watched small droplets of water from the shower touching her intimately. My tongue slid forward and collected the droplets into my mouth, barely grazing her skin in the process.

The guttural groan from above me was as sweet as an angel's voice. I pushed forward hard with my mouth as I pulled her closer with my hands to taste her. I sucked on her clit, relishing the flavour of the water that cascaded around her. Her hands fisted against my scalp as she leaned back further into the stream. With my tongue, I swirled the water against her clit. She moaned as I stroked her pussy back and forth with the tip of my tongue, lapping up every droplet of water that trailed down her body. When I buried my tongue in her, I glanced up at her. Her eyes closed and she shook slightly in my hold. The sight was phenomenal and I wanted nothing more than to prolong her ecstasy.

Drawing away from her, I twisted her around to sit at the end of the bathtub. "Sit back," I commanded in a whisper. Adjusting the angle of the shower, I let the stream of water rain down on her hips and thighs. She squeezed her legs tightly together. Her breathing came in shallow pants, and shivers raced through her. I knelt in front of her before pressing her knees to the sides of the tub, allowing the warm water from the shower to cascade over her pussy. She dropped her head back, her breath shallowing out further.

"Oh, fuck," she cried.

With tender movements, I brushed my fingers around the tops of her thighs, eliciting a moan. When I pressed my fingers into her again, I worked them slowly, watching with great fucking interest as they slipped in and out of her entrance. My hard-on grew and demanded fresh attention. Desperate for more, I leaned down to press another kiss against her pussy.

"Fucking hell, Alyssa," I said. "I want you."

She shook her head before lifting it so that her eyes met mine. "I—I need you. So bad."

I quickly assessed her current position. She was against the hard tub, her legs spread wide, and the water was starting to cool. It wasn't a great position for some quality loving so I decided I would torture her with just one more move—for her own comfort.

I stood and turned off the shower before stepping out onto the bathroom floor.

She groaned in frustration, the sound drawing a laugh from me. I reached down and helped her up and out of the tub.

"I don't want you getting sick," I said as I wrapped a towel around her shoulders. She started to towel dry herself, but seeing the beads of water resting on her breasts and clinging to her pussy made me want to lick them off myself so I held up my hand to stop her.

"Just dry your hair," I whispered, my voice low and hoarse. "I'll get the rest."

She smiled wickedly at me as she fluffed the towel through her hair. I watched excitedly as one of the beads of water on her shoulder collided with another, growing heavy. My eyes followed it as it made its descent down her body. Lifting my hand, I followed the path with my finger until it reached her thigh.

I grabbed the towel off Alyssa and wrapped it around her back, using it to pull her into the bedroom. She sat down on the edge of the bed, and I gently pushed her to lie down with the towel beneath her. Kneeling in front of her, I collected the remaining droplets of water with my mouth, kissing, licking, and nipping her entire body. She was writhing beneath me before long, begging me repeatedly to take her already.

When I stood, she shuffled higher on the bed so I could lie down with her. I wrapped myself over and around her completely, pinning her to the bed, staring deep into her eyes as I entered her for the second time. A hiss left my lips as I slid into the warmth of her pussy.

Her eyes rolled back as she gave a fuck-sexy cry of relief and ecstasy. I moved with her slowly, unwilling to release her eyes, which were filled with a love and desire that damn near broke my heart.

How had I missed four years of this? I was a fool. A fucking arrogant fool. I was never going to get better than this ... better than *us*.

I kissed her softly on the lips and proclaimed again how much I loved her.

"I'm yours," was all she could mumble in response before her body clenched tightly beneath me. She cried out loudly again as she came hard. I continued to move so she could ride out her orgasm, but then I stilled. I wanted to remain in the moment forever.

I rose up onto my elbows and brushed her hair off her face. The depth of the emotions she'd shown as I'd taken her had burned through my lust and left the raw, exposed edges of my soul showing.

"I am so fucking sorry for everything I did to us," I whispered as I brushed my hand through her hair. My voice cracked as I spoke.

She raised her hand to my face and wiped away a tear I didn't even realise had fallen.

"I can't say it's okay, because we both know it's not. I've been to hell and back, Dec." Her own tears started to fall. "But I forgive you. I love you."

I dropped my head to her chest so she wouldn't see the tears that were now falling in earnest. Her heart thundered against my cheek, a reminder that she was there. It wasn't too late to change. To fix things. The understanding that washed through me at the thought was overwhelming. A sob overtook my body, followed by another. I clung to Alyssa's shoulders tightly as I sobbed against her chest. I never wanted to fucking let go again. I never would.

I HAD no idea how long I had clung to Alyssa before finally

succumbing to sleep, but obviously at some point I had. Morning light streamed into the bedroom, I was lying on my back and her hand ran through my hair as I came to my senses. I lifted my hand, snagging hers and bringing it to my lips. She gasped at my sudden movement, and I smiled with her fingers still pressed to my mouth.

Raising my eyes, I glanced at my fucking beautiful angel. She was on her side, with her head propped up by her other arm. I released my hold on her hand, and it resumed its strokes through my hair.

"Good morning, gorgeous," I said.

"Morning." She offered a small smile before tucking herself into my side and resting her head on my shoulder. "I still can't believe you're here, like this."

I held her tightly. "Believe it, because I'm not going anywhere, Lys. Not unless you send me away."

"What about my family?"

For a moment, her words concerned me, but then I understood the one thing that might win them back to my side. I curled my finger under her chin and raised it so she could look at my face and see how serious I was. "Do they want you to be happy?"

She nodded. "Of course they do."

"Well, do I make you happy?"

She smiled and it was so blistering and filled with genuine happiness that I'd want to kick my own ass if I ever made her lose it again.

I lifted my head and kissed her softly. "Then we'll work it out."

"I don't know how you can have such blinding optimism after the week you've had," she said.

"I guess it's just easy to be optimistic when I've got a fuck-hot woman in my arms."

She slapped my chest lightly. "And here I thought we were having a moment of honesty."

"I am being honest." I stroked my hand lightly up and down her side. "Are we really going to do it today?" I murmured, silently praying Alyssa knew what I meant without me having to say the words out loud.

She was quiet for a while, making me wonder if perhaps she hadn't understood. Just when I was about to clarify, she spoke. "It's up to you. I just don't want to tell her anything if you are going to disappear again."

"I've told you—"

She pressed her fingers to my lips to stop me from repeating what I'd said so many times since I'd started trying to win her back. "I know," she said. "And *mostly* I believe you. It's just—" She sighed. "—I guess history has taught me to be on guard."

"I know, Lys. I told you last night though, I'm sorry for all the shit I've done. Here's the thing though, my life hasn't been all roses and sunshine. I know it's nothing compared with what you've had to deal with, but I don't want to go back to it. At the time, I guess I thought I was doing okay, but I wasn't. I couldn't sleep, had nightmares most nights, and took copious amounts of sleeping tablets just to be able to function. I had panic attacks that I had to keep hidden from everyone or risk my job. Now, having you in my arms like this . . . sleeping like I did last night . . . it just makes me see how bad I really let things get."

She planted a soft kiss on my chest. "Let's not get into the past now. You've got something planned for us for today, right? Let's just go pick up Phoebe and get this show on the road."

I smiled and nodded. "Sounds good, although . . ." I trailed off deliberately.

"Although what?" she asked, the corners of her eyes pinching together with suspicion.

I rolled myself onto my side before pushing her over onto her back and climbing between her legs, resting my pelvis against hers. "Although I can think of something I wouldn't mind doing before going."

She grinned at me. "Yeah? And what's that?"

"You." I captured her lips as my hands began to wander.

A LITTLE over an hour later, we pulled up in front of Mum's house.

The kamikaze dive-bombing butterflies were back in my stomach as I thought about what the day would bring. To Phoebe, I would start the day as Mummy's friend, but I would finish it as her daddy.

Just thinking the word brought a lump to my throat. I didn't know how we were going to tell her. Didn't really know if we even should so soon. But I wanted to do it. I wanted her to know, even though it scared the shit out of me.

Alyssa and I had discussed it while we'd showered and dressed. We discussed it again in the car on the way from Alyssa's house. Still, we were no closer to a decision. Instead, we agreed to simply wing it. To tell her together when we both thought the moment was right.

When we entered the house Phoebe practically launched herself into Alyssa's arms with a squealed, "Mummy!"

I held my breath as I watched their interactions. It damn near made my heart explode. I felt breathless and anxious, but I wasn't having a panic attack. At least, not yet. I had to stop myself from wrapping them both up in a group hug, choosing to walk over to Mum instead.

"Did you two have fun yesterday?" I asked.

Mum nodded. "How was your date?"

"It was fucking awesome, Mum." I beamed. I saw Alyssa give me the evil eye when I said "fucking." Shit, I'd have to watch my language.

"I need to talk to you before you go," Mum said, wringing her hands together.

She turned toward the bedrooms, obviously wanting some privacy, which had the butterflies in my stomach kicking up their aerial acrobatics another notch. What could be so bad she didn't want to say it in front of Alyssa? Or was it about her? I began to picture all the worst-case scenarios. The optimism Alyssa had accused me of having that morning seeped away as I followed Mum.

She walked into my room and shut the door behind us.

"You and Alyssa," she prompted. "You seem to be getting back on track."

I nodded, not willing to attempt to speak through the emotion and fear constricting my throat.

"I mean, I know you've got a long way to go, but she's there for you, right?"

"I guess," I squeezed out. "At least, I think so. I hope so."

Mum sighed and seemed relieved. I felt the anxiety slip away a little. It couldn't have been anything bad to do with Alyssa and me if Mum was relieved we seemed okay . . . . could it?

"I've decided . . .," she started, but trailed off.

"What is it, Mum? Tell me?" I spoke as softly as I could, trying to coax her around whatever nerves she was feeling.

"I'm leaving your father." The words fell out in a tumble and seemed to take the last of her strength. She sat on the edge of my bed and stared into space.

Without thought, I sat next to her. It was probably a strange reaction, but I was happy for her. No, I was more than happy. I was fuck-arse thrilled for her. She needed to get away from that prick for her own confidence and sanity. More than that, she needed to burn him for everything he had. While I ran through the thoughts, I decided I'd have to talk to Alyssa to see if she knew any good divorce lawyers. No, not good ones—great ones. Ones that would take everything Dad owned except the shirt off his back, and maybe even that. I would cover the retainer if I had to. I didn't care. It wasn't about the money. It was about ensuring that bastard got what was coming to him for lying to me for so long.

"That's great, Mum," I said as softly as I could manage. I could see the look of devastation on her face, and realised that me whooping it up in celebration probably wasn't such a good idea. At least, not for the moment. "If you need anything—anything at all—I'm here for you."

She shook her head slightly and looked up at me, as if she'd forgotten I was there. "I was actually thinking of going away for a while. Far away."

"Where?"

She shrugged. "Anywhere. I've just taken everything out of the savings account. That should keep me going for a while. I was thinking maybe London to start."

"That's sounds good," I said. A smile lit my face. "It worked fucking wonders for me."

"You're not upset?" She sounded surprised.

"Why the fuck would I be upset?"

"Because I'm breaking up our family."

"No, Mum, you're not. That arsewipe broke up this family long ago when he began cheating on you." *Plus insulting and spying on Alyssa*, I added mentally. I still owed him an arse whooping over that. I wondered if he understood that he'd be better off staying as far from me as possible while I was still in Brisbane. Just the thought of him being in that bathroom with Alyssa made my hands curl into tight fists that longed to connect with something.

"Declan, please don't—" She was going to defend him.

I cut her off with an incredulous glare. "Look, Mum, I'm happy you're leaving him. Ecstatic even, because he is a fucktard of a human being. He seriously needs to get a personality realignment or something. Until then, he can go to hell."

"I don't want to cause problems between you and your father."

"*You* aren't. Any problems are of his own doing."

She shook her head. "Declan—"

"I don't want to talk about it anymore," I cut her off. It was clear that arguing with her wasn't going to help either of us. "I think it's great you're going away. Do this for yourself. Alyssa and I will be fine without you. Like you said, we're heading down the right track at least. You need to be selfish for a while. So book your fucking ticket and go."

"It's booked," she whispered.

"Excellent. When do you leave?"

"Wednesday week."

Fuck! I looked around the room in a blind panic, trying to calm myself. If Mum left a week from Wednesday, that meant I only had a week and a half of accommodation in Brisbane. I couldn't stay with Dad on my own. I'd beat the living shit out of him on the first day.

I shuddered as I considered whether he'd use the opportunity to move Hayley, his little tramp, into our family home. Would Mum want to leave the house sooner? I wondered for a second if Alyssa would let me stay with her, but it was too early for that still. As much as I slept better when she was beside me, it wasn't fair to Phoebe to tell her I was her daddy and then force myself into her life and into her house within a week.

"Have you talked to Dad?" I asked, tentatively.

"Not yet. I'm going to tell him not to bother coming home though. He's got an apartment near the city he doesn't think I know about. He can stay there."

I nodded, breathing a sigh of relief for myself. "Is that where *she* lives?"

Mum nodded sadly and wiped an errant tear from her face. "But I'm ruining your day here." She plastered on a fake smile. "I'll be all right. You go have fun with your two beautiful girls."

I pulled her into a hug. "You don't want to come with us?"

She shook her head. "No, I want you and Alyssa to have some alone time. Lord knows you need it. And you need to bond with that precious little thing, Declan. Don't make the same mistakes your father did."

"I won't." I couldn't. Whenever I thought of Phoebe, I felt nothing but regret for how much time I'd already lost. Fatherhood might not have been the plan, but I wasn't going to shirk away from it—from her—now that it had found me.

I stood, helped Mum to her feet, and then gave her shoulders a quick squeeze.

Alyssa turned to me with a confused expression when I came back into the living room.

"You okay?" she mouthed.

I smiled and nodded. I was about to spend the day with the two most precious things to me.

Who wouldn't be okay?

CHAPTER NINETEEN

WIGGLE ROOM

ANXIOUS TO GET the day underway, I helped Alyssa load Phoebe and her gear into the car. When I got the car on the road, my hands shook and my mouth was dry.

Glancing in the rear-view mirror as Phoebe wiggled in her car seat to the music on the radio, I wondered whether it was possible I was actually more anxious to get the white elephant out in the open than the events of the day. Each time I looked at her, my heartbeat ramped up a notch, and I grew more terrified of her possible reaction to the news. The truth was, she didn't know me. Hell, *I* barely knew me anymore. The concerns I had over telling her the truth raced around my head as if running laps on a track.

How could I force myself into her life so fast? How were we even going to begin to tell her? Would she even understand when we did tell her? Would the word "daddy" mean anything to her?

The question brought to mind the afternoon I'd spent in the park with her and Alyssa. From what I recalled of that day, it was clear she would absolutely understand. She would know what the word meant, at least in the broader sense. Which meant she would either accept what we told her, or reject me outright. Either way, there was not a damn fucking thing I could do about it.

My heart could be crushed under the heel of a three-year-old's boot. What would I do if she said she didn't want me to be her daddy?

From across the car, Alyssa's hand reached for mine, snapping me from my thoughts. She must've sensed my blind panic creeping up. Taking my hand in hers, she gave it a light squeeze. It was her silent way of letting me know she was there for me. With her touch, the fear dissipated. The anxiety still ran as an undercurrent through me, but the suffocating terror disappeared. I gave her a small smile of thanks before turning back to the road.

"Where are you taking us anyway?" Alyssa asked. I still hadn't told her exactly where we were going, even though she'd insisted I needed to let her know the details so she could pack Phoebe's bag. All I'd told her was that we were going to be out for the whole day.

"You'll see." I kept my eyes trained on the road. The truth was at that point, I had so many conflicting emotions and thoughts in my head that it wouldn't take much for her to get the answer from me. She'd find out soon enough anyway. We were already over halfway to the Gold Coast and about ten minutes from my planned destination.

I hoped to give Phoebe the best day out I possibly could, and the theme parks in Queensland were world renowned. I had done a little research to find out the best one for kids under four, and all fingers pointed to Dreamworld or Sea World. I didn't want to spend the entire fucking day watching sea animals doing stupid tricks, so that left Dreamworld. The moment I took the Coomera exit off the highway, Alyssa knew our destination.

"Dreamworld, Dec? Really?"

"I figured you two deserve a fu—" I caught myself just in time. "—treat."

"But this is too much. I haven't brought any food or anything with us. It'll cost a fortune. I—I can't afford it." She almost seemed ashamed.

I frowned. The last thing I'd intended to do was make her feel inadequate. She also didn't seem to understand one fundamental aspect. "It's my shout."

"No, I can't expect you to pay, it's too much. Have you seen—"

I put my finger on her lips to cut her off. "I said my shout. Now, we're going there, no arguments, and no worrying about what anything costs."

She regarded me for a minute.

"Please?" I asked. "I'm sure Phoebe will love Wiggles World."

Phoebe squealed and jumped around at the mention of the W word, and Alyssa was caught. It was a dirty trick on my part, but I didn't care. Not if it got me what I wanted.

"Fine."

With a victorious grin, I climbed out of the car.

It wasn't until I reached the queue to get in that I discovered my mistake. I'd been so focused on Alyssa, and on Phoebe, that I hadn't grabbed my usual coverings. Without a hat and sunnies, my trademark auburn hair and turquoise eyes drew the attention of everyone around. Almost instantly, I was plagued by people wanting my autograph. I wanted to tell them all to fuck off, that I was trying to have a day with my daughter, but I couldn't. I was stuck between looking like an arse if I said yes and looking like a prick if I said no. Instead, I stood and signed everything that was pressed in front of my face. In the end Alyssa came to my side, brandishing the entry tickets.

"You didn't have to do that," I said. Then I dropped my voice, "I'm sorry, I've ruined it already—haven't I?" I ruined everything just by being Declan fucking Reede.

She shook her head. "It's not your fault. Besides, look how happy you've made them."

She indicated a family nearby. One of the men who'd got me to sign something passed it to his young son. At a guess, I would have said the boy was nine or ten, fucked if I knew for sure, but the smile on his face as he looked at the grubby pen mark I'd left on his hat was mind-boggling. It actually meant something to him.

Watching the look of rapture on the little boy's face, I was awed, and more than a little humbled. I'd honestly never really paid much attention to the aftermath of an autograph frenzy. Usually, I was always more concerned with the cramp in my hand and the time I'd wasted. Trust Alyssa to notice the smaller, but infinitely more important, things like the look on one little boy's face. I wrapped one arm around her waist and kissed the top of her head.

"Thank you," I murmured into her hair.

"For what?" she asked, clearly bemused.

"For being you."

She smiled and dropped her head onto my shoulder.

After enjoying the hold for a moment, I clapped my hands. "Let's get this show on the road."

We walked through the entry gates, and I watched as Phoebe's face lit up in excitement when she saw the fountain in the middle of the entrance. I didn't get what the big deal was, it was just a fucking fountain, but the way her face exploded into a smile was just perfect. My own enthusiasm took over in response to the sight.

I crouched down in front of her. "Where would you like to go first, Phoebe? ABC Kids World or to see the animals?"

"Umm . . ." She looked around at the signs; the pure choice was obviously overwhelming.

"You've got tigers or the Wiggles and Giggle and Hoot."

"Wiggles and Hoot." She jumped a little as she spoke.

"Wiggles it is, because today, little miss, *you* are in charge."

I stood and looked around to figure out which way we needed to go. I pointed in the right direction. "Thataway."

Phoebe ran off excitedly. Linking hands with Alyssa, we followed closely behind. I wondered if Alyssa understood just how nervous I still was. She seemed to be letting me take charge and control the situation though, and for that I was thankful. I felt like I was being given the opportunity to bond with my little princess. Or maybe I was being monitored to see whether telling Phoebe was a bad idea.

When Phoebe came to a dead stop upon seeing the entry into ABC Kids World, I couldn't help but chuckle. She turned to Alyssa, with eyes as wide as saucers. She was just too fucking cute.

Alyssa nodded but hung back, as if waiting for me to step up.

When she caught my glance, she nodded slightly in Phoebe's direction. My heart was in my throat as I crouched in front of Phoebe again.

"What do you think?" I asked her.

"Hoy there, hearty," she said, moving her arm across her chest. Alyssa laughed, and I looked at them both like they'd gone nuts. In fact, I was sure they both had.

"It's what Captain Feathersword says," Alyssa explained. It still meant shit to me, but they both seemed to be enjoying the laugh they were having. I wasn't about to spoil it by asking who the fuck Captain Feathersword was supposed to be. "That's his boat behind you."

I turned and there was a bright green-and-red cartoon-like pirate ship. Phoebe danced around, hopping from one leg to the other.

"Did you want to go look?" I asked.

She smiled brightly and nodded. "Yes, please."

I held out my hand, and she took hold of my pinky without question before running off in the direction of the boat. Walking quickly to keep up with her, I let her drag me along everywhere she wanted to go.

Even though there wasn't much for me to see in the area I didn't care. Phoebe bounded from one end of the ship to the other before stopping at a porthole. Even standing on tiptoe, she was just a little too short to look out of it. I knelt next to her and let her stand on my leg to get the extra height. I saw a flash out of the corner of my eye and glanced in that direction. Alyssa was standing with a smile on her face and a camera in her hand.

"Sorry," she said. "I couldn't resist a photo op like that."

I just smirked at her. The day would be full of shit I wouldn't dream of doing on my own—kiddie rides and boring animals—but I knew I would endure every minute of it to keep the smiles fixed firmly on my girls' faces.

"Declan—look." Phoebe tugged on my shirt collar and pointed in the direction of a man in an over-the-top pirate costume. He had black pants and boots, a puffy white pirate shirt, and a red-and-gold vest. In his hand he clutched a massive purple-and-pink feather. On his head he wore a pirate hat with a matching feather. I couldn't stifle the chuckle this time. Phoebe raced off toward him, dragging me along behind her.

Alyssa skipped up to my side. "*That's* Captain Feathersword," she whispered with a chuckle.

"Ahoy there, me hearties!" he exclaimed as we closed in on him. He crossed his hand, and "feathersword," in front of his chest. Phoebe's little action suddenly made perfect sense; obviously it was some sort of catchphrase.

As I drew closer, I saw a gleam of recognition in his eye. He knew who I was so I figured he couldn't have been all bad. Kneeling down, he started talking to Phoebe and in an instant had her eating out of the palm of his hand. He was damned good at his job.

I saw the camera flash a couple of times before Alyssa called, "Group photo."

Fuck me dead. I could only imagine the damage photos of me next to a children's entertainer might do to my career. When I saw how excited Phoebe was though, I sighed and manned up. I crouched on one side of Phoebe, while the good Captain took the other.

Alyssa took five or six damn photos before finally declaring she had a perfect one. To his credit, the poor sucker in the costume didn't complain about the time Alyssa had taken, even though he had other kids practically clamouring to talk to him. Once she had the photo, he stood and whispered something to Alyssa; she giggled and nodded. Then she passed him a pen and paper. He handed it back a second later. Alyssa smiled at him again. I was beginning to wonder if I needed to kick some pirate booty.

Alyssa was back with us less than a second later.

"What was that about?" I asked, unable to completely remove the suspicious edge to my voice.

"He wants a copy of the photo." She giggled again. "Apparently he's a fan."

I watched as he was mobbed by another family.

Two hours later, after going on every slow and child-friendly ride in the area, we headed on to the animals. I managed to convince Alyssa and Phoebe to go to the tigers at Tiger Island first. At least they were *proper* animals. Their strength and agility made for more interesting viewing than some damn ball of fluff stuck to a tree. When we got in front of the glass overlooking the enclosure, I lifted Phoebe on my shoulders for a better view. We watched as the keepers played with the tigers. I could have paid a little extra to get us in there with them, but there was no way in hell I was going to let my daughter near something that dangerous and I didn't want to spend time away from them either.

Over the next few hours, we covered most of the park, except the extreme rides that I would have done if I'd been there with anyone else. Listening to the screams and shouts of amusement coming from them, I actually felt a pang of jealousy. The Tower of Terror was a near-constant rush of noise during the day as it zipped back and forth along its track, while we puttered underneath it on the steam train or walked alongside it on our way back to the kids' rides. Alyssa took photos at every possible opportunity. It was almost as if she thought she'd never get the opportunity again. Perhaps she did. It was clear that at least some part of her still didn't believe me when I said I wasn't going.

At least once an hour, someone new hounded me for an autograph. Each time Alyssa just patiently waited off to the side for me to finish up, and then she and Phoebe would come back to my side. When Phoebe complained of being hungry, we found somewhere that served chicken nuggets for her.

During the day we had our photos taken with an array of people in odd-looking costumes and took up every photo opportunity on every ride. We finally got to go on something halfway decent by going on the log ride. Phoebe giggled the whole time, and in the official photo, snapped on the way down, she wore a smile I would treasure forever.

It was barely two o'clock, still hours before the park closed, when Alyssa told me it was time to head home. Phoebe was getting tired, or so Alyssa said. All I knew was Phoebe was getting louder, crankier, and clumsier. She'd tripped over her own feet no less than ten times in fifteen minutes. Each time, she'd been able to collect herself relatively quickly and with no tears.

While we prepared to leave, Alyssa ducked into the ladies' room, leaving Phoebe outside with me. I watched as Phoebe ran loops around one of the direction signs. On one loop, she tripped and went sprawling across the ground. She landed in a heap with a scream ready on her lips.

I didn't know if she'd done any major damage, but my first instinct was to run over to her and scoop her into my arms. Even as I comforted her, she screamed for Alyssa.

"Shh," I whispered as I rocked her gently against my chest. "Daddy's got you. You're all right."

It was only when I heard a soft gasp behind me that I realised what I'd said. Spinning on the spot, I passed Phoebe to Alyssa. I paced away from them, running my fingers through my hair. It wasn't how I'd wanted to do the big reveal. Blowing out a breath, I turned back toward the pair.

Phoebe had her face buried against Alyssa's neck and nothing more was mentioned about the D word. Either she hadn't heard what I'd let slip, or hadn't understood the significance of it. I wasn't sure if I was relieved or not. Alyssa smiled at me, reassuring me that she wasn't upset. I was over beside them both in a flash, my hand resting on the base of Alyssa's spine. I pressed my lips to her hair. "Let's go home, hey?"

"Sounds good," she responded.

"But first . . . we have to get an ice cream."

Phoebe lifted her head off Alyssa's shoulder and grinned at me through her tears.

We headed back to the main gate, stopping to pick up a copy of every official photo we'd had taken throughout the day. It cost a fuckload of money, but was worth every single cent for the permanent reminders of the log ride, the river rapids, and the big red car.

Once we'd finished there, I led the two of them to the ice-cream parlour near the exit.

"What's your favourite flavour?" I asked Phoebe.

"Umm, pink."

I raised an eyebrow and Alyssa smirked.

"Pinks not a flavour," I whispered conspiratorially to Phoebe.

"Pink! See," Phoebe said, pointing to the strawberry ice cream with a victorious grin.

I sighed in defeat. "Fine. Pink it is."

"I'll have the usual," Alyssa said, and I wondered if it was a test to see if I remembered.

As if I'd forget her favourite ice cream. I ordered two strawberry ice creams and one hokey pokey, all smothered in chocolate fudge but no cream.

"You remembered," Alyssa said as I handed her the hokey pokey. Despite her words, her voice was clear of surprise and brimming with confidence. It felt like she trusted my promises more with every passing hour. I wasn't going anywhere, and she was finally starting to understand that.

I twisted a loose strand of hair back into her ponytail. "How could I forget?" I asked.

Alyssa chuckled, no doubt as the memories returned. When we were twelve, she'd gone on a skiing holiday to Queenstown in New Zealand with her parents and Josh.

When they'd arrived back in Australia, Alyssa had raved non-stop for three months about hokey pokey ice cream, chocolate fish, and some drink called L&P.

For Christmas, I'd forced Mum to hunt around so many different stores trying to find that shit just for Alyssa. In the end, we'd paid a small fortune to get them from a specialty ice-cream parlour in the city. Now, just ten years later, it was everywhere.

"You'll have to come to New Zealand with the team when we race in Hamilton next year," I said to her. "You'll be able to get the proper stuff, direct from the source."

She nodded but didn't say anything. Her confidence from moments earlier seemed to falter. The hesitation was still there. I wondered what I could possibly do to try to convince her I wasn't ever leaving. A ringing on my mobile pulled me back to the present.

Because I didn't recognise the number, I answered it hesitantly. As soon as the caller spoke though, I recognised Ben's chipper tones. I walked from the table so that Alyssa and Phoebe didn't have to listen to my conversation.

"Hey, man," I said enthusiastically. "It's great to hear from you."

He chuckled. "To be honest, I wasn't sure whether or not you were serious about me calling you. Jade pushed me to do it."

"I'm glad you called, we have to arrange that catch-up. Maybe you can bring Jade and the kids 'round one day. I'll have to double-check when's good with Alyssa though."

"No problem. Just let me know the details."

"Cool, man." I wanted to hang on the line and talk to him some more, but I was growing desperate to get back to Phoebe and Alyssa. As I hung up I heard a bit of a whispered conversation. Alyssa was smiling, but looked nervous as hell. I wondered what had changed in the last few minutes.

"Really?" Phoebe asked Alyssa in a whisper. Then she looked over to me—her eyes were as wide as they had been when she'd seen the Wiggles sign. It was like all her fucking Christmases had come at once.

"What's up?" I asked, but neither of them would answer. "Fine . . . keep your secrets," I said, then instantly regretted it as Alyssa's face fell.

"Declan, I—"

I cut her off. "Don't worry. It was a stupid thing for me to say." Something I seriously needed to wipe from my lexicon. "Are you guys ready to go?"

Alyssa and Phoebe both nodded.

Scooping Phoebe up onto my shoulders, I carried her out to the car that way. Alyssa walked beside me with her hand resting on my back. We felt like a family, even if we hadn't yet told Phoebe exactly who I was. Instead of handing the task over to Alyssa, I put Phoebe in her car seat. I'd watched Alyssa enough that I finally had it worked out . . . mostly.

"Did you have a good day today?" I asked Phoebe.

She nodded and beamed. Her smile was so wide it had to have hurt.

"Declan," she said, before pausing to regard me for a second. Finally, she learned forward and whispered, "You're a good daddy."

My heart skipped a beat.

CHAPTER TWENTY

INNOCENT TRUTH

"YOU'RE A GOOD daddy." The four words ran on repeat through my mind. Seconds had passed since Phoebe had uttered them, and yet it felt like centuries as I tried to figure out how to react. When my brain didn't respond fast enough, my body took over. My face had broken into a smile to match hers. Then I leaned forward and planted a tender kiss on her forehead. "I'm glad you had a good day."

I backed out of the car and saw Alyssa watching our interaction intently. She had the ends of her hair twirled around her fingers. I reached out to still her actions.

"Well . . .," I started, my heart still hammering in my chest, my smile cemented on my face. "That was unexpected."

Even though I'd said the words when she'd fallen, the delay in her response had thrown me.

"She's very observant."

"She takes after her mother then," I whispered.

When I climbed behind the wheel, the silence in the car was absolute. My own thoughts were centred on Phoebe's words. Alyssa stared out the window, her mouth smiling, but her eyes filled with concern. I wondered whether she still doubted whether I'd stay. In the backseat, Phoebe passed out before we even hit the highway.

"Is she all right?" I asked, concerned, as I glanced in the rear-view mirror, watching her little head resting against the side of the car seat. Her head rested at such an odd angle it looked like it must hurt.

"She's fine. It's just been a long day for her," Alyssa replied.

"And for you?" I asked, hoping desperately that I hadn't fucked anything up with my slip or with my choice of destination.

Alyssa continued to look out the window for a few more seconds before turning back to me. "It's been a long weekend."

"And?"

"And I'm ready to go home and climb into bed."

I wondered if it was an invitation. If so, I would be there with bells on.

Or nothing on.

"But I think we need to talk to Phoebe first," she continued. "I want to make sure she really understands."

I nodded. "What do we say?"

"I think we tell her the truth."

"Which is?" I asked, terrified of what Alyssa would have me say—and whether it might change Phoebe's opinion of me.

"That her daddy made a mistake and wants to make up for it. That's about right isn't it?"

"It's an oversimplification, but it just about sums it up, I guess."

Alyssa laughed. "Declan, she's three. She doesn't need complicated. All she needs to know is whether you will be there for her."

"Always," I said without hesitation.

"Then there's nothing to worry about, is there?"

I shook my head. "I guess not, it's just . . . I worry about, when she gets older, you know."

She gazed at me questioningly.

"Well, if she finds out more about what happened when she's older . . . will she hate me?"

"I don't think she'll hate you."

"How do you know?" I asked, my stomach twisting into knots at the thought.

"How did you feel when you found out about Phoebe? Specifically about the fact Kelly knew?"

I couldn't figure out the best way to answer her. Mostly because I didn't know what she wanted to hear. In the end, I settled for the truth. "I was fucking pissed off," I whispered.

"Did you hate her?"

"What?" I was thrown by the question. "No, of course not. I was annoyed, but I could never hate her . . . she's my Mum."

Alyssa quirked her eyebrow at me. "Exactly. It's hard to hate your parents. The love is unconditional."

"I hate my father," I seethed.

Alyssa suddenly found her hands very interesting. "You might be angry with him, but I doubt that you hate him . . ."

"But?" I asked. I could sense the 'but' a mile off.

"Well . . . he's done some pretty horrible stuff, and he's hurt people you love. Plus, he knew he was hurting people when he did it, but he did it anyway."

"I knew I was hurting *you* when I left." I rubbed madly at my face, trying to wipe away the tears that were pooling in my eyes and obstructing my vision. I tightened my grip on the steering wheel and clenched my teeth to stop the flow. "I mean, I never imagined . . ."

She caught my hand in hers. "I know."

I pulled my hand free and stroked her cheek. "I love you. So much," I croaked.

"I love you too." She leaned into my hand. I could feel the warmth radiating off her and desperately wanted to get her home. I needed to hold her in my arms and wrap her in my embrace. She controlled my sanity; all it took was a word, or a touch, from her and my thoughts would calm. I owed her more than she would ever know, and I would spend the rest of my life making up for everything I'd done.

We fell into a comfortable silence as I drove us back. All the while four little words ran on repeat through my head. *"You're a good daddy."*

Phoebe woke just as we stopped. There were a few minutes of awkward silence as the car was unloaded and we headed inside.

"I'm just going to put some dinner on," Alyssa announced. "Phoebe, why don't you go get a book that Declan can read to you while you wait."

Phoebe shook her head and grabbed my hand. "Come to my room, I'll show you my toys."

I shot Alyssa a quick look of concern. Entertaining Phoebe at Dreamworld was one thing—being alone with her on her turf was something else entirely.

"Go on," Alyssa said. "I'll be down once this is on."

I nodded, before gulping down on a lungful of air. The unspoken words "and we can talk to her" hung between us.

Phoebe pulled on my hand and led me into her room. I spent the next half hour being shown every doll, teddy bear, puzzle, and book she owned.

"You've got lots of cool stuff," I told her. I was sitting cross-legged in the middle of her floor with my back to the door. "What's your favourite?"

"That depends on the day," Alyssa announced from behind me. She walked over and sat on Phoebe's bed. She patted the pink comforter in invitation, and Phoebe ran over to sit beside her.

My heart began to pound, knowing what was about to happen. Something shifted in the atmosphere of the room as a quiet tension seemed to settle over everyone.

"Sweetie, you know how Mummy always told you that your daddy wasn't around, but that he loved you, wherever he was, and nothing could change that?"

I closed my eyes and clenched my teeth. Alyssa could have easily spent the last three years telling Phoebe her dad was a fucking arsehole who needed his head read; she wouldn't have been lying. Yet, even through her darkest time—even after I'd fucking abandoned her—she'd been kind when speaking to Phoebe about me. It might have been more for our daughter's sake than mine, but I was still touched.

When I opened my eyes, Phoebe was looking at me. Her gaze seemed to reach right down to my soul. Alyssa inclined her head in Phoebe's direction, silently instructing me to take over. She wanted me to be the one to say the actual words. I knew I already had earlier, but that had been some weird instinct to soothe a crying child. Now it was just so fucking difficult to find the right thing to say. How did you even broach the subject? Should I just come out and say, "I'm your daddy, and I'm a fucking idiot for ever leaving your mummy?"

I opened my mouth to speak, but closed it again and took a deep breath. My eyes were prickling so I closed them.

"I'm sorry," I whispered finally. "I . . ." I was going to say I couldn't find the words to make it right; that I didn't know what to say. Even at this simple task, I failed.

A tiny set of arms wrapped around my shoulders, and I felt Phoebe's hair against my cheek. I wrapped her in an embrace and tried to force back the tears. I couldn't even open my eyes for fear the traitorous tears would escape.

"I'm sorry I wasn't there for you, Phoebe, but your mummy is right. Your daddy loves you. I—I'd do anything for you." The last part of my sentence was so choked that I didn't know if she understood or not, but I didn't care; saying the words out loud to her was a hundred times better than any therapy session.

"Can I say a question?" Phoebe asked and I finally grew brave enough to look at her. Her green-blue eyes, near perfect replicas of mine, were clear and untroubled. She wore a small smile. "Can you be my daddy for always?"

I choked back the lump in my throat and looked away from her captivating eyes. It was only then that I saw Alyssa was gone. I didn't know at what stage she had left, or why. I reached my hand out to stroke Phoebe's cheek gently as I nodded. "Forever and always, baby. I'm never going to leave you again."

Phoebe gave a little jump with a double-handed fist pump. "Yay!"

I smiled through the threatening tears and a chuckle left my lips. "Why don't we go see what Mummy is doing?"

She nodded sweetly at me and walked from the room. I sat on the floor a second longer, trying to gather myself. My heart was thumping and my stomach twisting, but I'd done it. I knew without a doubt that Phoebe understood who I was and what that meant. She accepted it. Fuck, she even seemed to be excited about it.

After a few more breaths to let the fact that I was on my way to becoming a card-carrying member of the father brigade settle over me, I picked myself up from the floor and wandered out to find Alyssa and Phoebe.

They were both in the kitchen when I found them. Alyssa stood at the bench and Phoebe had climbed onto a little stool behind her, watching as she worked her magic. Alyssa's breathing was a little erratic and a moment later, she lifted her hand and swiped her cheek. Obviously hearing me approach, she turned around to smile at me. The remnants of tears wet her lashes. I walked up to her and wrapped my arms around her waist from behind.

"Dinner smells good," I said out loud. Then I whispered in her ear, too quietly for Phoebe to hear, "Thank you."

She nodded. "It'll just be a few minutes. Phoebe, did you want to show Declan where everything is so that you guys can set the table?"

"Daddy," Phoebe corrected Alyssa, her voice was full of awe. I couldn't imagine her being more excited, even if she'd woken on Christmas morning to see Santa himself delivering her presents.

"Of course," Alyssa said, her voice strained and filled with emotion. Despite how well Phoebe was taking it, I could tell it'd been a long-arse day for Alyssa. It'd been a fucking long day for me too. "Can you show *Daddy* where to find the plates?" She rested her hands against the counter and ducked her head down a little before drawing a couple of short, quick breaths.

Had my conversation with Phoebe upset her?

Maybe she regretted the decision to let Phoebe know. I wanted to reassure her once more that I wasn't leaving, but Phoebe was practically shouting at me in order to get my attention.

Dinner was a fairly quiet affair for Alyssa and me, but Phoebe kept up a near-constant stream of chatter to fill the silence. She told me all about her friends at day care and about her Nana, Pop, Aunt Ruby, and Uncle Josh, letting me know she couldn't wait to tell them that she had a daddy now. During that part of her speech, I could have sworn I saw Alyssa wipe more tears away. Under the table, I rested my hand on her thigh to give her what comfort I could. She startled a little at the contact but didn't pull away so I figured she wasn't too upset with me.

It must have been overwhelming for her. I was fucking overwhelmed too.

We spent the rest of the evening just hanging out on the couch. We watched some TV and movies, and generally avoided any extra talk about the D word. I didn't approach Alyssa to find out whether she had any regrets about the day or the decision. That conversation could wait until after Phoebe was asleep.

When it came time for Phoebe's bath, I waited on the couch while Alyssa handled it. I might have signed up for the name and the responsibility, but I wasn't up for doing any of that shit just yet.

When they were finished, Alyssa called out to me from Phoebe's room. I wandered down but stopped short in the doorway when I saw Alyssa reading a story to Phoebe. Even though I'd known that Alyssa was a mother for weeks, even though I'd interacted with her with Phoebe, it wasn't until that moment that I truly saw how much of herself Alyssa gave. How much love she had to give. It made my heart weep for the time I'd lost. What would it have been like in the early days of Phoebe's life? I had no fucking clue what babies did, or what looking after one involved, but I somehow just knew Alyssa would have been a natural mother even while she was dealing with her own heartache.

I was lost in thought when Alyssa used a nod and soft touch to my hand to call me out of Phoebe's room. She led me into her bedroom and half-closed the door. Without a word, she closed her eyes and leaned back against one of the walls. A long sigh escaped her perfect lips, breaking the silence that surrounded us.

Following her, I pressed my body against hers, leaning my hands on the wall on either side of her head for support.

"Are you okay?" I asked in a whisper.

She nodded and gave me a small smile. "It's funny, you know, part of me never thought this day would come. But the other part? God, I've been hoping, wishing, and praying for this for so long, but kind of dreading it all at the same time. It just," her voice dropped to a whisper, "changes everything."

To offer her what comfort I could, I ran one hand along her cheekbone. Then I moved closer to her, so that my lips almost brushed against hers. I could feel the warmth of her body pressed against me.

"I know," I murmured. "I get it. But it's for the better, yeah?"

She nodded. "Yeah. At least, I hope so."

I closed the space between us. Her mouth was warm and inviting as I moved my tongue inside. She moaned against me, and I felt the wetness of fresh tears fall against the hand that still cupped her face.

"You are happy though, aren't you?" I asked as I pulled away, terrified of the answer.

"Yeah, I am. It's just so much to deal with."

"I know." Jesus fucking Christ did I know. Taking in Alyssa's obvious stress, I decided to do the one thing I absolutely didn't want to do. "Look, it's been a long day for everyone. I think we just need some space tonight, and I need some fresh clothes anyway. Maybe I should go back to Mum's now." I rested my forehead against hers.

Her arms lifted around my waist, holding me to her. "You're probably right," she said. Instead of letting me go though, she held me more tightly than ever.

"I can stay for a little while . . . if you'd like, that is?"

She nodded and rested her head on my shoulder. "I just really don't want today to end."

I smiled to myself, knowing I'd achieved my goal. She was mine again. My heart swelled with pride at being able to say that. I could never let her go again. If I were to lose her it would break me. Lifting her in my arms, I lavished soft kisses along her cheek and neck as I carried her across to her bed and laid her down gently.

Even though I needed her, it was clear she needed comfort and closeness, not sex. I curled around her and pulled her against my body.

"Can you stay until I fall asleep?" Alyssa asked the darkness.

I nodded and kissed her cheek once more. "Of course."

We lay in silence. For my part, I just enjoyed being wrapped around her, hearing her soft breaths in the near silence of the night. An hour passed before her breathing steadied, and I knew she was asleep. As I carefully extracted myself from the bed, she moaned and grumbled a little in her sleep before clutching the pillow.

"Declan." She murmured my name on a breath. A smile crept onto her features, and I found it almost impossible to leave the room.

After watching her for a moment more, I managed to withdraw from the magic of Alyssa, leaving the room and heading down the hall. When I passed Phoebe's room, I paused to peer inside. She was stretched out on her back, her arms raised high above her head and her lips parted in a small pout. With her eyes closed, she looked so much like Alyssa. As I watched her sleeping, I couldn't help but remember the first time I had ever seen Alyssa sleeping. I was eight at the time.

"DECLAN, MAKE sure your room is clean. We're having guests tonight," Mum called out. My thoughts immediately went to my cousins who stayed over much too often for my taste. I hated when they came because Toby always smelled like pee and even after he'd gone, the house stank for a week.

"Aw, Mum, do we have to?" I whined. "I don't like Toby and Scott."

"Who said anything about Toby or Scott?" Mum asked, her voice full of secrets and smiles.

"Who then?" I asked, running to find her.

"I guess you'll have to wait and see."

She laughed when I pouted.

"Always so impatient," she said, scuffing my hair fondly. "Curtis Dawson is rostered on tonight and Ruth has just been called in to work, so they've asked if I can watch Josh and Alyssa. If that's okay with you, of course?"

My excitement burst from me. Josh and Alyssa were my best friends. Well, Alyssa was my best friend and Josh was the cool older brother I always wished I had. Racing down to my room, I made sure all my stuff was packed away. Not that Alyssa would actually sleep in my room, she'd get the guest room, but I would have to share with Josh.

For the rest of the afternoon, I couldn't relax. Ruth and Curtis turned up just after six with pizza and my two closest friends. We all wolfed down our pizza and ran to my room to play with my Xbox and watch some movies. We stayed up until Mum finally put her foot down and shooed us all into bed.

In the middle of the night, I woke to the sound of a soft whimpering. Climbing out of bed, I stepped around the trundle where Josh was sleeping to investigate. I walked through the darkened hall until I located the sound. It was coming from beneath the guest room door—where Alyssa was sleeping.

I pushed the door open before sneaking into the room. Glancing down at the bed, I could see the ghost of her outline. Her hair was spread out on the pillow behind her. Her face was drawn into a frown and she was whimpering and kicking. Still, she looked like a sleeping angel.

I knelt next to her bed and gently stroked her cheek. "Shh, Alyssa, I'm here."

Her whimpering quietened and her movement stilled. I climbed onto her bed, staying above the comforter but determined to stop her nightmares.

I slept there the rest of the night and Mum found me the next morning.

I STOOD watching Phoebe for what I thought was just a few

minutes, but must have been longer because I felt arms stretch around my waist, drawing me back to the present. My hands found their place over Alyssa's hold as she rested her head on my back. "You didn't leave?"

I shook my head. "I guess I got a bit distracted."

After another glance in Phoebe's room, I turned in Alyssa's embrace. I was so overwhelmed with emotion, and there was only one way I could think of to release some of it. I captured Alyssa in my arms and pushed her back against the hallway wall, kissing her deeply. When she didn't resist, I cupped her arse with my hand and pulled her against me. She moaned into my mouth, and I carried her back down to her room.

I spent the next hour devouring her body in every way I could, burning the taste of her lips and skin into my memory so that I could make it through Monday morning without her. After we were both satiated, I held her tightly to me and told her how I felt about her, Phoebe, and life in general. There was really only one way I could sum it up.

"Things are finally on track," I whispered.

THE EARLY dawn light was just rising when I woke again. I leaned over and kissed Alyssa's cheek softly.

"I'll be back later today," I whispered.

Obviously still fast asleep, she mumbled something incoherent in response. I wrote a quick note, letting her know I would be back later in the morning after my phone call with Dr. Henrikson. Then I crept out the door, pulling it locked behind me.

The shit-eating grin wouldn't leave my face the whole way back to Mum's.

When I pulled up in front of her house though, I saw a figure slumped on the doorstep. I recognised the shape at once and nearly ripped the car door off in my haste to get out.

"What the fuck are *you* doing here?" I shouted as I ran across the lawn.

CHAPTER THIRTY-ONE

DADDY ISSUES

I COULDN'T BELIEVE my eyes. Lying prone in front of Mum's front door, using his suitcase as a pillow, was my father—a man who'd always been proud and strong, and the man I had once looked up to. He leapt up from the position he'd been in when he heard my voice. In a series of short strides, I crossed the lawn and grabbed the front of his shirt.

"What the fuck are you doing here?" I repeated in a menacing whisper as I got right up into his face.

"This is my house," he replied, trying to draw himself up to my height and assert some level of authority. In reality, he just looked pathetic.

"Not anymore," I hissed in reply. "Mum made it very clear to me that you are no longer welcome."

He slunk back down again, his shoulders slumping and his head bowing. "I know."

"All that shit you fed to me about respect. You're fucking scum."

He pressed his hand to his face, and if I hadn't known he was a fucking heartless bastard, I might have thought he was crying.

"Just go, before you hurt her more." I pointed toward his car.

"I have nowhere to go."

"What about back to that fucking little whore that you had the nerve to call the love of your life?"

"I can't." His voice broke.

Not that I cared, but his statement took me by surprise. "Why not?"

"We had an argument, and she wants her privacy. I . . . gave her the apartment a little while ago, it's in her name. She doesn't want me to live with her."

I didn't know what I was more pissed about. The fact that he had given her an apartment, or the fact that he had thought he could just come begging back to Mum when he fucked it up with his whore.

"Mum doesn't want you here either."

He growled before turning his back on me. He kicked the door in frustration and I thought I heard a quiet yelp from inside the house.

"Really, Declan? You don't think I realised that from the voice mail she left me? Or the fact that she changed the locks? Or maybe the fact that she drained our savings account?" His voice was full of sarcasm. Then he dropped his head. "I just need to talk to her. To work this out." His voice was broken, despondent.

I almost felt sorry for him. Almost.

If I didn't think he would only be faithful as long as it suited him, I might have found a solution to help him, but I knew his type.

I also remembered his words at the cafe and what happened with Hayley. The look on Mum's face and the pain in her voice when she spoke about what happened between them. Most importantly, I remembered what he'd done to Alyssa.

I took a deep breath. "I am going to give you three seconds to get the fuck out of here."

"Declan, I need to talk to your mother."

"One!"

"This isn't all my fault, I just want her to listen—"

"Two!" I roared, cutting him off. I clenched and released my fists in anger.

"It's never mattered before."

Launching myself at him, I grabbed the cuff of his shirt and pressed him into the door. Tears of rage pricked my eyes as I allowed the emotions I felt to flow through me. I was in his face, screaming, "How dare you say that, you sick son of a bitch! Does the fact that you have a family at home not matter? How can you come home at night extolling the virtues of fucking respect when you have none yourself?"

He cowered against the screen door.

"How many were there?" I asked, my voice dropping low and dripping with venom. The hatred I felt for him rose in my throat like bile.

He shook his head and raised his hands protectively.

"How many?" I shouted. No doubt all the neighbours up and down the street could hear me, but I didn't care. I raised my fist to force an answer, but was distracted by the wooden door behind the security screen opening just a crack. Mum's face appeared through the mesh.

"Declan, don't," she whispered. Her face was streaked with tears, and it looked like she hadn't slept all night.

"What the fuck, Mum? Are you going to defend him now?"

She shook her head, her eyes never leaving my face. "No, but I don't want you to fight with him," she whispered, her gaze steadfastly ignoring the shape of my father's head in front of her.

I used my grip on his collar as leverage to twist him away. I threw him onto the grass before shoving his suitcase after him with my foot.

"Go back inside, Mum," I ordered.

"Declan . . .," she started with a voice laced with worry.

"Just shut the door. I'll deal with this."

"Please, don't," I heard her whisper behind me.

I turned back to look at her. "I won't do anything stupid," I reassured her. "I just have to get rid of him."

She nodded and closed the door.

I walked over to where my father was lying prone on the

ground. Nothing remained in him of the man I'd once admired and loved.

"Get up," I hissed, nudging his side with my foot.

He pulled himself into a sitting position.

"Get up!" I screamed.

He scrambled to his feet.

"Now fuck off and never come back. Leave Mum alone."

"What if she wants me back?" he challenged, even as he grabbed his suitcase and backed toward his car.

"Then I will be advising her to go see a fucking shrink." I stalked in his footsteps, my fists clenched tightly at my side. It took everything in me to allow him to walk away unscathed.

He threw his suitcase into the back of the car before climbing into the driver seat and winding down his window. "You'll never understand," he spat at me.

I reached into the car and stopped him from turning the ignition. "You're right . . . I never will. Because I couldn't imagine ever hurting Alyssa that way."

"You think you have it all worked out, don't you?"

"No. But I have it worked out a damn sight better than you do," I murmured, preparing to pull my arm from the car and let him go. I was going to be the bigger man, I wasn't going to let violence or alcohol be my first resort anymore. For Alyssa and Phoebe, I would be the bigger man.

"That slut will take your money and leave you dry." His voice was so soft I almost missed what he said, but it registered enough for my elbow to snap back sharply into his nose. I listened with satisfaction to the wet sounding crunch as it connected.

Although I wasn't going to let violence rule my life, I wasn't about to let him trash talk Alyssa that way either.

I pulled my arm back out of the car and watched as he clutched one hand to his nose.

"You're fucking crazy," he said as he switched on the ignition.

"Yeah," I scoffed. "I get that shit from my father."

"Mark my words, boy, you will regret this. I . . ." He stopped himself short, glancing at the damage I had caused in the rear-view mirror. "God, to think I was about to throw it all away . . . for you," he muttered into the hand he held up to his nose to stem the bleeding.

I didn't want to listen to any more of his bullshit and lies. "Just fuck off, and stay away this time."

He scowled at me before pulling out of the drive. Unable to resist, I stuck my middle finger up at his car as it retreated into the distance.

Covering the distance back to the front door, I knocked lightly on the screen.

"Mum?" I called out. "He's gone."

The wooden door opened and Mum stood in front of me. She looked terrible as she unlocked the screen door. Her eyes were red-rimmed with huge black bags circling underneath them, her skin was pasty and white, and her always-perfect auburn hair was dishevelled. She handed me a key.

"I . . . I changed the locks."

"Good." I nodded as I gave her appearance another quick assessment. "Are you going to be all right?"

She nodded.

"How long was he there for?"

"Most of the night. I told him to leave, but he wouldn't. He said he would stay as long as he needed to until I spoke to him again."

My mouth twisted and I frowned at the fact that she'd let him hassle her all night. "You should have called me."

She shook her head. "You were with Alyssa. It's important that you two sort through everything. I need to know that you two at least are okay before I leave."

I grabbed her hands in my own, and my face broke into an involuntary smile. "We're better than okay. Mum, it's great," I gushed. Then I continued, my voice dropping lower, "In fact . . . we told Phoebe last night."

She looked shocked. "So soon."

"Why wait?" I asked with a shrug. "I wouldn't want to lie to her. I know how that bullshit feels. And I think Lys gets that."

Mum looked away. "I'm sorry for the mistakes I've made,

Declan. I should have tried harder to tell you about Alyssa and the twins."

I shook my head. "Don't. The truth is I probably wouldn't have listened. I certainly wouldn't have been ready to know. To be honest, I probably would have run a mile if I'd found out differently. It sucks that I've missed so much of Phoebe's life, but . . ." I raked my hand through my hair. "I feel like I'm in a better place now, you know?"

She touched her finger to my chin. "I can see that, I think anyone could see how good Alyssa and Phoebe are for you."

"What can I say?" I said as a loopy grin formed on my lips. "They're my girls."

Mum smiled through her obvious exhaustion.

"If he comes back, call me. Anytime. Alyssa will understand." I patted her back gently. "Now go to bed," I ordered softly, kissing her cheek. I turned my back to her, walking toward the kitchen to get some breakfast.

She laughed. "Look at you, Mr. Responsible."

With a grin on my face, I shrugged and continued on my way. When she'd headed to bed, I fixed myself my favourite delicacy — vegemite toast. Holding one piece of toast in my mouth, I carried the other in my hand and went to the living room. Leaning my toast on my knee, I sat on the couch and flicked on the TV. I couldn't get into anything that was on. Weekday morning TV held little that interested me, especially when my head was filled with thoughts of Alyssa and Phoebe.

With the mood I was in, I doubted even motorsport would've held my attention. Instead, I allowed the drone of the TV to fill my mind as I clutched my phone, anxiously waiting for Dr. Henrikson's call. Once he'd called, I would shower, change, and head back to Alyssa's arms. I trailed my hand through my hair as the time ticked by so goddamn slowly.

When my phone finally started to vibrate, I had it to my ear almost before the first ring could escape.

"Doc!" I almost shouted down the line, excitement ringing in my tone. I couldn't wait to tell him about my weekend and everything that happened between Alyssa, Phoebe and me.

"Declan," he greeted cautiously. "You seem particularly cheerful this morning."

"Fuck, Doc, why wouldn't I be? The sun is shining, the birds are chirping, and I'm in love with two beautiful girls."

"So I'm guessing you talked with Alyssa after our phone call on Friday."

"Yeah, Doc. We talked." I couldn't help the double entendre that came through when I said the last word, but visions of the weekend and everything Alyssa and I had done came into my mind. I considered how much had changed between us in just a few short days. On Friday, I would have thought it would be months before we'd enjoy that kind of fun. There were still so many obstacles for us to overcome, but at least it seemed like she was on my side now. Or more specifically, that we'd formed our own side.

"Why don't you tell me about that conversation?"

"I don't know what to say, but we talked, we had fun, we both got some things out of our system." I was trying to will away the erection that was building quickly as I thought about the type of things Alyssa and I got out of our system. It was highly inappropriate for me to be talking to my shrink with a raging boner, but I couldn't help myself.

"What did you talk about?"

"About everything."

I spent my hour on the phone giving him the clean version of the weekend, all the while the real events played over and over in my head. Halfway through the call, I moved from the comfortable confines of the couch and headed to my room to start packing a fresh bag of clothes. I threw all the ones from my night in the hotel with Eden and my weekend with Alyssa into the clothes hamper. I wasn't sure what Alyssa would have to say about me staying at her house for a few days, but figured it couldn't hurt to pack for it . . . just in case.

I sat on the bed just as I began to tell him about Phoebe. "We even told my daughter. Who I am, I mean." I choked on the last part.

"How do you feel about that?"

"Honestly? I don't think ecstatic is too strong a word. I mean, she took the news so well. She was excited about it."

"Children are very resilient."

I wondered what he'd meant by that, but decided to let it roll off my back. "She was happy. That's all that mattered."

"You're right. So what's next for you and Alyssa?"

"Well, I have some plans. Then I guess it's a matter of working out our timing. She's moving to Sydney." I was beaming inside, excited about my plans for Alyssa at the Suncrest Hotel and her move to Sydney. We hadn't discussed what would happen after the move, but I knew that moment would be pivotal to our relationship.

"Have you spoken to her family?"

"God, no," I exclaimed. "I'll be happy if Alyssa and I can move to Sydney without me having to see them again."

"You know that's no way to start a relationship."

I laughed. "I know, Doc, it's just . . . well, to be honest, her brother scares the shit out of me."

"That's understandable, considering your past."

"But he has nothing on Curtis." Killer Curtis would have my balls on a silver platter if he had half a chance. He was shorter, thinner, and had less brute strength than Josh, but he also knew ways to dispose of a body without getting caught.

"Is Alyssa close to her family?"

"Fuck, yeah. She always has been. They're a fucking tight-knit group." A group I was once part of many years ago. There was a time I had been Ruth and Curtis's quasi-son. That had changed when I'd left. If I'd had any doubt over whether they did indeed hate me, the meeting with Ruby in the city had made it abundantly clear. "But it'll be all right, Doc. Once they see how happy we are, they'll leave us alone."

"Declan?" Dr. Henrikson asked, ignoring my statement.

"Yeah, Doc?" I replied, wondering why he had changed tack.

"It's good to hear you this way."

"What way is that?" I was confused.

"Almost optimistic."

I laughed. "You're not the first one to call me that this weekend."

"I have to admit I am a little concerned though. Please . . . take this slowly." I could tell he was choosing his words carefully.

"Who's the pessimist now?" I asked.

"I just don't want to see you falling into any of your"—he paused—"old patterns."

"You mean running?"

"Amongst other things, yes."

"I'm never running from her again."

"I believe that you feel that's the case." He was obviously trying to placate me. "But I would like you and Alyssa to come in for couples' therapy when you can."

I laughed at the concept. Sure, I had issues which impacted on Alyssa, but Alyssa and I, we didn't have issues. "You're just trying to sting me for more money."

He laughed in reply, but it was hesitant and forced.

I sighed. "What makes you suggest that?"

"It is a little," his voice was slow, careful, considered, "concerning how insular your relationship with Alyssa seems to be. And how fast things are moving. You describe a world where everything is perfect, but only so long as there is no one else around. That is not a realistic scenario in the long-term. There will always be other factors impacting on the two of you. I would just like to see you both equipped with the right tools for having a relationship that will survive the real world."

I grew irritated. I had just told him about the fuck-awesome weekend I had with Alyssa and Phoebe, and his first suggestion was that we needed help?

"Fuck you," I said. "You don't know a fucking thing."

"Declan," he replied, with a calm voice. "I'm going to leave this here. But please, think about it. I'll call you tomorrow."

"Don't fucking bother," I murmured, but he'd already hung up the phone. I threw the phone onto my bed. "Fucking quack!" I screamed at no one in particular.

CHAPTER TWENTY-TWO

QUALITY TIME

GRABBING AN OUTFIT to change into, I stormed into the shower. I slammed the door shut behind me. The doc's words had planted seeds of doubt in my mind and I was anxious to see Alyssa again. Once I'd finished, I dried myself off and dressed in a rush, before grabbing my bag and writing Mum a quick note to let her know where I was going.

By the time I arrived at Alyssa's again, the small seeds had grown into weeds that tangled themselves around my memories of the weekend. I began to consider that maybe I was misreading the situation between Alyssa and me. Maybe things weren't as resolved as I wanted to think. With my heart in my throat, I knocked on Alyssa's door, unsure how she felt about the way I'd left earlier or whether my absence had given her time to reconsider everything that had happened.

The door pulled open and Alyssa mouthed, "Hi," to me and smiled. She had a phone handset squeezed between her shoulder and ear as she stepped backwards from the door to allow me entry.

"Daddy!" Phoebe squealed from in front of the TV before leaping up to give me a hug.

The sound of the word made my stomach clench and my heart

pound. A nervous excitement raced through my veins as she wrapped her tiny arms around my legs.

"Nothing important," Alyssa said into the phone, turning her back to me and heading down the hall toward her bedroom. She continued her conversation the whole way. By the time she reached the end of the hall, I could barely make out the words but I heard "Can't someone else?" and "You are absolutely certain?"

I sat on the couch and Phoebe climbed up beside me.

"You were gone when I woke up," she accused.

"Sorry," I said to her. "I needed to go get some more clothes and have a shower."

Her eyebrows creased together and she was silent for a minute.

"We have a shower here," she said eventually, the confusion in her tiny voice clear.

"I know," I replied. "But I'll have to go away sometimes. But never for long, and I'll always come back, okay?"

She considered it for another minute then nodded and turned back to the TV, laughing loudly at Tom and Jerry. I didn't know that shit was still on TV; I remembered it from when I was young.

Watching her as she watched the TV, I was soon laughing along with her. She would turn to me whenever something happened that she found particularly funny and tell me what she'd seen, as if I wasn't sitting right next to her. I could have found that irritating—and if it had been anyone else, I probably would have. For some reason, I found it endearing coming from the little angel perched next to me. Every now and then, I would hear a snippet of conversation float down from Alyssa, but I still couldn't hear many words.

"Declan?" Alyssa called, before appearing behind me. She was dressed in her work uniform and I frowned at the sight. She hadn't said anything about needing to work. "I've been called in to work. It's an emergency, and they've got no one else who can take the shift."

"Okay." I tried not to let my disappointment show in my voice. I'd been hoping to have some fun and extend the weekend.

"I, well, I don't have anyone else to watch Phoebe. Would you mind? It'll only be for a few hours at the most. I'll be at work until at least six, but Mum can drop in and pick Phoebe up earlier."

I heard what she wasn't saying as loudly as what she had. She didn't trust me to watch Phoebe. She'd checked every other resource and had no other options. I was the last fucking person she'd asked to babysit my own fucking daughter.

Dr. Henrikson's words began creeping through my mind again. I wanted to scream and shout that we would be all right. That we didn't need help. But I saw in that instant that I would be wrong. Terribly wrong. As much trust as I had gained from Alyssa over the weekend, I still had to work my arse off to earn the rest. There was only one way to do that.

"Lys." I stood and wrapped my arms around her. "I can handle it. It'll be great. What better way for us to get to really know each other?"

It was hard to sound reassuring. Even in my own ears my voice was weak and pitiful, and full of fear. I drove heavy, high-powered vehicles around a racetrack at high speeds for a living without batting an eyelid, and yet the idea of spending the day alone with my own three-year-old daughter frightened the living shit out of me.

I could do it though.

I *would* do it. If only to prove to everyone that I was committed to Alyssa and to Phoebe.

"You want me to get Mum to come over when she's free? She can take Phoebe back to her house and give you a break."

I shook my head. The idea of speaking to Alyssa's family any time soon frightened me much more than spending a day with Phoebe.

"We'll be fine. I can handle it," I repeated, as much to reassure myself as Alyssa.

Alyssa raced around getting ready, calling out instructions for Phoebe's routine as she went. Before long, she'd told me when to feed her, when to put her to sleep—apparently she needed to sleep at midday but couldn't sleep for any more than an hour or she wouldn't go to sleep later in the night. I was fucking exhausted just from Alyssa's explanations of what I needed to do—and I hadn't even started yet. My apprehension grew with every passing second. There wasn't an opportunity for me to change my mind though, because with one last kiss and a whispered warning to Phoebe to be on her best behaviour, Alyssa was gone.

I stood staring at Phoebe, and she stood staring at me. I smiled a tight smile at her. "What would you like to do?"

"I want to go to Nana's."

"No, baby, we promised Mummy we'd stay here," I said in my gentlest voice.

"But this house is boring!" She stamped her foot and crossed her arms.

Shit. Alyssa hadn't explained any of this to me. I knew the whens of her routine, but had no idea what to do if she didn't want to do something.

"Why don't you watch a movie?" I suggested.

She nodded before turning and running into her room. She came out a few seconds later with a Wiggles DVD. We sat and watched it.

And then we watched it again.

And again.

By the fourth run-through I was going utterly crazy. I even knew the words to some of the goddamned songs. When Phoebe tried to get me to get up and dance with her, I drew the line. Like she had with *Tom and Jerry*, every time something came on that she liked she turned to me and told me all about it. Even on the fourth run-through.

Needing a break from the endless cheer on the TV, I looked at the time. Time for lunch, and then a sleep, according to Alyssa's schedule. I checked the fridge, where Alyssa said she'd left some tuna sandwiches. I pulled them out and arranged them on a plate for Phoebe. I put them on a little table that was obviously designed for Phoebe to eat at. Then I headed back into the kitchen to fix something for myself.

"I don't want stinky fish." I turned to look at Phoebe when I heard her voice. She had her arms crossed again and a frown on her face.

"That's all I've got," I replied.

"I don't want it," she said more loudly, shoving the plate away from her.

Fuck! I wondered if Alyssa would be upset if I called her at work to find out what to do.

I couldn't do it. Whether or not it was intentional, the day was a test. Alyssa might decide I wasn't worth keeping around if I couldn't even look after Phoebe for one day. If I failed now, I might lose them both.

"Please, baby?" I turned on my charm. It worked on retail workers and hotel managers but I wasn't sure if it would work on her too.

She shook her head.

"What do you want to eat then?"

"A lollipop."

"You can't have a lollipop for lunch." I laughed at the absurdity of the request.

"I want a lollipop."

"After you eat something else?" I countered.

She shook her head.

I fixed her with a stern look, trying to let her know I wouldn't back down.

With a little frown scrunching the skin between her eyebrows she stared back at me, equally unwavering. Then she put her hands on her hips and pouted. Just when I was about to relent, she spoke again. "I want a vegemite sandwich."

"Now *that* I can help you with," I said with a smile. "I just happen to make a mean vegemite sandwich."

I whipped around the kitchen for a few minutes making the vegemite sandwich for her. I cut it into four squares and placed it in front of her. She took one look at the plate and pushed it away.

"I don't want it."

"That's what you asked for," I said, exasperated.

She shook her head. "I want it in triangles."

What the fuck difference does that make? It's a fucking vegemite sandwich for fucks sake. Vegemite is vegemite, regardless of how it's cut. I bit back the words and swallowed down the frustration rising in my throat.

"Just eat that," I said, trying to keep the annoyance out of my tone.

"No." She turned her head away.

"Eat it."

"I want triangles."

With a sigh, I grabbed the plate and turned back toward the kitchen. I spent the next few minutes remaking the vegemite sandwich. This time I cut it into fucking triangles. I placed it down in front of Phoebe. She took one bite.

"Yuck," she said, pushing the plate away.

Wondering whether I'd done something wrong, I grabbed one of the quarters and took a bite. "There's nothing wrong with that. It's a vegemite sandwich cut into triangles."

"I don't like vegemite."

With a great effort, I resisted the urge to growl at her. I tried to remind myself that she was just a child.

"Then what do you want to eat?" I asked.

"Ice cream."

I sighed. "You can't have ice cream . . ." I started, but then decided it wasn't worth the argument. After all, I didn't have to tell Alyssa that I'd fed Phoebe ice cream for lunch. "You know what— fine. Have ice cream."

I dished up the strawberry ice cream from the Neapolitan tub in Alyssa's freezer. Phoebe ate it all quickly and smiled at me. That smile alone was worth a thousand uneaten vegemite sandwiches. We watched the Wiggles . . . again . . . before I told her it was time for a sleep.

"I don't want to sleep."

I sighed. "Mummy said you have to sleep."

"I. Don't. Want. To," she said forcefully.

"Please?"

"No!"

"Please, baby?" I pulled out the charm again. "For Daddy?"

She shook her head violently and recrossed her arms.

"Mummy said you needed to sleep though." Alyssa had been very clear on the need for Phoebe to sleep. She said it had to happen no matter what.

Phoebe shook her head forcefully. Her brown hair flew around her face.

"Phoebe, we are having a sleep," I said, trying to sound forceful but not scary. How the hell did anyone do this shit?

She shook her head again.

I stepped forward and picked her up gently to carry her into her room. She kicked her legs out and screamed. When I tried to put her back on the ground, she was still kicking and screaming and wouldn't get her legs underneath her. Her cries were so loud the neighbours must have heard them.

Fuck me dead, I thought. *How the fuck do people deal with this?*

I couldn't ring Alyssa. As desperate as I was for assistance from someone, I knew no one who could help.

Then I remembered there was someone I could call who had experience with children. I dialled Ben's number and spoke to him briefly. Somehow through Phoebe's screams, he was able to decipher the reason for my call. He told me some techniques that he used. Basically it boiled down to bribery and distraction. Too bad I couldn't get a word in edgewise to try to distract her. I hung up the phone with a promise to call him later. For the moment, I had to deal with the still-screaming child who was now flailing on the floor.

Picking her up, and holding her as gently as I could while avoiding the hazards that were her arms and legs, I carried her to her room. I lay down on the bed with her and began playing a game Ben had suggested, Round and Round the Garden. Eventually, Phoebe began to calm, and even giggle, and I was able to convince her to lie still with me while I read her a story. Then I began to hum a tune to her. I couldn't remember the words, but it was something Mum used to sing to me.

After what felt like hours of battling her, her eyes began to drift closed, and she fell asleep leaning against my chest. I didn't want to move for fear of waking her. Allowing the peace and quiet of the now still house to wash over me, I closed my own eyes. Phoebe's rhythmic, soft breathing made my mind drift slowly into slumber.

My eyes snapped open when I heard the front door click unlocked. A second later I heard a voice, that wasn't Alyssa's, call out, "Only me!"

Fuck. I knew that voice. It was a voice I hadn't heard in over four years. The voice of a woman I'd once considered my second mother. I panicked, not sure whether I should call out in reply or not. In the end, I remained silent and hoped that she'd think no one was home.

After what felt like an eternity, Phoebe's bedroom door cracked open.

I heard a sharp intake of breath.

"Declan?" Ruth exclaimed.

Fuck me.

CHAPTER  TWENTY-THREE

MY APOCALYPSE

AFTER THE SMALLEST of glances at Ruth, I felt the panic and terror brand my face as it twisted into a contorted mask. I hadn't felt a surge of fear so strong since hearing Josh's voice at the airport. Working to pull my thoughts together, I put my finger to my lips to instruct Ruth to stay quiet. Which wasn't entirely necessary because she just stared at me with her mouth gaping slightly anyway.

I shifted position, gently rolling Phoebe away from my chest. Silently, I stroked her cheek a couple of times to ensure she was still in a deep slumber before pointing to the door, indicating to Ruth to leave the room. Watching Phoebe the whole way, I backed out and pulled the door shut behind me. With the tones of the death march ringing through my mind as I went, I began the slow walk out to the living room.

By the time I spotted Ruth again, my heart was pounding as if Lars Ulrich was using it to practice his percussion. The more I thought about the things Alyssa and Ruby had said, the more I was certain I could hear the beat of "My Apocalypse" drumming against my chest. The words began to echo through my head.

Clenching my fists at my sides, I tried every technique I knew to stave off the panic attack I felt building within me. My chest was tight—my lungs too small to draw the correct amount of oxygen from the air. The room slanted to the left and began to spin.

Through the haze of fear that was rising within me I sensed, rather than saw, Ruth come from behind and circle around in front of me. A cacophony of sounds hit me. My own heartbeat became amplified in my ears. I could hear Ruth's voice echoing above it, just slightly louder. It felt like she was screaming at me.

Louder and louder.

Words I couldn't understand or hear properly. I crossed my arms on top of my head, using my biceps to block the violent rush of noise. The room skewed further off balance, and my breaths grew shallower. Hands clutched at me from what felt like all directions, pulling and tugging while the screaming and thudding continued.

I shut my eyes tightly and tried to chant my mantra silently to myself. *I can get through this. I've had one before, and I made it through then. I can get through this. I've had one before, and I made it through then.*

I became aware of a second voice mixing with Ruth's. It took me a moment to realise it was mine. Slowly, the rushing sound in my ears quietened. Something soft hit the back of my knees and they gave way beneath me. What felt like a large pillow stopped my descent before I hit the ground. Fingers closed around my hands and the yelling slowly abated, although the voice didn't quieten, it just began to sound less harsh in my ears.

"Declan . . .," was the first clear thing I heard, but then the voice faded back into obscurity.

I dropped my head down to my knees and began to rock softly. My mantra wasn't helping. There was only one thing I knew for certain that would help and unfortunately she was at work.

"Declan." Ruth's voice broke through the haze again. She sounded . . . *worried?*

Curiosity brought me back to the present. I tried to breathe again and was relieved when I found that my lungs seemed almost regular-sized once more. Lifting my head, I opened my eyes. Ruth was sitting on the couch beside me. She held her hands out toward me and her face was traced with concern.

"Declan?" she asked again as my eyes focused on her face. "Are you all right?"

I nodded, then shook my head, then nodded again. I honestly wasn't sure whether I was all right or not. Whether I ever would be.

"Panic attacks?" she queried.

My lip quivered and I couldn't find the word yes.

Her face softened. "You really did miss her, didn't you?"

Tears welled in my eyes as I nodded again.

"Aw, baby." She held her arms out in invitation. I crawled across the couch and into her embrace before letting the sobs overrun my body as it recovered from the rush of adrenaline that my panic attack had inspired. The last time she'd comforted me that way was when I was sixteen. It was after Alyssa and I had fought at school, over something as stupid as not saying I love you.

Despite our past, and how much she had been like a mother to me at times, I couldn't fathom why Ruth was being so nice to me now. After everything I'd put her daughter, and her granddaughter through, why wasn't she kicking my arse? I didn't want to break the spell and ask, but eventually I had to. Extracting myself from her arms, I sat beside her on the sofa.

"Don't you hate me?" I asked.

She brushed the hair off my face. A small frown graced her brow and her lips turned downward. "Sweetie, I may be disappointed in some of the decisions you've made, but I could never hate you. And it's obvious you are in pain right now. That trumps everything else. Do you want to talk about it?"

"I was . . . scared," I admitted. "When you came in. I thought . . . I didn't know what you'd do. Everyone else hates me."

She laughed, just a soft chuckle. It reminded me of Alyssa. "Curtis and Josh have thick heads, that's all. You hurt their baby girl. But you know that, right?"

I nodded.

"And you hurt yourself just as much, didn't you?"

Swallowing down the lump in my throat, I nodded again. Ruth had always been intuitive and there was no point lying to her.

"Ruby told me about your talk, and Alyssa told me about your dinner at McDonald's. I can tell you're trying to do the right thing.

That means something. I wanted to see you sooner, to talk to you, but Alyssa asked me not to. She thought you might need your space."

"Thank you," I managed. I wasn't sure whether to feel touched that Alyssa had thought to ask for space on my behalf—or offended because it was another sign that she still didn't trust me. Did she think I could be run off? "But why are you here now then?" It wasn't until after the words had escaped that I could see how rude they might sound. "Shit, fuck, I didn't mean it like that."

She smiled. "It's all right, Declan. I usually drop by to see Alyssa a couple of times a week when she's not working. Where is she, by the way?"

"She got called in to work. Apparently, it was a big emergency."

Ruth raised her eyebrow at me. "And she left you alone with Phoebe?"

I bristled. Her amazed tone pissed me off. Was it really that hard to believe that Alyssa would trust me to look after my own fucking daughter? Okay, so I was apparently the last resort, but it wasn't that unthinkable was it? After all, I'd had to endure the mother of all temper tantrums and I'd survived. With my mouth twisted in distaste, I went to say something but Ruth cut me off.

"I just meant that Alyssa very rarely leaves Phoebe with anyone. Me, Flynn, Ruby, and occasionally your mum. That's it. We practically had to drag her down to enrol Phoebe in day care. She's very protective of her. I think sometimes Lys still sees Phoebe as the broken baby who wouldn't have survived without her brother's gift, and not always as the strong, smart child she has grown into."

Her words came as a shock. The thought of how hard it was for Alyssa to trust anyone else with Phoebe had never even crossed my mind. It dawned on me just how big a deal it was that Alyssa had allowed me to babysit at all so soon after coming back into their lives. A smile crossed my face as Ruth's words cemented the fact that Alyssa did in fact trust me.

"Would you like to stay for the afternoon?" I asked Ruth.

"I wouldn't want to intrude. I didn't realise you would be here or I wouldn't have come."

"Don't fucking worry about it. I'm glad you are here."

"Alyssa was right about you," Ruth said, as the corners of her lips lifted again.

"What?" I asked, wondering what Alyssa might have told her mum about me.

"You've lost none of your charm, but gained a real potty mouth."

I laughed. "There's nothing fucking potty about my mouth," I joked.

"Come on," she said, rising to her feet. "Why don't I make us a cup of tea and you can tell me what you've been up to?"

"That, well, actually that sounds great. Thanks, Ruth."

Without thinking about it, I hopped up on the kitchen counter while Ruth busied herself making the tea. I rarely drank the stuff these days, but she was being cordial to me and I didn't want to fuck it up. If I made an effort, I had no doubt Alyssa would find out. Not to mention the fact that being on Ruth's good side would help my cause with Josh at least—he was nothing if not a mama's boy.

"So what have you been up to in Sydney?" Ruth asked as she set one of the steaming mugs on the dining table and sat in the seat across from it.

I smirked. "You really don't want to know." There was no way I could tell her about the scores of women I'd bedded, the alcohol I'd drunk, or any of the horror that was my first few months down there.

"Something must have been real fascinating to keep you away from our little Alyssa?"

"Not really. That was just me being a stubborn arse. I—" I took a deep breath. "—well, I almost had myself convinced that I was over her. It was only in the dark of night that I knew I wasn't."

"You dreamt about her?" she guessed.

Shrugging, I leaned forward for the hot mug and cradled it in my hands. "If I was lucky. If not, I'd lie awake for hours staring at the ceiling while memories of our time together ran endlessly through my head."

"When did the panic attacks start, sweetie?" Her voice was still full of concern. I just wanted to hug her and say thank you again.

"Almost immediately," I admitted, my voice almost silent. These were things I'd barely covered with Alyssa. "It started small. Alyssa would call and I would listen as she left a message. Within a week, I found I had to actually clutch tightly to something to stop myself from answering the phone. I honestly thought she'd be better off without any ties to me. I thought she'd move on eventually. Do the things she always wanted to do, you know?"

"That was never going to happen though, you should have known that. Even without the twins, she could never have forgotten about you any more than you could forget about her."

"I know that now," I whispered. "But I thought I knew better. Eventually, holding on to something wasn't enough. That was when the insomnia started. All within a few weeks of being in Sydney. I should have known then that what I really wanted was to be back by her side. But the real problem was that I wanted to be at Sinclair Racing too. It was my dream job, and I couldn't just walk away."

Ruth glanced over the rim of her mug as she waited for me to continue the story.

I put my own mug back on the table and stared into the milky-brown liquid.

"That's . . ." I sighed. "Well, that's when things became dark." I wasn't going to tell her exactly how dark, I wouldn't be able to bear the look of disgust or pity that might cross her face. "I began to manage the only way I was able."

"Alcohol and women?" Ruth asked.

I nodded because there was no point denying what she clearly knew. It was pretty much public record after all. "For a while I tried sleeping tablets too, and they worked, but they just became another in a long line of addictions. The more time that passed, the harder it was just to pick up the phone. I think I knew that if I did, I'd be back in her arms in an instant."

Not for the first time, I wondered what life would have been like if I had succumbed to the urge to reconnect sooner. Would I have had to give up racing, or would we have found a way to make it all work?

Glancing over at Ruth, wordlessly absorbing my confession like a priest, it became clear once more that the hole in my life hadn't just been Alyssa-sized. There had been so many other connections I'd severed to avoid a reunion.

"I kept all her phone messages though," I continued. "I would play them occasionally when I was unable to sleep. I did such a good job of convincing myself that I didn't need her—I told myself it was only a piece of home I was missing, not her—that hearing her voice reminded me of easier times." My words reminded me of my temper tantrum with the answering machine. I'd lost all of the messages because I'd thrown the damn thing against the wall. I hung my head. "I was a fucking fool."

"But you're here now," Ruth said.

Raising my head again, I met her eyes. "And I'm not leaving her again."

She smiled at me. "That's all I need to know. Alyssa has made it clear to me what she wants and if my baby girl wants you, I'm not going to argue. I just need to know you're not going to hurt her again."

I shook my head. "Never."

She stood and took her mug to the sink. "Then I wish you both well. And Declan?"

Twisting in my seat, I glanced at her.

She turned and gave me a small smile. "Don't leave it so long before you talk to me again, yeah?"

"Yes, ma'am," I said, giving her a mock-salute.

A noise from the bedroom—a small voice calling out—indicated that Phoebe was stirring.

"Shall I?" Ruth asked.

"Do you mind if I do?" I didn't want to cause problems between Ruth and me, especially when I'd just aired my dirty laundry, but I was the one Alyssa asked to babysit and didn't want to shirk my duties. Ruth shook her head and gave me a little smile.

When I poked my head into Phoebe's room, she beamed at me. I wondered if she'd thought I'd be gone when she woke. She stood on her bed and held out her arms. "Cuddles!"

I walked over and collected her into my arms. "Did you have a good sleep?"

She nodded and snuggled into my chest, and I carried her out into the living room. When she saw Ruth she almost squealed the house down.

"Nana!" She wriggled out of my arms and was across the room and into Ruth's an instant later.

Ruth gave me an apologetic look, but I waved her off. If she made Phoebe happy, I was happy. The fact that Ruth was smiling and hadn't ripped me a new arsehole like I'd thought she might, helped to keep me in a good mood.

HOURS LATER, the three of us were set up on the floor in the living room playing with Phoebe's toy cars, car mat, and her dollies when Alyssa came home.

When she walked in the door, her eyes widened in surprise as she caught sight of us. "Mum? What are you doing here?"

"I decided to drop in and see you, to find out how your date went, considering you never called me."

Alyssa blushed scarlet and I chuckled.

"Are you two all right then?" Alyssa asked warily as she glanced between us.

"Thick as thieves," Ruth answered as she cast a conspiratorial glance in my direction.

Alyssa looked over at me and I smiled and nodded. She breathed an audible sigh of relief. "Well . . . all right then. Shall I set the dinner table for one more?"

"No, sweetie, it's all right. I've gotta get back and feed your dad. You know how he can get if he doesn't eat."

Alyssa laughed, but I made a mental note to ensure Killer Curtis was well fed before I met him again. Ruth hugged everyone goodbye and was gone within ten minutes of Alyssa's arrival. Although a slight paranoia built that Ruth had only hung around because she didn't trust me, the truth was she'd never once made me feel like I couldn't take care of Phoebe.

While I kept Phoebe entertained, Alyssa set about preparing a meal in the kitchen. I felt like an arse for not even thinking about dinner before then, but Ruth, Phoebe, and I had been getting along so well that nothing else had crossed my mind.

I snuck up behind Alyssa while she was at the sink washing some vegetables and wrapped my arms around her from behind. She leaned back against me and gave a small, delectable moan in response. I used one hand to brush the hair away from her neck and began trailing small kisses along her skin. The things she inspired in me. Every nerve ending sang with a need to be closer to her. I spun her around and captured her mouth. She kissed me back ferociously. If I hadn't been hyperaware of the little ears in the next room, I would have taken her then and there.

I released her lips, but held her waist. "I was thinking, maybe I could stay here for a few days. I mean, that is if you don't mind."

She let out a shaky breath and shook her head. "I don't mind."

Moving one of my hands around her body, I caressed her crotch through her pants. "That's good. Because I have a number of plans and it might take some time to work through them all."

I pressed her into the bench so that she knew what she'd done to me. I was solid as a rock.

Alyssa breathed into my ear, "I like plans." She grabbed my erection and it was my turn to groan. Her skilful fingers wrapped around it even through my shorts. God, I was so ready for her. She knew it and she smirked as she dropped her hand. "Unfortunately, I have to prepare sustenance for everyone and then get a certain little someone off to bed first."

I blinked but was unable to do anything more. Not with the promise of hot sex burning in my mind. I wanted her so badly, even more after the little things I'd learned today. Gritting my teeth, and breathing through my nose, I willed away my erection. I just had to wait a few short hours. Finally, I gathered up enough strength to move my mouth and ask how her day was.

The night ran smoothly from there. We all ate and then

watched a bit of TV. Phoebe—the little Judas—ratted me out to Alyssa, telling her about the ice-cream lunch, but thankfully Alyssa didn't seem too upset. She cast me the evil eye for a moment, but then smiled and shook her head a little in a slightly mocking way. As if that was what she'd expected to happen. It should have made me feel like a failure, only it didn't.

Fuck, she was good for me.

Alyssa bathed and dressed Phoebe again, and then at bedtime we both read Phoebe some stories until her eyes shut, and we left the room in silence.

The instant Alyssa had pulled Phoebe's door shut, Alyssa attacked me. Her hands were in my hair, then tugging at my pants, and then pulling at my shirt. Even as her fingers worked their way over my body, her lips touched my lips, then my neck where she nipped and sucked at my skin. Her whole being was in constant motion in my arms. I held her as close as I could, grinding myself against her as we connected. She turned to head toward the bedroom, but I stopped her. There was something else I wanted to do.

The thought of screwing her near the kitchen sink, of finishing exactly what she'd started earlier, had been playing through my mind, and I wouldn't be satisfied with anything less.

Leaving the light off, I moved her into position and worked my zipper down, leaving the button done so my shorts didn't fall around my feet. Then I pushed down my boxers just far enough to release my erection. I propped Alyssa up on the bench, pulling her skirt up and pushing her undies to the side. Lining myself up, I drove hard into her.

She cried out a little, her voice thick with lust. "Oh, fuck me, Dec." She bit her lip and dropped her head as her hands gripped my shoulders, holding me as I followed her instruction.

Reaching down between us, I rubbed my thumb along her clit while I continued to slam against her. Before long, she came around me, and I followed just moments later.

Without breaking our connection, I started to love her the way she deserved. First kissing her lips, and then trailing my mouth along her neck and shoulders. I pulled her shirt open and caressed her breasts softly.

"God, I can't help myself around you. I need you so bad," I whispered.

"It's okay. I needed that too." I could see her small smile even in the darkness. "More than you could know," she added in a whisper.

Lifting her off the bench, I carried her to the bedroom where I would spend all night loving her if she allowed me to.

CHAPTER TWENTY-FOUR

DO-OVER

AFTER A LONG sleep-in and pancakes for breakfast, Alyssa, Phoebe, and I finally emerged from the house around noon. The doctor called my phone while I was in bed, but recalling his words of doubt, I didn't want to talk to him so I let it go to message bank.

When our day finally got underway properly, I took them both to Ben and Jade's. I had, despite Alyssa's concerns, organised for the pair to watch Phoebe for the evening while Alyssa and I had our date in the city—the one I'd planned with the concierge at the Suncrest Hotel. Phoebe, for her part, was overjoyed by the idea of staying somewhere new. When she saw their baby, her eyes lit up with excitement. It was an un-fucking-real experience.

I stayed for about an hour with them all, but then I had to leave—there was still too much to be arranged. When I left Alyssa with everyone else, it was with the promise of arranging a car to pick her up and bring her to me when everything was ready. It meant that she and Phoebe had to stay with Ben and Jade for the better part of the afternoon, but that played perfectly into my plan.

Alyssa still had no idea what I'd arranged. The only clue she had was that it required dressing up, and that was only because I'd arranged to have a dress delivered to her a little after three.

The truth was, I was as nervous as fuck about my plan, but I was also determined not to fuck up the opportunity. If I could, I would have actually rewritten history.

Because that was impossible, I was instead going to try replacing it with something a little happier.

When everything was nearly ready, I glanced around the room and surveyed the handiwork of the team of staff who were still running around doing the final preparation for the night. Fairy lights covered almost every inch of the ceiling; they were the only thing lighting the room. Sheer white curtains enclosed the dance floor, making it into a private oasis. Satisfied, I walked around the table and dance floor one last time, greeting everyone personally. I could tell the racing fans from the others—they were the ones with a star-struck look when they shook my hand.

Finally, I called everyone together for a quick explanation of how the night would run. I ensured the DJ had the playlist I had created as well as strict instructions not to play a single damn song that wasn't on that fucking list. Everyone nodded and agreed, and I smiled.

It was going to be perfect or heads were going to roll.

With nothing else left to do, I pulled out my phone for the fifteenth time. Ben was supposed to call me the instant Alyssa left their house so that I would have time to change without being dressed too early, and he hadn't called yet. For a few more minutes, I watched the screen, before throwing the phone in my pocket again and heading to the toilets to get changed anyway. It wouldn't matter if I was in the monkey suit for a few minutes longer than absolutely necessary. For the night, I'd gone all out and bought a proper tuxedo, with a bowtie and all. The suit was sharp lines of black and white, but the bow tie was bright red and matched the dress I'd bought for Alyssa. Or more specifically, the dress the shop assistant had assured me would be perfect based on the photo I had of Alyssa.

I was halfway through doing up my shirt when my phone finally rang. I stumbled around after it, pulling it loose from the pocket of the pants I'd cast off moments earlier. "Hello?"

"Young Declan," a female voice I didn't immediately recognise said. It had a certain calm menace to it.

"Who is this?" I asked.

The voice laughed and a shiver ran down my spine. The cougaresque tones gave away who it was. "I'm hurt, Declan."

"Ms. Wood," I said coolly.

"Please, I've told you before, call me Paige."

"What do you want, Ms. Wood?" Calling her by her first name would indicate comfort and familiarity. Despite the moment between us at Bathurst, I felt neither.

"I'm calling to see if I can borrow your star power."

I pinched the bridge of my nose. "Why?"

"There's a little fundraiser in town tomorrow night and I'm trying to drum up some extra interest."

I was confused why she was calling me, and for more reasons than just the obvious—that I'd turned down every offer she'd ever made to join her team. Bathurst hadn't exactly been the first, it had just been the first I'd even partly stopped to listen to her. "Aren't you supposed to be in Bahrain?"

"Ah, see my boy, that's where the problem comes. I promised I would front a driver for this charity thing in Brisbane, but I didn't realise how close it was to the Bahrain race. Unfortunately, Hunter has already left the country and is unavailable to attend."

How the fuck is that my problem? I remained silent.

"Then it occurred to me that you had some spare time on your hands, and I wondered if you might like to go in his place?"

I blinked, uncomprehending. "You want me to go to some charity event to represent you? I drive for Holden and Sinclair, not for Ford or Wood."

"I know," she said, her voice almost soft and musical. Her attempt at seductive. Once, it might have worked on me. Now, it had nothing on Alyssa's voice, which was sexy without her even trying. "Alas, you are my last resort. I hate to let down a charity. They wanted to raffle off signed ProV8 merchandise to raise vital funds."

I closed my eyes and rubbed my thumb and forefinger across

my eyelids. I was getting tired of this dance of hers. "Look, Paige," I relented, using her name in the hope she'd think I'd seriously considered her request. "I'd love to help. I really would. But I've got my own stuff going on right now, and frankly, I don't think they'd like a Holden driver signing Ford merchandise."

"Young Declan," I could hear the condescension in her voice, "I will ensure they have ProV8 materials only, nothing to reference either Ford or Holden."

"I just don't think I can make it, I'm afraid." I was still trying to be polite, but my voice was cold.

"Oh, that is a shame. Especially when it's such a worthy cause. Those poor sick children."

I knew I was going to regret it as soon as the thought came to mind, but I had to ask. "What kids?"

"The money is for the children's hospital. They're raising money to help save the lives of children and babies. You know Danny loves that it when you show your support for those sorts of causes."

I pulled the phone away from my face and let loose a stream of vitriol. With a growl, I banged the fist that held my phone against my forehead. How the fuck was I supposed to say no to something that would help the people who helped my baby? Who had saved her life? "Fine," I murmured into the phone. Generally I would have ran this past Sinclair's PR team, but I was certain they'd be too busy with the Bahrain race to worry about what I was doing. Plus, how could they disagree? So long as it was generic ProV8 items, there wasn't any bad publicity that could come from a fundraiser for a children's hospital.

"Wonderful news," Paige said, her voice full of quiet confidence, as if she'd expected that result all along. She probably had. Manipulative bitch. "I have two spare tickets at the table. I'm sure, based on your *reputation*, that you shouldn't have too much trouble finding someone to attend with you. We can't have our leading man turn up alone, after all."

I gritted my teeth. "First, I'm not your 'leading man,' and don't worry I won't be alone. Just send the details through to my phone."

"Absolutely," Paige's delighted voice was as soft and creepy as her persuasive tone.

"Is that all?" I asked.

"Yes. Although I do wish you would reconsider my offer? I know you'd be very happy here, and we would definitely benefit from your unique talents."

"Thanks, but no thanks. I'll help out for charity, but that's it. I've told you, I'm still Sinclair through and through."

"Such loyalty." She chuckled before disconnecting the call.

"Fuck!" I shouted into the empty room, my temporary state of undress forgotten. My phone beeped and I noticed I had a missed call from Ben's number. Ten minutes earlier. He must have called just as Paige had.

Shit. Fuck. Damn.

It meant that Alyssa was already on her way and I had about twenty minutes to finish getting ready. I spent another couple of minutes giving Ben a quick call back to apologise and thank him for helping out. I ended the call asking how Alyssa was when she'd left.

Ben laughed. "She was a bit pissed about the car you got."

I joined in with his laughter, easily able to picture the look on her face when the hot pink stretch Hummer rolled up in front of Ben and Jade's house.

"And can I just say wow! You should see her. If I wasn't married . . ." He gave a low whistle. I heard Jade laughing in the background.

After hearing Ben's words, I was even more excited to see Alyssa. She was beautiful to me anyway, but I had a feeling tonight she would look extra special. I pulled on the tuxedo as quickly as I could. Then I checked everything in the ballroom one last time before walking down the stairs to the lobby. My original intention was to wait near the staircase, but because I was so anxious to see her, I soon moved just outside the entrance to greet her there instead. As the minutes dragged on, I kept edging closer to the road until I was standing right next to the bellhop who was helping people from their vehicles.

Fidgeting with my suit, playing with the bowtie around my neck, and raking my hands through my hair, I counted the seconds as I waited for her. When the huge pink monstrosity turned off the street to head to the hotel, I couldn't stop myself from leaping forward, knowing that my heart rested inside. I had the door open the instant it stopped.

When I saw Alyssa, my breath caught. She was too beautiful for words. As I helped her from the Hummer I noticed just how soft and silken the floor-length dress was. The colour made her skin appear almost luminous. The material clung tightly to her body, showing off her curves and leaving nothing to the imagination. I could already envisage peeling it off her later. Her hair was swept up into a loose bun, some curls falling loosely around her face. Her make-up was light and natural.

Once we were both on the footpath, I guided her into my hold before sweeping one hand from her shoulders to her thighs. "Fuck, Alyssa, you look—" I struggled to find the appropriate sentiment. "Fuck."

She flushed a deep shade of crimson before she looked me over. "You look great too, Dec." She eyed the hotel apprehensively. She whispered, "What are we doing *here*?"

"I'm exorcising my demons, and humbly requesting a do-over." I held out my arm to her. When she linked her arms around it, I led her into the hotel.

Ignoring the looks from the staff and other visitors, I headed straight for the stairs and walked her into our private function in the ballroom. As soon as the doors opened the sounds of Chicago's "Hard for me to Say I'm Sorry" filled the room.

She glanced around her in awe. "What is this?" she asked in a hushed tone.

"I wanted to tell you what you mean to me. To show you what you've *always* meant to me."

"What do you mean?" She looked up at me, her eyes soft and trusting. I led her to the enclosed dance floor, pushing the curtains out of the way. They fell back in place around us, wrapping us in their soft cocoon. I pulled her close and began to slow dance with her while the words I needed to say played around us.

I looked into her eyes. "I never told you that this is what it felt like when we danced at the school formal."

She cocked her head to the side but remained silent.

"Just the two of us. In our own little world. Everything else around us just . . . faded away." I pointed to the gossamer curtains, explaining their relevance.

"I . . . I don't know what to say," she whispered. Tears deepened the brown in her eyes, but she was smiling widely.

"You don't have to *say* anything. Let's just dance for a while, shall we?"

She nodded and then rested her head on my shoulder.

I tucked her even closer into me, until her hair brushed softly across my cheek. The song ended and the next one began. Song after song came on as we danced in our own little circle, never breaking contact. I didn't know if Alyssa realised the significance of the playlist. Each song was a message of apology, or a promise that I wasn't going anywhere.

We swayed to our own unique beat regardless of the tempo of the music. I closed my eyes and allowed everything else to fall away. The rhythm of our synchronised breathing was more beautiful than any sounds musicians could compile.

Finally, it was the time in the playlist for "The Reason" by Hoobastank. It was the message I wanted to deliver more than anything else. I whispered the lyrics against Alyssa's hair, trying to impart to her exactly how much I meant them. I felt small sobs wrack her body as the words reached her. When I got to the chorus, I pulled back and stared into her eyes.

Our bodies stopped moving as we pulled back and stared into each other's souls. I felt that some part of me was repairing slowly. That some place that had gone dark years ago was filling with light. I could only hope Alyssa felt the same way.

I'd arranged with the DJ for there to be a pause in the apology songs for some instrumental music so we could sit and talk for a while, over dinner. But before we did though, there was one last thing I needed to do.

I brushed away the remnants of her tears with my finger. Then, after kissing her tear-stained cheeks, I stepped away from her and pulled a small box from my pocket. I sank to my knee in front of her.

She shook her head a little in disbelief.

"Lys, I know it's only been a few weeks that you've been back in my life, but you've changed me, even in that short amount of time. I feel better about who I am when I'm with you. I love you with all my heart, and I know there will never be anyone else for me. I have no doubts anymore."

She shook her head more fiercely and started to talk. I held up a finger and pleaded silently with her to wait. She closed her mouth again.

"I know this is fast, and I know it is the backwards way of doing things, but I would love for you to move in with me when you come to Sydney." I flipped open the lid on the box and showed her the set of keys I had arranged to be cut especially for her. The key ring that held them was a smooth, unending silver circle that looked vaguely like a snake eating its own tail. The sales assistant had informed me it was an eternity circle. It was the perfect gift for Alyssa. Of course I could never tell her that it cost almost $300. She would freak if she knew.

She laughed, relieved. "Oh my God, Declan! You arse. I thought—" She cut off as she slapped my shoulder.

I stood back up and closed the lid again. I held out the box for her, but she just stared at my hand.

It was clear what she thought, and I decided to put her worries at bay. "Maybe one day," I responded wistfully. "But we're not ready for that just yet."

She looked from my hand to my face and back again. "Can . . . can I think about it?"

I nodded but pressed the box into her hand. "Keep the keys regardless. I want you to be free to come and go as you please. I want you in my life. All of you, or at least, as much as you'll give me."

"Thank you. For the weekend. For tonight. For being here. For everything. This . . . this is something I never even dared to let myself dream of."

I pulled her close to me again and put my lips to her ear. "I just want you to be happy. I love you."

"I love you too. And I am happy."

After pressing my lips to hers for a fraction of a second, I pushed aside the curtain and announced it was time to eat. Half the fairy lights had been turned off and a candlelit table for two had been set up in the room. I had to hand it to the hotel, they were doing everything right, and I hadn't even noticed them making the changes they had while they set up the dinner table.

I pulled Alyssa's chair out for her. When she sat, I kissed her cheek before taking my own seat.

"Do you ever do anything that is just plain and simple?" she asked, looking around again.

I grabbed the champagne from the cooler and popped it. As I filled our glasses, I responded, "Why would I do something plain and simple for someone so extraordinary?"

My words had the desired response—a red flush crossed her cheeks and ran down her chest. She dropped her eyes to the table and fidgeted with the loose strands of her hair. A moment later, she brought her eyes back up to meet mine and gave me a smile.

"Are you telling me I should just be quiet and accept what you do for me?" she asked.

"Yes, that's exactly what I'm telling you." I clasped one of her hands in mine, bringing it to my lips before placing it back on the table, still entwined with my own. I didn't know if you could eat grilled barramundi with one hand, but I was willing to give it a try if it meant not breaking the connection with Alyssa.

"So what are your plans for tomorrow?" I queried, as we began to pick at our meals.

"I probably should have told you sooner. I work every Wednesday through Friday, while Phoebe goes to day care. I was on holidays until last Friday and this is my first full week back. So . . ."

"So, I'll have to fend for myself." I quirked my eyebrow at her.

"That's what you're telling me?"

She smiled. "However will you cope?"

"I'm sure I'll manage . . . somehow," I joked. I thought now would be the perfect time to tell her about the fundraiser that I had agreed to attend. "Although, there is a way you can make it up to me."

Her fork stilled halfway to her mouth and she eyed me warily.

"I've agreed to attend a fundraiser. You know the sort of thing—sign some V8 gear that's going to be raffled off, have some dinner, and schmooze with the wealthy and wannabe elite. I was wondering whether you'd like to come and be my date. You can help keep me sane."

"Well, if your sanity is on the line," she deadpanned.

"Absolutely it is," I argued. "Two hours in a room full of strangers—knowing all the while you are at home waiting for me—may just be enough to destroy my last hold on reality."

"We wouldn't want that."

"Exactly. So will you come with me?"

She tilted her head to the side and then smirked at me. She put the forkful of fish in her mouth and chewed it slowly, as if deliberating. She swallowed. "Okay, but only on one condition."

"What's that?"

"You pick me up from my parents' house. Mum'll grab Phoebe from day care like usual so it'll be easier for me just to get ready and go from there."

"Oh, I see how it is," I joked. "You're sick of me already and don't want me around anymore, but you just don't know how to tell me that."

"No," she said adamantly. "Why would you think that?"

"Because you know full well Curtis is going to kill me if I go anywhere near your parents' house."

"It'll be fine," she said. "He won't do it while Phoebe's in the room."

I made a mental addition to my list—Curtis needed to be well fed, and Phoebe needed to be around, when I saw him next. Which was going to be tomorrow. I drew a shaky breath. "Okay."

"Okay?" she asked, surprise evident in her voice.

"Okay. I'll be there at six thirty to pick you up. Curtis be damned."

She smiled and reached for my hands. "It'll be fine, Dec."

"No," I argued. "It won't. He hates me."

"You're probably right. And he'll probably have a million and one questions and demands."

"I'll do it," I said. "Or at least—I'll try. For you."

"Thank you, Dec."

"I'll get a dress delivered to their house. I'll just need the address." I figured that they must have moved because their phone number had been disconnected when I'd tried it in London.

She rolled her eyes. "I can pick my own clothes, Declan."

"I know. I just know you won't have time—and I want you to look stellar . . . not that you don't always."

She laughed. "You're hopeless."

"Hopelessly in love."

"Fine, if you have to buy me a dress," she said the words in disgust, "Do it. But no damn pink Hummer this time."

"No problems, baby." I brought her hand up to my lips again and suddenly had no appetite, except my insatiable desire for her. "Are you done?"

She nodded.

"Did you want to dance some more—or can I show you something?"

She shrugged. "I'm ready to go if you are."

I nodded as I stood. The concierge suddenly appeared at my side. "I trust everything went to plan this evening?" he asked.

"Absolutely," I said, but I couldn't tear my eyes off Alyssa long enough to glance in his direction.

"Well, enjoy the rest of your evening, sir, madam."

"We will," I said. My voice was probably laden with carnal promises, but I couldn't have cared less.

"Your car will be waiting out front."

"Thank you," I said, without a backwards glance. "Be sure to leave yourself a little something when you charge my card."

Alyssa glanced back, no doubt beginning to wonder just how much it costs to hire the ballroom of the Suncrest Hotel for a private function like the one we'd just shared. I didn't want to tell her, because the answer was a fuckton of money. But it didn't matter to me, it was only money, and if I had achieved my goal of erasing some of the pain of the high school formal, it was worth every cent.

Once Alyssa and I were in the car, I drove across to West End, close to the spot where I had taken Ruby—or more specifically, she had taken me.

I helped Alyssa across to the railing, and we sat side by side with my arm wrapped over her shoulder, watching the moon over the city. We stayed still for almost half an hour, just revelling in each other, in our relationship, in the quiet.

"It's beautiful," she whispered.

"It's nothing compared to the beauty I can see in front of me," I said, staring at her.

She smiled at me before nuzzling in closer for a moment. "Let's go get Phoebe and go home."

I pulled her in to me, kissing her hard. Then I nodded. "Sounds good."

Even though I'd had another plan for the spot, I'd realised earlier that she still wasn't ready for what I wanted. I was glad I had done the bait and switch with the key ring. It had given me the perfect opportunity to see how she would react to the more important question.

I now knew that the ring burning a hole in my pocket would have to wait for a little while longer.

I HELD Alyssa in my arms, a satisfied smile on my face. Helping her from the dress had been every bit as enjoyable as I'd thought it would be. Phoebe had fallen asleep before we'd arrived home, so we'd just carried her into the house and put her straight into bed. Then I'd enjoyed every part of Alyssa—repeatedly. I still marvelled that I had ever sought comfort in the arms of anyone else. No random encounter could ever match what we shared.

"Declan!" Alyssa called unexpectedly, her voice filled with terror. "Don't go . . .," she whimpered.

I pulled her closer and kissed her mouth softly. "I'm not going anywhere. You're my reason to live," I whispered, to comfort her. "I want to be with you forever."

She smiled in her sleep and curled in to me.

I watched as her emotions flitted across her face. Even though I was starting to grow tired myself, I fought the urge to sleep, more content to watch her sleep.

"You want me to marry you?" she asked.

My heart thudded as I held her tightly, waiting for the answer to the dream proposal.

"Yes," she breathed.

I kissed her cheek and settled down to sleep, comfortable in the knowledge that eventually—when the time was right—I might get the response that had once scared the hell out of me, but that I now wanted more than anything in the world.

CHAPTER TWENTY-FIVE

CREATIVE VISUALISATION

THE NEXT MORNING, I woke to an empty bed and a silent house. A note from Alyssa rested on the bedside table, thanking me for the previous night, and again for early that morning. She also reminded me to pick her up from her parents' house, leaving their address at the bottom. I folded it up and put it into my wallet, but not until I had taken an extra minute to read the words a second time.

Taking a moment to relax, I rolled over onto Alyssa's side of the bed, relishing in the smell of her that clung to the blankets and sheets. I began to imagine what it would be like if—no, *when*—she was living with me. When I could roll over in the morning and she would be there. Her presence would be stamped on every surface of every room in my house. I could already picture which room I would change to give Phoebe a toy room as well as planning out a dream bedroom for her. It was easy to imagine a swing set beside the pool in the backyard. Everything was going to be . . . maybe not perfect, because nothing ever was, but it would be real.

With those images in my mind, I stood and began to get ready for the day. First, I made a mental list of everything I needed to achieve before the time came to collect Alyssa from her folks' house. I tried to put the actual reunion with Killer Curtis out of my mind, because when I allowed my mind to brush across that subject, my knees began to quiver, my heart began to pound, and my palms grew sweaty.

Despite pushing it from my thoughts as best as I was able, the worry remained buried inside me, waiting for the worst possible moment to strike me down with panic. Each time I'd thought I was finally free of the panic, it clawed down my throat and clenched my heart in its icy grip.

Getting ready for the day, I grabbed a change of clothes. As I yanked them out of my bag, it struck me that I really needed to get some more casual clothes. Especially as I was planning on an extended stay. With things working so well with Alyssa, there was no need for me to return to Sydney until I absolutely had to for preseason preparation.

The shopping trip Alyssa and I had taken a week earlier hadn't exactly stocked up my wardrobe. I had two choices: wear the same outfit every few days and learn how to wash my own clothes, or buy more shit. The "buy more" option won hands down.

After I'd set my plan, the first thing I did was ring the dress shop I'd visited the previous day. I asked for the assistant who'd served me and was in luck, because she was on. When I had her on the phone, I double-checked that she remembered me. It was a stupid question really, because how many blokes came in, ordered an Armani tux off the rack plus demanded a dress—which must be available immediately—with only a photo and a borrowed dress to work out sizing.

The clerk asked how our evening had gone, and I politely told her it went well—which was the understatement of the century— then I told her I needed a favour. A new dress, exactly the same size, delivered to a different address. I explained the basics of the type of event it was for but left it in her court to select what Alyssa would wear. I also ordered a new bow tie to match the dress. It was going to piss me off that I couldn't be completely ready for Alyssa when I picked her up, but there was little I could do about it if I wanted us to match.

I packed my tux back up into the bag it came in, getting it ready to take to the dry-cleaners. With those two items ticked off my to-do list, I climbed into the car for the rest of my tasks. I was halfway down the street when the phone rang. I pushed the Bluetooth button to answer it.

"Declan." Dr. Henrikson's voice filled my car.

"Doc," I replied as I pulled the car over to the side of the road so I could give him my full concentration. "Sorry I missed your call yesterday. I, uh, wasn't sure whether you'd call back today."

"I told you I would in my message."

I didn't say that I'd told him to fuck off last time we spoke, and that was part of the reason I hadn't answered when he rang while Alyssa and I were having our lie-in. That and the fact that I was buried balls-deep in the woman I loved. But, now that he was on the phone, I was happy to ignore the issue of our last phone call and the things he'd said. At that moment, I actually needed to talk to him. A moment passed in silence while I tried to think of the best way to raise my problem.

"Did you want me to stop calling?" he asked tentatively, when I still hadn't spoken.

"Fuck, no, Doc. I mean I *was* pissed off over your suggestion." *Couples' therapy.* I wanted to laugh, especially considering how well our last two dates had gone.

"I still think it's a good idea," he said. "Even if you do it just to prove me wrong."

"I dunno, but I'll talk to Alyssa about it," I conceded.

"I think that would be a step in the right direction. You need to keep the lines of communication open between the two of you if you want to have a stable relationship."

"I do."

"Okay," he said, and I knew the matter was dropped. "Why don't you tell me what has happened since we last spoke? Are there any new developments?"

I smiled to myself. "Are there ever," I said enthusiastically. "I asked her to move in with me."

Although I wanted to be honest with him, I refrained from telling him about the engagement ring I'd purchased. He would be about as supportive of the idea as Alyssa had been when I was down on one knee.

"And what did she say?" His voice was still tentative, as if he was uncertain what to say—or maybe he was just unsure how I would react to his question.

"She said she needs to think about it."

He breathed in relief. "She sounds like a wise woman."

"What? Why?" I wondered why her needing to think about it was such a good thing.

"Because, as I said the other day, I think you need to be careful about pushing things too far too soon. You've only just come back into her life. You're still adjusting to the idea of being a father and of being in a committed relationship again. Don't misunderstand me, I think it's commendable that you want to make up for past mistakes. I would just like to see that you don't make an even bigger one in the process."

"There are no bigger mistakes than leaving Alyssa," I snapped. Then I pinched the bridge of my nose and sighed to calm myself down. "Sorry, I'm just . . . on edge."

"What about, Declan? Remember you have the ultimate control in our conversations. We can discuss anything that is bothering you."

"I'm seeing Alyssa's parents again tonight, or at least her dad. It'll be the first time since . . . well, since everything happened. I saw her mum, Ruth, the day before yesterday, not long after our last conversation actually, and it went pretty well, but I don't think a reunion with her dad is going to go nearly as smoothly. He hates me, both Lys and Ruth have said as much." I had a major case of verbal diarrhoea, but I couldn't stop the word vomit once it had started.

Dr. Henrikson chuckled a little. "Yes, you do sound a little nervous. What worries you most?"

"You mean besides the fact that he's a prison warden who knows entirely too many criminals and police? So many in fact that he would probably know how to murder me and get away scot-free?"

He laughed. "Yes, besides that."

"I guess my biggest concern—besides the fact that I honestly think he may very well kill me—is that I'll disappoint Alyssa somehow."

"Why do you think that?"

"I just . . . well, what if I have a panic attack and then pass out or something? I'm going to look like a fool."

"You've been having the attacks more regularly lately?" he asked.

I nodded, even though he couldn't see me.

He must have guessed at my answer because he continued. "Have you been using your mantra when you've experienced the attacks?"

"I've been trying, but sometimes it's hard to focus on the mantra with the thoughts and images in my head. I just feel so tightly wound, like someone is crushing every part of me." I felt the sensation begin to build in my chest even thinking about it.

"Maybe we need to work on some other coping techniques. I don't think they'll help you tonight, unfortunately; generally it takes time to be able to exercise your mind to the point where it is able to work logically through the panic."

"What sort of tools?" I asked. Anything that would help me, even a little, was a good thing. I was sorely tempted to have a glass or two of scotch before picking Alyssa up—just a little something to help take the edge off—but I knew I couldn't. I owed Alyssa more than that. And I definitely owed Phoebe more than that.

"Creative visualisation techniques."

"What the fuck?" I asked.

"Imagining that you're in your happy place," he explained.

I smiled—and then groaned—when I thought about what I would regard as my happy place. How was I supposed to not panic around Killer Curtis when I was picturing myself between his daughter's thighs? "I don't think that will help."

"It won't in the short-term. As I said, you need to train your brain to react to stimuli the way you want it to. It's not an instant fix, but unfortunately there are no instant fixes."

Typical quack talk to try to leech as much money from me as possible. He spent the next twenty minutes talking about various coping strategies and how I could implement them.

"Doc?" I asked, as he began to wind up.

"Yes, Declan."

"I just wanted to say thank you. I know I've given you a hard time about some things, but I do think you've helped me. I just wanted to tell you that."

"That's what I'm here for."

"And, well . . . I'm not sure if I'll be needing daily sessions anymore."

"You don't want me to call anymore?"

"No, it's not that. I think, in fact I know I'll still need to talk to you. Just maybe only once a week for a while."

"No problems, Declan. I'll have Lucy arrange a regular appointment for you. Once you get back in Sydney, we'll make it our face-to-face time too."

"Thanks, Doc. That sounds great."

As I hung up, I felt marginally better about the night. Nothing would save me when faced with the wrath of Alyssa's father, but at least I had a feeling that *someday* things would be all right again. I would be able to cope with the panic when it built. After all, I could do it on the track—the focus I needed to drive the car usually put all thoughts of panic attacks out the window. I considered what the doc had talked about as I drove the rest of the way to the Grand Plaza before my mental to-do list took over my thoughts.

I found a dry-cleaners and put my suit in, insisting they have it ready for me in no more than four hours. To ensure it happened, I promised them a huge-arse tip if I had it back in time. Then I went through the small collection of surf shops that Browns Plains had to offer. It was a reminder that I hated shopping for clothes. No, I *despised* shopping for clothes. The only reason my last shopping trip had been bearable was because of Alyssa.

As if things weren't bad enough—having to trudge from shop to shop to stare at mindless, repetitive fashion—I found I was followed by stares and whispers wherever I went. Everyone seemed anxious to celebrate the return of the small-town boy who made it big.

I was in City Surf, or Beach Biz, or something surfer-wannabe sounding like that, leafing through their meagre selection of shorts, when hands came to rest over my eyes.

"Guess who," a horrid, nasally voice whined in my ear.

It wasn't Alyssa, that was clear, so whoever it was had no fucking right to be touching me. Twisting roughly out of the hold, I dislodged the hands from my face. When I spun around, I found an overly tanned face smiling up at me from beneath too-blonde hair.

"Darcy," I said in greeting.

"I heard you were back in town," she purred. "I was hoping for a reunion."

She took a step toward me, and I retreated straight into the clothing racks. When she reached for me, I twisted out of her grasp. Stepping away as far as I could, I watched her constantly. I couldn't believe her gall. Of course she knew I was in town—I'd beaten her husband to a bloody pulp on my first night back.

Yet she was coming on to me in the middle of their local shopping centre. It said a lot about the state of their relationship.

"How's Blake?" I asked. I didn't really care, but I wanted to remind her of her marital vows—not that they'd mattered much to her during the masquerade ball when she'd let me fuck her in the cloakroom.

God, I was a fucking idiot.

She giggled—fucking *giggled*—before she replied. "He'll be fine. He has a thick head, so it's hard to do much permanent damage. But I don't want to talk about him. I want to talk about *us.*"

She lunged toward me again, her hand reaching toward my crotch.

I jumped backwards. Because there was nowhere for me to go, I just smashed against the rack, dislodging a few pairs of shorts. "Whoa! Back the fuck up, bitch," I said, as the plastic hangers clanged against the ground. "There is no *us.* There never was, and there never will be."

She ran her finger down my chest; her nails were like talons and were painted fairy-floss pink. "Honey, you know you've never had it as good as I gave it to you. And *that* was just a sampler."

Her voice sounded like she was aiming for seductive, but it simply came out sounding needy and pathetic.

I smiled at her—a genuine panty-dropping smirk—before leaning in to her a little. Placing my lips against her ear, I whispered, "You think we were good together?"

Her breathing hitched and she nodded.

"You want a repeat performance?"

She nodded again before tilting her face toward me a little as if to claim my lips.

"What about Blake?" I asked, still in a hushed tone.

"What he doesn't know won't hurt him." Her voice was so breathy it was almost silent.

Her body inched closer to me. I would have felt sorry for her, having delusions that anything was ever going to happen between us again, except I remembered she'd used our one-night random fling as a way to hurt Alyssa. She used *me* to hurt Alyssa—as if I hadn't caused enough suffering.

Worse, Darcy didn't even seem to regret it. She didn't care that she was hurting her own husband. Any empathy I might have had for her evaporated.

My voice changed from a throaty whisper to a low growl. "You don't have a fucking clue what good is. You were nothing more than an easy lay who threw herself at me like a slut while I was too drunk to care what I was fucking. Why don't you just back the fuck off?"

I used her surprise at my words to push past her. Without stopping, I walked straight from the shop without a backwards glance. My heart hammered in my chest and I could feel my blood pressure rising. How dare she come on to me publicly like that? As if she had some kind of claim on me. I huffed out a breath and tried to release the anger with it. There were bigger things, more important things, than Darcy happening in my life. Like seeing Curtis again. If I could remember those other things, anything she did was insignificant.

As I headed for the food court, I heard high heels clicking against the hard flooring at a rushed pace behind me. They were following me. I wheeled around as soon as Darcy's hand tugged at my shirt. She was red-faced and her eyes flashed with madness. Her mouth twisted into an angry knot, but somehow her forehead didn't shift. The look on her face was almost too funny, and I had to bite the inside of my cheeks to stop from laughing.

"Blake was right," she spat at me. "You're a fucking arse, Reede. I could have given you pleasure unimagined, but you've chosen the path of pain. Enjoy it, wanker!" She turned on her heel and stomped off.

Whatever, Psycho Bitch. I'd seen similar displays from so many women in the past it almost didn't bother me—except now I was with Alyssa and I knew it would bother her that I'd treated the women I'd been with so badly. Darcy retreated into the distance, her faux-blonde hair swaying around her shoulders. For a moment, I debated going after her and apologising but thought better of it. Alyssa might care if I treated women badly, but I figured even she'd make an exception for Darcy.

As I went about the rest of my day, I pushed thoughts of Darcy and Blake out of my head. No matter what I did though, I just couldn't shake the dread that was building in the pit of my stomach.

AT THE appointed time, I arrived at the Dawson residence. I'd been cool, calm and collected the whole time I was getting dressed, and remained so right up until I reached the turnoff for their street. In the time it had taken me to drive from the corner to their house— less than a minute—a series of tremors had broken out across my body and sweat dampened my shirt. The ache in my ribs, which had finally dropped to a dull, manageable pain, grew more pronounced—demanding attention.

When I climbed from the car my knees almost buckled beneath me. I took a moment to lean against the Monaro and do some of the deep-breathing crap that Dr. Henrikson had suggested.

I closed my eyes and tried to visualise positive things. Happy things. The problem was the only happy thoughts I could summon involved Alyssa and me in various tangled positions in her bedroom.

My fingers running over the curve at the base of her spine. My tongue tickling the spot right behind her ear—which always earned me the most perfectly sexy moan. Her hands clutching me as I pushed myself inside her. Her fingernails digging in to my arse cheeks as she came.

None of those thoughts helped to calm my breathing or stop my shakes. Instead they just gave me an instant raging hard-on and a rising sense of guilt that I was thinking about her in those positions moments before greeting her family.

I made my way slowly down the path, walking carefully so I wouldn't fall on my arse but also so my erection would stop rubbing painfully against my zipper. Even when I knocked on the door, I was still sporting a sizable lump in my pants.

When I heard Curtis call out, "I'll get it," I immediately grew flaccid. I felt like running. Even though I was too old for a game of ding-dong-ditch, I couldn't help the flight instinct that struck me.

Then again, running while my knees were jelly probably wouldn't do me much good anyway.

Plastering what I hoped looked like a confident smile on my face, I tried to ignore the fact that my insides had turned to liquid. The door swung open, and I was face-to-face with my worst nightmare. Killer Curtis in all his glory.

"Declan," he sneered at me from behind his beard. His hair, which had been the same colour as Alyssa's when I'd left, had greyed considerably and his beard was filled with salt and pepper streaks.

Fuck! I hadn't planned properly for this. I had no idea how to address him. Years ago, before I left, he was just Curtis to me. He was just a father figure whom I'd looked up to and who'd treated me as one of his own children. I gaped at him. *Curtis*. Would calling him that now be interpreted as a sign of disrespect? But then I worried that I would look like a bigger tosser if I called him sir, or worse, Mr. Dawson.

I shuddered at the thought. After blinking a few times through my blind panic, I just stared at him. His sneer morphed into a scowl and he stepped closer to me.

Oh fuck.

He closed the door behind him. Leaving me outside with him.

Alone.

In the dark.

With no Alyssa or Phoebe between us. I took a step back, wondering if it would be rude to ask whether he'd eaten yet tonight.

"Aren't you going to say anything?" he asked.

Fuck, he was a scary bastard. It wasn't that he was bigger than me. Physically, I probably could have taken him in a fight. He was just . . . intimidating. There was something about him that made him seem ten feet tall and bulletproof. He worked with hardened criminals all day, so nothing frightened him. Nothing I could do could ever hurt him. Unless I hurt Alyssa, which I never wanted to do again.

"I'm sorry," I squeaked. Fuck, I sounded as terrified as I felt. Worse, it was a grossly inadequate way of expressing how much regret I felt over everything I'd done to Alyssa.

He tilted his head to the side before walking away from the door and down an alley at the side of the house with only a metre of space between the brick wall and the fence. I eyed his outline as he walked, trying to see if I could make out the shape of a Taser or truncheon. Anything that he might use to murder me before Alyssa could come to my rescue. I couldn't see anything obvious, but that didn't mean he didn't have something hidden away.

My gaze lingered longingly on the door. Alyssa and Phoebe were behind it, waiting. My entire life in Browns Plains was being blocked from me by that piece of wood. With one more wistful glance, I turned away and followed Curtis into the dark. I knew whatever happened next had to happen for Alyssa and me to move on to the next phase of our life together.

Curtis pulled open the side gate to the house and indicated that

I should go first. I took three steps inside before I hit something solid. It would have been okay if it had been a brick wall, but it wasn't. Instead, it was Alyssa's big lug of a brother. I turned back the way I came in just in time to see Curtis pulling the gate shut.

The soft click sent chills down my spine. I swallowed hard and put my hands up in surrender.

CHAPTER TWENTY-SIX

FOR WHOSE BENEFIT

"WHAT ARE YOU doing here, Declan?" Curtis asked. His voice was gruff and without any warmth.

I turned to face him. He was blocking the gate with his arms crossed tightly across his chest and his mouth pulled into a frown. The sound of the gate clicking shut still echoed in my ears, along with the thunderous rush of my own heartbeat.

"Alyssa was doing fine without you," Josh chipped in from behind me. I couldn't decide whether or not I should turn back toward him—largely because I couldn't figure out who was the greater threat.

"You hurt her so fucking much. Yet you waltz back into her life and immediately expect everything to be fucking hunky-dory again?" Curtis barked.

"I can't believe your nerve," Josh added.

"I know," I whispered. "I fucked up. I fucked everything up. I'm trying to fix it."

They both scoffed at me.

"Trust me, I know I don't deserve a second chance after everything that's happened since I left—"

"That's right," Josh interrupted. "You don't."

Ignoring him, I stared at Curtis. "But Alyssa has been gracious enough to offer me one. And I'm not going to hurt her again."

"I've heard that before," Josh snapped. "You won't hurt her, because she's too important to you. It's all bullshit isn't it? You wouldn't know real love if it jumped up and bit you on your fucking arse."

"That's not true." I turned, glaring at Josh, raising my voice. "I love Alyssa. I love her, and she loves me."

"I won't let you hurt her." Curtis's voice was strained. The menace in it dripped off every syllable. "It's better that you go now before she gets her hopes up any higher."

"I'm not going anywhere."

"You are," Josh said, taking a step closer.

"I don't want to leave."

"I don't care." Josh was in my face. I could see his fist clenching and releasing by his side. It was clear he was getting ready to hit me, but as scared shitless as I was of him, I wasn't ready to back down. Not when it concerned Alyssa.

"What about what Alyssa wants?" I retorted. "Doesn't she get a say before *you* decide that I should be run out of town?"

"I know what Alyssa wants," Curtis said.

"What's that?" I challenged.

"Not to have her heart broken again. We were barely able to pick up the pieces last time. I won't see my baby suffer through that again."

My fingers raked into my hair and I tugged it roughly. "What do I need to say to convince you?" I sighed in exasperation. "I'm in it for life. Fuck, I'm in it for forever if she'll have me that long."

Josh laughed; one single hard laugh.

I was getting dizzy from spinning back and forth between them. Leaning against the house, I scrubbed my face with my hands. "I don't know what else I can say that will convince you." My voice was broken, but I was determined to keep it together. No tears. No panic. Just facts.

"You may have fooled Alyssa, but you can't fool me," Josh said.

"Or me," Curtis added.

"Alyssa's happy with me. Can't you be happy with that? For her sake. Or for Phoebe's."

"Don't you *dare* bring my granddaughter into this. She's better off not knowing who her father is."

"She already fucking knows who I am."

"How dare you decide something so life-changing on Alyssa's behalf," Josh said, cracking his knuckles.

I sighed. "Lys *wanted* to tell her. She doesn't think I'll hurt her. If you can't trust me—trust that."

"Alyssa is a lovesick fool," Josh said.

"You're your father's son, that's for sure," Curtis muttered in disgust.

"I am *nothing* like that fucking bastard!" I roared, pushing off from the house and stepping up to him.

"Sure, I mean you've got nothing in common, do you? Screwing random people without concern for who you are hurting?" Josh scoffed.

I whipped my head around. "That was before. I . . . I've changed. For Alyssa." My voice was a hoarse whisper as I repeated myself. "*I've changed.*"

"Well, that's quite the turnaround in a month," Josh scoffed. "From a threesome in a fucking club to a lifelong dedication to one woman."

I felt the weight of his words. They pressed in on me so heavily that I couldn't even stand up straight. Staggering backwards, I came to rest against the wall again. I shook my head weakly as it drooped on my shoulders. Once more, I tried to argue in my own defence, but spoke without conviction because he was right. I wasn't any good for Alyssa. I'd hurt her so much and every girl I'd screwed while we were apart was another fucking nail in the coffin. By now, it must have looked like a fucking sieve.

"No. That wasn't *me*," I protested weakly. "It isn't who I am, or who I *want* to be. It was . . . a mistake."

"How many women have you made your *mistakes* with over the years?" Curtis's voice was low and menacing.

"I don't know," I admitted.

"Exactly, son." His voice softened, sensing my weakness. "Can't you see that you're no good for her? She needs to be with someone who treats women with more respect than you do. Phoebe needs a chance to have a father who can show her the way she deserves to be treated."

I sagged further into the bricks, wishing that the house would open up and swallow me whole—removing me from the situation and the pain from Alyssa's life.

He was absolutely right. I didn't deserve her. I didn't deserve any of her sunshine to brighten my dismal days. I didn't deserve the life I'd pictured when I'd woken that morning. The urge to go built in me. I needed to leave before I dragged her down with me.

If only I had the strength to move my legs. If I tried to stand, to support my own weight, I would either collapse in a heap or vomit.

"Just go," Curtis said, even more softly than before. It was almost as if he was trying to give some sort of much-needed fatherly advice. "She'll be better off once you're gone."

I nodded, barely aware of anything around me. All I could think of was the myriad of ways I'd hurt Alyssa over the years. The things I could remember doing and the things I couldn't. The sorrow I'd intentionally inflicted and that which had been forced into her life by the wicked hand of fate. A single tear ran down my face and dropped off my nose onto the ground.

A gasp alerted me to the presence of another, but I couldn't raise my head to see who it was. I was sinking into an ocean of despair and I was drowning. Everything I saw, heard, and felt was black and edged in pain.

My first fear when I'd been cornered by Josh and Curtis was of being physically beaten. However, as I leaned up against the wall— physically unable to move due to the emotional weight on me—I began to think it would have been preferable. *That* I could have fought against.

But I couldn't fight my mind viciously projecting images of the broken look on Alyssa's face when I'd left her. Nor could I fight the memory of the ghost of pain that continued to live behind her eyes, despite everything I'd done to try to remove it.

I couldn't breathe. I couldn't cope. I couldn't be there anymore.

"Dad! Josh? What the hell are you doing?" Alyssa's voice broke through the darkness like a light. I turned my head in her direction, needing to tell her they were right.

That I was sorry.

That I couldn't stay.

"Oh, God, Declan," she whispered, when her eyes locked with mine. She could obviously sense my revelation. I wasn't worthy of her. I would never be worthy of her, no matter how much I did to improve myself. She shook her head disbelievingly, her mouth forming the word "no" over and over again.

My eyes filled with tears. Even in my sacrifice for her, I was going to hurt her more. I could do nothing right by her. She would've been better off if I'd never existed.

In a heartbeat, she was next to me. Her scent overwhelmed me, giving me the ability to breathe again. Her hands became warm centres I could concentrate on. I knew I was all wrong for her, but I couldn't help but cling to her desperately and pray for absolution.

"I'm sorry," I whispered. "I'm so sorry."

"Lys," Curtis said, touching her shoulder. "Why don't you go inside? We can handle this."

"Just go, *Dad*," she hissed. "I think you've done enough damage."

"But Lys—" Josh started.

"You too!" she snapped.

Josh and Curtis made no move to leave.

"Go!" she yelled.

They both took a step back.

"Now!" She sobbed as the word left her mouth.

"Lys . . ." Josh's voice was hesitant.

"No! Just leave Declan alone. Leave us both alone. You've got no clue what he's been through, or what he's done for me."

"They're right though," I whispered to her as she gathered my face between her hands. The tears began to fall in earnest, both of us shedding our share. "I've done everything wrong by you. I should go so you can find the happiness you deserve." I blinked rather than focus on the pain in her gaze. "You'd be better off without me."

She shook her head again before staring hard into my eyes. Her voice was firm but full of sorrow when she spoke. "I haven't had a *day* of true happiness since you left. Even the days that were good would have been so much better with you by my side."

I shook my head in disbelief.

She brushed the hair from my face before pulling me away from the wall and further into her embrace. "I love you, Dec. Only you. Stay. Please? For me." Her voice was softer as she said the final words. She met my gaze; her eyes searched mine for something. Tears pooled around her lashes, no doubt reflecting the ones in my own eyes.

With our gazes locked, one thing became clear. I couldn't deny her a single fucking thing. If she wanted me to stay, I could never leave again. My eyes closed as I nodded once. A sigh passed her lips and she rested her forehead against mine.

"Thank you." The words were silent and perfect. Meant for only me.

My stomach clenched at the thought and I reached for her hand, clasping it in mine.

Curtis took a step toward us and touched her arm. "Alyssa—"

"Get away from us," she spat the words at him as she shook off his touch.

Leaving her forehead resting against mine, she brushed her hand across my cheek and touched a soft kiss to my lips. After a moment, she turned away from me.

"Lys," Josh said.

"How *dare* you!" she said, whipping around to face her father and brother. "Both of you! I've made my thoughts on this matter very clear."

She turned back to me, and I cupped her face between my hands. Her tears ran down my fingers.

"I love him," she said, as she met my gaze again.

"I love you too," I whispered back.

She turned her full attention to me. I lifted my head a little. The faith she was putting in me provided me with strength.

Her hands came to rest against my neck.

"Why don't we go inside?" she asked. "I know there's someone in there who's been asking for you."

"Are you sure?" I asked in response. "If I just disappeared now, she'd forget me. Maybe—"

"No! Stop. It wouldn't be better. We wouldn't be happier. It wouldn't be preferable. She needs you. Goddammit, I need you, Dec. Now's your chance to step up and be a fucking man."

I chuckled despite the gloom that had settled on me. I nodded. "There's just one thing I need to do first."

A grin twisted my mouth as she tilted her head in confusion. Without waiting for permission, I pushed my hands into her hair and drew her face closer to mine. I kissed her hard, trying to show her my need and desire—even my fears—in that one kiss.

WAITING FOR Alyssa to finish getting ready was a subdued and uncomfortable experience. An uneasy truce had settled over the house. Curtis and Josh made themselves scarce, but at one point I'd heard Ruth chewing them both out in another room. It was the type of thing I would have usually found hilarious, but I couldn't find any amusement in it with the doubts that were playing in my mind.

Even Phoebe seemed to absorb the sombre atmosphere. Although she was excited to see me at first, she quickly fell into thoughtful silence. I could easily say it was one of the most unpleasant experiences in my life—which really was saying something considering how fucked-up parts of my life had been. Thankfully, Alyssa didn't take too much time to finish dressing. Just before we left, I stopped to give Phoebe extra cuddles, trying to draw comfort and composure from her. I had no idea how I was going to cope with being on display all night. Pressing the flesh and playing nice with the charity crowd seemed an impossible task with the dread still coursing through my body.

The drive to the city was just as awkward; the conversation stale and stilted. Even though I'd promised Alyssa I would stay, the urge to run still built within me. It weighed down my limbs and made every action more difficult than it should have been.

"I'm sorry about Dad and Josh," Alyssa said. It was the fourth time she'd tried to apologise on their behalf.

I shook my head. "They were just looking out for you."

I couldn't meet her eyes, because if I did, I would falter. I would have broken down. The problem was that nothing Curtis and Josh had said was a lie. Every word was the truth—a truth I needed to remember so I didn't hurt Alyssa worse than I already had. With the choices I'd made, I'd damaged her in ways I couldn't possibly begin to fix.

Glancing across the car, the thought that staying with her would cause her more problems in the long run ran on a loop in my mind. To stop the words coming out of my mouth, I sighed and raked my hand through my hair.

"They're wrong!" she said. Each word was pitched higher than the last. "Ask me again."

The insistent tone in her voice drew my attention. As I parked the car, I watched her carefully as I spoke. "Ask you what?"

"What you asked me last night. On the dance floor. Ask me again."

"Move in with me?" I asked, trying to confirm whether that was the question she wanted me to ask.

"Yes, Declan. Yes. I want to."

"But what about—" I wanted to raise all the concerns the doc had raised, the points her father and Josh had made. I wasn't to be trusted. I was poisonous. Because of me, she would be hurt again. She pressed her fingers to my lips to cut me off.

"I don't care about anything else. The details will work themselves out in the end. All I know is that I don't want to be apart from you again. I let you walk away once, and I'll be damned if I'm going to do it again. These last few weeks have been un-fucking-believable. I've dreamt about you sweeping me back into your arms so many times during the years. That's why I needed another taste of the forbidden fruit in London. How could I resist it? Resist you. You're every dream I ever had. But this, Dec, everything you've done and become since coming home, it's all been so much more than I could have ever imagined."

"But, Lys—"

"No, no buts. It's my fault we had a bad start to the night. I thought my father would be more mature than that. He seemed to understand . . ." She trailed off and then sighed. "Let's worry about that later. For now, let's go inside and enjoy ourselves."

I scrunched my nose in disgust—it might have been for a good cause, but at the end of the day, I was still going to be stuck as the "celebrity du jour" for the night.

Alyssa laughed a little, the melodic tune helping to lighten my mood. At least a little.

"Okay," I whispered.

"Okay," she repeated with a firm voice. "Let's do it."

I took a deep breath and pushed open the car door. As she came near me, I eyed Alyssa's shoes. They were fuck-hot and made her legs appear longer, but they weren't exactly practical. Especially considering I'd had to park under King George Square secure parking, and we'd have a short walk to City Hall, where the benefit was being held.

"Aren't those a bit of a health hazard?" I asked, nodding at her feet.

She lifted one foot and twisted it left and then right. Fantasies of fucking her with those shoes on raced through my mind as she did. "They're just shoes," she said, after a moment.

At first, I thought she was responding to the fantasies playing through my mind.

"No, I mean you used to have a habit of tripping over thin air," I teased. "Do you really think stilettos were a good choice?"

She poked her tongue out at me and I narrowed my eyes.

"Do that again," I dared her, wrapping my arms around her waist and holding her tightly.

When she stuck her tongue out again, I captured it between my lips. With a small moan of delight rumbling in my throat, I sucked it into my mouth before pushing my own forward to meet it. She melted into me as our kiss grew hotter and less PG-13. She shivered in my hold, and I backed away. "Let's get you inside. It'll be warmer in there."

She nodded.

I slung my arm around her shoulders, and together we walked to City Hall. As we came up onto the top of the square, two thoughts struck me. The first was that the last time I'd been to City Hall was for the New Year's Ball—the one where I'd fucked Darcy in the cloakroom. It made me sick to my stomach to think that I had ever stuck my dick into that skank, but the thought that sickened me the most was that she was by no means the worst. I'd sunk to much deeper depths during my time away from Alyssa.

The second thing that struck me was that by going into the fundraiser with Alyssa on my arm, I was announcing to the public that I was a changed man. I was *arriving* at a function with a date rather than just leaving with someone else's. It might have seemed insignificant, but I was telling the world that Alyssa Dawson owned me completely. That I was trying to put my past behind me for a better future. The doubts and concerns, which had threatened to drown me all night, lifted with the thought. I stole a glance at Alyssa and saw she was watching me intently.

"Wow," she whispered. "What just happened? You look . . . lighter somehow."

"I just realised I love you."

She chuckled. "Good, because I love you too."

I moved my hand so that it rested on her hip and pushed her into the room slightly ahead of me. A few heads turned to look at her, before looking away. Then many turned back for a second glance. She was stunning, so I wasn't surprised by the lingering gazes, but it was the way the realisation of who she'd arrived with seemed to domino around the room that surprised me. Whispered conversations broke out everywhere. I felt like hoisting Alyssa up onto my shoulders and declaring to everyone in the room that yes, she was mine. Or perhaps more appropriately, that I was hers. And always had been.

I held my head up high—unable to stop the huge-arse grin that crossed my features—as I led Alyssa to our assigned table. It was sitting empty, and I cringed when I saw the sign on the table that read *Wood Racing*. I should've known Paige would do something like that to set me up somehow, but I'd already promised. I didn't want to let the kids down either, so I didn't make a fuss. However, I did grumble about it in Alyssa's ear when I pulled her seat out for her.

"Don't stress," she whispered back. "You still have your autograph session or whatever is going to happen. You can mention your true colours then."

"You're not only beautiful, and sexy, but wise too." I kissed her on the cheek and took my own seat. "What did I do to deserve you?"

"You got lucky, I guess." A small grin crossed her lips.

I leaned across the gap between us, placing one hand in her lap and the other on the back of her chair so I could get close enough to her that I could whisper in her ear without anyone else listening in. "Do you think I'll get lucky again later?"

Alyssa flushed and squirmed in her seat before glancing around the room. After a moment, her eyes grew wide as she looked at some of the other attendees—she was clearly in awe of the B-list celebrities and obvious money in the room.

I'd neglected to tell her that to get a ticket for a fundraiser such as the one we were at generally cost between two and five hundred dollars a seat. Not to mention it was upwards of two grand for a table. It was where the wannabe rich and powerful came together to show how willing they were to unite for a good cause. This one was for a children's hospital, but another night it might be for cancer research or the RSPCA. At the end of the day, it was often more about showing how philanthropic they could be than it was about the specific cause.

Usually I hated having to attend them, but with Alyssa at my side, it wasn't so bad.

The seats at our table filled slowly. With each new arrival, my heart sank further. I recognised each and every one of the faces who had taken seats near us, and they were all associated with Wood in one way or another. Alex, the Wood PR agent, walked in with her business partner, Ross. They sat across from us at the table. Alyssa gave Alex a small smile but earned nothing but a glare in response.

"Do you know her?" I asked Alyssa, even though I had my suspicions about the reason for the look. After all, being driverless, and forced to rely on the competition for help, was no doubt a PR nightmare for Alex. That made me, for all intents and purposes, the enemy at the table. Unfortunately for Alyssa, she was tarred with the same brush by association.

My suspicions were made stronger when Alyssa shook her head and whispered back, "Never seen her before in my life."

Right before the doors were due to close and dinner was to begin, another couple entered. I watched as they walked across to our table, filling the two remaining seats. One of them I recognised instantly. Felix Wood—Paige Wood's son. He'd gone into football instead of cars. Despite that, I wasn't overly surprised to see him representing his mother's team at the fundraiser. He was as big a drawcard as anyone else at the function after all.

I didn't immediately recognise the woman on his arm, but there was something vaguely familiar about her. Her bright red hair was twisted into a loose mess at her nape. She wore a tight-fitting green dress that hung so low on her chest that only her nipples were covered, and they were so erect they almost held the material away from her skin anyway. I pondered the familiarity of her a little more, watching intently as she sat down beside me.

While I was still starting at her, she turned to face me, her face forming a small smile.

"Declan," she purred. "What a surprise to see you here."

She sounded anything but surprised, and I wished I could place where I knew her from. A sinking suspicion grew within me that she was a one-night stand come back to bite my arse.

Alyssa gasped beside me. At first, I thought it was purely because of the obvious note of recognition the woman's voice held as she'd spoken to me. When I turned to look at Alyssa though, she was staring at the other woman as if they were old acquaintances. I stole another glance at the vaguely familiar stranger—who seemed to know me—for a moment, trying to figure out where I knew her from.

And where Alyssa might know her from.

She took Alyssa's hand and introduced herself as Matilda, and in that moment, I understood exactly who she was. And just how dangerous it was for her to be at my table with Alyssa.

Fuck me. I wanted to groan into my hands and then drag Alyssa from the table. To go anywhere else.

It didn't make sense. Why the fuck was "Tillie from the club" at the fucking fundraiser? Tillie from the magazine cover. Tillie of the fucking infamous public threesome after Bathurst that had been a major catalyst in everything that followed.

Even though I probably should have thanked her, because everything that had happened after that had led me back into Alyssa's embrace, I couldn't. All I could think about was whether she might be the reminder that would force Alyssa to understand the truth in her father's words.

I felt a strong urge to apologise for dragging her to the event and making her have to sit across from the woman from my past. The last thing either of us needed was any further reminders of my prior indiscretions after the way our evening had started. There was no way for me to do that without drawing further attention to the uncomfortable situation though. I turned my face up to the ceiling so I didn't have to look at either woman and begged the ground to open up and swallow me whole. When that didn't work, I excused myself from the table and almost raced into the men's room.

For a few minutes, I paced the room, screaming obscenities at the mirror before splashing my face with water to try to force myself to focus. When I walked back to the table, I found Alyssa and Tillie in conversation. Alyssa was actually smiling—either she was a better actress than I thought or she didn't actually know who she was talking to.

"Dec," Alyssa said, looking up at me with a smile. "I never told you about my flight home from London, did I?"

It seemed a random statement, and I didn't know what to make of it. With the question dancing on the tip of my tongue, I shook my head as I squeezed myself back in between the two of them.

"I—I was on the same flight as you," Alyssa admitted.

My jaw fell open as all of the near misses I'd written off as impossible came flooding back.

"I'm sorry," Alyssa continued. "It was childish, I know, but I just couldn't—" She cut herself off. "Well, you know."

With my jaw still gaping and my mind still racing over where she might be going with her admissions, I nodded. I understood her need to run, to protect herself and Phoebe. I'd been an arse to her and she had every right to avoid me.

"Anyway, Tillie here rescued me when I was in desperate need of a coffee."

My stomach plummeted as I recalled seeing Tillie order the drink, and exactly what happened after when she returned to my table.

"Declan and I actually had a conversation after I got your coffee." Tillie placed her hand on my arm.

I wanted to snatch away from her hold, but there were too many gazes levelled in my direction to do anything stupid.

"Of course, I had no idea he was the one you were trying to avoid." Tillie's mouth stretched into a Cheshire grin.

My plea for the world to swallow me up grew louder in my head.

"We really must continue that conversation one day," Tillie said, turning her grin onto me.

It was a no win situation. If I went as far to admit the conversation wasn't a conversation at all, but her trying to suck my cock in the middle of a busy airport, Alyssa could assume the worst. But if I entertained even the slightly possibility of a continuance, I would risk Tillie getting the wrong idea and not understanding that my cock, and every other piece of me, belonged to Alyssa now.

I plastered on the best fake smile I could muster. "I think I've said all I needed to say about that subject."

"That's a shame. Then again, never say never. You don't know when opportunities for *conversations* will *arise*." Her hand grazed my thigh under the table and I leapt away from the touch, banging my elbow against the table and causing the drinks on the table to splash around in their glasses.

All gazes at the table, and at the ones on either side, turned to me. I just gave them the fake smile that was still twisting my lips and then proceeded to ignore them all.

"So what do you do for a living?" Alyssa asked Tillie politely, no doubt trying to cover for my faux pas and move the conversation along.

"I'm in publishing," Tillie responded.

They continued their conversation, barely acknowledging my presence any longer. Burying my face in my hands, I sank down in my chair. From across the table, I heard Alex snicker. When I looked at her, she was wearing a barely concealed smirk.

Fuck me. It was going to be a long night.

CHAPTER TWENTY-SEVEN
WINE AND DINE

THE NIGHT WENT from bad, to worse, to downright horrendous. Alyssa and I endured a three-course dinner with snickers and murmurs all around us.

At one point, a TV sports journalist even came over and asked why I was at Wood's table. As the question and follow-ups left his lips, his eyes lit up as though he was thinking he was about to land himself a major scoop. Not wanting to let him jump to any further conclusions, I explained that I was the only driver available because I was on hiatus and not needed in Bahrain.

He smiled and nodded as if it made sense, but I saw him glancing at me covertly throughout the evening, watching me intently every time I opened my mouth to speak to anyone at the table—which wasn't often given the company I was in.

The night seemed to drag on forever, but there was nothing I could do to speed it along. I couldn't leave until I'd fulfilled my signing commitments, especially not when the silent auctions were already underway. All I could do was wait.

Eventually, I got tapped on the shoulder and told it was time. Together with the other celebrities at the event, I was ushered away from my table fifteen minutes before the auction started to be debriefed on the events. After the debriefing, I would be led to a desk and handed a pile of stuff to sign. Some larger pieces, like a framed ProV8 poster, were to be auctioned off. But the rest were all being sold individually, and I had to be available for an hour to sign personal autographs.

It was only then that I found out that there was going to be a slide show of some of the families the foundation had helped over the years. I kicked myself mentally for being so fucking stupid because they always did something to show where the money went. I should have realised sooner, but I hadn't and Alyssa would be unprepared for what she might see.

Being at the benefit to help raise money because of my children was one thing, subjecting Alyssa to what was sure to be a heartbreaking display considering her personal experience of dealing with Phoebe's condition and Emmanuel's death, and not even being there to help her through it was something else entirely. I couldn't even go back into the room to warn her. On top of everything else, I was given strict instructions to sign autographs and do nothing else. I wasn't to leave my post, and each winner only had a set time limit at my stand. It meant I wouldn't even have an opportunity to explain to anyone that I was still Sinclair through and through despite sitting at Wood's table for the night.

As soon as I was directed back into the main hall, and onto the makeshift stage, I looked around for Alyssa. She was sitting at our table with a small smile on her face. I didn't even think when I broke rank and ran to her. I whispered a quiet warning in her ear, telling her of the slide show and reassuring her that no one would think any less of her if she stepped outside while it was on.

That was all I had time to say before Alex stalked over to me and told me that I was to get back into place and not step out of line again. I went to tell her to fuck off because I was doing *them* a favour and not the other way around, but Alyssa stopped me with a quick shake of her head and a kiss on the cheek. It was almost as if she was telling me without words that now that I was here it would be easier if I just cooperated. I gave her a quick kiss on the lips in response. It earned a few murmurs around the room as I headed back to the stage.

When the slide show started—filled with picture after picture of kids lying in hospital beds, babies in incubators, and kids wrapped in bandages—I turned to check on Alyssa. Small tears ran along the side of her nose but her eyes were glued to the screen. I followed her gaze and saw beyond the images on the screen. I saw Phoebe in the face of every child. Saw echoes of Alyssa's pain etched into the face of every parent.

On the table, my fingers clenched to form fists at my own stupidity. How could I be so fucking dense? I wanted to run over to her and pull her against my chest. To hold her tightly and tell her it was okay. It would have been a lie—it would never be okay—but it might have helped her.

She locked eyes with me and something unspoken passed between us. In that second I understood. I felt the loss, the devastation, more acutely than I ever had before, but I also felt the hope and the love. I couldn't say what happened from that point on because I was so focused on Alyssa. Even as I signed autographs, I glanced at her as often as I could.

She surprised me by getting up from our table and purchasing a poster.

I chuckled when I saw what she was doing. She brought it over to me to sign.

"You don't need my autograph." I laughed.

She shrugged. "It's for a good cause though."

"That it is," I said, as I signed the poster.

"Besides, one day you might be *really* famous, and then this could be worth something," she deadpanned.

"If I'm ever that famous, you'll be right there alongside me, so you won't need the money."

I rolled up the poster and Alyssa reached for it, but I snatched it away at the last second.

"You need to give me something else first," I said.

"And what's that?"

With a smile, I tapped my lips. She leaned across the table and touched hers to mine for a brief second. Too brief. I couldn't wait to be done with this night so I could take her home.

A sigh escaped me as I watched her walk away.

"Do we all get to pay the extra price?" It was Tillie who'd asked the question.

I shook my head and offered her an apologetic smile. "I'm afraid I'm a one-woman man."

She looked surprised. "Even though I've seen it myself, I still don't know that I believe it." She looked toward Alyssa. "So tell me, what does she have that the rest of us don't?"

"My heart."

She laughed. "Some people might think that's romantic, but between you and me it's all just crap, isn't it?"

I scowled at her. "What the hell is that supposed to mean?"

"It means that we all know what you're like, Declan. You think it was your exceptional pulling skills that had me interested in the club?" She laughed. "You were a guaranteed lay, and rumoured to be a good one at that. The great Declan Reede screws around. That's what he does. That's *all* that he does. Even if you've forgotten that for the moment, it won't be long before you remember. Maybe you just need the right *women* to remind you." She raised her eyebrow at me as if I might change my mind at any second and beg for a repeat performance with her and her friend.

I shook my head. "Nope. Never again. She's it for me."

Tillie laughed. "If you say so."

She moved the glass of water I had stationed beside me to another part of the table and placed a shirt in front of me. She opened it out fully and showed me where she wanted the autograph. I complied quickly, mostly because I wanted her away from me as quickly as possible. Even after I'd finished though, she lingered.

"Why are you even asking me things like that anyway?" I asked. "Aren't you with Felix?"

She gave a throaty, seductive chuckle. "He's just my ticket in and a bit of arm candy. A girl can hardly come to an event like this alone." She sighed, glanced around quickly and then leaned in close to me. "If you must know, it's his sister, Talia, who holds my attention. You remember her too, don't you? I just like a little dick every now and then. We both do in fact." Her voice made no secret of the fact that she was actually giving me an open invitation to have a do-over of our fateful night in the club.

"Well . . .," I said, unsure how to end the conversation after her comment. "Good luck with that."

I signalled for the next person to come forward, cutting Tillie off before she could make another lame attempt at seduction. I took a sip of water before signing the keychain that was thrust in front of me, noting the odd taste in the water. Swallowing down the foul mouthful, I grimaced. There was a reason I never usually drank unfiltered water in the city. I had few other options though, at least until I was free to leave the signing table again.

Twenty minutes later, I was finally finished and was able to leave to try to find Alyssa. I hoped I could convince her to go now that the official shit was done.

When I stood, my legs almost collapsed beneath me and my head spun. I reached for the table, but my arm felt too long. My tongue felt heavy in my mouth.

I tried to figure out what was going on, but my brain refused to work right. It wasn't normal, and the sensation that something was wrong built within me. I took a step and stumbled. I couldn't have been drunk . . . could I? I'd had two rum and Cokes with dinner, but that had been much earlier, and I hadn't had anything more since then.

Even as the thoughts chased each other through my mind, I staggered back toward Alyssa at our table. My stomach roiled and pitched with every step.

"Declan?" she asked, her voice filled with concern. "Are you feeling all right?"

I looked at her—trying to make the three Alyssas I could see combine into one. When I failed, I shook my head. "I think I need the bathroom." My voice was slurred and unsteady even to my own ears.

She placed her arm around my waist and held me steady as I headed for the bathroom.

Pushing the door open with my shoulder, I stumbled inside

and headed straight into a cubicle. At first, I vomited, then when I had nothing left to bring up, I heaved until my chest ached and my stomach burned. When I finally got myself under control, I wanted nothing more than to curl around the base of the loo and rest my head against the cool tiles, but the unhygienic nature of a public pissing hole turned me off.

I struggled to get my legs under me again before dragging myself to the sink. Barely holding myself upright, I splashed my face with cold water. When I raised my head again, I was shocked by what I saw. My eyes were bloodshot and glazed. With rising horror, I recognised the face reflecting back at me. It was someone I hadn't seen in a long time. A face I hated—the face of my darkest days.

The walls started to close in on me, drawing closer together with every second. I had to get out of there. Staggering to the door, I pulled it open. I'd expected to find Alyssa waiting for me, but she wasn't. Stumbling as I went, and unable to make out anything with the haze blurring my vision, I headed toward the front door. Even though I wasn't thinking straight, it was clear to me that I needed some fresh air.

"Declan . . .," a voice whispered to me.

I spun on the spot, almost losing my footing and narrowly avoided falling on my arse. I looked around to find the source of the voice. The door to the cloakroom was open a few inches, and the voice within called out to me once again.

"Alyssa?" I asked, trying to work out whether the voice was actually in my mind or was coming from the darkened room.

"I'm in here," she whispered. Her voice sounded off. Deeper, and more infused with desperation than ever before. I wondered if it was the effect of whatever was flowing through my veins.

Wanting to find Alyssa, I stepped toward the room, pushing the door open and taking a few steps inside before pausing and turning around. The door closed, and I looked to see who had closed it but my head swum too much to make out anything in the darkness.

"Alyssa?" I repeated. I didn't know if it was some kind of sick joke. I couldn't understand why she would go into that room. She knew what'd happened in there with Darcy. Why would she want to share any time with that memory?

"Come here, Declan."

I stepped back toward the door and suddenly lips were on mine. A warm tongue pressed forward, seeking entrance to my mouth. My lips parted slightly while my brain struggled to catch up.

Something was wrong.

Alyssa was taller than usual. A memory flashed in my mind of her sky high heels. Maybe that's all it was. When I wrapped my arm around Alyssa's waist to respond to her kiss, it seemed to skinny — too lean.

Something was off.

Something was stroking my dick.

I moaned instinctively in response to the touch, but warning bells were going off inside my mind. In slow motion, my brain finally caught up with everything happening and it screamed at me that the touch was wrong. The taste was wrong. Whoever had their hand around my cock and their tongue in my mouth wasn't Alyssa. That realisation left me reeling and I jerked away from the touch. Too quickly. All of my balance went out the window and I fell backward into a rack of coats. I retreated as far back as I could and shouted, "You're not Alyssa."

Whoever was with me shushed me, but I couldn't be quietened. Someone'd had their tongue down my throat and it wasn't Alyssa. I wasn't *that guy* anymore, and I didn't want to be. I never wanted to be again.

I couldn't do that to her. My emotions spiralled out of control faster than my heartbeat raced.

Through it all, I shouted for Alyssa. My voice didn't seem to be making it through the swirl of noise around me, and I knew if I didn't shout as loud as I possibly could, Alyssa would never hear me. She'd never come rescue me.

I held my hand up to shield myself from the light that started small but soon grew to encompass the whole room. People barged in around me. More and more spilling in until it was suddenly full. In all directions I saw men and women; some confused, some scared.

My angel cut through the crowd and knelt in front of me.

"Shh, Dec," Alyssa—my personal angel—said. "It's all right. I'm here now."

Without thought, I reached for her and rested my head against her chest. She held me tightly, and calmly directed everyone else to leave. There were murmurs of dissent at first but somehow she convinced them all to leave us alone for a moment.

After a while she pushed me off her and stared into my eyes. "I'm going to ask you a question, and I don't want you to lie to me."

"I never—" I was going to tell her I would never lie to her again, but she cut me off with a wave of her hand.

"Just promise me."

I nodded.

"Did you take anything tonight? Anything to take the edge off?"

I shook my head.

"Are you feeling okay now?" she asked.

I shook my head again. "No," my voice sounded broken, even to me.

"Can I have your car keys? I want to drive you home."

I looked at her incredulously for a second. I wondered if she realised *no one* drove my car. Certainly no one else drove it while I sat in the passenger seat. The night of the drags, I had made a once-off exception for her.

Regardless of that, I reached into my pocket and fished out my keys. I placed them into her hand, twisting her fingers into a fist around them.

She stood and helped me up. As she led me from the cloakroom to the front door, I heard whispers all around. I didn't know what they were saying, and frankly I didn't give a fuck. I just wanted to go, to be home, with Alyssa. That, and maybe to vomit a few more times before bed. I had no idea who had lured me into the cloak room, but it was clear they'd intended on seducing me. Fucker.

Why couldn't people take, "I'm happy leave me the fuck alone," as an answer.

With her shoes off and carried in her hands, Alyssa supported me as we walked back to the carpark. As she unlocked the car, I rested against it and tried to stop my head from spinning. Alyssa came back to my side and she helped me into the car.

I crawled into the passenger seat, leaning my head against the headrest as Alyssa fastened the seat belt around me. Even though I'd been worried about handing over the keys, I was too far gone on the ride home to acknowledge whether Alyssa was treating my car right.

I didn't even realise we were home until I woke up in bed with Alyssa fast asleep beside me the following morning.

When I went to climb out of the bed, it became clear I still wasn't fully recuperated from whatever had happened the night before. My hands shook and my head spun. My lips were dry, so I slicked my tongue across them. It didn't help because my mouth was just as parched.

Standing as still as I could for a few moments, I thought about the night before. The more I considered the way I'd felt, the reactions I'd had, the more certain I grew that I'd been slipped something. It was the only logical explanation, because I sure as fuck didn't take anything. Nor had I had enough to drink to cause that sort of response.

With a glance down at Alyssa, lying peacefully in the bed, a thought formed in my mind. Had she truly believed me when I'd said I hadn't taken anything? Had our relationship really grown that strong again? Or did she think I was lying to her?

I snuck out of the bedroom quietly. It was only when I'd made it halfway down the hall that I realised I was wearing nothing more than a pair of boxers. I didn't know if Phoebe was at home or still at Alyssa's folks' house, but I was glad I had something covering my arse just in case.

Heading straight for the fridge, I grabbed a glass of orange juice to get rid of the taste in my mouth and relieve my desiccated throat. It honestly felt like I'd spent the night licking an ashtray. After I downed my first glass of orange juice, I hunted through Alyssa's pantry for some paracetamol, or anything that would at least reduce the throbbing in my head to a dull ache. I threw a couple into my mouth and downed them with a second glass of O.J.

"You popping pills again already?" Alyssa asked from behind me.

The sound of her voice startled me—I'd thought she was still fast asleep. I spun around to face her. Her words confirmed my fears from earlier; she didn't believe me after all. She thought I'd fallen back to my old patterns. I had to convince her otherwise or she might run.

"I . . . um . . . I really didn't . . ." I shook my head furiously, fighting back the fear.

Her face dropped and she stepped over to me quickly. "I'm sorry, poor choice of words. I know you didn't take anything last night." She pressed her lips to mine, and I relaxed into her. "At least not knowingly."

"But how?"

"When was the last time you took drugs? And I don't mean sleeping tablets or prescription medication."

I dropped my head to my chest and murmured, "Over three and a half years ago."

"Exactly," she said, nodding. "I know you have . . . issues . . . with alcohol. But that wasn't alcohol that made you act like that last night. I think someone might have spiked your drink."

I met her eyes and smiled slightly. The faith she showed in me was one hundred times more powerful than the doubt Josh and Curtis had brought back to the surface.

"But what I can't figure out is who or why?"

I shrugged, too happy that she believed me to worry about the reasoning behind the sabotage. That was something we could worry about later. Closing the small distance between us, I cupped her face in my hand and brought her lips back to mine. She pushed her tongue forward into my mouth, and I was reminded of the surprise that was waiting for me in the cloakroom.

My brow furrowed. The two events had to be connected. I told

Alyssa about it—about the tongue and the hand. My heart broke as I watched her expression drop, and her brows pinch. I didn't want to hurt her, but I needed her to know. Not only because it might be important to figuring out who the fuck slipped me something, but also because I didn't want to lie to her. I didn't want her to find out some other way and know I'd omitted the truth. When I finished, I explained that the kiss was the reason I was bundled in the corner of the cloakroom calling out for her.

She placed her fingers over my mouth when I started to apologise for the fifteenth time. "It wasn't your fault, Dec. You didn't ask for it. I'm glad you told me though."

I pulled her close to me. "Let's get all thoughts of last night out of our heads for a while," I suggested. "What's on the agenda for today?"

"Work," she said, with a grimace.

"Of course," I said. "Work." The word was a curse as far as I was concerned.

I stood staring into her eyes. "Where's Phoebe?" I asked softly, leaning my lips down toward her.

Alyssa's eyes fluttered closed. "She's still with Mum. I didn't want to pick her up last night . . ."

I'd heard all I needed to. Even though I was happy to have Phoebe in my life, I was a little relieved she wasn't going to walk out of her room at any second. I closed the distance to Alyssa's lips and kissed her fervently. I continued to step forward as my tongue battled with hers. Cupping her arse, I pulled her legs around my waist and walked toward the bedroom. If I only had a limited amount of time with her before she started work, I was going to make damn sure we got the most out of it.

I didn't stop walking until I hit the bed and tumbled on top of her. My lips went from hers to her neck, trailing kisses down to her sternum. My fingers worked the buttons on her pyjamas, pulling them open one by one. Each one that I undid revealed a new expanse of skin for my mouth to explore. Her legs remained hooked around my waist as she ground her hips up to meet mine and moaned in response to my touch.

Leaning all my weight onto one hand, I used the other to start exploring. I kneaded her breasts before bringing one of her nipples into my mouth. I swirled my tongue around the tip, eliciting a panted "oh God" from Alyssa. With my eyes closed, enjoying every sensation, I moved to give the other side some attention.

Alyssa's hand came to rest on my chest, and then she pushed me away from her. I worried that it was because the memory of what I told her had happened last night was still too fresh.

She stood, pushing me backwards, before twisting me around and pushing me onto the bed. She ripped my boxer shorts off in one fluid motion, and I sat completely motionless while I waited for her to execute whatever it was she had planned. She knelt down on the floor and pulled me to the end of the bed. Before I could really process what was happening, her mouth surrounded my cock.

I threw my head back and groaned. The sensation of her warm tongue flicking across the top of my dick was fucking amazing. I grabbed a pillow and propped myself up, because I didn't want to miss another second of watching myself slide in and out of her perfect mouth. The sight and feeling were enough to push me to the edge.

"Fuck, Alyssa, you're fucking amazing," I whispered, my voice stolen by desire. She sucked the whole of my length in, and I felt myself brush against the back of her throat.

When she pulled back, I stopped her. As much as I wanted her to keep going, there was something more I had a sudden desire for. I sat on the edge of the bed and wrapped my arms around her. I took a moment to explore her skin with my mouth again before pushing her pyjama bottoms off.

"Come up here," I whispered, pulling her hand to lead her onto the bed. I lay back down and guided her so her legs were straddling my shoulders. I licked her inner thigh while my hands ran up and down over her arse. She moaned at the sensation, but seemed to catch on quickly to what I wanted to do. While her pussy hovered over my mouth, she leaned forward and took my length back into her mouth. I hummed against her skin before turning my head to the other side and gently nipping the delicate skin near her perfect pussy.

I spent a little time running my fingers and lips around her hips and thighs, taking great care to lavish attention on everything but the one spot I really wanted to touch. She moaned around my cock and bucked her hips, presenting herself to me.

Needing to prolong the moment for both of our benefits, I rubbed my nose along one lip before pushing my tongue forward to meet her clit. The instant I made contact she gasped around my dick. I pressed forward more forcefully, running the flat of my tongue across her arousal in long, slow motions as her breath hissed around my cock.

The louder she groaned, the more daring and ambitious I grew. One of my hands ran up and down the small gap between our bodies while the other joined my mouth on her pussy.

With practised, unhurried movements, I pushed one finger inside her, rolling it around in a slow circle until I could feel her muscles tighten around the digit. The harder I worked her body, the harder she worked her mouth. I took her clit gently between my teeth and rubbed it with my tongue, all the while moving my fingers in, around, and back out in a slow cycle.

Alyssa's legs tensed around my shoulders, and I began to work my fingers faster. Even though I sucked and nipped at her body, and it was all fantastic, my focus was somewhere else—lost to all sensation but Alyssa's mouth around my cock. Speeding my movements, I worked her body hard to ensure she got off before I did, but it was a damn close race.

As she came, her entire body fell apart around me in a series of tight spasms—including her mouth and throat. Nothing felt better than her coming over me. The sensation was enough to finish me off. I blew my load into her mouth and her tongue caressed my length as I came.

"Holy fuck!" I cried as Alyssa dropped her head onto my thighs.

With her whole body boneless and pliant on my stomach, I stroked her back for a few minutes, trying to gather myself back up. My headache was gone, replaced with a general feeling of bliss.

Eventually, Alyssa climbed off the bed, grabbing my hand and pulling me up as she went.

"Come on," she said. "I have to have a shower if I have any chance of getting to work on time."

It didn't escape my attention that she was pulling me with her into the bathroom.

After starting the water in the shower, she pulled her hair out of the loose bun it was in. I leaned against the door, watching her perfect, naked body as she went about her tasks. After she'd climbed into the tub and stood under the water she turned back to me, granting me a great view of her incredible tits.

She smirked. "Are you just going to stand there and watch, or are you going to join me?"

She extended her hand to me. I took it, thinking there were many, many worse ways to start a day. It was too bad I wasn't going to have enough time to completely get my fill of her—then again, that was probably an impossibility anyway.

CHAPTER TWENTY-EIGHT

ALONE

IT WASN'T UNTIL after Alyssa had left for work that panic over the previous night's events set in. For hours, I obsessed about everything that had happened. I couldn't help contemplating the various possibilities of whether someone could have spiked my drink, and who. Who had the means, motive, and opportunity? Who had the most to gain by publicly humiliating me, if that was their intention? The fact was any one of the people at my table could have slipped something into a drink while I wasn't looking.

Unable to stay still while my mind was so active, I paced around the house. My mind ran circles on itself, twisting down ever-darker paths as I considered the possible suspects. But regardless of how often a name came back around in my mind, I was still unable to answer two key questions: why, and was it connected with whoever was in the cloakroom? The more time I spent fixating on it, the more confused I grew.

After pacing for hours, I gingerly tried some exercises, mostly push-ups and sit-ups, because it had been too long since I'd paid proper attention to my fitness. If I went back to Sinclair unfit for racing, I'd get my arse kicked by my personal trainers.

With only my own thoughts and panic to keep me company, the day passed as slow as treacle. At one point, I ordered pizzas for dinner, specifying a delivery time about half an hour later than Alyssa was due home. Talking to the operator was the highlight of my day.

Finally seven o'clock crept around, the time Alyssa was due home. When I heard a car pulling up out front, I practically ripped the door off the hinges to get to her. I was at her car door in the next second, ready to pull her into my arms. After kissing her to let her know how much I'd fucking missed her all day, I turned and helped Phoebe from the car. As I worked, I asked her about her day. Freeing her from the car, I slung her onto my hip the way I had seen Alyssa do. Phoebe giggled and grabbed on to my shoulders.

"I missed you so much today," I told Alyssa.

"I missed you too. Unfortunately, real life gets in the way every now and then. I've still got bills to pay."

"Let me," I said.

"What?"

"Let me pay them. I fu—I owe you. I owe both of you. It's the least I can do."

She laughed. "I can pay my own bills."

"But . . ." I trailed off, readying arguments so I could get them right. "If you're going to move in with me, then what's mine is yours. So it won't matter if I give you some now, will it?"

"I can pay my own bills, Dec," she huffed. A frown pulled her eyebrows together and I saw it was an issue of contention.

"All right." I held up my free hand as a peace offering. "But the offer's there."

She sighed. "Thank you, but I'm happier paying my own way."

I put Phoebe down just inside the door.

"What's for dinner, Mummy?" she asked.

"I don't know, sweetie. I'll have a look shall I?"

"Don't bother," I said proudly. "I ordered pizza."

Alyssa laughed. "That's hardly healthy."

I shrugged. "It's a treat. Besides, I wanted to cook and I didn't have a clue where to start. This just seemed easier."

"Well, I guess it shows you are thinking about us at least," Alyssa whispered, as she stepped closer to me.

"I always think about you," I replied. Her mouth met mine with a soft, warm kiss. A proper welcome home. It was strange how comfortable I felt being so . . . domestic. If someone had told me two months ago that I would be back with Alyssa, that I would be a father, and that I would be the fucking happiest I'd ever been, I wouldn't have believed them. In fact, I probably would have turned around and smacked them in the mouth just for daring to mention her name.

Now, I was ready to do anything to have a life with her.

To have both my girls permanently by my side—the sooner, the better.

"So!" I exclaimed, clapping my hands together for emphasis. "Who's up for some games before dinner comes?"

We spent half an hour playing with Phoebe's toys before the pizza arrived. Then we settled down and watched a little TV. Phoebe drifted off to sleep sitting beside us on the couch so I carried her to her room. As I placed her in the bed I placed a delicate kiss on her forehead.

"I love you, baby," I whispered, before turning to follow Alyssa into our bedroom.

Friday passed in much the same fashion as Thursday. Except it was even less exciting, and my mind had more time to contemplate all the darkness I'd experienced lately. I still wasn't any closer to figuring out the culprit behind the drugging at the charity event. My mind kept vacillating between Alex and Tillie, but I couldn't figure out a motive. Somehow Tillie didn't strike me as the sort of person who needed to spike drinks to get what she wanted.

Thankfully though, there had been minimal fallout on TV and in the newspapers. It was the third headline of the sports segment on the morning news, but they didn't talk about drug use or alcohol, instead rehashing old press statements regarding the "stress" that had seen me go on hiatus from Sinclair Racing, and speculating if it was the cause of my breakdown. It made page five of the sports pages in the newspaper. I knew enough to know that negative front-page headlines were bad news when it came to sponsors, but buried on page five hardly rated a mention—maybe a slap on the wrist.

It was heading into the late afternoon before my boring peace, and non-stop inner monologue, were silenced by a phone call. Danny's voice came down the line.

"Declan, I need you back in Sydney," he said, without any introduction or small talk.

"Uh, sure . . .," I replied. It was unlike Danny to not make at least a little small talk before launching into business.

"I've arranged a flight for you for tomorrow morning. It's imperative you come straight here on arrival. I need to see you as soon as possible." His clipped tone was so unlike the last time we'd spoken, and it made my breath catch in my throat.

"Sure thing," I said, trying to stop my heart from racing in my chest and stealing my voice. "Can I ask why?"

"We can discuss that when you arrive. Your itinerary is on your email. See you tomorrow."

He hung up, leaving no room for discussion. I stared blankly at my phone for a number of minutes until it beeped a few times and switched off. I'd spent so little time on it lately that I hadn't realised the battery was so low. I found a spare outlet in the bedroom and plugged in my charger, not bothering to turn my phone back on. There was no need for it if all it was going to offer was more confusion and questions.

As I stood, a sick feeling crept up on me. Trying to force it down, I reminded myself that page five was not a big concern. I'd seen drivers get worse and not be reprimanded. Fuck, I'd done worse without rebuke.

Working to avoid a panic attack, I even tried to convince myself that Danny wanted to see me just to run some tests with the new car. It didn't work. There was no need for a test so early, and even if there was, all of the engineers were still in Bahrain. Fuck, even Danny was supposed to be in Bahrain. My heart pounded and my head spun with possibilities.

The worst thing was, no matter whether the reason Danny wanted to see me was good or bad, I wouldn't find out until the next day. Familiar feelings crept up in my body. My heart raced, my palms grew clammy, and my throat constricted. My stomach twisted, and I couldn't contain the food I'd eaten any more. I ran to the toilet and hurled. Falling onto the floor of the bathroom, I curled into a ball. I couldn't get my breathing back under control, no matter how hard I tried.

Alyssa found me a few hours later, curled into a corner in the bathroom experiencing a full-blown panic attack. As soon as she came near me—as soon as her skin made contact with mine—my breathing calmed and I was able to open my eyes. She helped me to my feet, and I held her close to me until my heart rate returned to normal and I was able to function again.

She brushed the hair away from my face. "What happened?" she asked in a quiet murmur. "What's wrong?"

"Danny Sinclair called today," I said. "He . . . he wants me back in Sydney, but I don't know why."

"Are you okay?"

"I'm fucking terrified, Lys. I don't know what to do." My words ran together and fell out of my mouth in a jumbled mess.

"Do you think it's because of the other night?"

"I . . . I don't know." I raked my hand through my hair. "But I just can't help feeling that something's wrong. Very wrong."

"How are you going to get to Sydney?"

"He's arranged flights. I need to go online and get the details. I just don't know what to do." I rested my head on her shoulder.

"You get the details. You fly to Sydney and find out what he wants. We'll work out the rest after we know what it's about." She brought her lips to my cheek.

A mirthless chuckle left me. "As easy as that, huh?"

She smiled. "I never said it would be easy. But we can get through anything together, right?" It was as if she was trying to confirm I wasn't going to run.

Holding her more tightly in my arms, I confirmed in a hushed whisper against her hair, "Together."

Phoebe interrupted the moment by running into the room. "Mummy! I'm hungry!" she exclaimed.

Alyssa laughed and dropped her arms, grabbing my hand in

one of hers. "C'mon, Dec."

We walked to the kitchen, and she started throwing together a meal.

After dinner, we put on a movie for Phoebe before retreating to Flynn's room, where the computer was. As Alyssa booted up the system, I looked around the room. I hadn't noticed before, but it was surprisingly sparse. Besides the computer, there was a bed and a very small chest of drawers. Half a dozen shirts and a winter coat hung in the cupboard, but there was nothing to suggest a living arrangement of any permanence.

"How often does Flynn stay over?" I asked, trying to keep the jealousy out of my voice.

"It depends," Alyssa answered distractedly. "But generally one night a week, I guess. It's helpful, especially if I have to work late."

"Are you going to miss him when you move to Sydney?"

Focusing on the screen, her fingers found the end of her hair.

"What is it?" I asked, knowing her well enough to know that was her anxious face.

"Well, before—" She cut off. She took a deep breath before continuing, "Before *us*, he was talking about moving to Sydney with me. To help with the costs and everything."

There was more, I knew it. "And if you'd moved to London?"

She sighed. "He was planning on trying to come too."

I was floored, but it helped me see one thing more clearly than I ever had before. He and his brother had what appeared to be a successful business in Browns Plains, but he was willing to move to help Alyssa out. "He really does care about you, doesn't he?"

She nodded. "And Phoebe is his world."

The reminder that due to my own stupidity someone else had been playing dad to my daughter for the last three and a half years stung.

"Please, don't be jealous," Alyssa said, turning to me. "I know how you feel about him and everything, but I've relied on him for so long. He's my best friend."

One day, I would earn that mantle back. "What's going to happen now that there is an *us*?" I asked.

"I don't know." She turned away, her face thoughtful. "I guess we'll have to cross that bridge when we come to it. I still need to finalise all my plans when it comes to the move."

I nodded. She stood and offered the computer to me. The browser was open, and all I needed to do was log in to my webmail. Somehow, the minutes that it took to do that were the longest in my life. It wasn't long before I found the airline itinerary amongst the pile of unread emails. My hands were shaking by the time I pushed the print button.

When I turned back toward Alyssa, she was staring into space, seemingly lost in thought.

"What is it?" I asked, touching her arm.

She started a little and dropped her gaze. When she spoke, her voice was so quiet I had to strain to hear it. "I was just thinking that perhaps, well, maybe, we should investigate getting the birth certificates amended."

The emotion in her voice was so thick it was painful to hear, but it also spoke to me of the trust she'd started to feel toward me. Trust I'd thought I might never earn back, and yet ran deeper than I ever would have guessed. A wave of emotion crashed over me. To avoid sinking under it, I stood and pulled her into my arms.

"I'd like that," I whispered. "If you're sure?"

She nodded against my chest. "I'm sure. I think, well, I think I would like it too."

In that instant, it was clear that having to put Flynn's name on the birth certificate had hurt her as much as it had hurt me to see it there. If things had gone differently, if she hadn't needed to grieve and hand the reins over to someone else for a while, she might have never done it.

After the conversation, I felt braver. In fact, I almost felt ready to face Danny and anything he could throw at me. After all, how bad could it be?

When Phoebe was tucked in and asleep, I lay in bed with Alyssa curled in to my side. My mind ticked over with all the changes that'd happened in such a short time frame. Despite the pain they'd caused me and my loved ones, I struggled to regret a single thing that'd happened. Each event had led me one step closer to being right where I was. Back to Alyssa. Back to love. Swallowing down the rush of emotion rising within me, I squeezed her more tightly.

"What are you thinking about?" she murmured in a sleepy tone.

I'd thought she'd already drifted off to sleep. "Nothing. Everything. Life," I said cryptically.

"Fair enough," she murmured.

I held her close until sleep finally claimed me.

"COME ON, you two, or we're going to be late!" Alyssa ordered from the living room. She seemed keener to get me on the flight than I was to go. I'd decided it was much more enjoyable to continue playing in Phoebe's room, even though she was making me dress and re-dress all her dollies repeatedly. I didn't want to leave the known safety of Alyssa's house. At some point over the last few days, it'd become my sanctuary. Part of me feared that being back in Sydney would make all of this seem less real. That it might somehow lessen Alyssa's trust. It wouldn't change the way I felt about Phoebe and Alyssa, but being in their house made the whole thing less dreamlike.

Every minute closer to the time of the flight was a minute less I could spend with my family. I was dreading the moment when I had to tell Phoebe I was going away and I didn't know how long I'd be gone for. Even though I hoped I wouldn't need to be away for too long, I wouldn't know for sure until I'd talked with Danny. Watching Phoebe play, I decided it was better to tell her now before we got in the car. At least I could make sure she understood.

Swallowing hard, I bit the bullet.

"Just give us a minute," I called back to Alyssa, then I turned to Phoebe. "Honey, you know your daddy loves you and is sorry he hasn't always been here for you, right?"

She nodded and then stood to wrap her little arms around my

neck. "I love you too."

"And you know that I never want to leave you or Mummy again, right?"

She squeezed tightly and I wrapped one arm around her waist.

"But Daddy needs to go away for a little while, okay? I promise I'll be back as soon as I can and that I'm never going to go away for a long time again. I'll always come back for you and Mummy."

Her mouth turned down into a frown. "Why are you going?"

"I have to do something for work, but I'll come home as soon as I can."

She wrapped her arms around me again and pulled my neck so hard it almost choked me.

"I don't want you to go," she whined.

"I know, and I don't want to go either. But I'll leave my car here, hey? That way I have to come back."

She perked up a little. "When?"

"I don't know, but I'll ring you and Mummy and tell you both as soon as I know, okay? And I'll ring every day when I'm gone."

Her bottom lip remained extended into a pout, but she nodded a little.

"Shall we go?" I stood and swung her up onto my back.

She giggled as she wrapped her arms around my neck before I jogged out to the living room.

"Aren't you ready yet?" I called to Alyssa as I raced past her and out the door.

She followed me out the door and locked it behind us. "Nervous?" she asked.

It was clear she could see straight through my bravado, so I nodded. I placed Phoebe in her car seat and then turned to see Alyssa watching me.

She stepped closer and linked her fingers with mine. "Whatever happens, I'll be right here waiting for you."

I nodded, and then lifted our joined hands to my mouth before brushing my lips across the skin on the back of her hand. "Thank you."

We climbed into the car, and I pulled out of the driveway

slowly. A solemn silence seemed to fall over the three of us. Any attempt to break the quiet, whether through conversation or music, seemed to thicken the atmosphere further. Or maybe it just felt that way to me. For some reason, I couldn't stop feeling like I was on my way to a hanging, and it would be my neck in the noose.

Finally, we pulled in to the airport, and I stopped the motor but left the keys in the ignition. We'd already agreed Alyssa was just going to drop me off and keep the Monaro while I was away. After we'd both climbed out of the car, I gave her a lingering embrace and a kiss worthy of a goodbye. Even though I didn't want to let her go, eventually a security guard came to wave our car on. With a sigh, I released Alyssa from my arms, but clutched her hand as she hopped back into the car, only letting go at the last second. She wound the window down, and I leaned into it.

"Take care of my baby," I whispered to her as she started my Monaro.

She rolled her eyes. "Your car will be fine."

I looked in the back seat. "I wasn't talking about my car."

Her face softened into such a sweet expression. "We'll be okay, Dec, just . . . call when you can, okay? As soon as you can."

I nodded and gave her one more quick kiss.

The flight was painful. I buried my head in my hands and ignored the world at large as best I could. But every kilometre closer to Sydney was another stake in my heart. The minutes passed in a vague blur as I drew nearer to whatever fate waited for me at the end of my journey. I couldn't even recall disembarking the plane or climbing in the taxi.

The drive to Sinclair Racing headquarters was a blur of shadows and greenery. Despite the speed with which the morning had passed, time stopped as soon as I was standing alone in front of the building.

During the steps from the footpath to the front door, my feet were weighed down with doubt and fear. I reached my hand into my pocket to pull out my phone and call Alyssa but there was nothing there. I tried to recall the last time I'd seen it, but the thought made my heart plummet. It was when I put it on to charge back at Alyssa's house. I had been so concerned with spending time with Phoebe that morning that I hadn't even thought to check for it. Which meant I had no immediate way of calming myself down before heading inside.

I sighed before I swiped my security card to gain entrance. My footsteps echoed off the marble floor of the vast entryway. I had never been there on the weekend; at least not without other people around. It was altogether eerie.

I walked up the stairs toward Danny's top floor office. No one else was in any of the other offices, but Danny's door stood open. I took that as an invitation to walk straight in. He wasn't behind his desk, but I crossed the room anyway to wait.

As I neared his desk, I saw something sitting on the green leather. My heart dropped to the floor, and my stomach twisted when I saw what it was. There was no doubt in my mind about this trip anymore. Any tiny semblance of hope I'd felt dissipated in a fraction of a second.

I was absolutely, completely, and totally fucked.

CHAPTER TWENTY-NINE
THAT'S ENTERTAINMENT

WHAT HAS PROV8 bad boy Declan Reede done now?
   The fights. The drugs. The alcohol.
   Only Gossip Weekly *has detailed coverage of Declan Reede's wild week in Brisbane. You don't want to miss a single detail. Don't stop reading until the end of our eight-page article.*

The headline was splashed across the front of the magazine, lying almost innocently in front of me on Danny's desk. It was emblazoned across a collage of photos of the time I had spent in Brisbane, but by far the biggest photo on the page, taking up the majority of space, was a photo of Eden and me on the hotel balcony during her one-night stay. I was shirtless, her arms were wrapped around me and her head rested on my back. If I didn't know the truth of the moment, I would have thought there was something romantic about the embrace.

   It was bad—very, very bad—but I had to know just how terrible it got. I took a deep breath and turned to the first page.

Declan Reede's Wild Week in Brisbane
   By: Miss M. (Photos by W.T. Entertainment)

Prominent V8 driver and notorious bad-boy, Declan Reede—currently on leave from Sinclair Racing *due to his disastrous on-track performance—has dipped to new lows during a recent trip to Brisbane. Now his off-track performance has been called into question as well. His descent started with his public sex act in* Firebird, *the renowned nightspot for the young and upcoming stars in Sydney* (featured in Gossip Weekly issue 294). *During the past week there have been repeated reports of violence, drug-fuelled rampages, and public womanising.* Gossip Weekly *has secured exclusive interviews with close family friends and people central to his downward spiral.*

The short paragraph introducing the photos was terrible. It was as if someone had been following me around specifically gathering information, and twisting everything that happened to show me in the worst possible light. I glanced around at the photos printed on the page. My eyes locked on one set, and the block of text that they centred around.

The Cafe attack:
"I was so scared," Hayley Bliss, formerly a close personal friend of Declan Reede, has revealed to us.

"I was sitting at a cafe with Robbie, Declan's father, talking about my new role with the bank. He's my work mentor, you see. He came out of nowhere, screaming like a lunatic. The next thing I knew, he was throwing tables around and threatening us both. It was terrifying."

Hayley told us she was thankful that Reede's father was there to control the situation. "Declan really respects his father. If he hadn't been around, I just don't know what might have happened."

Having gone to the same school as Declan, Hayley was able to tell us about the changes that have taken place in Declan's life lately.

"He used to be a sweet, caring person. But in the last few years he's been slowly losing it. I know for a fact that he started taking drugs shortly after he left for Sydney."

When asked who was the worst influence Hayley's answer was surprising. "By far the worst influence is the floozy who claims to be the mother of his child. Despite repeatedly telling her he didn't want children, she apparently tricked him into getting her pregnant. Personally, I think that's what started this whole spiral. It's all Alyssa Dawson's fault." (For more revelations about Alyssa Dawson, turn to pages 7 and 8).

I growled at no one as I read through Hayley's interview. Close fucking family friend my fucking arse. She was a fucking whore who no doubt had my fucking father's dick in her mouth every fucking night. My fingers trembled and my heart beat louder with every second, pounding so hard I could barely focus enough to keep reading. I couldn't believe a photographer had been close enough to get these specific angles without my knowledge. They had to be mere fucking metres away. I tried to recall that day. I knew my anger had blinded me to everything besides my father and his godawful fucking slut.

Recalling that day, I remembered seeing the sun flashing in my eyes as I was being pulled away. I couldn't believe how fucking idiotic I'd been for not fucking realising it was a fucking camera flash. Maybe it was because I wasn't a complete narcissist and I'd assumed I could get through one fucking day without a camera crew on my arse.

Even though all I wanted to do was to slam the magazine shut and declare it all fucking bullshit, it was clear Danny had seen it all. It explained the phone call and the terseness. It didn't, however, explain his current absence.

I recalled the last words my father had issued to me. *"Mark my words, boy, you will regret this."* Had he tried to stop this? Had he agreed to let Hayley paint me in such a harsh light after I'd thrown him out on his arse? It was all too obvious that he was the one filling Hayley's head with nonsense about Alyssa. I hadn't thought it was possible to hate my father more than I already did, but somehow he had just reached new lows.

I turned the page, not knowing what else would cover the next three double spreads.

The Women:
Declan Reede has always been known for his womanising ways,

355

however during his week in Brisbane he took it to new heights. He was seen in public with three different women within the space of twenty-four hours. Our sources reveal he told each of these women he was changing his ways and was interested in monogamy.

It seems even his teammates aren't off-limits for Reede, with our sources spying him at the Suncrest Hotel with team strategist, Eden Bishop. The pair were seen freely embracing on the hotel balcony before heading off for an intimate dinner at the Sunshine Room. They were spotted much later stumbling through the streets back toward the hotel.

Despite spending the better part of the evening with Miss Bishop, Reede later met up with an unknown blonde to drive to a secluded location at West End. The two were seen in an embrace. Our sources have confirmed Reede was later seen returning to the Suncrest Hotel room he shared with Miss Bishop.

Early the next morning, Reede saw Miss Bishop off to the airport and met up with his third apparent conquest, Alyssa Dawson.

Photos were lined up across the page, one after the other after the other. Me with Eden on the hotel balcony. Me with Eden at a table in the Sunshine Room. A grainy shot of me with Ruby at West End—whoever had taken that one had managed to capture the one second where we were actually touching. Me with Alyssa at the Queensland Raceway.

The Racetrack Romance:

Insiders reveal Reede was granted exclusive use of Willowbank Raceway to keep his on-track skills honed during his time away. It has been revealed to us, however, that he decided instead to use the time to arrange a rendezvous with his sometimes lover, Alyssa Dawson. The two were oblivious to prying eyes as they were all over each other, both on and off the track. He even handed control of the vehicle over to her for a period, allegedly ignoring instructions to the contrary.

A handful of photos accompanied the article, including one of Alyssa and me kissing up against the car. There was even a handful taken while we were on our private picnic. I sank down in the chair, my anger giving way to exhaustion as I turned the page again and grimaced at the next part of the article.

Planning on jumping ship?

Our reporters spotted Declan sitting with Wood racing hierarchy at a fundraising event at City Hall. When asked about his future he seemed to indicate changes were coming and that he had a new focus. When we asked Sinclair Racing officials about Reede's appearance, they claimed to have no knowledge of the event or why their star driver was in attendance.

Combined with recent rumours of discontent in the Sinclair camp, this suggests there may soon be a changing of the guard at Wood racing. We spoke to PR representatives who indicated that a switch might indeed be on the cards. Although they would neither confirm nor deny the rumours, they made it clear it was no secret the team wanted Declan Reede and had been courting him for months.

One has to question, however, whether any potential offer at Wood racing will remain on the table after the apparent drug-fuelled paranoia exhibited by Reede during the night. Multiple sources have confirmed that after the official part of the evening had concluded, Reede exhibited various signs of intoxication ending with a tryst in the cloakroom with an unknown woman and an apparent psychotic episode. Staff psychiatrists have expressed concerns over Reede's mental stability.

The question remains: where will Reede race next year? But perhaps the better question is: should he be allowed back on the track at all while exhibiting such dangerous and destructive behaviour?

Photos of Alyssa and me dressed up for the benefit accompanied the spread. As did photos of me in the corner of the cloakroom and of Alyssa helping me out the door and back to the car.

I was almost too scared to turn the page. Even without knowing the full details of what was on the last spread, I could see these eight pages ruining my life. There was no way Alyssa would think that things were innocent between Eden and me. How could I possibly explain to her that we were just friends? Especially with my history. Everyone who read the damned magazine would be on watch for "dangerous and destructive" behaviour. With my past, would Mum believe me if I said I wasn't taking drugs anymore?

To top it all off, no doubt Danny now thought I was planning on switching to Paige's team. My breathing was ragged. I needed Alyssa. I needed her to tell me that everything would be all right. I wondered whether she would still feel the same as she had before she saw me off. Would we still be as strong? Would we still face anything that came along *together*?

Closing my eyes, I yanked at my hair. Then I blew out a breath, opened my eyes, and turned to the last two-page spread of the article.

Mother of all lies:

By far the most shocking of the revelations our sources have provided is the existence of a love child between Declan Reede and his on/off lover, Alyssa Dawson.

"Oh, Alyssa was well known in school, if you catch my drift," former school friend, Darcy Cooper, revealed to us. "Everyone knew she was the go-to girl for the boys if they wanted a good time."

Darcy also provides an insight into the relationship Reede and Alyssa Dawson had while still at school. "They were always fighting. It seemed like they broke up every other day. But everyone knew Alyssa wanted to get her claws into him permanently."

"That's why she hatched the scheme to fall pregnant; she thought it would make him stay with her.

"Because I used to be her best friend, she told me what she planned to do one day. I tried to convince her not to, but no matter what I said, she wouldn't change her mind." Darcy told us of her sorrow at the loss of a once close friendship due to the deception Miss Dawson planned. "But then he left town. He made the smart choice and left her for his career."

Darcy told us that a few months after Declan left town it was discovered that Miss Dawson was pregnant. "She never said who the father was, but it was obvious she was trying to pin it on Declan. I was never sure though—the timing always seemed a little off to me."

The scandal has apparently torn apart families, and even Darcy's devoted husband, Blake Cooper, was pulled into the fray. Darcy confirmed a fight had broken out between Reede and Cooper on Reede's first night in

Brisbane. The exact reason for the altercation still appears to be unknown, but it is clear from the video that Reede was the aggressor, attacking a defenceless Cooper without warning.

"All Blake did was make one little comment about Alyssa's pregnancy," Darcy told us. "Declan Reede is a loose cannon. And he doesn't understand commitment. In fact, he's propositioned me repeatedly even though I am a happily married woman."

My eyes burned with unshed tears as I read the spiteful lies of Darcy. She'd promised me pain, but I never thought she would use Alyssa as the tool to deliver it. I didn't believe a single word of the article, of course. There was no way Alyssa would have planned for the things that had happened. Sure she'd wanted kids, but on the horizon, not straight out of school. Regardless, Alyssa's reputation would be marred by the words. It could cost her the job she wanted. It would hurt her. It killed me to think of Alyssa in pain. I leaned forward in the chair, burying my face into my hands.

"I see you've found the *interesting* reading material that was delivered to my office yesterday." Danny's voice was hard and cold as he spoke behind me.

I didn't bother twisting around in my seat. There was nothing to be gained from meeting his eye. I didn't need to see the disappointment on his face, not when I could hear it in his voice. I didn't even bother lifting my head. Instead, I just nodded into my hands.

"Do you care to offer an explanation?" he asked.

I shrugged. "Will it make a difference?" I asked. My voice was broken and almost silent, because I already knew the answer. And it was echoed through my body before he'd even issued it.

"No. But I want to know how long you've been lying to me."

"I haven't—" I started.

"Bullshit!" he exclaimed. "Look, I know some of that article is rubbish. I'd be willing to overlook half the crap they've written. But Wood? How the hell could you not tell me about her trying to court you, goddammit?" He slammed his fist down on his desk on the last word. "I asked you outright and you lied to me."

"I'm sorry," I whispered. "I've had a lot on my plate."

He scoffed. "*You've* had a lot on your plate? I was supposed to be on a plane to Bahrain yesterday, but *this*—" He indicated the magazine. "—arrived. So instead of watching my loyal driver who doesn't ruffle too many feathers actually make me money, I had to stay here and deal with *you*." His voice was filled with such venom as he said the last word that I knew I was done for.

What was left of my career was fast flying away from me. I pinched the bridge of my nose.

He stood inches from me, his grey hair dishevelled and out of place. Clearly, he'd been working his hands through it repeatedly. "The worst part, Declan, is how many chances I've offered you. Any other owner probably would have kicked you off the team a hundred times by now, but I didn't. I saw the value in you and offered you chance after chance. And *this* is how you repay me?"

I shook my head vehemently. "Can I please explain?" I asked.

"No." He said the word with such finality. My career at Sinclair Racing was over and there was no room for negotiation.

Even though I wanted to explain, I didn't push the issue. Instead, I bit my tongue and held back my tears as I handed over my security pass and other possessions. His words, his lack of forgiveness, had torn a fracture through my heart, but I couldn't blame him. He was right. I'd been given so many chances, and I'd fucked up every one.

I fucking loved my job with the team. Despite it all, I was still Sinclair through and through. The entire way back out of the building though, my heart clenched with fear. There was every possibility that losing my job would be the least painful of the losses I would suffer as a result of the article. Alyssa could believe every word written and never want to see me again. She could take Phoebe out of my life, and because I wasn't listed on the birth certificate there wouldn't be a damn fucking thing I could do about it without fighting. Only now, I had no means with which to fight.

As I trudged through the foyer, with Danny following my every footstep, my anger grew. It wasn't some fucking coincidence that there was a photographer at all of those events.

Someone had fucked me over big time.

Someone had taken everything precious in my life away, and I had no damn fucking clue who it was or why. All I wanted to do was destroy something—to rip something, or someone, apart with my bare hands. I waited under Danny's watchful eye for a taxi. We stood in silence while I debated whether or not to say anything.

In the end, I turned to him right before climbing into the taxi and said, "Thank you, for the opportunity and for everything. I'm sorry I'm nothing but a fuck-up."

I turned away before I could see the look on his face. Mostly because I didn't want him seeing the tears in my eyes. For the first time since making my choice to go to Sydney, I had no idea what the fuck I was going to do with my life. I was facing my first night as an unemployed person with no future and no hope. Worse, I had no one I could talk to. No friend I could ask for help. It was just me. And that's all it would be.

In my mind's eye, I could already see Alyssa's reaction to the article. To the sight of Eden and me on the hotel balcony in Brisbane.

I'd already had two chances to make things right with Alyssa—I didn't deserve a third.

I threw my credit card at the taxi driver as I barked out my address. Trying to make it obvious I didn't want to make small talk with him on the way home, I turned to face the passenger window.

Once he'd dropped me back at my house, I ran inside. I picked up the phone to call Alyssa. I had to explain about the magazine before she saw it and jumped to the wrong conclusion. Although I had no way of making her believe me, I had to try.

After I rang directory for her numbers, I phoned her house. When her home number rang out, and her mobile went straight to message bank, I rang Mum and begged for Ruth's number again. I didn't tell her what was happening though. She didn't even know I'd gone home to Sydney, and I didn't want to break her heart again.

My leg bounced as I waited for someone to pick up at the damn phone. Finally, I heard Ruth's voice at the end of the line.

"Declan?" she asked when I'd said hello. "What the hell is going on?"

My heart sank. From the tone in her voice, and the fact that she'd cursed, it was clear she knew something.

"I have to talk to Alyssa," I said uncertainly. I wasn't sure what I would do if she refused to come to the phone. I couldn't afford to waste money anymore, so I couldn't exactly get a return flight in a hurry. I would probably have enough cash available to get me through to the end of the year, but then I would have to talk to my broker about liquidating some of my other stocks after that. Maybe the house too.

"She's not here."

"Where is she then? Can you please give me the number? It's urgent. I need to talk to her."

"No," Ruth whispered. "I can't."

"Why not?" I demanded, ready to challenge any excuse.

"Because she isn't here."

"What?" My blood froze in my veins.

"She's not here." Ruth sobbed.

"Where is she?" I felt a shroud fall around my mind. I couldn't process anything. Ruth's quiet sobs only added to my stress. Where could Alyssa be when I needed her so desperately?

"Alyssa's *gone*, Declan."

My stomach plummeted. I needed to vomit. She couldn't be gone, she just couldn't be.

"Why?" I asked, my voice cracking halfway through the word.

"I don't know. She called here a little over an hour ago, shouting about a magazine or something. I couldn't get a straight answer out of her—except that she was leaving town. She hasn't answered her phone since."

"No," I whispered, my brain refusing to believe Ruth's words. "She can't."

"I'm sorry." I heard the line click as Ruth hung up the phone.

"No!" I shouted to the empty room and silent phone. I yanked on the base for the phone, tossing it across the room. "She's not gone! She can't be!"

My voice fell as I repeated it again and again, trying to convince myself while knowing the truth. I'd hurt Alyssa too much this time—she was gone. Lost to me forever, right when I needed her the most.

I sank to the floor as the last of my sanity seeped away from me. I couldn't believe it. Out of everything I'd experienced over the past few weeks, this was the worst. The life I'd convinced myself I could have, that I might even deserve, was over.

She was gone.

THE STORY CONTINUES IN

DECLAN REEDE: THE UNTOLD STORY #3

ABOUT THE AUTHOR

Michelle Irwin has been many things in her life: a hobbit taking a precious item to a fiery mountain; a young child stepping through the back of a wardrobe into another land; the last human stranded not-quite-alone in space three million years in the future; a young girl willing to fight for the love of a vampire; and a time-travelling madman in a box. She achieved all of these feats and many more through her voracious reading habit. Eventually, so much reading had to have an effect and the cast of characters inside her mind took over and spilled out onto the page.

Michelle lives in sunny Queensland in the land down under with her surprisingly patient husband and ever-intriguing daughter, carving out precious moments of writing and reading time around her accounts-based day job. A lover of love and overcoming the odds, she primarily writes paranormal and fantasy romance.

Comments, questions, and suggestions for improvements are always welcome. You can reach me at writeonshell@outlook.com or through my website www.michelle-irwin.com. Thanks in advance for your correspondence.

You can also connect with me online via
Facebook: **www.facebook.com/MichelleIrwinAuthor**
Twitter: **www.twitter.com/writeonshell**